SF Books by V

LOST STARSHIP SERIES:
The Lost Starship
The Lost Command
The Lost Destroyer
The Lost Colony
The Lost Patrol
The Lost Planet

DOOM STAR SERIES:
Star Soldier
Bio Weapon
Battle Pod
Cyborg Assault
Planet Wrecker
Star Fortress
Task Force 7 (Novella)

EXTINCTION WARS SERIES:
Assault Troopers
Planet Strike
Star Viking
Fortress Earth

Visit VaughnHeppner.com for more information

The Lost Planet

(Lost Starship Series 6)

By Vaughn Heppner

ISBN-13: 978-1542345989
ISBN-10: 1542345987
BISAC: Fiction / Science Fiction / Military

-1-

Captain Maddox ducked at the shrill sound of a high-energy buildup. A millisecond later, a pulse-bolt flashed over his head. The bolt struck a tunnel wall behind him. The energy sizzled through the metal plating, scouring the planetoid rock behind it.

Maddox drew a long-barreled gun. He should have brought a higher-caliber weapon. The pistol was a marksman's tool. He believed an android had just fired at him, and they were notoriously difficult to kill with anything but the biggest weapons. Had Ludendorff planned an assassination attempt *together* with the androids, or had the androids found the professor's hideout and were they now trying to stop the captain from reaching Ludendorff?

The tunnel's overhead lights flickered once, twice, and then abruptly went out. It turned the deep corridor pitch-black.

In his imagination, Maddox could hear Sergeant Riker's disapproving voice. The sergeant had told him less than forty minutes ago that it was rash to go down alone. Maybe the sergeant had had a point.

Maddox shifted positions as he slipped a pair of goggles over his eyes. They contained advanced sensors that recorded data from his surroundings and turned it into something his eyes could recognize.

He was deep underground on Saturn's largest moon, Titan. These were old tunnels, dating back more than two hundred years. He was in a large access tube several hundred meters before reaching a huge storage area filled with old machines. He was too deep for Galyan to communicate with him. He was even too far from Riker's position many levels above.

The captain studied the darkness. Junk littered the way. There! He saw movement. A man—an android?—peered over a rusted machine. The humanoid drew back his arm. The hand clutched a grenade-sized object.

Instinctively, Maddox fired three quick shots. He knew each shot would give away his position, but he had to stop the grenade before it became airborne.

Two bullets went wide. The third hit the wrist as the hand moved forward, stopping the arm's forward movement. It caused the fingers to spasm open. The grenade lost its forward momentum and fell.

Maddox dove from his location, rolled across the floor and struck an old machine on the other side of the corridor. The dive was in case another assassin had pinpointed him because of the pistol shots.

Up ahead, an explosion caused metal to blast apart, raining everywhere. The concussion blew debris as far as Maddox's location.

The captain was crouched low, with his hands over his ears. The blast and heat told him that had been a military grade grenade, not a mere police tool for subduing criminals.

Cautiously, the captain peered up from his new spot. He was a lean individual, taller than most, with angular features and a high metabolism due to his dual nature as half human and half New Man. He was a captain in the Patrol arm of Star Watch. Not so very long ago, he had been in Intelligence. He wore his uniform now, along with several special items on a utility belt.

Starship *Victory*—the ancient alien vessel he commanded—waited in Titan orbit for him. He had left the ship in the hands of Lieutenant Noonan and Galyan, the vessel's alien AI, for this mission.

"Captain Maddox," a voice—man or android—called from the darkness.

Maddox grinned to himself. Did the second assassin believe he would answer and give away his position?

"This is the end of the line for you, Captain. You have fought valiantly for many years but your use is at an end. Do you understand what I'm trying to tell you?"

With infinitesimal deliberation, Maddox peered from around the lowest part of the side of the machine that served as his cover. That gave him a limited view, but it was hopefully the unexpected move as far as the assassin was concerned.

"Do you know…?" the assassin said, pausing for effect.

Maddox could not see him.

"That I know your father's identity?" the assassin finished.

The captain's gut clenched as his breathing tightened. Could this be true or did it merely mean the enemy understood one of his motivations? Maddox would bet on the latter. Still, if the assassin did know this…

"You are quiet, Captain. Are you afraid of me?"

Maddox debated with himself. Slowly, he peered over the machine. The man or android peered around a larger machine fifty meters ahead, with a scoped rifle aimed in Maddox's general direction.

The captain ducked behind his machine, doing so barely in time—thanks to his speeded reflexes. Something hissed overhead. Unseen in the darkness, the captain's smooth forehead furrowed with furious thought.

The assassin used spring-driven ammunition. The shots would not give away the assassin's location as the pistol had done with his.

"I know where you are now," the assassin said. "You are doomed, Captain. I merely adjust my weapon so—"

Maddox heard faint clicking. He clutched his gun with manic strength. Was this it? Did the assassin have grenades? Should he try to retreat? Maybe he should charge the assassin and try to close—

A loud report sounded from behind Maddox. He flinched in surprise. So that had been the assassin's game. The enemy had spoken in order to cover the approach of a third assassin from behind. He should have understood the ploy sooner.

An explosion sounded from farther ahead.

Maddox cocked his head in surprise. That was odd. What could have—?

"Captain?" a gruff-voiced man called. "Are you hit, sir?"

"Sergeant Riker?" Maddox asked in amazement.

"Yes, sir," Riker called from behind. By the sounds, the sergeant was forty meters or so to his rear.

"What did you just do?" Maddox asked.

"I used a grenade-launcher," Riker said. "I believe your attacker is dead. At least, he's not moving and he has a big machine lying on his head."

Maddox ingested that. "I gave you explicit orders to remain behind."

"You did, sir. But Brigadier O'Hara countermanded the order and told me to hurry and find you. She had reason to believe you were in danger, and it seems she was right."

"The brigadier is on Titan?"

"No, sir," Riker said. "She's in Titan's orbit."

Maddox nodded. That seemed implausible and much too fortuitous. He might be *di-far*, but this was stretching the bounds of luck beyond reason.

Di-far was a Spacer term for a person who could change the destiny of worlds and civilizations. Such a one could lift a world's fate, as it were, and set it onto other tracks with a completely different future outcome. Such a one often had lucky breaks.

"What are your orders?" Riker called.

Maddox cocked his head in the other direction. Was the sergeant being insistent? That seemed odd, and off. The man was his subordinate, a solid plodder, usually waiting for orders, not insisting he receive them. Hmm…maybe something else was in play here. It was time to find out. Yes, it was time to play this new hand.

"Keep a sharp lookout, Sergeant."

"Sir?"

"Do you see anyone else?"

Several seconds passed until Riker said, "I do not."

"Then come up and join me," Maddox said.

"Where exactly are you?"

"Just hurry along, Sergeant. I believe Time is our enemy, particularly if we're going to save Ludendorff from the androids."

-2-

In the darkness, the two men stood near the dead android. One of them was tall: the captain. The other was shorter, with the beginning shoulder-hunch of an older man. Despite the darkness, Maddox could see Riker's weathered features. The sergeant's left eye and arm were bionic.

The sergeant wore a pair of goggles similar to his own. The captain knew that Riker's bionic eye could see just fine in the dark. Why, then, did the sergeant wear sensor goggles like him?

Could the androids have committed an oversight?

"Is something wrong?" the sergeant asked.

"I notice you've closed your top button. Is your throat feeling better then?"

"My throat?" Riker asked. "Oh, yes, it is. Thank you for asking, sir."

Maddox kept his features bland despite the realization that he was alone with the enemy and deep from any quick help. Why would the androids destroy one of their own in order to try to foster this pretense? It must have something to do with Ludendorff.

There was nothing wrong with Riker's throat, of course. The captain had just made that up. And he was nearly one hundred percent certain this was an android play because…

The pseudo-Riker's grenade had knocked down the second assassin and caused the machine to fall on the individual. Tiny sparks still sizzled within the crushed cranium, showing the circuitry of an android brain.

Maddox knelt on one knee as he studied the dead construct. He did not know why—but the crushed head did not strike him as an ancient Builder-made android. This construct seemed to have been manufactured within the last few years on some human world. In other words, this dead android was a throwaway.

Did that mean the android acting as Riker was the real deal—an old Builder android? It was an interesting possibility.

Maddox noticed the crushed rifle. That was too bad. He had planned to take the weapon. There was no point now.

Standing, Maddox decided on his options. The pretend-Riker android would be hard to kill with the pistol. He would have to shoot it in an eye to do so, and that task was made more difficult with the thing's goggles.

The captain did not glance at the pseudo-Riker. He was not sure he could hide his revulsion. If the android had harmed his faithful sergeant—

"Follow me," Maddox said abruptly. "And keep a sharp lookout for others."

"Begging your pardon, sir," the pseudo-Riker said, hurrying to catch up. "But is it wise to continue? The brigadier gave me strict orders to find you and bring you back up. Besides, what can your gun do to other androids if we find them?"

Maddox did not respond to the question. Instead, he continued down the old corridor, with his long-barreled gun ready. He could hear the construct's footsteps as it followed behind him.

Old and discarded machines from an earlier space age littered the tunnel. These tunnels and machines came from the time before Laumer-Drive technology. These days, Maddox realized that Methuselah Man Strand had given mankind the liberating jump technology. Strand was the evil Methuselah Man. Professor Ludendorff was the…well, maybe not the good one. Ludendorff was the more helpful of the two, and he was supposed to be down here in the old Titan mines.

Ludendorff had called Maddox several days ago, asking him to come immediately. Maddox knew that the Methuselah Man had a reason, an intense one, according to the professor's hints. Ludendorff had also asked Maddox to come down alone. That was suspicious, but a gut instinct caused him to trust the professor in this, this time.

The two of them—Maddox and the Riker fake—sidestepped derelict, rusty machines. The air was colder down here and stale in places. Maddox had a rebreather ready, but he had not yet put the mask over his mouth and nose.

Maddox wondered if the pseudo-Riker truly believed he did not suspect the real situation. What was the thing's game?

As Maddox strode purposefully, he started scratching his stomach in order to keep his hand near a special weapon. It was a prized monofilament knife with a hardened alloy blade. It had an unbelievable edge of interlocking molecules, the reason why it was called a monofilament weapon. It could literally cut through anything, and that would include the unique Builder metal that often lay underneath an android's fleshly disguise.

"How much farther is our destination, sir?"

Once more, Maddox did not respond to the question. He did not like people asking him too much. He had ordered Riker to follow him. If the sergeant asked too many questions, it smacked too closely of insubordination. Maddox detested that in underlings. He had come to believe that others viewed this behavior as part of his New Man heritage. He did not like to believe that was what caused the feeling of dislike. He was his own person. He was not some *mini-replica* of the New Men. What he disliked, he disliked, and that was that.

"Sir..."

"Shut up, Sergeant," Maddox said.

The pseudo-Riker quit talking.

Two minutes later, Maddox reached a floor hatch. He knelt, tapped a code into an old but surprisingly dust-free keypad, twisted a handle and opened the hatch. Holstering the long-barreled gun, Maddox slid his feet onto a steel ladder and began to climb down.

Above him, the pseudo-Riker followed.

***

Three levels down, the ceiling lights glowed dimly. Maddox no longer wore his goggles, although he let them hang at his throat just in case he needed them quickly.

The pseudo-Riker did the same thing with his goggles. The fake sergeant carried a dual-purpose weapon known in Star Watch slang as an over-and-under. The under part was a grenade-launcher. The above part fired heavy caliber slugs. Those would be android-killing bullets.

The tunnels had narrowed down here, and the air had grown staler. They no longer passed regular hatches. The doors were more like ancient bank-vault entrances, each with a keypad to the side.

"Why do you think Ludendorff is hiding down here?" the pseudo-Riker asked.

"You can ask him soon enough," Maddox said curtly.

A hundred meters later, they turned a corner. Maddox stiffened.

"Is something wrong, sir?"

Maddox silently filed away the data that the supposed android watched him closely.

"It is," the captain said, leaving it at that.

Like a stalking jungle cat, Maddox continued down the corridor. He passed another vault-like entrance, and then one more. The third heavy entrance was ajar the slightest bit. What was worse, it was the entrance to Ludendorff's hidden location.

Was this what the fake Riker wanted from him: the entrance location? Maddox scratched his stomach and twisted around to check on the sergeant.

The pseudo-Riker glanced at him. The twin barrels of his over-and-under were aimed at the floor per regulations.

That surprised the captain.

"Trouble?" the Riker double asked.

"We will assume so. I'll open the door. You get ready to fire at anything suspicious inside."

The pseudo-Riker nodded, and did not seem distrustful regarding Maddox's orders.

Soon, Maddox stood by the vault-like entrance, latching onto the handle with both hands. The fake Riker took up his position.

"It's lit in there," the sergeant whispered.

"Now," Maddox whispered, pulling the heavy vault-like entrance.

The sergeant scanned the chamber until his shoulders slumped. "I don't believe this."

Maddox waited.

"Professor Ludendorff is dead," the sergeant said.

-3-

Maddox followed the sergeant into the spacious chamber. The lights were brighter in here than outside.

There were worktables along the sides and advanced computer equipment. There were also several strange machines, one of them a large aquarium with an android skeleton floating in a green solution. Wires and cables sprouted from the metallic-gleaming construct.

A medium-sized corpse lay sprawled in the middle of the room. He wore a white lab-coat, had tanned skin and a neat burn-hole in the center of his forehead.

There were others dead in the chamber, two androids with huge craters in their chest areas. A big melted gun lay near the dead scientist.

"I cannot believe this," the sergeant said, as he stood over the dead man.

Maddox approached, making a show of holstering the pistol. He knelt beside Ludendorff, staring at the corpse, and realized immediately that it was not the professor. It was a close approximation of the Methuselah Man, but it clearly was not him. That was a relief, but it didn't surprise the captain. He had long since learned to distrust notices of the professor's death. The Methuselah Man loved employing body doubles and he'd proved exceedingly difficult to kill for those who had tried in the past.

"Why do you think the androids killed him?" the sergeant asked.

Maddox thought about motives, but not the motives of those who had slain the Ludendorff look-alike. He considered the motives of the pseudo-Riker. Why had the android gone to this elaborate charade? Why show him this? The best reason Maddox could suppose was to identify the corpse. The fake Riker had said, "Ludendorff is dead." Then, the sergeant had gone straight here. If this wasn't Ludendorff, was Maddox supposed to say so?

Instead of commenting, Maddox stood, going to one of the slain androids. He did not study it in detail. He let his subconscious tell him—

It was a Builder-made android. He was certain that was true. According to the android Yen Cho of last voyage, there were few of these kinds of androids in Human Space. Two dead ones here meant something vital.

"You are quiet," the sergeant said.

Maddox ignored the comment. He went to the large aquarium with the floating metal skeleton. Had Ludendorff done this? Maddox suspected so. What had the professor hoped to achieve?

"You have discovered something," the sergeant said.

Maddox glanced back at the construct. The sergeant aimed the over-and-under at him.

"You don't seem surprised," the construct said.

"At your treachery?" asked Maddox.

The thing watched him. It seemed impassive now. Whatever program had run the "Riker" interface had stopped.

"When did you realize I was not your sergeant?" the android asked.

Maddox said nothing.

"Do you want to die, then?"

"No," Maddox said.

"The requirement to live longer is that you answer my questions," the android said.

"I think the opposite is true. Once I've given you the answers you desire, you will kill me to cover your tracks."

"In that case, I might as well kill you and leave. I do not know why, but I feel that this is an exposed position."

"You're right about that," Maddox said. "I wonder if that means you're developing a sixth sense. Wouldn't you agree that that would be a metaphysically interesting proposition for an android?"

"Is that Ludendorff's corpse?"

"You already said it was," Maddox replied.

"Come now, Captain. You are not stupid like most humans. You have—"

A high-pitched whine began in the room. It rose sharply in volume. Maddox clapped his hands over his ears, and he dropped to the floor.

The android pulled the trigger. A grenade flew. It smashed against the aquarium, breaking through into a sludge-like substance. A tiny green glob oozed through the breakage. At that point, the grenade exploded. Something about the green sludge retarded the process. A bit more of the substance oozed through the breakage, while the rest of the aquarium glass starred. That was it, however. The android skeleton rode out the muffled explosion inside the aquarium.

Maddox might have scrambled to his feet. The high-pitched whine had worsened, however. It made him lethargic, his muscles weak. Slowly, he looked at the pseudo-Riker. He expected to see the thing targeting him. Instead, the android stood frozen like a statue.

At that point, a hidden hatch opened. A man, or possibly an android, stepped out. The individual wore a crinkling silver-suit with a fully enclosed helmet, one with a darkened visor. The suited person approached the frozen android. As he did, he withdrew a knife much like the monofilament blade Maddox carried. The suited individual made a deep incision in the back of the pseudo-Riker's neck. Blood flowed, but less than there should have been if he'd been human. The silver-suited person took out a small tool, reached into the incision and wrestled with something at the base of the skull.

Abruptly, the android collapsed onto the floor.

The suited individual clicked something on his belt. Immediately, the whine cycled down until it ceased altogether.

Maddox felt exhausted. Gingerly, he removed his hands from his ears and sat up slowly.

As the captain did this, he saw the suited individual take hold of his own helmet. He twisted until it clicked, and removed the helmet from his head. It was Professor Ludendorff, or a perfect replica of him. The man was bald with a hooked nose and deeply tanned skin.

"Well done, Captain," Ludendorff said. "I do believe I have finally acquired the android I've needed for some time. I'm hoping you'll assist me, though. We have to patch the aquifer before the solution drips out, and we have to scan the high-grade brain before it deteriorates beyond recovery."

Maddox worked his mouth, until he was finally able to speak. "There must be more androids nearby."

"Of that I have no doubt, my boy. Thus, you should take the construct's weapon. Check the ammo supply, of course. Go seal the door afterward. It will take anyone some time before they can break through that."

"We're trapped down here."

"Nonsense," Ludendorff said. "I always have an escape hatch. Now get up, please. We have much to do and little time to do it in."

"You used me as bait," Maddox said, finally able to climb to his feet.

"Please, no recriminations. I did what I had to. It worked, and I may have just saved humanity by doing so. You may negate my tremendous advantage if you dilly-dally, though. Thus, I encourage you to get moving, my boy. The clock is ticking on the human race, and I believe I am the only one with the brainpower to save it—with your help, naturally, and that of your wonderful ship."

Maddox studied the Methuselah Man. The professor had a plan. How much of it helped humanity and how much of it helped Ludendorff? The captain shrugged. He might as well get on with it, as the professor had suggested. When the Methuselah Man was like this, he loved to boast.

Maddox went to the pseudo-Riker and picked up the over-and-under.

"Did the android kill my sergeant?"

"What?" Ludendorff asked. The professor had knelt and he was busy detaching the android's head from its body.

"Is Sergeant Riker alive?" Maddox asked.

"That is an interesting question. Now, quickly shut the door. I feel naked with it open. Oh, quit fretting about Riker. We'll find out soon enough. We have to interrogate the android's circuits before the others realize I've tricked everyone. I have a clue, a tantalizing idea, but only the oldest androids can give me confirmation. That is why I've gone to such lengths to draw such a one to me."

Maddox made his decision, hurrying to the vault-like entrance and closing it. He wanted to know if Riker was alive, but he also wanted to know the professor's plan. As far as he could see, this was the fastest way to finding out both.

-4-

Two days later, Starship *Victory* parked in Earth orbit.

Captain Maddox had traveled as fast as possible from Titan once he'd learned Ludendorff's plan. He had not sent a message ahead regarding the plan. He hadn't dared to risk someone intercepting it.

He had debated using the star drive to make the short hop from Saturn to Earth. Building up velocity the normal way and then decelerating wasted too much time. Valerie had argued otherwise.

"If you use the star drive," Valerie had said, "that will alert whoever is watching us that you've found something critical."

It was good thinking, and the captain had followed her advice.

Fortunately, a few of Maddox's assumptions in the Titan tunnels had been wrong. The android had been lying about Brigadier O'Hara being in Titan orbit. Nothing had happened to Sergeant Riker, either. Each was a relief, although Maddox had not informed anyone of his feelings in that regard.

The captain did vocalize his concerns regarding android interference. Last voyage, Maddox had learned that the androids had competing factions. Some wanted nothing to do with humans, distrusting them intensely. The smaller but older group helped humanity from time to time. The androids were, for the most part, Builder-built. Those had escaped Builder service throughout the centuries and led independent lives. All of these androids wanted to continue that way. Thus, for the most part, the androids remained hidden, living their lives as humans. A couple of voyages back, some of the androids from an ancient Builder base at the bottom of the Atlantic Ocean had moved openly. They had tried to take over Earth's government, but Star Watch had eventually crushed them.

Last voyage, Yen Cho—probably the oldest android in existence—had informed Ludendorff and Maddox that some of the oldest models had lived as Methuselah Men.

Maddox did not know Yen Cho's present location. Yet, the captain was certain the old and cagey android had learned, or would do so soon, what had transpired down in the oldest Titan mine.

"The brigadier is waiting to see you, sir," Lieutenant Noonan said over a shuttle's comm.

"Roger that, love," Lieutenant Keith Maker answered in lieu of the captain. The small Scotsman piloted the shuttle, lifting off *Victory's* hangar deck and heading for space.

Maddox sat in his seat, deep in thought. He wondered what the Iron Lady would make of Ludendorff's proposal. She would have to go to the Lord High Admiral with this.

"Shall I take evasive maneuvers?" Keith asked.

Maddox nodded.

"Are you expecting trouble, sir?"

"We've always had trouble when we're carrying delicate information like this," Maddox said. "Why would it be any different now?"

"Right you are, sir," Keith said, grinning. "I suggest you hang on tightly then. This is going to be fun."

***

With the Eastern Coast of the United States showing below them, Keith maneuvered the shuttle as if they were an eccentric comet. They burned through the atmosphere, juking, releasing decoys and making sudden and nearly impossible redirections. Otherwise, the ride was uneventful. No androids, no New Men spies—if any were left on Earth—made any attempt against the shuttle.

Faster than ordinary, Keith landed in Geneva, Switzerland.

Maddox unbuckled and headed for the hatch. Just before exiting, he said, "Take her back up, Lieutenant."

"No shore leave?" Keith asked.

The slightest of frowns touched the captain's brow.

"Aye-aye, sir," Keith said. "Straight up is where I'll go."

Maddox nodded before exiting. The ease of the landing had surprised him.

He drew his long-barreled gun once on the tarmac and he sprinted for the buildings in the distance. He ignored the hovers heading for the shuttle, deciding to use misdirection and surprise just in case the androids were being subtle in their approach.

***

An hour later, divested of all his weapons, Maddox waited in a chamber deep under Star Watch Headquarters. He had undergone a thorough scan—the new procedure when Star Watch personnel suspected an android double might be involved.

The captain sat at a large round table. There were several chairs and many screens on the walls. Otherwise, the chamber was bare.

He disliked having this kind of paranoia directed at him. For too long, he had been the outsider in Star Watch. His dual heritage made many powerful people uncomfortable with him. He had learned to live with that, but he didn't like it. Now, though, someone doubted his real identity.

Maddox kept himself perfectly still. Of course, observers watched him through some of the screens. He thus attempted an android-like stillness. In his heart, he resented this suspicion. Thus, he stoked it. Galyan would have undoubtedly told him he did this for nefarious psychological reasons.

A door slid open and Mary O'Hara, the head of Star Watch Intelligence, walked into the chamber. She had an unassuming appearance, with gray hair and a matronly image, slightly offset by her uniform.

She stopped and studied the captain.

Maddox sat perfectly still, watching her out of the corner of his eye.

The Iron Lady motioned to someone unseen outside the chamber. The hatch slid shut and O'Hara headed alone toward the round table.

As she neared, Maddox twisted his head slowly, allowing himself a slow blink, but keeping his features impassive.

O'Hara sighed. "It isn't what you think, Captain."

He raised an eyebrow.

"We had to examine your data first," she said. "Although, I do wish Ludendorff had come himself. Sometimes his paranoia against us is tiring. Where is the professor, anyway?"

Maddox unbent, shedding the robotic manner. "I'm afraid I can't say, Ma'am."

"Nonsense," she said.

"I gave him my word I'd keep mum."

"You took an oath to Star Watch first," O'Hara said.

"In this instance, the two do not conflict," Maddox said.

"And if they did?"

Maddox stood, gave her a short bow and pulled out one of the chairs for her.

"Please," O'Hara said, sweeping past the chair to him. She gave him a hug like a mother would to an errant young boy.

Maddox endured the hug, his features never changing, although he did pat her lightly on the back. He had never told anyone, but he would go through fire for Brigadier O'Hara. He would hunt down like a dog anyone who ever harmed his…former commanding officer.

O'Hara released him, looking up into his face. The smile slowly drained from her features. She nodded and finally sat down.

He helped push in her chair before going back to his own.

"An android would act happier if I gave him a hug," O'Hara complained. "Your robotic response confirms the tests. I am speaking to the real Captain Maddox."

He realized those words were not for his benefit, but for whoever watched the exchange on the screens.

"Professor Ludendorff sends you his regards," Maddox said.

O'Hara frowned slightly before snorting out a small laugh. "I suppose the professor is wise to keep his distance. In this way, I am not tempted to run a battery of tests on *him*."

"I'm sure he agrees with your assessment, Ma'am."

"Do you trust him?" O'Hara asked suddenly.

"That is a loaded question. If you mean, do I trust his motives for wanting to join the projected expedition, the short answer is no. If you mean, do I believe his idea is a sound and reasonable one, then the answer is yes."

"So you think this...*junkyard planet* of his exists?"

"I do."

O'Hara put a small blaster on the table. That surprised the captain. He had not noticed it in her hand before this. The Iron Lady could be more devious than he realized. It also showed that she might have had a smidgen of doubt concerning his identity, despite the screening.

O'Hara cleared her throat. "I, on the other hand, am unconvinced that Ludendorff's idea is sound."

Maddox waited.

Professor Ludendorff had made an incredible discovery. The germ of the idea had come from Yen Cho's data "gulp" last voyage. *Victory* had gone into the Deep Beyond, finding a Golden Nexus. Before escaping the nexus, the advanced android had downloaded ancient data stored in the Builder computer. Yen Cho had given *Victory's* crew the data "gulp" in exchange for a head start from Star Watch Intelligence. So far, little of the data made sense. A few Kai-Kaus chief technicians had had the most luck deciphering certain files. Galyan had also helped in that regard. The best translator of ancient Builder data had been Ludendorff.

Unfortunately, Ludendorff did not trust Star Watch. The professor had reams of priceless knowledge in his head. He was certain Mary O'Hara would like nothing better than to get him in a small room and pump him of all his knowledge. The brigadier's words suggested that the professor was correct in thinking this. The skittishness on Ludendorff's part meant he'd only had limited access to Yen Cho's data "gulp."

Deep underground in the Titan tunnels, Ludendorff had downloaded the latest captured android's knowledge. The professor had run an extremely delicate and advanced program on the captured brain, and had hit upon the location of what the professor had termed, "The Junkyard Planet."

This planet was far from Human Space, out in the Beyond. As the name implied, it was full of junk, of derelict machines and equipment. Only…these were old Builder machines. The Builders were ancient and highly advanced aliens, responsible for the Methuselah Men, jump technology, nexus pyramids floating in space, the victorious war against the Destroyers millennia ago, a thousand burned Swarm worlds…the list of their accomplishments was long.

"Ludendorff cannot know he will find this…*scanner* on the Junkyard Planet," O'Hara said. "It is a fancy, a dream, a—"

"Do you distrust him personally?" Maddox asked.

O'Hara looked up sharply. "Yes! He has schemed endlessly for his own goals. He has—"

"Helped give us Starship *Victory*," Maddox said quietly.

"That is imprecise," O'Hara said. "His notes proved critical. But the professor did not acquire the alien starship in person. You did that."

"Without his notes, it would have proved impossible."

O'Hara studied the captain. It seemed as if the question was torn out of her. "Do you think we should race off to this derelict world?"

"I think Starship *Victory*, the Destroyer, the Kai-Kaus and their fund of high technology have all greatly aided us in one way or another. Each of those things came about in part because of the Builders."

"I cannot deny that," O'Hara said.

"The Swarm is out there," Maddox said, remembering the terrifying fleet he had seen last voyage. He shook his head. "Star Watch, all the human races combined, cannot face the full might of the Swarm. *Victory* was able to race home last voyage because of the Golden Nexus's hyper-spatial tube. What if the Swarm conquers the Golden Nexus, taking it from its Chitin defenders? In time, Swarm scientists could discover how to create their own hyper-spatial tube. Commander Thrax Ti Ix could already have taught the Swarm the means of using nexuses."

"That is a guess," O'Hara said.

"Yes," Maddox said, "but not altogether an unreasonable one."

Mary O'Hara stared at her wrinkled hands.

The captain sat back, waiting.

Commander Thrax Ti Ix, he mused. He'd encountered the modified Swarm creature on the Builder Dyson sphere *Victory* had visited two voyages ago. Thrax had infected the Builder on the sphere with Swarm viruses. That Builder had helped Thrax and many of his modified Swarm creatures escape the exploding Dyson sphere. Thrax had led his small fleet into a hyper-spatial tube, fleeing to the Swarm Imperium.

That Imperium controlled as much as one-seventeenth of the Milky Way Galaxy. The Swarm worlds were concentrated in the Orion and Perseus Spiral Arms. The nearest point of the Imperium to the Commonwealth of Planets was 2027 light-years. Until now, it had appeared that the Swarm used sub-light-speed drives, taking incredibly long amounts of time to go from one star system to another. Thrax could have given the Imperium Laumer Drive, star drive and now hyper-spatial tube tech. That would dramatically change the balance of power between the Swarm and humanity.

"There are so many variables to this," O'Hara said in a pleading tone.

"Reality doesn't care about variables," Maddox said. "What is is. If the Swarm launches a fleet at us, we must know that as quickly as possible. We must use our hoped-for mobility against their larger but slower fleets."

"You are making many assumptions," O'Hara said.

"Logical assumptions," Maddox said. "I saw the Swarm fleet. It would take time to refit their warships with star-drive systems. Even giving every tenth ship Laumer-Drive tech would be time-consuming for them. If the Swarm is going to make a quick stab at us, they would likely use Commander Thrax's vessels alone or add hordes of sub-light traveling Swarm vessels to his ships."

O'Hara frowned, becoming thoughtful.

Motion caught Maddox's eye. He looked up. The Lord High Admiral regarded him from a wall screen.

Admiral Cook was a large old man with a red face and gruff features. He wore a white uniform. The Lord High Admiral ran Star Watch. He had not always trusted the captain, although that had changed lately.

"How…likely do you think it is that such a scanner is still in existence at the Junkyard Planet?" Cook asked.

"As to that, sir, I can't say," Maddox replied. "But I think gaining anything like that is worth the effort."

"You are forgetting about opportunity costs," Cook said ponderously. "If *Victory* attempts to race to the Junkyard Planet, it cannot be somewhere else. If this is one of Ludendorff's scams…"

"I understand," Maddox said.

The captain could still hardly believe what Ludendorff claimed to have discovered. The implications had been there all along, though. Maybe that was what he should be emphasizing to the Lord High Admiral.

"Sir," Maddox said. "I spoke to the Builder on the Dyson sphere. He showed me an amazing star field. He had what seemed to be up-to-date knowledge regarding far-flung territories. We have the long-range communicators. Well, Ludendorff has one, and a few New Men have others, and I believe Star Watch possesses two, at least. That shows it is possible to communicate across many light-years. That is something we believed impossible just a few years ago."

"True," Cook said.

"A hyper-spatial tube can send a ship a thousand light-years or more in a moment," Maddox said. "That is Builder technology. Why, then, couldn't there be a scanner that can see hundreds of light-years in a moment? With such a scanner, we could create an advanced warning system, knowing the instant an enemy invasion fleet entered our territory."

"It is a tantalizing possibility," Cook admitted. "Yet, such a scanner seems more magical than technological."

"I won't dispute that," Maddox said. "Yet, if Star Watch had such a scanner, able to view a hundred light-years away, we could use it powerfully to our advantage."

"Hmmm," Cook said. "The obvious move, if we possessed such a scanner, would be to create a giant, centrally located fleet. The moment the Swarm appeared, we would know and could begin a counter-assault against them."

Maddox knew when to fall silent, letting the idea and the possibilities do the arguing for him.

"There must be other marvels on this Junkyard Planet, as well," Cook said with a far-off, contemplative stare.

"Undoubtedly," Maddox said.

That refocused the Lord High Admiral. He studied the captain. "Ludendorff will want some of these marvels for himself."

"Agreed," Maddox said.

Cook sighed deeply before regarding O'Hara. "Are you dead set against the voyage, Brigadier?"

O'Hara looked up. "No, sir, not dead set. I just wonder why…" She glanced at Maddox, then quickly away.

"Yes, I understand," Cook said in as soft a voice as he could manage. "Why must we always send the captain? The answer is obvious. He has the best ship for such ventures, and he has proven himself as the best man for these missions. Perhaps it would be wiser to deliberate about this, but the possibility of gaining a Builder scanner is too urgent." The admiral fixed Maddox with his stare. "You must begin the voyage at once, Captain."

"I have a few requirements before I leave the Solar System," Maddox said.

"Waiting to leave for any reason is dangerous," Cook said. "Androids might use that to sneak aboard your ship."

"We'll have to double security."

Cook nodded slowly. "Do you have anything to add, Brigadier?"

"We could use the Spacers in this," O'Hara said.

"Tell me where they're hiding," Cook said.

"I have no idea," O'Hara said. "No one has seen a Spacer for the past few months."

Cook waited several heartbeats before he said, "Is there anything else, Captain?"

"Not that I can think of, sir."

"Then it is decided," Cook said. "I charge you with finding this Junkyard Planet and returning to Earth with the Builder scanner Ludendorff claims is there. Do it quickly, Captain. The sooner we get such a scanner operating…"

"I understand, sir. If it's there, I will—"

"No!" O'Hara said, alarmed. "Do not boast. Do your best. That is all we ask. I do not want you to jinx the expedition by making grandiose boasts."

Maddox raised an eyebrow before nodding.

Victory had its newest destination. It would no doubt prove to be a highly interesting voyage.

One thing he would try to learn, however, was the professor's real reason for wanting to go to this dead Builder world. Ludendorff would try something nefarious there. Of that, the captain had no doubt.

-5-

A week later and well over a hundred light-years from Earth, a cloaked star cruiser moved through an uncharted system—uncharted in relation to Star Watch maps at any rate. It was the Star Cruiser *Argo*, named long ago by its unique commander.

Deep inside the *Argo*, in a heavily armored chamber located there for maximum protection, a wizened old man hunched over a computer console. He had hellish embers for eyes and muttered softly to himself as he worked.

He was the Methuselah Man Strand, and he ruled like a tyrant aboard the carefully modified vessel. The crew was composed of golden-skinned New Men, each of them controlled through mind-altering brain surgeries.

Strand manipulated the computer screen, which held a dizzyingly complex mathematical formula. It was his latest endeavor as he tried to calculate the Emperor's response to his offer.

There were so many factors to consider. If he added a threat here—Strand tapped the screen, waited, and watched a rippling change throughout the complex formula.

This was not good. If he went that route, three years from now, the indicators showed—

A *beep* broke Strand's vaunted concentration. With an irritated scowl, he glanced up at the intercom system.

"Yes?" he growled.

"Excellency," a New Man said from a small screen. "A star cruiser has entered the system."

"Is it fully intact?"

"Excellency, you ordered—"

"I know very well what I ordered," Strand snarled. "I expect passive sensor-scans only."

"Yes, Excellency," the New Man said in a rote manner.

Strand studied the individual. The New Man's name was Dem Darius. He was taller than average and of a more noble bearing than ordinary. He was the acting commander in Strand's absence. Once, Darius had commanded a flotilla of star cruisers. He had run across Strand back in the day, and made a routine visit to the *Argo*. Darius's arrogant manner had angered Strand. Thus, he had kept the flotilla commander, using his cloaking to slip away from the other star cruisers.

"The sensors do not indicate any battle damage to the approaching vessel," Darius said. "However, the star cruiser's furtive manner indicates otherwise."

"Maintain our position," Strand said. "I'm coming up."

***

Several hours later, the *Argo* adjusted its course.

Strand sat in the commander's chair in the center of the bridge. Dem Darius was at the gunner's seat, checking the ship's weapons.

Whenever the Methuselah Man felt ill at ease or downcast, he would eye the noble-looking golden-skinned superman. Strand would recall Darius's arrogant words from that long-ago time. It settled Strand's unease to see that even the proud broke under his genius and cunning. He was the ultimate man. He always rose to the supreme position.

Feeling better, Strand focused on the latest situation.

The system possessed a G-class star with four planets, one of them terrestrial and the rest gas giants of various sizes. There were no appreciable asteroid belts or Oort clouds, and absolutely no comets in the system.

The enemy star cruiser had come out of the Laumer-Point nearest the star. The triangular-shaped vessel headed toward the jump point at the third planet, a gas giant with seething, swirling planetary-wide cloud cover.

Strand had been worried that the New Men had discovered his secret base here. For some time now, he'd expected more Throne World warships to tumble out of the star's jump point. None had, and this star cruiser traveled in a seemingly oblivious manner.

"Their commander appears to be unaware of my outpost," Strand said.

None of his New Men responded to the comment. They were not supposed to. Even so, their silence rankled.

It was true that he maintained iron discipline aboard his ship so that he had complete control. If he gave any one of them any independent thought at all, that one might foment a rebellion. That would mean Strand's death, at best. It could mean his subjection, at worst. However, he still occasionally missed normal back-and-forth conversations. He had not had one of those since—

Ludendorff! That had been the last time. It had been via the long-distance communicators they both possessed.

He would crush the professor one of these days. Presently, he had more important fish to fry.

At his signal, the vessel began an intense burn. He wanted to build up as much velocity as he could while the regular star cruiser was behind the second planet in relation to them. That would be for less than an hour. The cloak only worked effectively without any burn or with the special "silent running" system. That allowed the *Argo* to *creep* from one location to another.

Strand's secret base was hidden on the extra-large moon of the third planet. The moon had an atmosphere, but a person could not survive in it without aid. Still, the "air" helped in certain regards. An underground complex holding several thousand people existed there. They were mostly technical people, with enough pay-girls thrown into the mix to keep the men from rebelling due to boredom. More to the point, Lore Fallows had worked there for quite some time. To date, the Kai-Kaus chief technician had manufactured several disrupter cannons. Strand's cloaked star cruiser possessed one of those, among its other armaments.

Strand had kidnapped Lore Fallows from the sub-men while in Neptune orbit. That stealthy maneuver was finally about to pay some real dividends.

The Methuselah Man grinned with genuine humor. He had many debts. Some might call them grudges. Strand prided himself on paying back those kinds of debts with interest. The Emperor of the New Men had expelled him from the Throne World. This was his chance to begin the payback against the ungrateful pretender.

Strand's breathing quickened as he considered the breadth of his grievance. He had created the New Men through an intense process. Originally, he had begun a eugenics program to develop superior soldiers. Those soldiers would defend humanity against the terrible menaces out there. That had been over one hundred and fifty years ago. The Thomas Moore Society—

Never mind about that!

The New Men had escaped his grasp. That had been in large part due to the present Emperor and that prissy-boy, Golden Ural. They would both learn what it meant to cross him. Professor Ludendorff would learn—the galaxy—

Strand balled his ancient fingers into fists, squeezing. He had to maintain his decorum. He had to control his rage. He had made too many mistakes lately. He was going to change that. He would turn everything around. First, he had to capture that star cruiser over there.

"Steady as she goes," Strand said, to no one in particular. He watched his bridge crew, though. He watched to see if any of them nodded to each other or secretly signaled in any other way. None did. Thus, the *Argo's* acceleration continued without any unwonted actions on the Methuselah Man's part.

***

Later, Strand left the bridge, slept for a spell, worked on his equation and finally returned to the bridge. Many of the personnel had changed to the second team, although Dem Darius remained at the gunner's console.

The *Argo* drifted on its built-up velocity. The enemy star cruiser continued to accelerate as it headed for the Laumer-Point.

Strand was not worried. He did not believe the star cruiser would attempt to enter the jump point at its present speed. It would have to decelerate first. That meant the two ships would reach the third planet at roughly the same time.

This was the essence of many space battles. It took time to maneuver into position. Space was vast. Missiles or drones often had to travel for days to reach the enemy. Beams were incredibly short-ranged, given interstellar and even star-system distances. Most beams rarely reached effective performance beyond one hundred thousand kilometers. Strangely, that made missiles the weapon of choice for long-distance conflicts. It was strange because missiles were so much slower than a speed-of-light beam.

For Strand's purposes, the *Argo* needed to be even closer than normal. He had a trick up his sleeve. Even though it would be quite some time before he could employ the trick, his gut had begun to squeeze in anticipation.

The Methuselah Man silently recited many mind-litanies to calm himself. Finally, he gave bridge command back to Darius.

Strand left the bridge and went to exercise. He read a book afterward, ate a tasty meal and thought about going to the sex-simulator. No. It was better to leave sex out of this for now.

As one of the oldest beings alive, he had learned that the great problem with long life was ennui or boredom. He could have anything ordinary he wanted. That meant none of those things satisfied him these days. Only difficultly acquire things brought pleasure. Revenge against the powerful was among the hardest to gain. Thus, it brought him the greatest joy when achieved.

What did a man want to make him happy? Just a little more was the answer. Well, Strand wanted a *lot* more. They would see. They would all see.

***

The third planet of the system, the second gas giant with its swirling atmosphere, grew larger by the hour. Strand looked out a viewing port, seeing the planet with his naked sight.

The enemy star cruiser applied massive deceleration, the exhaust a bright plume in the distance.

On the passive sensors, it was apparent now. The regular star cruiser had taken hull damage earlier. A thorough examination with the passive sensors indicated that the damage had come through heavy hammership cannons. That would seem to indicate the star cruiser had stumbled onto Admiral Fletcher's hunting fleet.

That troubled Strand. If Fletcher was out here, it could ruin everything.

Star Watch and its allies still wanted the kidnapped women the New Men had taken at the end of the invasion of "C" Quadrant of the Commonwealth. If Fletcher had made it this far, it was more than possible that he could find the Throne World. If Star Watch's Grand Fleet invaded the Throne World System, the New Men would boil out en masse. Did Star Watch truly desire a grand battle against the New Men before the Swarm arrived?

"Foolish," Strand muttered. *No. Concentrate on the main issue*, he told himself.

Strand forced himself to sit still. He studied the enemy star cruiser. It was three hundred thousand kilometers ahead of them. The gas giant loomed before the enemy vessel. The Laumer-Drive entrance was nearby. The tramline was part of the route to the Throne World.

"The ship is at extreme range of our disrupter cannon," Darius said.

Strand's head jerked before remembering that he'd ordered the gunner to inform him of exactly that information. The Kai-Kaus disrupter was an amazing weapon. It would revolutionize space warfare. He could understand why Admiral Fletcher felt so confident. But Strand would not snipe at the star cruiser at extremely long range.

"Steady as she goes," he said.

The minutes passed into a half hour. The half hour grew into a full hour and then two. The enemy vessel was now two hundred thousand kilometers away from them.

"They have turned on their Laumer-Point sensing gear," Darius said.

"Drop our cloak," Strand said. "Then go full ahead at maximum speed."

It didn't take long after that.

"Sir," a New Man said. "The enemy commander is hailing us."

"Ignore him," Strand said.

"Sir," the New Man said shortly. "He is threating to target us unless we identify ourselves."

"Open channels," Strand said.

As the comm officer tapped his controls, Strand donned a holo-mask. He fiddled with it until it showed him as a golden-skinned New Man. A moment later, Commander Lars Lark of the *Silver Tangier* stared at Strand from the main screen.

"What is the meaning of this?" Lark demanded.

The New Man had arrogant features like many of his kind. He had bristly black hair, sharp angles to his face and almost-gleaming eyes like a stellar eagle. He wore a black uniform with silver insignia on his shoulders and left pectoral, signifying that he was part of the Emperor's Guard, a chosen group of starship commanders.

"This, my fine fellow," Strand said blandly, "is a little surprise for the Emperor."

"You must be more explicit," Lark said.

"Oh, must I?" Strand asked.

The commander's eyes flashed. "Are you threatening us? If so, why?"

"Come, now," said Strand. "This is improper. You—"

"A moment," Lark said, as he held up a preemptory hand.

The commander turned his head as if listening to someone unseen on his bridge. Lark nodded curtly to the hidden someone and stared like a predatory beast at Strand.

"You are the Methuselah Man," Lark said coldly.

Strand barely concealed his surprise. He finally managed to ask, "Do I look like the—"

"Enough!" Lark said, interrupting. "State your intentions, Methuselah Man."

"Sir," Darius said. "The *Silver Tangier's* targeting systems are locking onto us."

"Take your weapons offline, at once," Strand told the commander.

"You are a traitor," Lark told him. "Prepare to receive a traitor's reward."

"You fool. I'm here bearing gifts."

"You are a notorious liar," Lark said. "I have no intention of ending my days as part of your heinous crew."

"Sir—" Darius said from the gunner's console.

Strand couldn't believe it. On the main screen, the triangular-shaped star cruiser opened fire. A red fusion beam speared from the hull-damaged vessel, heading straight at Strand's precious *Argo*.

-6-

The fusion beam struck the electromagnetic shield with greater energy than Strand had expected. This must be a new-and-improved fusion beam.

"The shield is absorbing the strike, Master," Darius said. "What are your orders?"

Behind his holo-mask, Strand scowled. He did not like Darius asking him anything. It indicated a struggling will that was attempting to free itself from bondage.

"Keep bearing in," Strand finally said.

There was a stir among his bridge crew. Strand noticed, and he almost quailed inside. What was going on here? He settled a forearm onto his lap. On the wrist was a dark pad with various buttons. He let the fingers of his other hand rest against those buttons. Several coded taps would send a signal to the embedded mini-bombs in his crew's skulls. That would instantly quash any rebellion, although it would also deprive him of his trained bridge personnel.

The fusion beam grew hotter. The shield kept absorbing, darkening in the area as it did so. Bit by bit, the darkening bled into more of the curving shield.

"I will hammer your shield into submission," Lark boasted on the screen. "The Emperor will reward me for ridding the Dominants of your plaguing presence."

"I have not come to fight," Strand said. "The fact that I refuse to open fire on you should prove my good intent."

"Why did you sneak up on my ship then?" Lark demanded.

"I turned off my cloaking device, did I not? That was meant as a sign of my good intentions."

"Sir," Darius said. "The shield is at forty-three percent capacity in the targeted area."

Strand appeared to ignore the information. The truth was otherwise. He did not like this.

"Why won't you believe me?" Strand said.

From the main screen, Lark studied him. The New Man cocked his head a moment. Someone unseen seemed to be urging him to a course of action, or to remain on the course he'd already chosen. Abruptly, Lark chopped a hand through the air.

Several moments later, the fusion beam died away.

Strand wanted to heave a sigh of relief. He wanted to mop his sweaty forehead. He did not allow himself to do either of those things.

"Thank you," the Methuselah Man said.

Lark studied him. What did the Dominant think behind those intense eyes?

"Perhaps I spoke hastily," Lark said. "I thought you were Strand. Yet, you do not speak as he does. Still, the Methuselah Man controls your vessel. If your intentions are peaceful, I must hear it from his lips. I will give you thirty seconds to get him. After that, I will renew my attack until his vessel is destroyed."

Strand seethed at these admonishments. Who was in the shadows over there, advising Lark?

Strand stood. "As you wish, Commander." He headed for the hatch. As he did, he felt an itch between his shoulders. Did that come from Lark studying him from the screen, or from his own New Men?

As soon as Strand stepped into the hall, he shut off the holo-mask. He composed himself, waiting several seconds. This was about buying time to work in close enough. Finally, Strand reentered the bridge, moving to the command chair, settling into it before looking up at the watching Lars Lark.

There was something unseemly in the New Man's gaze, and Strand realized two things that bothered him. Lark had free will. Worse, the New Man's free will permitted him to stare at Strand with revulsion.

"So, you are the Emperor's toad," Lark said in a sneering manner. "I have never seen you in person. I am awed, and I am sickened that such intellect as yours should reside in such an inferior body. Do you not tire of existence as such a small, weak old man?"

"I do," Strand said, deciding he wanted more than anything to make Lark part of his crew.

"If I were you," Lark said, "I would strive for bodily improvement or consider a glorious battle death. Living as you do, century after century in such a mangled form…"

"You tread on dangerous ground by insulting me."

"Why should you say this?" Lark asked. "You have spoken well of the Emperor. You have given me your word of peaceful intention toward my vessel. You have accepted my attack and pleaded for mercy. How then could I fear you?"

"I concede your point," Strand said stiffly.

At the gunner's console, Darius's eyes seemed to widen fractionally.

At the same time, Commander Lark fingered his mouth.

Suddenly, Strand knew what was going on. The New Man was trying to lure him into a trap.

Strand made a bland gesture.

Gunner Darius's back stiffened. A moment later, with practiced skill, he began to target the enemy.

On the screen, Lark's head moved as if he were reading something before him. He looked up sharply at Strand. "You are powering up your disruptor cannon."

"For one reason only," Strand said, "in order to forestall any treachery on your part."

"Do you declare our truce to be at an end?"

"I'm afraid so," Strand said. "You're not going to believe what I have to say in any case. Thus, here is a quick lesson in decorum. It is unwise to insult such a man as I."

An energy build-up whined throughout the *Argo*. Seconds later, a powerful disruptor beam slashed from the vessel. The beam reached across the closing distance, darkening Lark's shield.

Belatedly, a red fusion beam struck back.

It was an uneven contest. The more powerful and technologically advanced disruptor beam relentlessly battered the enemy shield. Soon, it was a black semi-circle before the star cruiser. By that time, Strand's shield had turned a cherry-red color, nothing more.

"Their shield is about to collapse," Darius said.

"Be ready to divert power from the beam," Strand said. "I wish to disable their ship, nothing more."

Darius swiveled around. "That could prove to be a difficult task, Master."

"I did not ask you how hard the process would be," Strand said. "I informed you of my desire. Your responsibility is to see that it happens. Or do you lack such skill?"

Darius seemed to struggle with the answer. His innate New Man superiority no doubt attempted to assert itself. Finally, he said, "I do not know, Master."

"I am not interested if you *know*," Strand said. "I am interested that you do."

A warning from other bridge personnel caused Darius to swivel back to his board. His golden fingers moved furiously across the gunnery panel.

Abruptly, the enemy shield collapsed, breaking under the hellish assault. The full-powered disrupter beam smashed against the armored hull. The beam began to chew through heavy armor plates. At the same time, the vessel's shield tried to reform. That proved impossible with the bar of destructive energy in the way.

Now, the disrupter beam chewed into ablative foam behind the breached armor plates. The beam broke down bulkheads, smashing into the vessel's living quarters.

Abruptly, the disruptor beam quit. It changed targeting vectors as it reappeared and began plowing into engine compartments. It was a delicate attack compared to a few seconds ago. Instead of merely battering down the armor and roving at will, Darius tried to use the destructive force like a scalpel. In truth, it was a fifty-fifty proposition that he could succeed. If the beam hit the wrong chamber, it could cause a massive, ship-wide explosion that would kill everyone aboard.

On no account did Strand desire that.

He fumed on his command chair. Strand's plan had been to close-in and use the stasis field against the enemy vessel. That would have proven so much easier, without this useless destruction. He needed the star cruiser intact. He—

"There," Darius said, with a flourish at his board. "I believe I have given you your wish, Master. I—"

"May have spoken too soon," Strand said in annoyance.

An explosion on the other ship blew away armor plates as well as the main thruster nodules. The debris tumbled away end over end.

Strand froze in harsh anticipation…would more of the star cruiser blow? Would he lose the prized vessel?

Several seconds later, after nothing more happened, Strand exhaled with a rattle in his throat. He coughed for some time afterward, struggling to repress it. He detested such signs of weakness.

Finally, he wheezed and took a drink of a thickened liquid. That helped soothe his sore throat. He noticed that the enemy star cruiser was still relatively intact.

Darius waited at the gunnery console. Did Strand detect pride in the New Man's eyes at his accomplishment?

Strand debated tapping his wrist control, ridding himself of this new source of vexation. Yet, that seemed wasteful. Darius had just proven himself as a skillful soldier, and Strand needed a skilled crew. Still, he wondered if Darius had developed a modicum of free will. Maybe that was why the New Man had handled the disrupter cannon so well.

Strand decided he had some questions that needed answering. First, though, he needed to secure the enemy star cruiser.

-7-

Fifty minutes later, Strand's highly modified *Argo* matched velocities with the drifting vessel. A mere two hundred kilometers separated the star cruisers. No doubt, the survivors over there were prepared for a valiant defense. It was possible that some of them were surprised that he had not yet called on them to surrender.

Strand would not ask them anything yet, nothing that allowed them a choice. He was going to make all the decisions now.

"Begin," he told the new gunner.

Strand had confined Darius to his quarters. He had to think about that one a little longer.

A strange emanation began throughout the craft as a stasis-field generator sucked up the ship's power. Outside, a triangular-shaped field spread from the locus of the *Argo*. The stasis field encompassed the enemy vessel.

At the same time, space commandos spewed from special ejectors. The New Men sped toward the stricken *Silver Tangier*. Each commando soon activated his thruster-pack, each applying terrific thrust in order to slow his velocity. The commandos wore special suits so they could move within the stasis field.

Strand watched from his command chair.

Like space mites, the commandos reached the stricken star cruiser's hull. They used magnetic boots to walk to various hatches. No one on the other side was awake to give them trouble. That was the beauty of the stasis field. The trick was to work the *Argo* in close enough to use it, as the stasis-field generator was an extremely short-ranged weapon.

Strand relaxed as the commandos entered the enemy starship. The Methuselah Man checked his chronometer to see how much time the crew captured by the stasis-field had left to live. If his commandos could not secure the star cruiser in time, those caught in the stasis field would die.

Strand looked around at his bridge crew.

"Sir," the comm officer said sharply.

Strand almost slid out of his chair in surprise. He got to his feet and raised his right hand to touch the control pad on his left wrist. The officer had startled him. On no account should the New Man be able to speak first.

"What is it?" Strand asked in a raspy voice.

"One of the enemy personnel has greeted your commandos. They have the greeter in custody."

"Someone is awake over there?" Strand asked in amazement.

"Yes, Master."

"How did the greeter find the correct sort of suit in time?" he wondered aloud.

"May I speak, Master?"

"Speak, speak," Strand said.

"The individual was not wearing a suit."

"And he's moving and talking within the stasis field?" Strand asked.

"Yes, Master," the comm officer answered.

Strand blinked several times. He didn't know what to say. This was impossible. How could…? Ah.

"My commandos have no doubt captured an android," Strand said. "I can conceive of no other possibility. Yet, what is an android doing on the *Silver Tangier?"*

"I do not know, Master," the comm officer replied.

"A mystery," Strand said to himself. "Tell the commandos to use restraints. I want the android alive. They must secure the star cruiser, and… Yes. They will bring the android to the retrieval shuttle. I have a feeling this creature wants to speak with me."

***

Strand waited until the stasis field went offline. He waited until his teams had secured the enemy star cruiser. By this time, the entire *Silver Tangier* crew was in their starship's brigs. The only person belonging to the enemy craft who was aboard Strand's vessel was its Commander, Lars Lark. Strand had not yet decided how to deal with him. The insults had been too savage for him to brush aside. Yet…if he hoped to lure the Emperor's people here—

"Come," he told his guard.

The five of them marched down a ship's corridor, soon reaching their destination. He allowed the guards to take up position in the scanning room. He sat in a chair and reflected for a moment on what he knew about the android.

His instruments told him this was a genuine Builder-made android. That made the construct incredibly dangerous. There was no telling why it had been aboard the *Silver Tangier*. The android was wise enough to know that greeting the commandos would have made Strand instantly suspicious. The construct was trying to tell him something by the action.

Strand had not survived the centuries by taking unneeded risks. Builder-made androids often possessed great intellect and could be exceptionally cunning. A small part of Strand's hindbrain was telling him to destroy the construct, to have nothing to do with it. And yet…sometimes risks brought fantastic rewards. He had not remained alive for so long by eliminating *every* risk.

Strand felt as if this were one of those moments to accept a dare.

He raised a clicker and pressed it. The big wall screen came on, showing him an android standing absolutely still in a cell.

Strand leaned forward, studying the construct.

They were not on the same deck. While his instruments had not detected a bomb on the thing, that didn't mean it lacked one.

The android was tall, with long silver-blonde hair and handsome features. She wore a gaudy reddish and slightly reflective uniform with a long cape and stylish boots. The android looked to be a woman in her thirties, but that meant less than nothing. The construct could be weeks old or it could be a thousand years old.

Strand pressed another switch on his clicker, opening communications between them. “Do you have a name?” he asked.

The construct moved, blinking, twisting around. It did not smile. The face lacked any emotion at all. It was more like a wooden mask. Did it lack the proper protocols for human behavior?

“You may call me Ms. Rose, or simply Rose if you prefer,” the android said in an emotionless voice.

“How old are you?”

“That is an indelicate question and shows a decided lack of breeding,” Rose said. “I will tell you that I am much older than you.”

Strand drummed his fingers on an armrest. He did not care for her cheekiness. What was the thing’s reasoning for it?

“Did you counsel Commander Lark during our confrontation?”

“I gave him information, if that’s what you mean.”

“What was the nature of this information?”

“That you were the Methuselah Man Strand.”

“Why would you tell Lark?”

“I desired a cessation of hostilities between your two vessels.”

Strand debated the idea. “No,” he said. “That does not ring true. We were not yet engaged in hostilities at that point. Your knowledge created the tense situation.”

“It appears I made an error in judgment,” Rose said.

“That also rings false. You must have known the commander would not…hmmm…regard me fondly.”

“I know that now. The commander hates you, if you will allow me to be blunt.”

“Maybe I hate him,” Strand said, nettled.

“That is quite possible. By the way, I think you might like to know that I suspected you would employ your stasis field.”

Strand rubbed his mouth. “How could you have suspected that when the stasis field is a secret weapon?”

"Oh," Rose said, somewhat vaguely. "That does seem to contain an error in logic, doesn't it?"

"Are you attempting to anger me by your manner of speech?"

Rose did not answer, but waited.

"You do realize that I am easily angered, don't you?" Strand asked, mimicking the other's way of speaking.

"I have heard reports, but few of us believe that."

"Why would you doubt it?"

"You are a Methuselah Man," Rose said. "That implies a measure of restraint and an understanding that survival demands an acceptance of harsh truths."

Strand did not care for the android's mockery. The construct seemed altogether too easy in her demeanor. Strand had stayed away from androids as much as possible. Thus, he was unused to dealing with them and wasn't sure what tack to take here.

"Did you seek out Commander Lark?"

"Of course," Rose said. She grasped the edge of her cape and swirled it. As she did, her features seemed to come alive, as if the human protocols were finally online. That brought animation to her face, and it made her seem truly alive and more beautiful.

"Sir," Rose said, with lift and lilt to her voice. "I believe I should get to the point. I joined the commander because of his route. I believed you would intercept his craft because Lark was going through this star system. I wanted to be here so that I could talk to you."

Strand could feel his skin stretching across his facial bones. This was preposterous on so many levels. The implications—

"You expect me to believe that?" Strand asked.

"My dear Methuselah Man, you work under serious misconceptions. The most egregious is that you think your intellect is the highest in this region of space. While you have many gifts, mine dwarf yours. Frankly, there are several other androids with astonishing capabilities, much greater than those you possess. I hasten to add that you know nothing about them, or about me, for that matter. I realize this is a shock to your pride, but there it is."

Strand blinked several times, feeling as if there was grit beneath his eyelids. He found this beautiful, cape-wearing android irritating in the extreme.

"You are my prisoner," Strand said, "I am not yours. Or do you deny that?"

"That is obvious. Why then would I want to make a false statement concerning it?"

"I don't understand how you can claim superiority to me," Strand said. "I can snuff you out like *that* if I so desire."

"You're implying that I think I can win a direct contest of might between us at the present time. Clearly, I cannot stop your human robots—correction, your ultra-men robots—from destroying me if you desire."

"Can you stop me from destroying you in any other manner?" Strand asked.

"I believe so," Rose said. "Otherwise, I would not have placed myself in your custody."

"How can you achieve this miracle?" Strand asked hoarsely.

Rose smiled. "Do you care to join me in my cell so I can tell you?"

"Certainly not," Strand said. "I will remain in my citadel of strength."

"Then, your guards will hear this truth as I utter it."

Strand glanced at his golden-skinned guards. They seemed attentive in one way only: they watched the prisoner. Did Rose possess some hypnotic power, perhaps? Is that why the android wanted him to send the guards away?

Strand squirmed in his chair. He hated this. The android was much too calm even for a Builder-made construct.

Strand smiled slyly. He believed he understood the psychological ploy at play. Rose must have a long file on him. Somehow, Rose understood that such confidence as she displayed would upset the Methuselah Man's equilibrium. Through an act of will, Strand would prove Rose wrong.

"If you have something to tell me," Strand said. "This is the moment. Otherwise, I will destroy you, as you strike me as a needless risk."

"I believe you," Rose said.

The android swirled her cloak a second time, and then cleared her throat. She stood as if she were a herald delivering a message.

"I have come to inform you that your brother in training and mental processes has begun a journey into the Beyond. He hopes to reach a derelict planet containing powerful Builder artifacts. Your long-range communicator is representative of such devices. Professor Ludendorff desires a long-ranged *scanner*, able to survey a cubic hundred light-years at any one time."

Strand's eyes glowed with anger. "You seriously expect me to believe such foolishness?"

"Not without evidence," Rose said.

"You possess such evidence?"

"Oh, yes."

"Produce it at once, and don't tell me I have to be in the same room with you."

"You do not," Rose said. "If you will give me a moment…I will show you."

Rose reached under her gaudy tunic and made several manipulations. Soon, a tiny holographic projector sprouted from her left palm. She began to play a holo-recording of the meeting between Captain Maddox, Brigadier O'Hara and the Lord High Admiral.

Strand watched the holo-vid with absorption. When it ended, the Methuselah Man sat back, wondering about the validity of the recording.

"I will need time to think about this," Strand said.

"I can appreciate that. However, you should know that it took me longer to convince Commander Lark to take this route than I had expected. It is important to remember that Starship *Victory* is possibly the fastest vessel in Human Space."

"I can travel just as fast."

"Then, you will have to hurry indeed," Rose said, "as they have a head start."

"I'm already in the Beyond."

"True. But you're on the wrong side of the Beyond. You will have to travel far and fast indeed if you hope to get to the Junkyard Planet while Maddox and Ludendorff are still there."

Strand studied the android. "What do you gain by convincing me to go?"

"That should be obvious," Rose said. "I want to go there with you."

Strand laughed dryly, shaking his head.

"I have much to offer you," Rose said. "I have considerable knowledge of the planet. Believe me when I say that I can help you."

"Perhaps that's true, perhaps it isn't. What do you get out of this?"

Rose smiled. "That is the crux, isn't it? Frankly, I need some help myself. There is a device I desire, and it is deep within the planet, hidden behind several troubling guardians."

"No. I'm not buying that. If you wanted this device so badly, why haven't you gone yourself in all this time?"

"Traveling independently through space has not been our way for hundreds of years."

Strand scratched his chin. "Tell me more."

Rose looked away as if she seemed to consider what she should say. Finally, regarding Strand once more, she said, "There is a hole in my…thinking, my logic processors, if you prefer. I do not understand the protocol that has kept me from repairing the damage. The answer to that lies on the Builder planet. I am unable to travel there on my own, as I've stated, but it appears that I can go with another."

"In that case, why didn't you join *Victory*?"

Rose shook her head. "There is a secondary reason for my warning to you. We androids do not want the humans to gain the scanner. It will make them too powerful, but more to the point, they might discover our comings and goings then."

Strand had already reasoned out why Star Watch wanted the scanner. Why was that bad for the androids? Wouldn't they fall in with humanity?

"What if a Swarm fleet shows up in Human Space?" Strand asked. "What if the scanner could help Star Watch defeat the Swarm?"

"I understand the thrust of your question. If the humans lose, we androids shall simply go elsewhere."

"Using spaceships that you claim you cannot use," Strand said.

"A Swarm victory in Human Space would change our protocols."

"If the New Men gained the scanner, they would win a renewed contest against Star Watch."

"That is not our projection," Rose said.

"Who is this 'we' you keep referring to?"

"The android collective, obviously," Rose said.

Strand stood. His brain hurt with all these seemingly conflicting revelations. He did not like Rose, although she was easy on the eyes.

"You can stew in your cell for a while," he said. "I must think, truly think."

"Time is critical," Rose said. "I haven't told you, but maybe you've already guessed. Admiral Fletcher is closing in on the Throne World. Given the admiral's present search patterns, he will find the Throne World in the next several months at the longest."

Strand gave the android a wintry smile. That was one way to pressure a man. Tell him he had to decide *now*.

"Remember this, *Rose*. You need me. I do not need you. You risked your person in appealing to me. I may go to this planet, but perhaps I will dissect you first. What do you say to that?"

"I have given you my case," she said. "I now await your will, Methuselah Man. Know, though, that this united effort will benefit us both. Logically, I would not have come to you otherwise."

"Perhaps," Strand said. He clicked his device. The screen went blank. Absently, he wandered to the hatch with his head already bent in thought.

-8-

Strand was hunched over his computer screen, tapping furiously and sipping strong coffee. He had saved thirty-eight different paradigms. Each had something in its favor. Each had something against it.

Deciding was the issue. Which way should he go? The problem was that he had no one to ask, no one to bounce his ideas off.

His course of action had been clear a day ago. He would capture a star cruiser, show its commander the outpost, the disruptor cannons and send the New Man on his way. That commander would scurry to the Emperor. He would inform the Emperor of everything he'd seen.

Strand scowled as he read the thirty-ninth paradigm. This one did not have anything good to offer.

The situation was thus. Admiral Fletcher led Star Watch's Grand Fleet. The fleet had many *Conqueror*-class battleships. Those battleships possessed long-ranged disrupter cannons, which were better than the New Men's fusion beams. If that wasn't enough, according to Strand's specs, the battleships had better shields than the star cruisers possessed. The only negative to Fletcher's *Conqueror*-class battleships were their numbers. He only had eighteen of the superlative warships.

Star Watch's Grand Fleet had other potent vessels, though. There were carriers with the latest jumpfighters, older battleships, slow but heavy monitors, missile ships that launched antimatter missiles and the rugged, hard-hitting hammerships from the Windsor League. It was a bigger, tougher and more self-sustaining force than had pushed the original New Men's invasion armada out of "C" Quadrant.

The truth was that Fletcher could do horrible damage to the Throne World with that fleet. Could he destroy the Throne World itself?

Strand doubted it. The Throne World possessed nasty surprises. But it would be a bloody mess. He didn't understand why Star Watch allowed Fletcher this madness with the looming possibility of Swarm attacks. But that wasn't his problem. It was the Emperor's problem. And that gave Strand his opening.

Thanks to Lore Fallows, Strand now possessed a small number of working disruptor cannons. Even more important, he could show the Emperor's technicians how to mass-produce more disruptor cannons. If the star cruisers had disruptors instead of fusion beams…that would shift the balance of power back toward New Men superiority.

The old-style humans—the sub-men—would likely have greater numbers for quite some time. The New Men therefore needed technological superiority as well as superior strategy and tactics.

Strand stood, moving to a station with a tri-dimensional holomap. With a pointer, he moved different symbols from one location to another within the holomap.

For quite some time now, Strand had wondered how he could lure the Emperor from the Throne World. His master equation had finally given him the answer. The possibility of gaining disruptor cannons had a fifty-nine percent probability of bringing the Emperor himself to inspect the possibility, especially with Star Watch's Grand Fleet in the vicinity.

Strand dropped the pointer and massaged his forehead. He did not want any distractions. Still, was Ludendorff really traveling to this amazing derelict planet?

The professor had made several bold threats to him not so long ago. If Strand could capture or kill the professor on the Junkyard Planet, Strand would no longer have to worry about his old adversary.

He rubbed his forehead. Was Rose as smart as she claimed? Could the android have predicted his actions with near certainty?

If that was true, he needed to figure out how the androids had done that. They were not smarter than he was in pure intellect. They must have superior equipment or some hidden Builder technique.

"What should I do?" Strand whispered to himself.

In the old days, he could have talked to Ludendorff about this. They would have mulled it over for days, weeks or maybe even months. They had done so much together, lifted humanity out of its backyard place in stellar civilization.

It was too bad that they had parted ways so many years ago. Ludendorff had become too cautious, too hidebound by old philosophies. The professor had suggested they not play God. "Men are not meant to wield absolute power," Ludendorff had said.

What a load of crap. He was Strand. There was no one he trusted more with power than himself. The power had not changed him. He had become wiser, more—

"What's the point in boasting?" Strand said softly. "I must think, really, really think."

He turned away from the holomap. He put the computer to sleep so he wouldn't see the equation waiting for him. He went to his cot, pulled off his shoes and lay down. He put his left arm over his eyes and began to work through one piece of datum after another.

He lay there for seven and a half hours, hardly moving. He weighed this with that. He tried to imagine the outcomes of one method versus another.

Commander Lars Lark waited for him. Should he release the commander or take him into the operating chamber? Should he try to tear apart Rose or attempt to trick her? Would it be wise to contact Admiral Fletcher, or should he lead the dangerous old fool on a wild goose chase?

There were so many decisions, so many ways he could do this.

Would the Swarm really bother coming into this part of the galaxy? The idea seemed wrong to Strand. The bugs had better things to do than worry about humans. And yet…

At the end of the eighth hour, Strand removed his arm. He sat up, padded to a pitcher of purified water and poured himself a glass. He drank deeply. He turned the glass in his hand.

With a thump, he set it on the table.

"Yes," Strand said. "That's what I'm going to do."

He felt tired, and his mind hurt. He would like to sleep for an age, but he had a lot of work to do before he implemented the next part of his long-term strategy…

-9-

Hundreds of light-years away from Strand, Captain Maddox stalked through *Victory's* corridors like a tiger on the prowl.

The starship had almost reached the limit of the Commonwealth and was coming upon the Beyond. Human Space or Known Space contained the Commonwealth of Planets, the Windsor League, the former Wahhabi Caliphate and the majority of the independent worlds. It also held some of the border regions. Throughout the years, people had coined the term "Beyond" for what lay beyond known space.

The New Men lived in the Beyond, hidden from the rest of humanity.

Captain Maddox wasn't unduly worried about entering the Beyond. He had done it many times before. As a Patrol officer, one of his chief duties lay in mapping the Beyond. In fact, Maddox had gone farther into the Beyond than any human, including Strand and Ludendorff, who had both gone to the Builder Dyson sphere for internal modifications a long time ago.

Maddox prowled the corridors—on the hunt—because so far, the security teams hadn't found any stowaways, spies or androids slipped-in among the crew.

That was highly unusual given the experiences of their last several voyages. Due to the secrecy and the importance of this voyage, Maddox felt in his bones that someone had stowed away on the ship. The fact that he hadn't found the stowaways only increased his certainty of their presence.

"There you are."

Maddox spun around, his hand dropping onto his holstered weapon.

Meta jogged toward him. She wore a tightfitting Patrol uniform, her jiggling breasts quite noticeable as she ran. Meta had a shapely figure, long blonde hair spilling out from under her cap and a face that could have launched flotillas of starships. She was a beauty. She was also one of the strongest persons aboard *Victory*. That came from her lab-altered genetic makeup, and that she had grown up on a 2-G planet. Meta had been many things throughout her life, including an inductee on a prison planet and an assassin. She was deadly, and she was the captain's girlfriend.

Maddox appreciated Meta for a number of reasons. She was different enough that he felt more comfortable around her than he did around others. He liked her toughness of character, and that it came in such a delightfully feminine package.

Meta ran up to him, twining both of her arms around one of his. She began to walk with him, squeezing his captive arm.

Maddox knew she wanted something, but he waited for her to ask.

"When was the last time you lay down?" she asked without looking up.

He shrugged.

"Don't give me that," she said. "I know you know."

"It could be thirty-seven hours," he admitted.

"And you're as alert now as you were then?" she asked.

"Maybe I'm more alert now."

"Maddox," she chided. "You have to rest."

"Not yet," he said.

"I've never known you to have a case of nerves before."

"It's not nerves," he said.

"What else could it be?" Meta asked.

He glanced down at her. "Let's switch arms," he suggested.

She looked up at him. He could see the worry in her eyes. She released him, walked around to the other side and clutched that arm.

Maddox flexed his gun hand. He didn't like anyone holding onto it, not even Meta in the middle of Starship *Victory*.

"Are you worried about androids?" she asked quietly.

He pointed his index finger at her and let his thumb drop as if it were a hammer, "shooting" her, to demonstrate that she'd hit the target.

"I thought you told me Galyan has gone over the crew rosters and the various medical examinations three times already."

"Four times," Maddox corrected.

"Has he found anything amiss?" Meta asked.

"You'd know if he had."

"Then why are you wound so tightly?" she asked. "You've quadruple-checked and everything is in order. Caution is good, paranoia not so much."

They walked together, turning a corner, passing several engineers on their way to the main engine compartment.

Maddox wasn't sure how to broach the topic with Meta. He mulled it over and finally cleared his throat.

"Do you recall Shu 15 calling me *di-far*?"

Meta glanced at him. The Rouen Colony beauty hadn't altogether cared for Shu 15, a petite Spacer who had been with them last voyage. Meta's introduction to Shu had been just after the Spacer had kissed Maddox on the lips.

"As a *di-far*," Maddox said, "I have begun to listen to my instincts more carefully. They tell me something is wrong."

"Don't tell Riker about your increased confidence in your instincts."

Maddox grew tightlipped. He knew he shouldn't have said anything about this to Meta. One of the truisms of command was to give people your decisions but never the reasons behind them. Others could accept decisions but often wanted to argue over the reasons.

"Dearest," Meta said, gripping his arm with considerable strength. "I fully agree with listening to the little cues in the backs of our minds. In my former line of work that often kept me alive. But becoming too reliant upon your feelings—"

"Gut instincts," Maddox corrected. "Those are different than mere feelings."

Meta raised an eyebrow. Instead of further conversation, she opened herself up. She let herself feel—

She looked up sharply. "Captain, you're wound tighter than I realized. You're hopping with this suppressed…I'd almost call it rage."

Maddox halted, and he pried his arm free of Meta's grasp. He flexed his hands and considered her words.

Rage. She had said rage. Abruptly, he turned, heading almost at a run for a nearby rec room.

Behind him, Meta trotted to keep up.

Halfway there, Maddox broke into a sprint. No one aboard the starship could keep up with Maddox once he ran full tilt. He flashed past surprised crewmembers, moving with economical motion.

In moments, he burst into a large padded area. Maddox pulled off his jacket and shirt, tossing them to the side. He yanked off his boots and socks. As Meta raced into the chamber, he went to a locker, took out tape and wrapped his fists. He slipped on sparring gloves and proceeded toward a heavy bag.

He let the rage in him bubble to the surface. The bag swung at each thudding blow.

Meta hurried around the bag, standing behind it, holding it for him.

Maddox began to pound the heavy bag with a flurry of blows. Meta winced at several of them. Sweat began to glisten on his torso. He gave combination after combination. Then he began to kick the bag. That caused Meta to hang on more tightly, grunting a few times.

The captain was a whirlwind of action, moving with astonishing speed. He hit with brutal strength. Meta was a hybrid. Maddox was even more so. Despite his lean physique, he had phenomenal strength.

At last, even the captain's famous endurance failed him. He staggered back from the heavy bag, with his shoulders slumped. He panted, and sweat was rolling down his stark muscles. His right arm quivered now and again.

Gingerly, Meta let go of the bag. She looked at her man with concern.

Maddox took a towel from the locker, wiping his face. His pants were a mess, sweat-stained, crumpled and torn in one spot.

"Feeling better?" Meta asked.

As he unwound the tape, Maddox studied her without really seeing her. For the first time in several days, his stomach no longer seethed with anticipation. He no longer felt amped-up and jittery. He concentrated, trying to pinpoint the moment those sensations had taken hold.

It had been at Saras 7, a Star Watch depot. They had taken on a cargo of jumpfighter spare parts. He tried to recall when he'd made the decision to stop at the depot, and couldn't. If that was true—

Maddox snapped his fingers. "Galyan," he called.

A moment later, the Adok holoimage appeared before him as a small humanoid with ropy arms and deep-set eyes. Galyan had fine lines crisscrossing his face, the way he'd looked a few moments before his death six thousand years ago.

"Yes, Captain?" Galyan said.

"Why did we stop at Saras 7?" Maddox asked.

Galyan's eyelids fluttered. "We needed spare parts for the jumpfighters."

"Who reported that?"

"Checking..." Galyan said. "Checking... Captain, there was no formal request. A day before we passed through the Saras System, a notice appeared in the maintenance manifest."

"You cannot trace the person who logged the information?"

"I do detect a trace—Captain, someone hacked into the computer-maintenance system."

"Doctor Rich was a hacker once," Maddox suggested.

"It was not Doctor Rich," Galyan said.

"How do you know?"

"Because Warrant Officer Davis is your culprit," Galyan said. "I know that because I have just run—"

"I don't doubt your process," Maddox said, interrupting. "I am unfamiliar with Warrant Officer Davis. Who is he?"

"She, sir," Galyan said.

"Where is she?"

"Checking…" The holoimage glanced at Maddox in surprise.

The AI's projection had become more emotional throughout the voyages as Galyan gained greater computing power and personality, becoming more like the original alien Adok, Driving Force Galyan. The original Galyan had been "deified," his engrams imprinted on an advanced Builder AI system loaned to the Adoks thousands of years ago.

"Captain, this is amazing," Galyan said. "Warrant Officer Davis is dead. Her body arrived in the ship's morgue several hours ago."

"What killed her?" Maddox asked.

"It appears she had an aneurism."

The captain bared his teeth. "Tell the medical team to take great care with her corpse. I think they'll find that Davis has a Builder device fused in her."

Galyan's eyelids fluttered. "Do you suspect that Warrant Officer Davis was a Spacer spy?"

"Either that or a plant," Maddox said.

"What has caused you to come to this conclusion?" Galyan asked.

"Shut down intra-ship communications and security systems," Maddox ordered. "Do it now, Galyan, before more people have to die."

-10-

Galyan eyelids fluttered wildly for five seconds. Afterward, the Adok holoimage said, "It is done, sir. The ship's comm and video systems are down. Do you suspect that Spacers have infiltrated the starship?"

"Galyan, confine yourself to this location," Maddox said. "Do not do anything until I personally return and reinstate you."

"Sir?" Galyan asked. "Did I do something to upset you?"

"You're doing fine," Maddox said. "This is merely a precaution. But you must do exactly as I say."

"Yes, Captain. I am shutting down until further notice."

Maddox waited until the holoimage froze. Then, he grabbed Meta by an upper arm and dragged her along.

"What's going on?" she said breathlessly.

"I believe we're being prepped for a Spacer assault," Maddox said.

Meta shook her head. "How can you possibly have arrived at that conclusion?"

The captain gave her a shark's grin. "It's a convoluted process, to be sure. You gave me the starting point. Now, speed is critical. I have to catch the Spacer operator before he or she knows I'm coming for them."

"I still don't understand," Meta said.

"Do you have a weapon?"

"Not on me," Meta said.

"From this moment on, you will always carry a weapon, preferably two or more. Here, take this."

Gingerly, Meta accepted the monofilament blade. "You're crazy for using one of these. One wrong slip—"

"That's the trick," Maddox told her, as they hurried down the corridors. "Don't make the slip."

"Can't you tell me where we're headed?"

"Not yet," Maddox said, as he drew his long-barreled gun. "Ready?"

"Hey," she said. "You're not even wearing your shoes or shirt. Shouldn't we go back for them?"

Maddox took a deep breath, dragged a forearm across his forehead, and trotted faster down the corridor with Meta doggedly following him.

Maddox believed he knew what had caused his earlier agitation. A hidden Spacer had used an inner Builder device against his mind.

Shu 15 was still on Earth, a political prisoner working for Brigadier O'Hara. Shu had two Builder devices inside her. One device had powered the other. The critical device had allowed Shu to use transduction. She could see electromagnetic radiation and electromagnetic wavelengths and process the data as fast as a computer. Shu had also been able to manipulate electromagnetic wavelengths.

Maddox believed a Spacer with similar transduction abilities had been agitating his mental processes. He didn't believe the Spacer could actually control his mind, but maybe it had been weakened in some manner by the constant stimulation.

That's why he'd had Galyan shut down the ship's video equipment. Through transduction, a person could use the video system and see the captain coming for them.

Where was the Spacer hiding? Using transduction, Shu could short-circuit weapons. Maddox wondered if it was merely a matter of time before Spacers learned how to attack a biological nervous system or pinch blood vessels.

The stowaway had clearly joined the starship at Saras 7. Would they take the risk of mingling with the crew?

Maddox doubted it.

"This way," he said over his shoulder. He glanced back farther when Meta didn't answer and saw that he'd left her far behind.

Maddox's bare feet pounded upon the decking as he sprinted once more. While he recuperated faster than ordinary, he'd still felt the effects of the strenuous exercise. He panted, and his skin was once again slick with sweat.

Logically, the Spacer would be in the hangar bay with the spare parts.

For the next ten minutes, Maddox pushed himself, receiving startled glances from various crew personnel. The conviction that he was right about this grew into grim certainty.

Finally, he dashed into the great hangar bay, veering from the parked shuttlecraft and the four jumpfighters. Mechanics looked up. The captain even heard a distant hail from Keith Maker.

With an increasing sense of urgency, he raced toward a supply depot. A crewman in a utility uniform was walking briskly away from the area. The man had pale skin and an indention on the back of his head that might have come from quickly removing a pair of goggles.

"You!" Maddox shouted.

The pale man did not turn around. He also did not increase his pace. If he was a spy, where did he think he was going?

Maddox aimed his long-barreled gun at the man.

That caused the pale utility worker to spin around in consternation.

"Stop," Maddox ordered.

The man turned and ran.

Maddox pulled the trigger, but the gun didn't work. That clinched it for the captain. Without holstering the sidearm, Maddox forced himself into a last sprint. He quickly gained on the pale man.

"Stop," Maddox called.

The man turned, snarling. He pulled something out of his utility uniform.

Maddox aimed the long-barreled gun at him, firing once more. The weapon went *click, click, click*. Maddox did not waver, although he readied himself to throw the gun as he neared the man.

"You're trapped," Maddox shouted.

The pale man's features were twisted with hatred. He had strange eyes, and it was clear he had a small but powerful hand weapon.

"Stay away from me," the man shouted.

Maddox continued sprinting at the man. He would attempt to dodge when the other fired. Maybe the other would wound him, but Maddox was determined to capture the Spacer.

"The Spacers will rise again!" the man shouted. Instead of aiming at Maddox, the man put the point of the weapon against the underside of his jaw.

"No!" Maddox shouted.

The Spacer pulled the trigger, sending a powerful beam up through his jaw and into his brain. He collapsed onto the decking.

-11-

Several hours later, Maddox called for a meeting in the briefing chamber. As he headed there, Galyan appeared before him.

Maddox had restored the AI shortly after the Spacer's suicide.

"Captain," Galyan said. "You're wanted on the bridge. Lieutenant Noonan has spotted an anomaly. It could be Commander Thrax Ti Ix or a Spacer starship."

"Is the anomaly saucer-shaped?" Maddox asked.

"Yes, sir."

"Tell her I'm on my way."

The intra-ship communications had malfunctioned. Maddox believed the Spacer had done that before his death or during the death process. In any case, they had to use communicators or have Galyan pop from one spot to the next to relaying messages.

The holoimage paused before disappearing.

"Is there a problem?" Maddox asked.

"There is, sir," Galyan said. "I have attempted to follow the trail of logic that led you to your conclusion regarding the Spacer spy."

"I'm sorry, Galyan. I can't explain the process."

"Is that because you intuitively came to the conclusion?"

"That's one way to say it."

"How else could one describe the process?" the holoimage asked.

"Humans have a conscious and an unconscious mind—"

"I am aware of the duality of human reasoning," Galyan said, interrupting. "Usually, however, once a human has followed his intuitive insight, he can reason out the logic of it. Why do you feel you have been unable to reason out your subconscious logic?"

Maddox debated with himself as he headed for the bridge. "I shouldn't have been so angry earlier. That was my first clue."

"Pardon me, sir, but it appears as if you have indeed reasoned out the logic. Yet you said you had not. I am curious as to which of those statements is true."

Maddox hesitated before saying, "The thought came to me as I hit the heavy bag that nothing should have made me so agitated. The duration of my unease also pointed to an outside source. We know that the Spacers have learned how to manipulate the electromagnetic spectrum. That seemed like the most rational explanation for my rage. So, I asked myself if the Spacers would want to agitate me? The answer was yes, particularly if they planned to show up in force."

"You have been waiting for them to appear?"

"Since the Spacer's suicide, I have," Maddox admitted.

The holoimage floated along as Maddox took a turn in the corridor.

"I have it." A moment later, Galyan glanced at the captain. "Are you not going to ask me what I have discovered?"

"I don't believe so," Maddox said.

"That could be considered as cruel, sir, as my psychological profiler gives it a ninety-six percent certainty that you know I want you to ask me."

Maddox said nothing.

"I am also quite certain, psychologically speaking, that you dislike my psychoanalytic analysis concerning your various behaviors."

"Then why do you do it?" Maddox asked.

Galyan's lined face might have held the hint of a smile.

Maddox noticed. "I suppose you believe that the psychoanalysis is for my wellbeing."

"If you will allow me to be blunt," Galyan said in a soft voice.

Maddox didn't want to, but he nodded.

"Mentally, you are the strongest individual I know," Galyan said, "and that would include the professor. However, you seem to believe that you are an island. Yet, during our repeated voyages, we have aided each other. We have stood together, stronger united than our individual parts would equal." The AI paused before continuing. "While you are the mentally strongest among us, you cannot survive alone. No human is structured for that kind of existence. You lean heavily on Meta, although you might not realize the extent to which you need her."

Maddox shifted uncomfortably.

"Here is the crux of the matter," Galyan said. "I have spoken to you like this in order to give you the opportunity talk about these things. Whether you know it or not, sir, you need to speak to others about your inner concerns. If those concerns remain bottled up, they will build in pressure and begin to cause a list in your mental stability. Your speaking to me like this is a safety valve, allowing some of that pressure to escape."

Maddox considered the idea. He even glanced sidelong at the little holoimage. If he didn't know better, he would think the AI cared about him as a friend. A new realization struck the captain.

Could the alien AI be lonely? Maybe playing the psychoanalyst helped Galyan feel that he was an important member of the team, a friend, rather than just a technical aid.

"Thank you, Galyan. I believe you're right. I doubt anyone else would have seen this."

"Doctor Rich might have," Galyan said. "Ludendorff—"

"No," Maddox said. "They're too busy with other matters. This is your insight. I'm grateful to you, my friend."

Maddox did not know how it was possible, but the little holoimage seemed to beam and even preen with delight.

"Was there anything else?" Maddox asked.

"I will relay your message to the lieutenant that you are on your way."

“I’m almost there anyway,” Maddox said. “We’ll enter the bridge together.”

“Yes, sir,” Galyan said, as if the idea pleased him.

-12-

Maddox stood on the bridge, studying the main screen.

They were halfway through the Ulant System, heading to a jump point near a supergiant red star. There were two terrestrial planets in the system and one vast super-Jupiter almost half a light-year out. Between the super-Jupiter and the inner terrestrial planet was a mass of debris. It wasn't an asteroid belt exactly, as the dust, rocks and planetoids covered a vast region of space, approximately a Mars-like orbit to a Pluto-like orbit. In that region of space was enough debris to make up the mass of the Solar System's Sun.

This meant that *Victory* had to travel with the shield powered at full strength. The shield was presently a dim red color. The majority of the shield-damage came from constant dust and occasional space pebbles.

"If I bet the way Keith does while on shore leave," Lieutenant Noonan said, "I'd wager that the Spacer vessel believes we can't see them through all the debris."

Valerie Noonan had long brunette hair, a taut body and the most professional air of any officer aboard *Victory*. She knew all the regulations, followed them closely, and she'd worked harder than anyone else to join Star Watch.

"We are using an Adok scanning technique," Galyan said. "It is based on the refraction principle coupled with—"

"It's impressive is what it is," Maddox said, interrupting, sparing them from an extended technical explanation. "How long have they been ghosting us?" he asked the lieutenant.

"I noticed the ship ten minutes ago," Valerie said from her location. "We've been in the system for five hours, though. I suspect they've had us under observation since we arrived. Shall I order a change in heading, sir?"

Maddox did not respond immediately. He put his hands behind his back as he studied the image out there. The Spacer vessel—if it was the Spacers, which seemed reasonable—was a mere dot near the super-Jupiter. It really was remarkable that the sensors had been able to spot it. Adok technology continued to surprise them in good ways.

"Are we scanning in all directions?" Maddox asked.

"Affirmative, sir," Valerie said. "As far as I can tell, there are no mines, no hidden drones, nothing else around us that could endanger the starship. I doubt that the ship back there can harm us in the foreseeable future."

"It could simply be an observation vessel and nothing more," Galyan suggested.

"Could be, but I doubt it," Maddox said. "Not with a Spacer spy killing himself to hide something aboard the ship." He wondered why the enemy vessel remained near the super-Jupiter. "We have a decision to make," he said finally. "Do we turn around and confront the possible Spacer ship to ascertain its motives, or do we employ our star drive to leave it in the dust?"

"Are you asking my opinion, sir?" Valerie asked.

"I am, Lieutenant."

Valerie sat a little straighter, biting her lower lip. "It would be good to know who they are, sir. The suicidal spy is troubling. Combined with that vessel in the star system—"

"Yes...?" Maddox said.

Valerie continued to chew on her lower lip.

"Sir," Galyan said. "I have intercepted a transmission. It is garbled—Sir! The transmission originates from the enemy starship and it is in code. A moment please, yes, it is a machine code of some kind."

"Does it strike you as a Spacer or an android code?" Maddox asked.

"My analysis...android," Galyan said.

Valerie looked up sharply. "Are you thinking what I am, sir?"

"That the so-called Spacer suicide was an android plant to misdirect us?" Maddox asked.

Valerie nodded.

"It has crossed my mind," Maddox said. "Yet, the corpse was definitely that of a Spacer. Now, though, I'm reevaluating the reason the spy directed his transduction abilities at my mind. I wonder if he did it *precisely* to agitate me. I believe he wanted me to hunt for him."

"So you'd find him?" Valerie asked.

"Exactly," Maddox said. "It's possible someone programmed him to run and kill himself before we could question him. His suicide would clinch our certainty regarding Spacer interference."

"Including causing us to believe that was a Spacer vessel out there?" Valerie asked. "On the off-chance that we spotted them."

"What do you think of my analysis, Galyan?" Maddox asked.

"It strikes me as too elaborate," the holoimage said. "This last message seems sloppy on their part."

"Did you detect it easily?" Maddox asked.

"No, sir," Galyan said. "I have been employing every safeguard. Otherwise…otherwise, I would have missed it." The holoimage appeared thoughtful. "Captain, if you are interested in my suggestion…"

"Let's hear it," Maddox said.

"We should investigate the starship," Galyan said. "I believe it has become imperative."

Maddox's grip tightened behind his back. He continued to study the super-Jupiter and the dot of a sensor ping. The system contained more dust than any place he'd ever been. Clearly, there was a mystery in play. He believed his adversary out there was subtle and dangerous. In some fashion, his adversary knew he had left on an important mission. Could the person or persons know the nature of the mission?

It would be wise to believe they did. Who would be most likely to know about the Junkyard Planet? Hmm…in this case, androids or Spacers were just as likely. Although, if he had to make a choice, he believed the androids would know more than the Spacers would, as the androids had been around longer.

"Galyan, can you set up a decoy reflection?" Maddox asked.

"A sensor ghost?" the holoimage asked.

Maddox waited for an answer.

Galyan's eyelids fluttered. "Yes, sir, I can do it. But it will take an hour before I'm ready."

"An hour will be sufficient," Maddox said.

"May I ask what you're planning, sir?" Valerie asked.

"I suspect our adversary wants us to invcstigate that starship," Maddox said. "I think there's a reason why it has remained so close to the super-Jupiter. I don't trust this star system. I don't trust the suicidal Spacer. If he had the ability of transduction, why did he kill himself so soon? He could have waited to do it."

"He must have panicked," Valerie said. "People do that, you know."

Maddox fixated on the distant sensor ping. "We're going to give them something to do for a time, something to watch. While they sit there, we will slip away."

"To come in behind them?" Valerie asked.

Maddox shook his head. "We will travel far and fast, Lieutenant. I have a...*suspicion*, if you will. We must get to the Junkyard Planet as soon as we can. And that is exactly what I plan to do."

-13-

Aboard the Star Cruiser *Argo*, Strand paced in agitation. The Methuselah Man was in the *modification* chamber, muttering to himself as he studied the latest readings.

He was not sure, no, not sure at all.

Strand tapped a board, made adjustments and looked up. A tall glass cylinder silently moved into position. Inside the cylinder was a wide-eyed Dem Darius, with electrodes attached to his shaven scalp and to his golden-skinned and quite nude body.

Strand had begun his newest plan. It was daring and would take masterful execution. Certainly, he was up to the task, though. He was determined to find out whether his New Men were secretly fomenting rebellion and whether Darius was the chief of the rebels.

"Are you frightened?" Strand asked the New Man.

Inside the cylinder, Darius breathed rapidly. He wore the appearance of fear, and he manfully attempted to control it. Sweat shined on his golden skin and several of his muscles twitched at odd moments.

Darius was tall and slender, but despite his leanness, his muscles looked like steel cables when they twitched. He was stronger than a champion power-lifter from Earth. That was because Darius was modeled on perfection, not on the mongrel sub-men infesting most of Human Space.

Strand tapped the panel. The cylinder slid into a giant slot and power energized the electrodes.

Darius groaned as he twitched more visibly, and drool slid from his compressed lips. The level of pain needed to cause a New Man to do that was intense.

"I will ask you a series of questions," Strand said casually. "You will answer quickly and without hesitation."

"Yes, Master," Darius whispered.

"Are you a Dominant?"

Darius stared at Strand. He almost seemed reluctant as he said, "Yes."

"Do you possess leadership capabilities?"

Again, there was hesitation before he answered, "I do."

"Are you superior to most New Men?"

"Yes."

"What was your highest achievement?"

"I fought to the Second Level."

Strand made a notation on a slate. He had thought it had been to the Third Level. Darius was even more of a prize than he'd realized.

"Who do you serve?" the Methuselah Man asked.

There was a momentary hesitation before Darius hissed, "Excellence and mastery."

"Ah…" Strand said. He had not foreseen this. The Dominant had betrayed himself. "You serve excellence?"

"I strive to achieve."

"And what is it that you wish to achieve?"

"Mmmmmm," Darius said. It seemed as if the New Man resisted himself, as if his lips would answer but his will struggled to remain silent.

"Please," Strand said. "Complete your thought. What is it you wish to achieve?"

Darius began to blink, and he appeared shocked.

Strand believed he knew why. The New Man must finally realize that he had breathed *Reveal*, a cocktail of chemicals that induced the breather to speak the truth, as he knew it. It seemed probable Darius had hoped to keep these beliefs to himself.

"What do you hope to achieve?" Strand asked.

"Mastery, Master."

"I am the master."

Darius said nothing, although it seemed he fought his fear.

"Do you refute the statement that I am the master?"

"No," Darius whispered.

"Why did you not speak my title as you said that?"

"No, Master," Darius said.

"Do you enjoy naming me the master?"

"It is not a matter of joy, but of fact."

"Tell me, then, how can a servant achieve mastery? Do you remember? You said you wanted mastery. Yet, I am the master."

"It is a conundrum," Darius said, as beads of sweat appeared on his scalp.

Strand found this interesting. He could see why Darius had achieved the Second Level. The New Man had a stubborn will indeed. Strand had never dealt with a Second Level New Man aboard the *Argo*.

"Doesn't one need freedom to achieve mastery?" the Methuselah Man asked.

"Most likely that is true, Master."

"It is certainly true, you mean?"

Darius did not speak.

Strand made another notation on his slate. Afterward, he tapped the stylus against his front teeth. "Are you attempting to gain freedom?"

"I would..." Darius's shoulders tightened, "appreciate freedom."

"Are you attempting to *gain* it?"

"I am your servant...Master."

"You are attempting to divert," Strand said. "Do you not realize that reveals your inner heart?"

"It is possible."

Strand made a third notation. Darius's answers had stunned him. The New Man had incredible inner resources. Where did he find the willpower to answer like this?

"It is more than possible," Strand said. "It is a fact. You are in secret rebellion against me."

Darius began to hyperventilate.

No, this would not do. Strand tapped a red dot on his panel.

Power energized Darius's pain sensors. The lean superman twisted in the glass cylinder. He clamped his lips together, but the raw sensations proved too much for him. He groaned like a deeply wounded animal. The groan grew until Darius howled, a nakedly animalistic sound.

Strand nodded as he listened to the noise. "Now, let us adjust your mental settings, eh."

It seemed unlikely that Darius even heard the Methuselah Man. The New Man howled and his eyes bulged. Mucus flowed from his nostrils and still he howled, the noise becoming hoarse.

Strand manipulated his board as he rerouted the obedience fibers in the subject's brain. The pain Darius felt flowed deep into his memory. It would act as a leash on the rebellion. This Strand knew from previous experiments.

Finally, Strand tapped a green dot.

Inside the cylinder, Darius gasped as sweat rolled off his limp legs and pooled around his feet.

"What is your primary goal in life?" Strand asked quietly.

"Obedience to you, Master," Darius said in a raspy voice.

"Do you wish to make a confession?"

Darius stared at Strand for only a moment. The New Man dropped his gaze, and he managed a bare nod.

"I have striven for free thought," Darius whispered hoarsely. "I have also plotted to become the best of your bridge crew."

"Why did you wish this?"

"For two reasons," Darius whispered. "One, I wished…"

"Continue, as you have not finished your thought."

"I wished to be the best Dominant aboard the *Argo*."

"That was your first desire?" Strand asked.

"It was, Master."

"And the second? Tell me about that."

"I desired to become indispensable. In this way, I believed you would give me certain allowances. In time, I believed, I could use the allowances to gain my freedom."

"That was a clever plan."

Darius did not respond.

"You are my highest achieving New Man. Perhaps there is a lesson for me in your striving. I may adjust you further so that you continue to strive for excellence. You will now do so, though, because you love serving me. Is that understood?"

"Yes, Master."

"Do you love serving me?"

Darius rubbed the back of his neck.

Strand knew it was a sign that the New Man attempted to lie. That was amazing at this point. It showed a fantastically stubborn will. That was both good and bad. A wise master would seek to harness such a will.

Strand rubbed his leathery hands together. Dem Darius could potentially become his masterwork. It would take more time in the cylinder, of course. It would be delicate work, and it could destroy the New Man's brain if done incorrectly. But that was a risk Strand was willing to take.

"Do you still desire to be the best?" Strand asked.

"Yes, Master."

"You want to be the best with every fiber in your being?"

Darius nodded.

"I am glad to hear it," Strand said. "It means that you will employ that stubborn will of yours to survive what is to come."

A shadow of fear marred Darius's perfect features.

"Do you understand that you have agreed to further retraining?"

"I did not realize," Darius whispered.

"Knowing this, are you still willing to be first?"

Darius hesitated only a second before he said, "Yes."

"The results, then, are on your head," Strand said. "Your ambition has brought this about. Remember that when you desire death to end the unbearable pain you will have to endure."

Strand began manipulating his panel. Thus, he failed to see the momentary blaze of hatred shine in Darius's eyes. It lasted only a second. Then, raw agony broke the concentration as the two entered into a more painful and intimate relationship of master inflicting pain to mold his chosen slave.

-14-

Back aboard Starship *Victory*, Valerie squared off against Keith in Rec Room 3. Valerie was wearing tight-fitting training gear, with her hair bundled under a soft padded helmet. Keith was barefoot and wearing an old-style karate Gi, which looked slightly ridiculous.

A few others trained nearby, but each group left the others alone. A few thumps and grunts sounded occasionally while bare feet shuffled against the floor padding.

It had been three weeks since the captain had slipped away from the mysterious starship in orbit around the super-Jupiter gas giant. That had been in the Ulant System. Since then, *Victory* had raced through the Beyond, straining to reach Ludendorff's find.

As Valerie shifted her stance, she realized she hadn't seen the professor much this voyage. He seemed to be keeping to himself more than usual. Did that portend anything ominous?

Valerie had a sneaking suspicion that it just might. She didn't trust the professor. She never had. The Methuselah Man was too self-centered and arrogant. The captain could be arrogant, too, but she had come to believe that had as much to do with his New Man heritage as having to go it alone most of his life. The captain's arrogance was psychological armor against a hostile universe.

Valerie could relate to that. She'd been a loner for a long time, too. That had made it particularly hard in the Space Academy.

"What's wrong?" Keith asked, with his grin slipping.

"What?" she asked.

"You're scowling."

"Oh. It's nothing. Are you ready?"

"I'm going to flip you onto your back, love," he said, the grin returning full force. "You know that, right?"

Valerie grinned back at him.

She liked practicing close-quarter combat with Keith because they were almost the same height. Keith weighed more, and he was stronger and quite a bit quicker. She'd been astonished on more than one occasion at his speed. His hand speed might even rival the captain's reflexes. Maybe that's what made Keith such a deadly jumpfighter pilot.

Just as she readied herself to lunge at him, Keith attacked.

He came in fast, jabbing, shifting positions, trying a leg sweep. She jumped over his leg, but that left her vulnerable as she landed. He punched her in the stomach, sending her staggering backward.

She knew what he would do. Thus, she jumped back farther to gain space. Then she lunged blindly, striking. Instead of hitting him, she tripped and landed on her face, thudding against the floor padding.

Keith stood to the side, with his arms folded as he grinned down at her.

"You're too obvious sometimes," he said.

Valerie climbed to her feet. The good feeling had evaporated. She didn't like people making fun of her, and she felt that was what Keith was secretly doing with his grin.

"Now you're serious, love," he said in a joking manner. "Now I'm in trouble, eh?"

Valerie shook her arms, twisted her neck until it popped and went into a new stance. She'd let herself get preoccupied. Keith never seemed to do that. The pilot seemed to live in the moment. Maybe that was one of his secrets. She thought too much. She brooded over problems and—

With a shout of surprise, Valerie went flying through the air as Keith flipped her. She landed on her back with a thud.

A moment later, Keith looked down at her, with his grin wider than ever. "I've been learning judo," he said. "I wanted to surprise you. Are you surprised?"

Valerie didn't say a word as she climbed back to her feet. She'd let herself get distracted again. That wasn't going to happen a third time. She was a better close-combat fighter than Keith. He shouldn't be able to do this to her. She'd trained far longer than he had.

Watching him, shifting to the left, striking to the right, she missed. He tried another of his sneaky maneuvers, but she was ready this time.

For the next twenty seconds, they lunged and defended, neither able to get an advantage over the other.

Some of her anger and embarrassment oozed away as they continued. Keith kept laughing, but in a good-natured way. He had a sunny disposition. He smiled a lot and he made some goofy faces at her. She almost had him twice, but his speed and reflexes saved him.

She smiled while thinking about Keith. She'd been spending more time with him lately. He'd held her hand once. She'd liked that, but hadn't let him hold her hand too long.

Star Watch regulations didn't prohibit onboard relationships, but it frowned upon them. It had various safeguards. Now that Valerie thought about it, the captain ignored almost every regulation regarding Meta. The captain pretty much did as he pleased in that regard.

Keith surprised her again, and she went flying, thudding onto the mat on her back. This time, Keith followed the maneuver by landing on her chest.

"I'm going to pin you," he boasted.

A surge of determination motivated Valerie. She fended off his first assault, wrestling like a wildcat.

"Hey," Keith said. He strained to keep her from reversing their positions.

Valerie pushed. He pushed back. For a moment, they were in perfect equilibrium. Then, Keith did something with his left foot. She fell back. He landed on top of her and their faces were centimeters apart.

"This is it," he said.

She strained against his pinning her. He leaned closer. Their lips almost touched.

"Valerie, love," he said in a husky voice.

Valerie became very aware of his proximity, of his body pressing against hers. Suddenly, this didn't seem to be close-combat training anymore. It felt more like—

Keith kissed her. As he did, he released pressure elsewhere.

Valerie went with the kiss. She liked it, until she wondered how this would affect their working relationship. Maybe this was a bad idea. Maybe this would cause complications. It might even jeopardize the mission in some way.

Without really thinking about it, Valerie used a new move Meta had shown her two days ago. She flipped Keith onto his back, looking down at him.

He grinned up at her as if he expected her to kiss him back. He practically lay there waiting for it. She considered kissing him. She wanted too, but regulations—

She jumped to her feet. "Why did you do that? That wasn't right."

"Sure it was," he said, getting up. "I know you liked it."

"That's not the point. You don't kiss your opponent."

"Valerie," he said, stepping closer.

She punched him harder than she meant to. It made him stagger back, and he tripped over his feet, sprawling onto his back.

"I win," she said.

He blinked at her, seeming confused.

Valerie almost admitted that she had liked the kiss. But if she did that, he would pursue her. They were on a mission. This wasn't the Love Boat. This was Starship *Victory*. They were officers in Star Watch. They had a duty.

Before she could explain any of this to him, Valerie spun around, walking away.

"Hey," he said. "Where are you going? It wasn't that bad."

Valerie ran for the exit. Some of the other sparring couples stared after her. It made her even more self-conscious, which made her stomach feel funny.

This was just great. Keith had ruined everything with the kiss. Now, they couldn't be friends anymore. Why had he done that? Why—

Valerie ran as fast as she could for her quarters, her skin burning as a full-force blush made her cheeks throb.

***

Several hours later, Valerie walked briskly down a corridor in the science section of *Victory*. She'd been doing some soul-searching. Her conclusion was that she needed a second opinion.

Valerie knew she was a stickler for the rules. Maybe she was taking this too hard. Maybe she could see Keith. Well, it didn't have to be anything official. So he'd kissed her. Did that mean they were girlfriend and boyfriend? It didn't have to go that far right away.

The truth was that Valerie did not have much experience in these things. She bet Keith had had strings of girlfriends. He'd been an ace in a civil war. He'd owned a bar in Glasgow. He might be in his room right now carving a new notch on his belt.

She wasn't going to be just another woman for anyone. Sure, maybe she was overreacting. But she'd seen firsthand that the old ways of courtship were better than fooling around with every joker that came a girl's way. People got into all sorts of trouble with casual relationships. When she settled down, it was going to be something special. It wasn't going to be yet another man in a long line of lovers. That's what sluts did.

Valerie fumed. She wasn't a slut. She was a good girl. If that's how Keith thought about her—

Her nose wrinkled. She would like to face Keith on the mat now. He wouldn't flip her or even get close to pinning her. He figured she got distracted too easily. Ha-ha, she'd show him concentration like he wouldn't believe. She would pound him, pin him and slap him across the face until he cried out for mercy. That's what she should have done to him in the first place.

"Valerie. What are you doing down here?"

The lieutenant's head snapped up and she almost took a close-combat stance.

Doctor Dana Rich recoiled, although she smiled to show that she meant it playfully.

"Are you going to hit me?" the doctor asked.

"What? No!" Valerie said. "I…I was thinking about something else."

Dana nodded understandingly.

Dana was wearing her lab coat. She was older than Valerie, with dusky skin and dark hair down to her shoulders. She was Indian—dot not feather—and she was as good-looking as she was brilliant. The doctor was the professor's lover, the two seemingly made for each other. Once, Ludendorff had been her professor. Dana had been the only female student in the university on Brahma. Dana had run off with Ludendorff as he went searching for what would become known as Starship *Victory*.

"Would you like to grab a cup of coffee?" Valerie asked.

Dana thrust out her lower lip for a moment before nodding. "Yes. I'd love a cup. There's a cafeteria nearby."

"I know where it is."

"Before we go," Dana said. "I have to know. Is this a professional courtesy call or did you just happen to chance by?"

Valerie adjusted her blouse nervously. "I'm not coming here as Lieutenant Noonan making an inspection. But it isn't a chance meeting."

"Oh," Dana said, sounding cooler than a moment ago.

Valerie wanted to hold it in, but it just tumbled out. "I need advice, Doctor. I couldn't think whom I should ask…" She thought about Meta and the captain. "I don't think I can talk to Meta about this. I-I… You seemed like the logical choice."

Dana studied her. "This sounds personal."

"Yes," Valerie said, miserably.

"Oh. You mean personal for you."

Valerie nodded.

"Come, come," Dana said, sounding relieved. "I would be glad to lend you my shoulder…ear…whatever. Let's get some coffee and you can tell me all about it."

***

Valerie drained her third cup of coffee as she finished explaining the situation to Dana.

The doctor had been more reserved in her drinking, stirring a half-full cup of cold coffee. She had nibbled on a pastry, barely eating any of it.

"I have to watch my figure," Dana had said after Valerie had stared at the pastry once too often. "The doctor likes me to keep slim."

Valerie set her empty cup in the saucer. She noticed that her hand trembled the slightest little bit. That was enough caffeine for her.

"You like him," Dana announced.

"What?"

"The signs are obvious. That's why you're…concerned."

"But…we're Star Watch officers. We're on a critical mission. Our behavior is highly inappropriate."

"Would you call the professor and me inappropriate?"

"Of course," Valerie blurted. "No, I mean—"

"Shhh," Dana said, patting one of Valerie's hands. "I know what you mean. My father would think exactly like you. Maybe you're both right. I've told the professor before that he should marry me. He just laughs and changes the topic. Sometimes I think I should leave him just to teach him a lesson."

Dana patted Valerie's hand again. "But we're not talking about me. We're talking about you. My dear, if you're worried about your professional behavior, I would take into consideration that you usually work in a different area of the ship. Keith is primarily a strikefighter pilot."

"He's on the bridge sometimes."

"True, but—"

"Oh, this is a fine mess," Valerie said. She picked up the coffee cup and made to sip before remembering that it was empty. She set it back in the saucer.

"I shouldn't have practiced with him," Valerie said.

"You're not in a nunnery," Dana said. "You're human. You're young."

"Not that young anymore."

"My dear," Dana said. "You are painfully young, and beautiful. I'm surprised you haven't had this problem more often."

Valerie shrugged.

"You've unbent a little," Dana said. "I remember the first voyage—" She laughed before frowning, looking away.

"Is something the matter?" Valerie asked.

Dana did not answer.

"I'm sorry," Valerie said. "Here I've gone on and on about myself, not thinking to ask you if everything is all right."

Dana kept staring off into the distance.

Valerie asked in a softer voice. "Is everything all right, Doctor?"

Dana gave her an agonizing glance. Her eyes brimmed with tears. She wiped them roughly, shaking her head.

"Everything is fine," Dana said. "It is I who apologize. I am embarrassed."

"Dana. Don't. I came to you. If you need something, I'd love to help. We're friends. We're a family, remember?"

"Yes," Dana said softly. "I do remember. I'm so glad you came to see me. I…I think you should talk to Keith. You should tell him how you feel."

"I don't know how I feel…exactly."

Dana gave her a sad smile. "That's what you work out together. My advice, my dear, is to keep being Keith's friend. See what happens. Take the risk of getting hurt. If you never take a chance, never risk, you'll end up an old lady with a houseful of cats. I do not recommend that for you."

Valerie nodded, filing away the advice. She was going to think this through carefully.

"Enough about me," the lieutenant said. "How can I help you?"

Dana was silent for several seconds. "I'm not sure anyone can help me."

"Does… I hope I'm not prying?"

"No," Dana said softly.

"Does this concern the professor?"

"It does."

"In a romantic way?" Valerie dared to ask.

"I'm afraid not."

Some of Valerie's shyness evaporated as her professional side began to reassert itself. Was Ludendorff up to his old games?

"What seems to be the problem?" Valerie asked.

Dana did not speak for a time. She picked at the pastry, crumbling it, seemingly unaware of what she was doing. Finally, she looked down, and seemed surprised. She jerked her hands from the demolished pastry and wiped her fingertips clean with a napkin.

"The professor is...distracted," Dana said softly. "He's alone in his workroom more than normal. He stares into space more often when we're together. I talk to him, but he doesn't pay attention. I've...I've spoken nonsense to him several times as a test to see if he's listening. He just says, 'Oh, how nice,' or 'hmmm, I see.'"

"Don't all men do that some of the time?" Valerie asked.

Dana smiled sadly. "Of course they do. But this is more pronounced. I know him. When he's like this..."

"Yes?" Valerie said.

"It's a clear sign he's agitated. Unfortunately, the only time I've seen the professor agitated is when he...well, when he has something up his sleeve, as they say."

"You think this concerns the so-called Junkyard Planet?"

Dana's eyes widened as she studied Valerie. "I'm a fool."

"What do you mean?"

"The captain sent you to do this, didn't he?"

"What?" Valerie asked.

"I should have realized. You would never get romantically involved with the lieutenant. You're too worried about regulations."

Valerie reddened.

Dana kept staring at her, finally putting several fingertips against her mouth. "I'm sorry I said that."

"No... That's okay."

"It isn't," Dana said. "You *did* come to me in good faith. You were just being...a good sister by asking how I'm doing."

She smiled. “Please don’t tell the captain what I said about the professor. I spoke to you in confidence.”

“Dana…”

“Please, Valerie. Let me confront the professor. Let me do this my way before you bring the captain into it.”

Valerie was more conflicted than ever. She had come to Dana for help. Could she just betray the doctor’s trust?

“All right,” Valerie heard herself say. It did not sit well with her, but that’s what friends did, right? “I’ll give you twenty-four hours to find out what’s going on.”

Dana reached across the table, gripping one of Valerie’s hands. “Thank you. And this meeting was for the best. I might have dithered about doing anything otherwise. Now, I have to act. I’ll get back to you in less than twenty-four hours. I love the professor. I dearly do. But I have a responsibility to Star Watch and to the rest of the crew aboard *Victory*.”

Valerie nodded, feeling a little better. Twenty-four hours, and then she could go tell the captain about this. Nothing bad could happen during the next twenty-four hours. She was certain of that.

-15-

Several hours later, Doctor Dana Rich paced back and forth in her room. She hadn't told Valerie everything. She was certain Ludendorff was up to something. Why couldn't the old coot act normally for once?

Dana smiled wistfully. She'd been asking herself too many questions lately regarding the professor. Was her time with Ludendorff ending? She'd felt his distraction before. He had brushed it aside and told her not to worry. Now, she wasn't so sure anymore.

Yes, the sex was fantastic. The Methuselah Man did things to her that no one else could even come close to doing. He was a master in the bedroom, a lover like no other. He'd boasted before of how he'd trained her to match him in the boudoir. He had also said on more than one occasion that if he hadn't molded her soon enough, she would have learned bad techniques and possibly never reached the heights she now regularly did.

Dana sighed, hardening her resolve. She'd beaten the entire male chauvinistic Brahma System with their Hindu attitudes about women. She had thrived on Loki Prime, the prison planet. She had thwarted the professor before in the Beyond, back when they'd been in the Adok System. She loved him. It was possible she even needed him. But she couldn't let him get away with whatever he was planning this time. He had such a narrow focus. This was about human survival, not—

Dana made a half-strangled sound and resolutely marched for the hatch. She was going to confront the professor and find out exactly what kind of mischief he had planned this time.

***

Dana pounded on Ludendorff's hatch. She had been doing so for thirty seconds already.

Finally, the hatch slid open and a slightly out-of-breath Ludendorff stared at her.

"What seems to be the problem, my dear?" he asked.

"Can I come in?"

"I'll come out."

"No," she said, pushing him, causing him to stumble backward into his private laboratory.

The professor caught himself, but by that time, they both stood in the large chamber.

The hatch slid shut behind her, and that made Dana jump. She stared about the room. A long and much too sinuous machine snaked around the counters. She'd never seen anything like it. It must have been over ten meters long, Dana thought. The snakelike machine made odd sounds as lights flashed in various places. At the same time, the long machine squirmed as if it were alive.

"What *is* that?" Dana asked.

"Nothing much," Ludendorff said in a hearty tone. "It's a pet project to while away the hours during our protracted journey."

Dana eyed him. "Don't lie to me, Professor."

"Dana," he said, with his hands on her shoulders. "Do you doubt me?"

"Yes."

He laughed, hugging her, patting her until he jabbed something pin-like against her back.

Dana jerked out of his grasp, staring at him in shock. "What did you do to me?"

"Dana, Dana, Dana," he said in a chiding voice. "Really, my dear, this is my fault. I haven't been able to hide my unease well enough. I knew I shouldn't have spent so much time in here. What you see is a hedge against the future."

"But…" Dana said, blinking drowsily.

"There," he said, taking hold of her, guiding her to a chair. "Sit, relax, take a load off your feet."

Dana felt woozy. "What's wrong with me, Professor?"

"Not a thing, my dear. You're tired. You've been overworking lately."

"That's not true. I've had too much time on my hands. If Valerie hadn't spoken to—" Dana stopped herself before she said too much.

"Oh, dear," Ludendorff said. "Valerie spoke to you?"

"What is that thing?" Dana slurred, trying to raise a hand to point at it, trying to change the subject.

The professor stood beside her, rubbing her back. That felt good. The professor was so thoughtful.

"Is Valerie well?" Ludendorff asked.

Dana tried to hold back. She knew Ludendorff was up to something. Why had he pricked her?

"Dana," the professor said. "Tell me all about Valerie. I'm very interested. You know I am."

"Yes…" Dana said. "It started like this…"

***

Valerie wondered what Dana had discovered. Thirteen hours had passed since she'd spoken to the doctor.

The lieutenant was checking the main sensor node in the forward part of the ship. She was making sure everything was up to code. Normally, Andros Crank would have done this. The Kai-Kaus chief technician had the flu, and was in medical, resting. She was doing him a favor by looking into it.

Valerie moved through a hatch, nodded to a tech specialist monitoring a panel and headed for a narrow access corridor.

She hoped Dana wouldn't take the entire twenty-four hours to find out. Valerie felt guiltier by the hour for not racing to the captain about this. She hadn't seen Keith since then, either.

Scowling, Valerie passed through another hatch. She began to study the various panels, tapping diagnostics. It was a tight fit in here, the air slightly stale.

For the next few minutes, the task absorbed her thoughts. It was a welcome relief from all the worrying she'd been doing. Keith, the professor—

A hatch opened behind her. A tech specialist stared in at her. It was, she noted, the same man she'd seen earlier. There was something slightly off about him.

"Is there a problem?" Valerie asked.

The tech specialist shook his head, entering the narrow chamber.

"Maybe if you wait until I'm done in here…" Valerie said.

The tech didn't appear to have heard her. At the same moment, the side of his head flickered. What in blazes—

"Holo-mask?" Valerie said, puzzled.

The tech specialist stared at her, and then he lunged with something in his hand.

Valerie swept an open palm at him, aiming for his chin. She struck it, feeling the shock against her wrist. That jolted the tech, sending him staggering back.

It must have done something to his holo-mask too, switching it off or shorting it. The holoimage wavered and went down. Professor Ludendorff stood panting against a wall, gingerly touching his chin.

"What are you doing here?" Valerie asked. Then, she realized she could be in danger. "Galyan," she called. "Come at once."

Ludendorff pushed off the wall, balancing on shaky legs as if he were groggy.

"You have a solid right," the professor told her.

"Galyan is recording all this," Valerie said.

Ludendorff smiled. "Not at the moment, I'm afraid. I have a little gadget that is hindering his access to us."

"Why are you doing this?" Valerie asked. "The captain—"

"You will remain oblivious to any of this," Ludendorff told her. "I want you to trust me."

"Get out of my way."

"No. I want you to—"

The professor must have spoken just to distract her. The next thing Valerie knew, the Methuselah Man held a small gun, aiming it at her. He fired three times—three soft *hisses*—sending three slivers into her.

"You shot me!" Valerie said as her eyes went wide.

"With extreme reluctance, I assure you," he said.

A second later, Valerie collapsed.

-16-

Starship *Victory* continued to travel deeper into the Beyond, leaving known space far behind. Using jump points and the star drive, the ancient Adok vessel moved through one desolate star system after another. It often passed strange planets, which the crew dutifully cataloged. More interestingly, the vessel passed odd contrivances drifting in space. While there was no sign of life or artificial energy, clearly, at one time, life and energy had flourished in this region of space.

Maddox sat in the command chair on the bridge. He'd felt better about the voyage for some time, but lately a nagging doubt had begun to plague him.

Had had overlooked something? Maybe he'd forgotten a warning. The feeling bothered him—

"Captain," Galyan said. "I believe you will find this interesting."

They had just come out of a star drive jump.

Maddox glanced at the little holoimage. Galyan seemed excited. He could hear it in the AI's voice. That was so different from the beginning when they'd first met. The change made the AI seem more human, but also more terrifying if he thought about it too much.

The Adoks had "deified" Galyan. That was such an odd term. Maddox wondered if it had held religious significance?

"Do you not want to know what is so interesting?" Galyan asked.

"Please," Maddox said, "tell me."

"I have detected an ancient space station. So far, I have not detected any energy readings on it. I have detected old bio readings, though. I suspect those are skeletons."

"Let's see the station," Maddox said.

Galyan looked at the main screen. A second later, a double-decker space station appeared. Two large "wheels" connected by a central column made up the station, which orbited a red dust world. Several chunks were missing from the station's wheels. That could indicate old battle-damage or more recent meteor impacts. The station looked old and long-abandoned, and seeing it gave the captain a strange feeling. Was this humanity's ultimate future, nothing more than ancient artifacts drifting uselessly in space? How long did humanity have in the universe? Would it be one hundred years, one hundred thousand or even a million until the last human became extinct?

There was another peculiarity about the abandoned space station. It was *huge* compared to the Earthlike planet it orbited.

"How big is it?" Maddox asked.

"Approximately a quarter of the size of Earth's moon," Galyan said.

"That's massive."

"I have been studying the station and its relation to the planet. I believe its location adversely stimulated the dead world's tides."

"There's water down there?"

"An ammonia sea," Galyan said.

"Oh. It's not a human inhabitable planet, then?"

"If you mean humans cannot breathe the 'air' unaided, you are correct, Captain."

Maddox checked the readings running alongside the image on the screen. The derelict space station was 2.6 million kilometers from their present location. Had the station been abandoned for centuries or it was closer to a millennia?

"You said it contains skeletons," Maddox said. "Are they Swarm skeletons?"

"I have analyzed them from afar to the best of my ability," Galyan said. "I could give you more accurate data if I were on the station. So far, the skeletal composition is alien, meaning they are an unknown variety of creature."

"They're a new species?" Maddox asked, becoming intrigued. They had just happened to stumble upon an incredible find. If this had been a regular Patrol journey, they would stop and investigate the station. Now, they would have to note it and let someone else examine and catalog the ancient wreckage later.

"'New' is a relative term," Galyan was saying. "The creatures are long dead, so they certainly are not new."

"What do you make of this, Lieutenant?" Maddox asked.

Valerie sat at her bridge station. She seemed quieter than usual, had been for several days. With some stiffness to her bearing, the lieutenant swiveled around to face him.

"The 'creatures' Galyan is referring to are dead and gone," Valerie said. "The skeletons are meaningless to our purpose."

Maddox eyed her askance, finding her last statement peculiar.

He'd heard about her little run-in with Keith on the practice mats. The pilot had gone to Riker for advice. The sergeant happened to have mentioned it yesterday to Maddox. Valerie was taking the mat incident much too hard. She was too wound up, sometimes.

"We could send a jumpfighter to the station so that a few scientists could study the skeletons and artifact for a few hours at least," Galyan said. "Maybe there is a new technology to discover that could aid us in our quest."

"That's an excellent idea," Maddox said. "Galyan, get the professor. Maybe he knows something about this dead station."

Galyan disappeared, and reappeared almost right away.

"That was fast," Maddox said.

"I was unable to reach the professor," Galyan said.

"Why's that?"

"I believe he is in his study, as I do not see him on any of the security cameras. Unfortunately, I cannot appear in his study."

"You're blocked from it?" Maddox asked, surprised.

"I am, sir."

Maddox stood. He didn't like the sound of that. "You have the bridge," he told Valerie. "I'm going to pay the professor a surprise visit."

As Maddox headed for the exit, Valerie moved from her location to the command chair. Once settled in, she pressed a singular button on the left armrest. Then, she proceeded to stare at the main screen, waiting.

***

With Galyan at his side, Maddox brushed past a protesting Doctor Rich. The captain tried the professor's hatch. It did not open.

Before Dana could utter another protestation, Maddox pulled out an override unit, forcing the hatch with it. He stepped into the professor's large chamber, ready for anything.

Ludendorff turned around in surprise. He held a bulky metal object and seemed slightly winded. Putting the object into a lower cupboard, the Methuselah Man straightened.

"Can I help you?" Ludendorff asked.

Maddox glanced around the room. It was full of computer equipment and scattered tools, and a few bolts, perhaps, or something like bolts that were lying on a long counter.

"Have I done something to upset you, my boy?" the professor asked.

"Galyan can't appear in your lab," Maddox said.

"That is true," Galyan said, from outside the hatch, peering in. "I would enter, but I find something hindering me."

Ludendorff chuckled. "I love my privacy, it's true. What's wrong with that?"

"Why are you winded?" Maddox asked.

"Do you not exercise to stay in shape?" Ludendorff asked.

"What did you just put away?"

"Would you like to see it?"

Maddox nodded.

"It's old, and interesting," Ludendorff said. He reached into the cupboard.

"Sir," Galyan said. "It appears I am in error. I mean regarding the harmlessness of the derelict space station. It has just activated."

Maddox regarded the holoimage outside the hatch. "What kind of activation are we talking about?"

"High-velocity missiles, sir," Galyan said. "The ship is under attack."

Maddox did not hesitate. He raced out of the chamber, heading for the bridge. Maybe this was why he'd been feeling antsy. He should have launched a probe at the station. That was standard Patrol procedure regarding unknown objects.

As the captain raced away, Dana entered the professor's chamber holding a strange unit.

"Well done, my dear," Ludendorff said. "Well done, indeed. That could have proven embarrassing, to say the least."

The professor held out his hand. Without a word, Dana gave him the activation unit. The professor smiled, pecked her on the cheek and took the activation unit to a counter. Picking up a tool, he proceeded to dismantle the thing.

He couldn't let the captain find this, or find the sinuous 'bot he would need on the Junkyard Planet. It was time to take even greater care. If he wasn't careful, the captain would discover what he planned. That would not do.

-17-

Maddox reached the bridge in time to witness the destruction of two hyper-velocity missiles. Terrific explosions whitened the screen.

"What kind of radiation are they emitting?" Maddox asked.

Valerie turned to regard him, blinked several times and finally vacated the command chair.

Once again, Maddox was struck by the difference in her bearing. Normally, she would have hopped out of his chair. These days, she moved as if she were drugged. Was she getting enough sleep?

"Galyan," Maddox said.

"I am detecting regular radiation readings, Captain," Galyan said. "Those were standard-issue thermonuclear detonations."

"They're Star Watch warheads?" Maddox asked.

"I did not say that."

"Do they match any known Star Watch ordnance?"

"They do," Galyan said, sounding surprised. "How did you know?"

"It was a logical deduction," Maddox said blandly. "Lieutenant," he said, regarding Valerie. "Did the space station give any warning prior to the attack?"

"Checking," Valerie said, tapping her board. She shook her head a moment later. "I do not detect any form of warning."

"The old station simply launched the missiles?" Maddox asked.

"Maybe we tripped a proximity sensor," Valerie said.

Maddox rubbed his chin. "Do you detect the station making any kind of scans?"

Once more, Valerie tapped her board, studying the results. "Negative," she said.

"Do you have a theory, sir?" Galyan asked.

"Not yet," Maddox said. "Do you?"

"I agree with the proximity sensor idea," the holoimage said.

"Yet, the lieutenant has not detected any sensor sweeps," Maddox said. "By what process did the 'dead' station know we had come too near?"

"Teleoptic scopes, perhaps," Galyan said. "That is the most logical deduction. It used visual cues."

Maddox rubbed his chin, wondering if that was true.

"Should I fire upon the station?" Valerie asked.

"No," Maddox said.

"Should I send a jumpfighter there to investigate?" Galyan asked.

"We don't have time for that," Maddox said. "And I don't want to send someone into danger without a good reason. We need to reach the mystery planet sooner rather than later. Helm, increase velocity for the next jump point."

With a few taps to his board, the helmsman complied.

"Do you still wish to speak to the professor?" Galyan asked.

Maddox removed his hand from his chin. The missiles had launched as he'd spoken with Ludendorff. Had that been a coincidence?

"I'll speak to the professor later," Maddox said. "Until we're out of the star system, I'm remaining on the bridge. Let's see if the station has any more surprises for us."

***

A day later, in the next star system, Maddox pondered the coincidence of the station attacking as he spoke to the professor. He stood before a viewing port, alone with his thoughts, with the stars shining in the darkness.

He hadn't gone back to see Ludendorff because if the Methuselah Man had had a hand in the missile attack, the captain doubted he would have found any incriminating evidence in the professor's laboratory. The likeliest reason Ludendorff would have staged the station assault was to gain time to hide something. And if any man knew how to hide evidence in plain sight, it was the professor.

That did not mean Maddox would forget about this. Instead, the professor had sparked his interest. He trusted Ludendorff to help humanity, but he would always help himself at the same time. Maddox had not forgotten about some of the professor's past partners, particularly the unsavory slarn hunters. Ludendorff was brilliant, but the man also made some terrible errors in judgment.

The captain wondered about androids—the Builder-made constructs in particular. The android on Titan said it had known his father. He longed to know his father's identity. Yet, he also feared to find out.

Maddox sighed. According to Ludendorff's calculations, *Victory* would reach the Junkyard Planet in another eight days. He recalled the Dyson sphere—that had been a challenging voyage. The sphere had been much farther from the Commonwealth than this derelict world was. In truth, Maddox was surprised at the Junkyard Planet's nearness to the Commonwealth. That had struck him as odd from the beginning of the voyage.

Had the place been a Builder outpost?

Whatever the case, it was time to plan for the Junkyard Planet. It was time to call a meeting. Could he trust Ludendorff to give an accurate picture of what he knew and, more importantly, what he surmised about the planet?

Maddox grimaced. He could trust Ludendorff to be Ludendorff. That meant the professor had something in play. The Methuselah Man would bear watching. No doubt, the professor would expect him to spy on him now.

The captain's grimace turned into a sinister smile. That meant it would be good for Ludendorff to find him—Maddox—spying on him. But the professor couldn't discover this too easily, or the Methuselah Man would realize that the first level of probing was meant to be found out in order to hide the second-level search.

It was an old intelligence trick, but it was often an effective tactic.

For the first time during the voyage, Maddox began to feel like his old self. He'd had a sensation of...something bad waiting for them. Now, he was beginning to act.

The game is on, he told himself. And there was one thing about games that never changed for the captain—he played to win.

-18-

The next day, Maddox was in the gunnery room, practicing his quick-draw firing.

A knife-wielding holoimage appeared to his left as he entered an area. He drew smoothly, firing before the holoimage could complete its slash.

Someone behind him clapped.

Maddox holstered the practice pistol before regarding Dana Rich.

"Hello, Doctor," he said. "What brings you down here?"

"I have a message to deliver."

Maddox noted her withdrawn manner. There was something else as well, an inner listlessness. He felt like that should have jogged a memory, but he couldn't quite latch onto what it was.

"Does the professor want to see me?"

"The professor would like to hold a briefing, Captain. He has an announcement to make."

"Of what nature?"

"Concerning our next jump."

Maddox took his time responding. "It feels as if the professor is up to something."

"Is that so unique?"

"Sadly, no," Maddox said. "Come. We will forgo any briefing. You and I shall talk to the professor now."

Dana made an exasperated sound. “Haven’t you hounded him enough? He has faith in you. Why does your faith in him keep slipping?”

The reaction surprised Maddox, although he kept his features bland. Her emotion seemed genuine, yet…

“You of all people should understand how being unique causes jealousies and backbiting from those around you,” Dana said. “Why do you have to suspect him all the time?”

Maddox made an offhanded gesture.

“I think you’re jealous of him, too,” Dana said.

“Yes. That’s it exactly.”

“Don’t patronize me, Captain.”

He nodded. This was a good act, but it was an act just the same. He decided to let her believe she’d persuaded him.

“Tell the professor he can have his briefing in an hour,” Maddox said.

Dana seemed to expand, almost like a cobra ready to strike. It seemed, he thought, as if she were…struggling internally. Finally, in a loud huff, she spun around and stalked away.

***

An hour later, Maddox entered the briefing chamber.

Professor Ludendorff sat at one end of a conference table. Dana sat on his right. Valerie sat beside her and then Meta.

Maddox moved to stand behind the open chair on the other end of the table. Riker sat on his right, then Keith Maker, Andros Crank and finally the professor on the other end. Galyan stood slightly behind and to the side of the captain’s chair.

Andros Crank was a stout and rather short man with blunt fingers. He had unusually long gray hair, which he seemed to take great pride in, considering its sheen and how well-combed he kept it. Andros seldom said much, but he had observant gray eyes that seemed to miss nothing.

“Thank you for coming,” the professor said.

“Excuse me,” Maddox said curtly. “I’m the captain. I run the meeting. Therefore, I will open it.”

Ludendorff looked annoyed, but he nodded.

Maddox stood at his spot, slowly taking his seat. "The professor has an announcement to make. He has asked if I could summon a briefing. This I have done. Professor, if you will."

"Thank you, Captain," Ludendorff said. He had several items on the table. "I'm not certain where to begin. Well, perhaps I'll begin with a confession. These do not come easily to me."

Ludendorff turned to Dana. "I hope you will forgive me, my dear."

The doctor looked at him in surprise.

Ludendorff withdrew a tiny vial from his pocket, holding it between his thumb and index finger. "I had to do something the other day that makes me ashamed. I drugged you. It has bothered me ever since."

Ludendorff handed her the vial.

"What am I supposed to do with this?" Dana asked.

"Drink it, please," Ludendorff said. "It will restore your memory of the event."

Dana weighed the vial in her hand, finally looking to Maddox.

The captain frowned. He hated to admit it to himself, but Ludendorff had surprised him. "I cannot counsel you in this. I am of two minds concerning it."

Ludendorff laughed. "I should have expected this. I finally make a confession, and the most suspicious man in the universe believes it's a ploy."

"Don't drink it," Maddox said, certain now.

Dana must have felt otherwise. She unstopped the vial and tossed the contents into her mouth. She swallowed, looked at Ludendorff and waited. A few seconds later, her shoulders hunched, she closed her eyes and groaned. She held that pose for a time, finally, gingerly, opening her eyes and peering at the professor.

"You pricked me in the back when you hugged me," she said.

"I'm sorry, my dear. I truly am."

Dana turned to the captain. "I surprised him in his laboratory. I saw something he wanted kept hidden."

"What did you see?" Maddox asked.

Dana blinked. "It was a holomap, a grim image of what is awaiting us." She turned to the professor. "Why couldn't you trust me? Why did you treat me like you treat everyone else?"

"I made a mistake," Ludendorff said, looking down, sounding genuinely contrite.

"He panicked," Valerie said in a rote manner. "It would seem that even Methuselah Men can panic."

The professor sighed, producing another vial. "I am afraid I must also apologize to you," he told Valerie.

Lieutenant Noonan stared at him.

"Please," Ludendorff said, handing her the vial. "I wish you would accept my apology."

Valerie did not accept the vial. She turned an agonizing glance to the captain. "I don't trust him," she said. "I don't want to drink it."

"Roll the vial to me," Maddox said.

Ludendorff blinked several times.

"Professor, if you please," Maddox said.

"Of course, of course," Ludendorff said. He flung the vial down the table. It slid quickly to the side, and it might have gone off and crashed onto the floor, but Keith caught it.

"There you go, mate," Keith said, beaming at the exhibition of his nimble reflexes.

Maddox accepted the vial, placing it upright before him.

"Don't you want your memories restored?" Ludendorff asked Valerie.

"I don't trust you," she said. "I don't like taking anything that messes with my mind. How do I know this isn't a trick?"

"Would I trick my own lover?" Ludendorff asked.

"You just admitted that you did," Valerie said. "What did you do to me?"

Ludendorff looked away, shaking his head. He told them what he'd done as Valerie had checked the forward sensors.

"While I appreciate you telling us this," Maddox said. "I wonder if you've done so only because you know I'm watching you more closely."

"I knew you had begun spying on me," Ludendorff admitted. "I could feel it, partly because I have devices that warn me and also because I have a sixth sense about these things." He shrugged. "Perhaps that had something to do with my confession. I like to believe it's because I've been feeling miserable for drugging the doctor." He looked at Dana. "I dearly hope you can forgive me, my dear."

"I need time to think about this," Dana said in a small voice.

"I understand completely," Ludendorff said.

"What is the nature of this grim holomap?" the captain asked.

"If you will permit me to show you..." Ludendorff put his hands on a square device.

Under the table, Maddox rested his gun hand on his holstered sidearm. Above the table, he nodded.

"Galyan, can you dim the lights?" the professor asked.

The lights dimmed as the professor manipulated the holo-box. It made a slight humming sound. Moments later, a projection burst forth over the conference table.

It showed a white dwarf star and its nearest planets.

"We are fast approaching the Ezwal Star System," the professor said. "In many ways, this is the most unique star system in the Orion Arm. As you can see, it has a white dwarf star. Once, the star was much like Sol's Sun."

"Why is the system unique?" Galyan asked.

"Ah..." the professor said. "That is a good question. Notice this region here." Ludendorff used a pointer to show intense darkness.

"Is that a black hole?" Galyan asked.

"It is indeed," the professor said. "It is far enough away from the white dwarf that it hasn't destroyed the tiny star yet. The black hole has devoured the farthest gas giants, however. The constant, nearly overpowering gravity has also created a unique tramline."

"You're suggesting that *Victory* go to this unstable system?" Maddox asked.

"We are presently on course for it," Ludendorff said. "In fact, we should reach the system in another three days."

"Why would we want to?" Maddox asked.

"The tramline, the link between star systems, is nearly four hundred light-years long."

"That's impossible," Valerie said. "Hartford and Spengler proved that no tramline is over seven light-years in length. As we know, there is no tramline that long in Human Space. The longest is five point three light-years."

"I am well aware of Frederick D. Hartford and Anthony Spengler's work," the professor said. "I nudged them in that direction, if the truth be known. Their analysis was good, as far as it goes, but it was also flawed. Strangely, they did not take into consideration what a black hole's event horizon can do. In the Ezwal System, it has elongated the tramline into a three hundred and eighty-four light-year tunnel."

"Why keep this information from Star Watch and why keep it from Dana?" Maddox asked.

The professor tapped the side of his nose. "For one thing, it is dangerous using the *stretched* tramline. I believe *Victory* can easily overcome the obstacles, but to deny any danger would be false."

"Why bother using a dangerous tramline?" the captain asked. "Three hundred and eighty-four light-years is a hefty jump, I agree, but—"

"If we attempt to reach the Junkyard Planet any other way," Ludendorff said, interrupting, "we will surely perish."

Everyone at the table stared at the professor.

"Perhaps you can tell us why that is," Maddox said dryly.

Ludendorff nodded. "Do you recall the derelict space station several days ago?"

"I haven't stopped thinking about it," Maddox said.

"Yes, it was unusual. Well, there are more of those along the way, not so many on our end of the four hundred light-years, but closer to the ancient Rull Empire end."

The captain drummed his fingers on the table.

"I'm sure I've told you about the Rull before," the professor said.

Maddox said nothing.

"Have I been remiss?" the professor asked.

Maddox still did not speak.

"I see," Ludendorff said. "I knew something had slipped my mind, I just couldn't remember what. Well, the Rull…they were an interesting species."

"Were those Rull skeletons aboard the derelict station?" Galyan asked.

"As to that, I cannot say," Ludendorff replied. "I rather doubt it. The Rull were extraordinarily secretive. You see, they were shape-shifters, able to appear as almost any other species. It gave them fantastic advantages regarding interstellar espionage. They were the bane of several other species. But you don't have to worry. The Rull will not bother us. I believe they've lcft a few artifacts behind, as I've said, but their day has passed. The last Rull perished when the Vikings were using their longships to raid Europe."

"Are you suggesting we use the Einstein-Rosen Bridge to bypass the majority of the dangerous Rull relics?" Galyan asked.

"What is this about an Einstein-Rosen Bridge?" Maddox asked.

"It is the technical name for the tramline," Ludendorff said. "Galyan is showing off, nothing more. Yes. We will use the tramline to bypass the worst problems and to speed the process. Ever since Thrax escaped from the Dyson sphere, Earth has been in danger from the Swarm Imperium. If there is one thing I've learned in my long existence, it is that knowledge is power. As the weaker party, humanity desperately needs knowledge. That is why we need a long-range scanner."

"That is all well and good," Maddox said. "I want to know why you've hidden this from us. Why have you drugged and reprogrammed Dana and Valerie?"

Ludendorff chuckled good-naturedly. "I have hardly *reprogrammed* them. I suppressed one memory and gave them another. I've already told you why. Nothing must stop our mission. It is vital to humanity. I was fearful that Star Watch, and possibly you, would object if you knew what really awaits us. Thus, when Dana surprised me—"

"I detect falsity in his words," Galyan told the captain. "I have studied your psychology, Professor. You are stating mistruths."

"Confounded AI," Ludendorff said. "No one is asking your opinion. I most certainly did fear that Star Watch would discover my deception."

Maddox glanced at Galyan.

"I do not understand this," the holoimage said. "He is telling the truth now."

Maddox glanced at Ludendorff, and something occurred to him. What was one way to divert or distract people? Confess to a lesser crime. It was true that Ludendorff hadn't told them about the Einstein-Rosen Bridge. But that might not be what Dana had seen in the professor's laboratory. Galyan was about to foil Ludendorff's likely deception, and that would not do.

"That will be all, Galyan," Maddox said. "I want you to begin scanning for this black hole. I want to verify the truth of the professor's words."

"Really," Ludendorff said. "I find that insulting."

"Galyan," Maddox said.

"Yes, Captain," Galyan said. The AI grew still.

Maddox cleared this throat.

"Is something wrong, sir?" Galyan asked.

"I would like you to do your scanning from the bridge."

"But, sir—"

"At once," Maddox said.

Galyan gave him an extra-long scrutiny before disappearing.

Maddox picked up the vial Valerie hadn't drunk. He would have Galyan analyze this later. Eyeing the professor, the captain said:

"I appreciate your candor, but I'm not sure I can fully trust you now. You can no longer keep your own lab."

"I understand," Ludendorff said.

Maddox nodded. "It helps that you can agree to the limitation. That shows your good will toward us. Now, I would like to know more about the Ezwal System."

"Of course," Ludendorff said.

Maddox sat forward, listening as the professor resumed his explanation. All the while, the captain was thinking. He realized that whatever Ludendorff was hiding, it was no longer in his laboratory. There was another thing. That Ludendorff had so readily agreed to the limitation meant without a doubt that the professor was hiding something else.

From this point on, Maddox would act accordingly.

-19-

Galyan analyzed Ludendorff's serum. There were no toxins, no memory suppressants or other suspicious drugs in it.

"Even so," Galyan told the captain. "I cannot tell what it does to the human brain. Dana has refused to submit to a brain scan."

"What did you find in Valerie?"

"A lingering drug known as HVDL," Galyan said. "It is commonly known as the Persuader, used by kidnappers, rapists and credit-card thieves. After ingesting the drug, the person readily accepts whatever advice he or she receives. The robber convinces his victim to empty his account. The rapist—"

"I understand the principle," Maddox said. "Does it have any aftereffects?"

"For a month or more," Galyan said. "The person remains uncommonly open to suggestion. That is one reason few politicians have adopted it as a stratagem for getting themselves elected. While they could convince a roomful of people to vote for them, that vote could change once the recipient watched the opposing politician's holo-vid ads."

"Ludendorff's serum erases the HVDL's effect?" Maddox asked.

"I have not been able to determine that. In this instance, I would have to run tests."

"No," Maddox said. "We will not run any human tests. Do you have any other antidote to HVDL?"

"I have read the computer file on the subject. I can synthesize one easily enough."

"We'll have the lieutenant take that once you've manufactured the antidote."

"Yes, Captain."

"On a different note, have you located the black hole?"

"I have, sir. It is in the location the professor told us it would be."

Maddox departed. For the remainder of this voyage, he would check everything before he ate or drank it. He would also talk to Meta and Riker about that. Those two could keep a secret—that he still watched and suspected the professor. He wasn't sure about anyone else, though. Thus, he would not risk having others give away his secret scrutiny.

***

The next couple of days passed uneventfully until finally they approached the Ezwal System.

Maddox was on the bridge. Valerie scanned the system from her station. Soon, she posted her findings on the main screen.

The white dwarf was a little bigger than the Earth but had the approximate mass of the Sun. The star was extremely dense, composed of electron-degenerate matter. Although the white dwarf was a star, it did not generate heat through fusion but through stored thermal energy. That made it comparatively dim.

"Do the nearest planets show any signs of a red giant phase?" Maddox asked.

The red giant phase would have occurred when the main sequence star expanded. That would have obliterated any tightly orbiting planets and seared others at farther orbits.

After a quick survey of the nearest planets, Valerie confirmed that they did indeed show the expected signs of red giant expansion.

The white dwarf had likely been Sun-sized once. Near the end of the red giant phase, the ejected ionized gas had likely turned into a planetary nebula. The black hole would have devoured the nebula, erasing all sign of it.

"I would like to point out," Valerie said, "that so far, I haven't detected any old Rull space stations."

Maddox decided the system appeared safe enough. Thus, Starship *Victory* proceeded on course.

Sometime later, they turned on the Laumer-Drive, searching for jump-point entrances. While Ludendorff had gone on about the Einstein-Rosen Bridge, it was essentially a longer Laumer tramline.

"I've detected an opening," Valerie said. She turned around. "It's near the black hole, sir."

"Will that be a problem?" Maddox asked.

Valerie studied her panel. "It might. While our engines are strong enough to force us through, the nearness of the event horizon could cause a time distortion."

"Can you estimate the extent of the distortion?"

Valerie tapped her panel. "It could add several weeks to our journey, sir. We won't notice it right away, but an outside observer would notice that we inside the vessel were slowing down."

"That would seem to negate the bridge's utility," Maddox said.

"Three hundred and eighty-four light-years would take us weeks to travel the normal way," Valerie said. "We'll still save time using the bridge. I'm sure you remember that the professor suggested there are old Rull artifacts along the way. Those artifacts will certainly make our journey more dangerous. We will avoid the artifacts and the danger if we use the bridge."

According to the professor, Maddox thought to himself.

The captain studied the main screen. Was it wise to trust Ludendorff about this? He did not like approaching the black hole this closely. Yet, if *Victory* perished or sustained damage, that would harm the professor. If Maddox knew one thing about Ludendorff, the Methuselah Man loved his own skin more than he loved anything else.

"We will proceed to the Einstein-Rosen Bridge," Maddox said.

***

The crew grew tense as the starship approached the black hole. They were alone in the Beyond, about to enter what could possibly be an unstable wormhole.

Maddox retired for a time, returning as the vessel neared the wormhole entrance.

"This is interesting," Galyan said. "I am actively trying to estimate the slowing progression of time as it occurs to us."

"We're in the grip of the black hole?" Maddox asked.

"That is an imprecise statement," Galyan said. "An immense gravitational force has begun to exert an influence upon us. Fortunately, the Laumer-Point draws near, giving us a means of easy escape."

"Could the Rull have left surprises near the entrance?"

"I cannot conceive of a way for them to have done so," Galyan said. "The black hole would have long ago drawn such a thing into it."

That made sense. *I should have thought of that.* "How long until we reach the Laumer-Point?" asked Maddox.

"Fifteen minutes," Valerie said.

Time passed slowly, and that wasn't because of the black hole.

Soon enough, Maddox began the jump procedure. Everyone had taken his or her shots. The equipment was primed. On one side of the ship was primordial blackness. On the other side were the stars. Maddox's gut told him to expect something bad.

We've made long-distance jumps before, Maddox told himself. It had been through a hyper-spatial tube, though, not an elongated tramline. Still, four hundred light-years, give or take, was a small jump compared to what he'd done before.

Maddox exhaled, wishing his brain would let his gut know there was nothing to worry about.

"Ten seconds to jump," Valerie said. "Seven…four, three, two, one… We are entering the wormhole."

-20-

For once, Maddox was aware of what was usually a split-second event. They entered the jump point. Everything became a blur of motion stretching…stretching…stretching. Maddox was aware that he held his breath. Could this really be happening? They traveled nearly four hundred light-years—

Maddox swayed on his chair. *Victory* exited the wormhole, expelled into normal space once more. They had made it, they…

Maddox frowned, trying to marshal his thoughts into a coherent line of understanding. The ship had begun in one star system and entered another… According to the chair monitor to his side, the system had a cool blue star and five terrestrial planets. The sensors, such as they were, indicated that the system lacked any gas giants whatsoever.

Maddox looked around. The bridge crew struggled to shake off what used to be Jump Lag. The modified drugs normally took off the edge. A few times, someone still had minor aftereffects. The machines also—

"Warning!" Galyan cried. "The ship is under a powerful sensor scan."

Maddox sat straighter, attempting to concentrate more fully. A warning blare sounded on the bridge.

"Raise the shield," Maddox said in a slow voice.

Valerie tapped her board. "The shield is not responding, sir."

"Galyan—"

"I am working on it, sir," the AI said. "I have discovered the problem. Along with the sensor scan, a foreign wavelength interference is attempting to overload our ship's systems."

"Lieutenant," Maddox said, speaking more crisply. "Can you activate the main screen?" It was presently blank.

Valerie worked on her panel, and abruptly gave up. "I don't understand this," she whispered lethargically.

Maddox was up out of his chair. In three strides, he was at her station. He manipulated her board as she sat inert. A second later, the main screen activated.

"I have an idea that could help, sir," Galyan said.

"Do it," Maddox snapped.

"Do you not wish to hear my idea first?" Galyan asked.

"Do it," Maddox said. "That is an order." He looked up at the main screen.

What seemed like bright flares moved across the screen. They were streaks of light gaining speed. Behind the lights—exhaust plumes from something, Maddox thought—was a large dark planetoid.

A loud whooshing sound occurred. It rocked the bridge. Maddox staggered, grabbing a station, holding on until the shaking passed.

"What was that?" the helmsman shouted.

"A powerful defensive pulse," Galyan said. "An unknown enemy is trying to cause more malfunctions to the ship. I knocked down their attempt, but it caused some disturbance to *Victory*. In case you are wondering, sir, they are still scanning us."

"Whatever your pulse was, it worked" Valerie said. "I'm raising the shield."

Maddox saw that, as a ghostly nimbus appeared on the screen, showing the electromagnetic protection around *Victory*.

"Raising our shield has blocked their scan," Galyan announced.

"Where is the scan's origin point?" Maddox asked.

"The armored spheroid," Galyan said.

"Do you mean the planetoid ahead?"

"That is not a natural object, sir," Galyan replied. "It is a vessel, a massive ship, and it appears—lasers, sir, heavy lasers are warming up."

Bright points of light appeared on the vast sphere. A moment later, lasers poured out of a half-dozen apertures.

"The enemy vessel is approximately twenty kilometers in diameter," Valerie said. "It's huge."

The streaks on the main screen had picked up velocity.

"Those are missiles," Valerie said. "They're homing in on us, sir."

"Target them at once," Maddox ordered.

The enemy sphere's lasers struck the shield more forcefully. The shield held, but the lasers began turning the targeted points red and then brown.

"The wattage of those lasers is most impressive," Galyan said. "They are several factors greater than Wahhabi *Scimitar*-class warships can fire."

"Try hailing the vessel," Maddox said.

"It is an automated ship," Galyan said. "I do not believe there is anyone alive to hail."

"Is this another Destroyer?" Maddox asked.

"Negative, sir," Galyan said. "I believe it is a primitive Builder robot-ship or possibly a Rull vessel. Certain functions lead me to the former conclusion."

"What is its purpose?" Valerie asked.

"That doesn't matter right now," Maddox said. "Target those missiles. Destroy them before they get too close."

Seconds later, *Victory's* neutron beam struck the first missile.

"It's shrugging off the beam," Valerie said in amazement.

"Activate the disruptor cannon," Maddox said.

"Sir," Galyan said. "I am having qualms concerning this battle. I believe *Victory* could be outclassed. Perhaps—"

"Lieutenant," Maddox said. "Can the ship use the star drive yet?"

"In five minutes or so, sir," Valerie said. "There appears—"

"Five minutes," Maddox said. "That should be enough. Galyan, is the disrupter cannon malfunctioning?"

"Checking…checking…I see the problem. Would you like me to tell the cannon operators—?"

"Go, inform them," Maddox said.

The holoimage disappeared from the bridge.

The starship shook. On the screen, large anti-missiles accelerated toward the incoming drones.

"What is that sphere?" Maddox said.

Galyan reappeared. "The cannon will be operative in three minutes, sir."

The large enemy missiles bored in. The neutron beam continued to hammer the first missile. The thing's outer alloy seemed utterly resistant to the beam.

"What is the enemy missile made of?" Maddox asked.

"I do not have a name for it," Galyan said. "I have never run across its like. This is most interesting."

"Have you recorded it composition?"

"Affirmative," Galyan said. "I have also run several internal tests. This might revolutionize Star Watch's ship armor."

"Only if we survive the battle," Maddox said.

Finally, the disrupter cannon came online. The powerful beam hit the nearest incoming missile.

"The alloy is heating up," Galyan said. "It is—Warning! The missile is about to detonate. The warhead—"

"Emergency jump," Maddox said in a commanding voice. "Helmsman—"

"The drive is not yet fully operational, sir."

"Jump anyway," Maddox said.

The helmsman twisted a ring on his finger.

Maddox strode to the helmsman's station and shouldered the man aside. The captain manipulated the board. From deep inside *Victory*, the antimatter engines whined near overload.

On the screen, an enemy warhead ignited. At nearly the same time, Starship *Victory* slipped away with the star drive. As the ship did so, power surged throughout the vessel. That did the impossible. It shorted the star drive.

Victory fell out of the jump before moving far. It placed the starship nearer to the gigantic spheroid. Now, only several hundred kilometers separated them.

Maddox shoved the helmsman completely off his chair, taking the man's place. The captain's fingers blurred across the board.

In seconds, every point-defense cannon on the Adok starship opened up. The shells hammered the alien spheroid. At the same time, Maddox launched more missiles and aimed the neutron and disrupter beams at the huge, automated vessel.

"Galyan," Maddox shouted. "Find out what happened to the star drive. We have to get out of here."

The holoimage disappeared.

Maddox studied his panel. According to the readings, the giant enemy auto-vessel had the same strange alloy as its outer skin. The PD shells bounced off the hull, although many left dents. The neutron beam had no apparent effect. Only the disrupter beam chewed into the highly resistant alloy.

"The enemy spheroid is finally beginning to react," Valerie said.

Maddox used his board, searching for a vulnerable point on the enemy vessel. It did not appear to have one. Even so, he would act as if it did. With a few taps, he focused every weapons system on one location. He hammered that location ruthlessly, hoping to break through. The only hope was to cause a massive explosion inside the enemy spheroid.

"Get me Ludendorff," Maddox said.

The seconds ticked away.

Enemy beams now smashed against *Victory's* shield. The ancient Adok vessel had the best shield in all of Star Watch, but it turned an ugly purple color almost immediately.

"Captain," Valerie said. "Professor Ludendorff is on channel two."

Maddox switched to it, seeing a harried-looking professor on his tiny helm screen.

"You must disengage at once," Ludendorff said. "That is a Rull Juggernaut. I doubt *Victory* can defeat it."

"You knew about this ship?" Maddox asked indignantly.

"I did not know it was at this location, if that is what you are suggesting," the professor said. "I assure you that this is a grim surprise to me as well. My advice is to use the star drive. Jump out of danger."

"Captain," Valerie said. "I detect enemy tractor beams."

"Yes," Ludendorff said, nodding on the tiny screen. "Those are indeed tractor beams. The auto-ship is trying to lock us into place. If it is successful, the Juggernaut's shearing beam will begin to cut our hull into ribbons."

Maddox's face screwed up. With several taps, he located the focus of the shearing beam. He redirected the disrupter cannon, firing there.

At that moment, *Victory* shuddered.

"The shield is about to collapse," Valerie said. "Enemy shells have begun breaking through. If they manage to slip a thermonuclear warhead through, we're finished, sir."

Maddox studied his panel. The enemy tractor beams were growing stronger. If the shield fell and the beams gripped the starship—

"Sir," Galyan said. "I suggest you reactivate the star drive."

"It works?"

"Yes, sir."

Maddox thought about that. "Won't the star drive cause an explosion if we try to jump while locked into place?"

"I give the maneuver a thirty-two percent probability of success," Galyan said. "That is several factors greater than if we remain to fight the spheroid toe-to-toe."

"Captain," Valerie said, "your instincts are correct. You can't jump with the tractor beams locking us into place. That would tear the ship apart."

"Thirty-two percent," Maddox said. That meant there was a sixty-eight percent chance of failure. Steeling his resolve, Maddox activated the star drive.

"Where are we jumping to?" Valerie shouted.

Maddox didn't bother to look. He—

A terrible grinding noise sounded. Explosions rocked the bridge. *Victory* shuddered.

"The tractor beams have caught us!" Valerie wailed. "We're doomed."

At that moment, everything blacked out as darkness enfolded the bridge. There was a shaking sensation. Then, silence made the darkness ten times more terrifying.

Are we dead? Maddox wondered. He didn't think so, because the dead didn't think...he thought, not knowing for certain of course. But if they weren't dead, what and where were they?

-21-

"Where did they go?" Strand asked angrily.

None of the New Men on the *Argo's* bridge answered or even acknowledged that they had heard the question.

Strand's star cruiser was in the same distant system where *Victory* had battled the automated spheroid. Strand had observed the fight with interest and relish. He had half-believed he was about to witness the destruction of Starship *Victory* and his nettlesome colleague, Professor Ludendorff.

Strand did not care for Captain Maddox. But he did not hate the captain to the same degree that he despised Ludendorff.

Now, the starship had vanished. It had jumped, clearly, breaking away from the clamping tractor beams. That was extraordinary.

The Rull Juggernaut was something else. If he could collect enough of the ancient relics, perhaps he could create his own fleet.

Strand studied the main screen, watching the Juggernaut. It was nothing like the Destroyer in size or capability. In that regard, it was a minnow compared to a Great White shark. Still, *every* warship in this region of the galaxy was a minnow compared to a Destroyer. If he could gather enough mutated minnows—Rull Juggernauts—he could defeat any other school of warships.

"Detection," Strand said. "Is the starship still in the system?"

A New Man tapped his panel. "I can find no sign of them, Master."

"Give me your estimation of the possibility that they are hidden somewhere in the system."

The New Man sat quietly, tapping his board for a long moment. "There is a seven percent chance they are hidden in the star system, Master."

"Keep searching," Strand said, as he stood. "Contact me the instant you discover them."

"Yes, Master," the New Man said.

Strand debated with himself. "Communications, contact Dem Darius. Instruct him to return to the *Argo*."

"Master," the communications officer asked, "will you desire Darius to shut down the Juggernaut before he leaves?"

"Is that not self-evident?"

"Not to me, Master."

"That is because you are inferior to me."

"Yes, Master," the communications officer said, waiting.

Strand sighed. "Inform Darius he is to shut down…" The Methuselah Man reconsidered. "Correction. Instruct Darius to await further orders. He will remain near the jump point on the Juggernaut. If the starship reappears, tell him he must await my orders before he reengages in battle."

"Yes, Master."

Turning, putting a hand on his bad thigh, Strand limped for the exit. It was time to revisit the android Rose.

***

Strand had been busy since capturing the android. He had decided to trust Rose after a fashion. If Ludendorff was traveling to this Junkyard Planet, he would too.

Rose had spoken about a need for haste. Strand doubted that anyone among the human races could travel as quickly as he could if he put his mind to it. For one thing, Strand knew that he was the master of the Nexuses. No one knew as much about the Builder pyramids—no one among humans—as he did.

Strand had used his star drive and used selected jump points to reach a Nexus unknown to Star Watch or the New

Men. With it, he'd used a hyper-spatial tube to leap far ahead of Ludendorff.

Given Rose's data, Strand had a good idea of the professor's route. The old bounder would use the elongated Einstein-Rosen Bridge—that had seemed obvious. The Rull and their annoying relics would prove too troublesome otherwise.

Strand doubted any Rull yet lived. He'd captured one long ago. He'd extracted interesting information from the creature. It had been a laborious process, but well worth the effort. The Rull had died, of course. It had tried many permutations in order to kccp its knowledge from him. That had been the first of the creature's many mistakes.

Several days ago, Strand had given Darius precise instructions. He had also loaned the New Man several of his brain-scrubbed colleagues. The Juggernaut had proven a tough nut to crack. Only Darius remained of the team he'd sent. That had been enough, though, to activate the ancient vessel so Darius could pilot the giant spheroid near the wormhole exit and wait for *Victory* to appear.

It had been a good plan. Actually, it had seemed foolproof.

Strand shook his head. Foolproof, what an interesting term. Nothing in this life was foolproof. Fools could wreck anything. The universe was a fantastic representation of that.

If *Victory* had slipped out of this little trap…it was unlikely that the professor would realize he was behind it. Ludendorff had never traveled as much as he—Strand—had. He knew far more about the Beyond than the old bounder did. Still, Ludendorff was a slippery devil. If he could finally eliminate him…that would make the rest of his plans much easier to implement.

Strand stepped off the turbo-lift and began limping down a corridor. The android was troublesome because she had been so accurate about everything so far. This meant Rose had deep knowledge. Could she be wiser and more slippery than Ludendorff was?

The ancient Methuselah Man made a wheezing sound that rose and fell in rhythm, the sound of him laughing at his own joke. No one was as slippery as Professor Ludendorff.

Besides, Rose was his captive. Strand would never give the android the slightest chance of escaping. He should have already destroyed her…except, she kept giving him interesting tidbits of data. Breaking onto the Juggernaut had simply been the latest and most impressive.

He should kill her. It was possible he was making a mistake by letting her live this long.

"It's a risk," Strand said to himself in a wheezy voice.

So be it. He accepted the risk because he would extract a fantastic advantage from the android.

Strand smiled as he headed for the screening chamber. It was time to apply a little pressure, time to remind the android that she lived at his sufferance…

***

Strand activated the wall screen.

Rose stood at attention in her cell with her eyes closed. She wore the same reddish garb and cape as before. She did not seem miserable. In fact, she looked like a store manikin. She did not even appear alive.

Strand activated communications between her cell and the screen.

Instantly, the android opened her eyes. That changed everything, as she began to breathe and do the other tiny things that made people and animals seem alive.

For a reason he couldn't catalog, that peeved Strand. He recognized his dislike for anyone with independent willpower aboard his star cruiser. That was part of the disquiet. But there was more to it than that.

"Is the Star Watch vessel destroyed?" Rose asked.

"What if I told you it was?" Strand asked.

Rose did not reply.

"Well?" Strand asked sharply.

"You are stating postulates," she said. "I doubt, therefore, that you are interested in my answer."

"You would do well to refrain from making any judgments concerning my statements."

"I see," Rose said. "*Victory* slipped out of your grasp. That has made you…peevish."

Strand kept his features immobile. Was it a coincidence that she used the same term he'd been thinking a short time ago? Bah. He dismissed the idea that she could read his thoughts as being a fantasy.

"You have laid down a card, as it were," Rose said. "It is possible Ludendorff will surmise your hand by that card. If you will recall, I cautioned you against the Juggernaut assassination attempt."

"You did," Strand conceded. "But I do not believe the professor knows I had a hand in the attack."

"What makes you so certain?"

"The probabilities of that are too low, for one thing."

"Has he used this route before?"

"Come, now," Strand said. "You know he has. So have I. I suspect you already knew that. Why try to deceive me into thinking you don't know?"

"I grow weary of my confinement," Rose said. "I could aid you better if I had greater access—"

Strand couldn't help it. He laughed at her.

"You are a supremely suspicious man," Rose declared.

"It is one of the keys to my longevity."

"No doubt true," Rose said.

Strand shook his head. "I cannot guarantee your safe conduct if you continue to make judgmental statements regarding my words."

"You have a rare sensitivity to such things," Rose said.

With an effort of will, Strand kept from making another threat. He realized she was mocking him. If one made too many threats without doing something, further threats became less meaningful. How could he hurt the android in such a way that she would feel pain but not turn against him?

It was an interesting dilemma.

"Can you function as well without arms?" Strand asked.

Rose did not reply right away. Finally, she nodded. "I take your point. I will refrain from antagonizing you further. My recommendation is to travel as fast as possible to the Junkyard Planet. I have detected your interest in the Rull Juggernaut. There might be one or two more in existence. Would you not like to own those?"

"I would," Strand said roughly.

"Then I suggest we travel while we can," Rose said. "I will also point out that there are more powerful artifacts on the planet than Rull Juggernauts."

That whetted Strand's interest. It also made him suspicious. "Why haven't the androids availed themselves of these artifacts?"

"But we have," Rose said.

"Such as…?"

Rose smiled. "You may remove my arms if you wish. I would not like that. But that will not turn me garrulous. Instead, I would realize my destruction was imminent. Then, I would deactivate my sensory inputs, as I would assume you would soon begin torturing me."

"I am not foolish."

"I am willing to work with you, Methuselah Man, but not if the outcome is my obvious destruction. If you hope to gain some of the valuable objects on the planet, you will have to release me. Otherwise, you will have to find them the old-fashioned way, searching like anyone else."

"Tell me this," Strand said. "Does the planet possess spaceborne sentinels?"

"Of course," Rose said.

"Can you deactivate them?"

"I have codes that will let your ship slip past them. Before I give you the codes, I will need my freedom."

Strand pursed his lips as he studied her. Rose calmly stared back at him. He found that irritating. Finally, however, he smiled.

"Soon," he said. "Soon you and I shall walk together on the artifact planet. I give you my word."

"That satisfies me," Rose said. She closed her eyes.

"But…" Strand said.

She opened them.

"I would also like to know what happened to Starship *Victory*."

Rose shrugged, shutting her eyes once more.

That more than irritated the Methuselah Man. It caused him to make a mental note that he would make the android suffer for her passive insolence when the time came…

Strand turned off the wall screen. He stood and began massaging his sore thigh. He'd missed his first strike at Ludendorff. The next attempt would be more deadly, and it would succeed. On that Strand silently vowed.

-22-

"Sir?" Galyan said. "Do you hear me, Captain?"

"I do," Maddox said. "But I can't see anything."

"I think I can rectify that."

A moment later, the little AI glowed with light. Nothing on the bridge was working. All power had ceased except for Galyan.

What had caused the lack of sound?

"How are you able to glow?" Maddox asked.

"To pass the time while in the Solar System, I worked out various emergency procedures. This is one of many."

"That isn't what I meant," Maddox said. "That you're glowing indicates you have energy. The bridge lacks all power."

"You are right, sir," Galyan said. "The air is beginning to grow stale as well. I will begin working on that at once."

"Galyan," Maddox said. But it was too late. The holoimage had left.

It meant pitch-darkness again, as Galyan had been the only source of light.

"Can anyone hear me?" Maddox asked.

No one answered.

The captain moved slowly, finally reaching Valerie's station. She was slumped over her panel. Maddox shook her, but she did not waken.

Had the others received some sort of jump shock? Were they in some sort of sidereal universe? Why could he function while the others had been rendered unconscious?

The captain straightened, testing the air. It did seem a little stale as Galyan had suggested. He negotiated in the darkness, finally reaching the exit hatch. It would not open.

He tried a manual override, but that didn't make any difference.

A small part of Maddox wanted to panic. He suppressed the impulse. Instead, he began to think. Had Ludendorff known about the Rull Juggernaut waiting for them? What purpose would keeping quiet about that have served the Methuselah Man?

Maddox shook his head. He couldn't fathom a purpose. Ludendorff could be exceedingly devious, but this seemed too out-of-bounds for even the professor.

Galyan reappeared. "Captain, I cannot—oh, there you are."

The glowing holoimage floated to him.

"You are I are the only two people awake on the ship, sir."

"That's interesting, no doubt," Maddox said. "How do we reverse this process?"

"I believe we must exit the—I am not sure what to call this place, sir. Is this hyperspace? Is this a shift in time and space? I am referring to a different dimension, I suppose, a side pocket if you will."

"I don't—"

"We must recreate the situation just before we jumped," Galyan said.

"Are the engines working?"

"Barely," Galyan said.

Maddox scratched his scalp, soon saying, "I doubt we can recreate the situation. The tractor beams had locked onto us. That must be the difference that caused the present situation."

"I believe you are right, sir. How does knowing this help us?"

"Is Ludendorff awake?" Maddox asked.

"He is unconscious like everyone else. Why do you suppose you are awake, sir?"

"First we would have to know why the others are unconscious," Maddox said, reluctant to admit his theory that it was due to his New Man characteristics. "Perhaps my speeded metabolism has something to do with my present consciousness."

"Eureka!" Galyan shouted.

"What does that mean and why are you shouting?"

"Eureka is a term, sir. Archimedes was the first human to say it."

"Who?" asked Maddox.

"Archimedes was a Greek scientist, sir. He lived in the ancient city of Syracuse, in Sicily. His king or tyrant believed the goldsmiths were cheating him. The tyrant gave the smiths gold, and they fashioned a crown for him. The tyrant believed the smiths had switched some lead with the gold. The tyrant wanted Archimedes to tell him if that was true or not."

"I don't see how that has any bearing on—"

"One day," Galyan said in his excitement, "Archimedes took a bath. He noticed that as he sat in the water, it rose. The idea came to him then. If he took an amount of gold and put it in water, it would lift a certain height. If he took the tyrant's crown and put it in water, and the water raised higher or lower than the correct height, that would mean the goldsmith had indeed cheated Syracuse's ruler. As the idea came to him, Archimedes shouted, 'Eureka!'"

"Do you know what happened to the starship?" Maddox asked dryly.

"I studied Earth history while orbiting your home planet. I—"

"Galyan."

"Yes, Captain. I believe I do know what happened to *Victory*. The tractor beams held us, but they did not do so perfectly. If they had achieved a lock, we would have either pulled the Juggernaut with us or been torn in two as we jumped. Neither of those events occurred—"

"A slingshot effect," Maddox said, interrupting. "We built up star-drive power, but did not move. More power built up and finally, we tore lose, catapulted like a stone from a slingshot."

"Yes, I understand your analogy," Galyan said. "That is the process by which we moved into this…shadow realm. This place seems to devour energy, both the ship's energy and that of the various individuals. I suspect one of us will soon succumb to the constant energy-drain. After a time, the other will also fall asleep. Then it will simply be a matter of time until all energy is gone from the ship and our bodies."

"We must escape from the shadow realm," Maddox said.

"I find that to be an excellent suggestion. But how do we achieve such a miracle?"

Maddox stood by the closed hatch. If the AI didn't know the answer—

The captain snapped his fingers. "You're glowing."

"Do you want me to dim myself, sir? My glow is causing a prodigious drain to the little energy the ship possesses."

"No. I want you to reroute the energy to the ship's sensors. Then, I want you to turn on Valerie's screen so we can see what's outside."

"Darkness, sir," Galyan said.

"That is what you surmise. Let us see if that is correct. Can you reroute the energy?"

"Give me a few seconds. There," Galyan said, as he grew dimmer. "I have done it. If you will go to her station…"

It had become dark except for a small blinking light at Valerie's station. The captain soon stood beside her. He tapped her board and began to scan—

Maddox stopped in shock. He could not believe what he saw. It was massive, according to his sensors, the hull constructed of neutroium. It was fifty kilometers long and—

The captain shivered as he realized he viewed a Destroyer of the Nameless Ones. Then he saw another of the terrifyingly ancient war-machines.

"Sir," Galyan said in a soft voice. "My processors are weakening. What do you see?"

Maddox could hardly believe that Galyan did not see this. Then the captain spied a distant source of light. From here, it looked like a pinhole in the universe. But because there was universal darkness, the light was magnificent.

"Galyan, can you reroute power to the thrusters?"

"I am losing coherence, sir."

"You are Driving Force Galyan. You once fought for your world. I want you to fight for humanity. Hold it together and give me impulse power. I need it immediately."

"I. Am. Trying. There… You have a modicum of power, sir."

Valerie's panel went dark. Now, a light blinked on the helmsman's board.

Maddox went there. He sat at the helm and inched the ancient Adok vessel toward the point of light. It was hard to know how much time passed. Galyan no longer spoke. The pilot board grew dimmer. Yet, still *Victory* headed for the pin-dot of light.

Something eerie had happened to the starship. The near lock, the slingshot effect—

"No," Maddox said in a raw voice. He jerked upright, realizing he'd been dozing. If he fell asleep, he doubted any of them would wake up on this side of life. He didn't know if there was an afterlife. It seemed more than possible. He certainly believed in the Creator. But the captain wasn't ready to find out if there was another life after this one. Not today.

Grimly, Maddox forced himself to stay awake, but he could feel his strength and determination draining away. He began to shiver. But he held his lonely post, refusing to give up. If he surrendered to his tiredness, he would never find his father. He would never avenge his mother. He must do those things before he died. He also wanted to protect humanity from the Swarm, from Commander Thrax Ti Ix. That bastard of a preying mantis was not going to defeat him or cause mankind's extinction.

Maddox clung to the helm, breathing raggedly. He saw the point of light expand. Or maybe the starship drew closer to what had once seemed like a pin-dot in the blackness.

That gave the captain a tiny extra something. He used the infinitesimal surge of strength to sit up and pilot the vessel. The light had become intensely bright. Some of the brightness seemed supernatural; it seemed as if the light seeped through the outer hull and bulkheads.

Maddox shielded his face with an arm because the brightness began to hurt. He cried out as everything became intensely white. He wanted to get to the Junkyard Planet. He wanted to reach the place…

Before he could complete his thought, Maddox slumped forward, unconscious. At the same time, Starship *Victory* passed through the intensely bright light.

-23-

Maddox wrinkled his nose, inhaled sharply and sneezed. That made his body shift and caused his head to slide across the piloting board.

With a start, Maddox sat up. His vision blurred. He rubbed his eyes and tried to recollect what had happened. He found it hard to remember. There had been a struggle, a dark planetoid with tractor beams—

"We catapulted using the slingshot effect," he whispered.

Maddox took his hands from his eyes. The blurriness departed. He saw the bridge crew sprawled on the deck or draped over their stations. A few of the people stirred.

There was light in here. That seemed—

The memories flooded back. Maddox recalled the darkness, the energy drain, the Destroyer, two Destroyers and the terrifying light. The starship had passed through the light...

Lieutenant Noonan sat up. Her hair was a mess. She ran her fingers through her hair, rubbed her face—she twisted toward the captain.

"What happened?" she asked in a thick voice.

Maddox surged to his feet. He tugged his uniform straight. "Are your sensors working?" he asked.

Valerie stared at him a little longer, finally turning to her panel. She tapped hesitantly. A few areas turned on. She tapped with more authority.

"We're no longer in the same star system," she said.

Maddox doubted she referred to the 'shadow realm,' as Galyan had called it. She must mean the star system with the Rull Juggernaut.

"We broke free of the tractor beams," Valerie said. "That's good news."

"How far are we from there?" Maddox asked.

Valerie used two hands on her panel, tapping, cataloging and studying. Finally, she shook her head. "I have no idea where we are—wait. I take that back." She tapped more and looked up sharply. "Sir, if this is correct—" The lieutenant swallowed audibly. "We're thirty-eight light-years from our last location."

"You mean with the Juggernaut?" Maddox asked.

"This doesn't make sense. How could our ship travel thirty-eight light-years? Our star-drive jumps are usually three light-years long, rarely much more."

"It is a mystery," Maddox said. "We can solve it later. At the moment, I want to know if there are any threats to *Victory* in this system."

"Yes, sir," Valerie said, going back to studying her sensor board.

Others began to stir. A flickering holoimage appeared, looking around as it coalesced.

"Captain," Galyan said. "You did it!"

Maddox motioned for Galyan to remain silent.

Valerie swiveled around. "What did he do?"

"He brought us out of the—"

"That will be all, Galyan," Maddox said. "Could you see to Professor Ludendorff? I would like him on the bridge on the double."

"Yes, sir," Galyan said, disappearing.

"What did you do, sir?" Valerie asked, looking at him strangely.

"Brought us out of danger, I suppose," Maddox said. He turned to the pilot and asked the man a question.

A second later, Valerie resumed scanning.

That allowed Maddox to go to the other personnel, inquiring about their physical and mental conditions.

Galyan reappeared shortly. "The professor is on his way."

Maddox nodded absently.

"I'm putting up my findings," Valerie said. "The second planet is strange. It has an Earthlike atmosphere, but that doesn't make any sense given the readings."

Maddox examined the main screen. The system had a G-class star, four terrestrial planets, seven gas giants, two asteroid belts and an extended Oort cloud.

"How far are we from the second planet?" Maddox asked.

"Approximately three billion kilometers," Valerie said.

"What is the second planet's composition?"

"That isn't the issue, sir. It's the planet's shell. It's completely metallic."

Maddox turned to Valerie. "What does that mean?"

"What makes it even more perplexing," Valerie said, as if she hadn't heard the captain's question, "is the high-quality metals that make up the shell."

Maddox absorbed the thought. "Are you suggesting it's an artificial shell?"

Valerie nodded. "I hadn't thought that far, but that makes sense. Yes. The second planet has an artificial metal shell. Large areas are rusted, and—"

The lieutenant's eyes widened. She tapped her panel. "Sir, this star system—it's at Ludendorff's location for the Junkyard Planet. Could the second planet of this system be our destination?"

A strange sensation passed through Maddox. It left him feeling uncomfortable. It was the same sensation he had if he thought too long about the universe having no end or the Creator having always existed. It left him feeling insignificant, something he despised.

How could they have reached the Junkyard Planet like that? The coincidence of reaching here from the shadow realm seemed…impossible.

"Helm," Maddox said. "Commence taking us to the second planet. Weapons, keep everything warm. We found the Juggernaut waiting for us earlier. Who knows what this system holds?"

Maddox eyed the main screen. Whatever else happened, he wasn't going to let anyone take the starship by surprise again.

-24-

The hatch opened. Maddox turned as the professor stepped onto the bridge.

"You requested my—" Ludendorff stopped talking as he looked at the main screen. "The Junkyard Planet," he whispered. "We made it. I-I hadn't expected the journey to be this easy."

Maddox shifted his stance as he put his hands behind his back. The journey hadn't seemed easy at all. What else had Ludendorff expected to attack them?

"The lieutenant's sensors show a metal shell," Maddox said, keeping his thoughts to himself.

"Yes, certainly," Ludendorff said. "I spoke about that earlier."

"Indeed you did not," Maddox said.

"I'm sure I have. Yet…" Ludendorff frowned at the captain before approaching the main screen.

"I don't believe the Rull ever controlled the planet. It was Builder protected. I'm a little hazy on a few points. It was a world. By that, I mean a normal civilization once controlled the planet and the star system. The race developed an overly mechanistic society, building, molding and expanding with ruthless zeal. In the end, they paved or built over the normal dirt and rocks, erecting roads, bridges, buildings—the metal shell that now rusts below us."

"They were normal," Maddox said, as if tasting the words. "What does that even mean?"

"The planet was earth-like, and the aliens were humanoid. I visited here centuries ago in my earliest days. It was very different then. The last Builder androids moved openly here. I recall from that time rumors of ancient artifacts stored deep within the planet. It was a Builder storage area, so to speak."

"You suggested the planet or star system could be dangerous," Maddox said. "Could you elaborate on those dangers?"

"I suspect many traps, many devices like the Juggernaut. We should advance upon the second planet with extreme caution."

"Post a yellow alert," Maddox told Valerie.

The lieutenant manipulated her board, sending out the message.

"You said the long-range scanner will be inside the planet," Maddox said. "Can you be more specific?"

"We need to find the Hall of Mirrors. In it, according to the android I questioned on Titan, will be a second passage of sorts. It will be an elevator down to a deep core mine."

Maddox shook his head.

"The deep core mine is one of the methods the aliens used to power the planet's industries," the professor explained. "A deep core mine taps the planet's core, using the thermal energy."

"You are quite the fund of knowledge...suddenly," Maddox said.

"I should begin my preparations," Ludendorff said, ignoring the barb. "Have you decided who will go onto the planet?"

Maddox took his time answering. "We will do this the Patrol way, which means I'll use probes first."

"We may not have time for a lengthy and cautious approach."

"You surprise me, Professor. One minute you urge caution. The next you counsel haste. Is there something you wish to share with me?"

Ludendorff chuckled ruefully. "This is...an historic occasion. I'm nervous, I admit. I'd never thought to come back here. My teacher..."

"This sounds interesting."

"It's not," Ludendorff said. "I had an android teacher long ago. It was a Builder creature through and through. My journey here was part of my original education. Before the Space Age, the British aristocrats used to send their children on a Grand Tour. That meant a tour of Europe. It was part of their education. My Grand Tour was considerably grander. I toured throughout this portion of the Orion Arm, seeing many civilizations. I never thought to come this far again—not with the mysterious Rull creating greater difficulties."

The professor clapped his hands. "If you'll excuse me, Captain, I have much to do before we go down."

Maddox let him go. They needed the professor, but the Methuselah Man clearly had his own agenda. Their encounter left the captain thoughtful. He took his chair, considering various tactics regarding the professor.

-25-

Starship *Victory* eased toward the second planet. During the final approach, Galyan asked for the privilege of naming the system. Maddox granted it to the AI.

Galyan named it the Pandora System for obvious reasons. They came seeking artifacts. What would they find when they opened the box?

That consumed everyone's mind.

Lieutenant Noonan was in charge of the first planetary survey. She launched the probes, and then her team studied the results. They grew anxious about the findings. Finally, Maddox held a briefing.

There were a few more people in the conference chamber this time. Those included a space marine lieutenant, a bio specialist and a xenologist. A tense feeling built as they waited for the captain to open the meeting. Most of them had already heard the news. The surface portion of the mission wasn't going to be a cakewalk, but not for the reasons anyone had suspected beforehand.

Maddox nodded to Valerie.

"This video is from the third probe," the lieutenant said.

A holoimage appeared above the table. First, there was a gleaming almost smooth-seeming surface far below. A few wispy clouds were in the way. The wisps vanished as the probe descended. The metallic ground-color soon gave way to large rusty patches that spread as the probe entered lower into the atmosphere. Finally, individual towers and block buildings appeared.

"Crazy," Keith said. "It looks as if someone nuked the place."

Everything was a ruin, with girders sticking out like broken bones. There were busted autobahns, rusting vehicles and many, many whitening skeletons. There was no open ground anywhere, just a vast ruin of a one-world city.

"What's the air like?" Meta asked.

Valerie manipulated a control, glancing at numbers flashing along the bottom of the holoimage. "The air is breathable but will probably taste like copper. The probe did detect toxic pockets like thick fogs, and it detected minute particles of biological agents drifting in the air."

People traded glances as if they knew something weird was coming.

Meta squirmed, asking, "Any sign of life?"

A few around the table held their breath as they waited for the answer.

"Indeed," Valerie said. "The first two probes found biologically formed waste product."

"Do you mean shit?" someone asked quietly.

"That's an uncouth name for it," Valerie said primly, "but accurate. The second probe analyzed one such mound of waste product and found a troubling amount of animal tissue in it. That would seem to indicate the feces of a predatory animal."

"Did you find any visual signs of life?" the marine lieutenant asked.

"Oh, yes," Valerie said, glancing at Maddox. "That's coming soon."

Everyone grew more tense, more interested.

"There," Keith said in a breathless voice. "I see it."

Others did, too. A few gasped. One man cursed quietly.

A muscular humanoid creature with a pink tail and elongated talons burst out of a sewer opening. At least, it might once have been a sewer opening. The creature ran on all fours, moving fast like a greyhound. At the last moment, it stood up in what seemed a difficult maneuver. Like a chimpanzee, it could walk on two legs, but neither elegantly nor easily. The creature launched itself at the probe, landing so it shook the machine and the recorder. Its talons ripped at the probe. Everyone saw talons splinter and break off, but the creature did not lessen its maniacal assault.

"Look," Keith said. "More are coming."

Three more of the hairless humanoid beasts rushed the probe. Soon, they too clawed and attacked the device. At some unseen signal, the newcomers turned their assault on the creature that had broken many of its talons. The spectacle was brutal. The others tore apart the first one. It happened fast, with each creature ripping meaty chunks out of the weakening creature.

Soon, the newcomers quarreled like hyenas over the remains of the slain humanoid. That allowed the probe to lift off. The three gazed upward at the probe, their faces bloody, fresh meat visible between their fangs.

At that point, something glinted in a tower window. A dark streak zoomed at the probe and—

The holoimage over the conference table abruptly quit.

"A shooter destroyed the probe," Valerie said into the silence.

"What were those creatures?" Keith asked. "Do we have any idea?"

"Unfortunately, yes," Ludendorff said. "I recognize them."

"What do you call them?" Keith asked.

"I should modify my statement," Ludendorff said. "Once, its kind would have been known as a Vendel. They are the race that created the industrial planet."

Maddox wondered why Ludendorff hadn't told them that earlier.

"Were the Vendels like that when you were here?" Keith asked.

"On no account," the professor said. "They were a kind race, cultured and slow to anger. They were smaller, less bestial and—"

Ludendorff glanced at Maddox. "I think I know what happened to them and their planet."

"Don't hold us in suspense," Valerie said. "This is horrifying. What caused your peaceful race to turn into cannibal monsters?"

"You said you detected toxic traces in the air…?" Ludendorff said.

"This is the toxin's composition," the lieutenant said, putting the formula on the holoimage.

Ludendorff stood, leaning closer to the holoimage. "Interesting," the professor said, shortly. "This confirms my suspicion. I don't know who did this, probably an alien race, most likely the Rull before they perished. I would not discount the Builders, although it does not seem to be their…hmmm, style."

"Professor," Maddox prodded emphatically. The more Ludendorff had a captive audience, the more he liked to draw out his explanations.

"This is a fascinating possibility," the professor said. "It is also grim and inhumane. But I cannot conceive another explanation that holds together so well."

"What are you talking about?" Valerie asked.

"Someone appears to have…hmm, sprayed the planet with toxins. In this instance, I believe a DNA-mutating substance. That caused the Vendels to mutate into what we have just witnessed. They regressed into brutal—"

"Zombies," Keith said, interrupting. "Their enemies turned them into zombies, into foul, cannibalistic creatures that will attack anything that moves. Do you think they've devoured everything else on the planet?"

The professor scowled at the small Scotsman. The scowl softened as the professor considered the question. Finally, he shrugged.

"I suppose your poetic term fits loosely enough," the professor said. "Yes. They are zombies, ghouls, cannibals, whatever term you prefer. The waste evidence seems to indicate the creatures overran the planet." Ludendorff faced the captain. "The creatures might boil out in their hundreds, possibly in their thousands. Landing and searching the interior of the planet has just become many times more risky than I'd anticipated."

"Don't worry," the space marine lieutenant said in a deep voice. "I can take care of them." He was a blocky man with a blond crew cut, thick muscles and a hard quality to his face but especially to his eyes. A year ago, he'd fought New Men on the ground. He was one of the few to have lived to tell about the encounter. His name was Karl Sims.

"Even if you're wearing exoskeleton marine-armor," Ludendorff told Sims, "you will not defeat a thousand such creatures."

"Some heavy shock grenades would flatten your thousand," Sims said. "A flamer would take care of the stunned beasts in short order."

Valerie shuddered. "That's brutal."

Sims did not reply.

"I do not have the same faith in firepower," Ludendorff told Sims. "These creatures—"

"What about the shooter?" Meta asked, interrupting. "Who was he? He couldn't have been a mutated Vendel."

"That is an excellent question," Ludendorff said. He turned to Valerie, "Did you happen to capture any footage of the shooter?"

The lieutenant shook her head. "Just that one glint," she said. "It was a tech weapon. One bullet, or whatever he fired, took out the probe. The surface probes are built to absorb a lot of damage, as you saw when the Vendel attacked this one. So, for the shooter to take it out with one shot is impressive."

"The shooter also seems to destroy the professor's theory," Dana said. "If there is one shooter, there are probably more. If there are more, can they have survived if thousands, possibly millions of these zombie-creatures exist? There's another problem. Why didn't the biological toxins deform the shooters as well?"

"There is a mystery here," Ludendorff said. "That is your area of expertise, Captain. Do you have any thoughts as to the mystery?"

"One thought," Maddox said. "Where is the Hall of Mirrors? It's time you told us, Professor."

"What about the mutated Vendels?" Ludendorff asked. "Don't those bother you?"

"They're a nuisance," Maddox admitted. "But we'll overcome them, if we have to."

"With shock grenades?" Ludendorff asked in a mocking voice.

"With disrupter beams, missiles and hell-burners," Maddox said. "If we wipe out a large enough area, we can explore it at our leisure."

"Bloodthirsty but effective," the professor said. "Spoken like a New Man, sir."

Lieutenant Sims stiffened, but he held his head steady, never glancing at the captain.

Maddox refrained from drumming his fingers on the table. How did the last statement help the professor? What was the Methuselah Man's game?

The professor cleared his throat. "In preparation for the meeting, I went over my notes in some detail. I have begun to suspect that the Hall of Mirrors is underground. There's also a good chance it is located in the Southern Pole Region."

"Just a moment," Maddox said. He opened communications with the bridge, instructing them to take *Victory* over the South Pole region. After he was finished, the captain regarded Ludendorff.

"You are eager to descend," the professor said.

Maddox said nothing.

"Er...yes," Ludendorff said. "May I?" he asked Valerie.

She slid the holo-imager to him.

Ludendorff slipped a data-stick into a slot, manipulated the imager and soon produced a new holoimage. They viewed vast domes and tall spires in a grand circular area many kilometers in diameter.

"This was the anchor for a space cable," the professor said. "The cable would have reached up into orbit, connected to an orbital station."

"You once saw this?" Meta asked.

"Many centuries ago," the professor said wistfully.

"We'll find the ruins," Maddox said. "The Hall of Mirrors lies under that?"

"I do not know for certain," Ludendorff said. "So please do not be angry if it turns out otherwise. But yes, that is my belief."

Maddox nodded, envisioning the next step. "Are there any questions or observations regarding this?"

There were many, and the discussion continued in earnest.

Maddox listened with half an ear. He wondered what they were going to find underground. The cannibalistic Vendels seemed daunting. He hoped Lieutenant Sims was right regarding how easy it would be to deal with them.

-26-

Several hours later, *Victory* was in a stationary polar orbit. To Maddox's surprise, finding the space-cable anchor proved harder than he'd expected.

Three more probes went down. Only one returned. Through it, they viewed more beastly Vendels. The southern variety was even bigger and more aggressive than the earlier cannibals had been.

Maddox and Meta went over the requirements of the landing party. They debated using nuclear weapons to clear the area first. The extent of the subterranean realm forced them to scrub the idea.

"What if we cause massive cave-ins?" Meta asked. "Besides, the deep caverns will protect the Vendels from the blast and radiation. That leaves us with the professor's dilemma. If tens of thousands of Vendels descend upon the landing party at once..."

Maddox shook his head. "Such large manifestations of Vendels strike me as unlikely. The creatures are predators and scavengers. That implies low densities at any one point. In order to have high population densities like an army, one needs good logistics to bring in masses of food to keep everyone from starving in a few days."

"That's a good point," Meta said. "There is one other thing, though."

Maddox studied her. "Do you mean Lieutenant Sims?"

"I don't know why High Command gave us a New Man-hating space marine commander."

"I do," Maddox said. "One, Sims is a good soldier. Two, I still have enemies in Star Watch. It's possible one of those saddled us with Sims as a joke."

"If someone hates you, they don't give you a killer like Sims as a *joke*. It is in the hope that the space marine will kill you."

"Maybe," Maddox said, with a shrug.

"Don't count on his training to slow him down."

"On the contrary," Maddox said. "I'm counting on his dislike to give him extra stamina and thereby produce more effort. Sims can't let me outperform him. His pride won't allow it. Thus, he'll work harder than anyone else to prove he's better than me."

"Your plan has one flaw."

Maddox silently went over his reasoning. "I fail to see it."

"Sims doesn't just dislike you," Meta said. "He hates you. There's a difference, one large enough to drive a battleship through."

Maddox was tired, and he didn't want to discuss this anymore. He would take a power nap. Afterward, the landing party would board the shuttles.

***

Ninety-five minutes later, the lead shuttle exited *Victory's* hangar bay. Keith Maker piloted the craft, with Maddox beside him. Three other shuttles followed carrying the exoskeleton-armored marines.

Maddox peered out the viewing port as the silver-colored world spread out below them. Meta was in the command cabin with him, along with the professor.

"Don't take anything for granted," Maddox told Keith. "The shooters live down there as well as the Vendels. The shooters may still have large sophisticated weaponry."

"We haven't detected anything like that," Ludendorff said.

"How did you manage to live this long?" Maddox asked the professor. "I doubt it was by taking stupid chances."

Having difficulty hiding his grin, Keith tapped his controls. "I've activated my radar and motion detectors. Nothing is going to take us by surprise, sir."

"Famous last words," Meta grumbled.

"Cheer up, love," Keith told her. "It's me flying. You have nothing to worry about."

Keith banked the shuttle and took them down toward the atmosphere. Behind them, *Victory* grew smaller as it serenely orbited Pandora II.

Maddox recalled maneuvering over Loki Prime, before Meta came into his life. Pandora II wasn't a jungle world. It was the opposite, a concrete and metal wreck. Yet, it seemed as if this place might be the more dangerous of the two.

Keith moved fast, jinking and deploying camouflage fibers. Soon, the shuttle began to shake.

"We've entered the atmosphere," Keith announced.

Maddox wondered again what they would find down there. They were a long way from home, a long way from help. The captain glanced at Keith. The pilot obviously loved his work. The Scotsman grinned as he made another maneuver. Then, he happened to glance at the captain and noticed him watching.

"This is the life, eh, sir?"

Maddox grinned faintly and nodded. He was surprised to realize he too was looking forward to this.

Maddox relaxed as Keith dove faster, maneuvered more violently and made the shuttle shake harder.

"Is this truly necessary?" Ludendorff asked querulously.

"Ab-so-lutely," Keith said. "Safety and caution are the bywords today. Thus, I fly like a madman. If shooters are targeting us, it won't be this shuttle they hit."

Ludendorff grumbled under his breath.

The ace's eyes gleamed, and his smile stretched across his face.

Shortly, the comm crackled, and a following pilot asked, "What are you doing, Tango One? How do you expect us to keep up with you?"

"No one can keep up with me," Keith boasted over the comm.

"Shows over," Maddox said. "We're a squadron, not a lone wolf. You will act accordingly."

Keith nodded a second later. "Aye-aye, mate, er, sir. I understand."

Meta and Maddox traded glances. Keith had said that just like a deflated little boy told it was time to come inside.

The violence of their descent lessened. The shaking grew tolerable and Keith no longer bubbled with excitement.

"Thanks, Tango One," a pilot said over the comm. "I can match that."

It was Keith's turn to mutter under his breath.

Soon, the metallic sheen down below changed as the rust spots and rust belts separated from the brighter areas. The Pandora star shined strongly, providing illumination. It was early morning on the southern polar region of the planet. They'd agreed that that should be the best time to explore, while the Vendels were still waking up for the day.

"There's nothing tracking us so far," Keith said, as he checked his panel.

Maddox peered out of the viewing port. He saw endless towers, block buildings, airstrips, what might have been malls, skyscrapers—the vastness of the one-world city spread out in all its misery. Why would the un-tampered Vendels have done such a thing? How had they fed their billions of inhabitants? The city had gone subterranean for a considerable depth. Maybe they'd had underground agriculture or vast synthesizing plants. Why had the Builder androids moved openly here? Had the intense urbanization had something to do with it?

Maddox glanced sidelong at the professor. Ludendorff seemed to have kept much more information hidden than he'd ever revealed. Yet, the Methuselah Man was the source for just about everything they did know out here. Why did he hold back so much? Wouldn't Star Watch work more efficiently if Ludendorff opened up?

It was possible the old dog couldn't change his habits. Ludendorff had operated like this for so long, it was all he knew. Maybe he just liked to keep something up his sleeve…

Maddox rubbed his chin. What were Ludendorff's ultimate goals? What did the Methuselah Man hope to achieve with his existence? Were there hidden Builder motivations buried deep in Ludendorff's subconscious? Maybe not even Ludendorff knew all those answers.

"There," the professor said. "That's the area. You should land somewhere over there."

Keith tilted the shuttle, and they dropped almost straight down toward huge round domes, skyscrapers and a dark mass of an indistinguishable something. At this rate, they would hit the surface in seconds.

The professor grabbed his armrests, shouting in surprise. "Are you insane?"

"Missile," Keith said crisply, as he tapped his board. "Coming fast. I'm activating our autocannons."

Maddox studied the tiny combat screen. He saw a cruise missile zooming several meters over the tops of towers and between the spaces of vast block buildings. The cruise missile must have used afterburners, because it leapt faster. As it did so, the missile zoomed upward at them, leaving the buildings behind.

"Right you are," Keith said, talking to himself. He pressed tabs. The shuttlecraft shuddered. A second later, antimissiles rocketed toward the incoming missile. At the same time, the autocannons barked.

"If it's a nuclear—" Ludendorff said.

"Hang tight, sisters and brothers," Keith shouted, interrupting. "We're going to do this…*now*."

The cruise missile must have had a proximity fuse. The warhead ignited a millisecond before the first antimissile would have slammed into it. A nonnuclear but lethal detonation created a massive fireball.

Ludendorff shouted in alarm. The shuttlecraft swerved violently, curving away from the powerful explosion. Afterburners kicked in, and they moved like a bat out of hell. It was not good enough to get them out of danger, though.

The blast-wave reached them.

Like a surfer on a tsunami wave, the shuttlecraft tumbled headlong. At the same time, intense heat baked the craft as the armored shell began to glow with the rising temperature. The air-conditioners hummed. Even so, everyone in the cabin sweated horribly as smoke rose from various panels.

Maddox knew Keith was shouting because he saw the ace's mouth moving. He did not hear a thing, though. A cyclone howl made that impossible. The captain could not understand how they'd survived the explosion so far. This must be the limit at which the shuttle could survive the near detonation. Perhaps only Keith's fantastic reflexes and decision-making were giving them this fighting chance.

The violent shaking lessened, although it was still rattling them.

"I see another missile," Keith shouted. His voice was barely loud enough to compete against the lessening howl.

Even as the ace pointed out the new cruise missile, Maddox saw a beam reach down from the heavens. The beam struck the cruise missile, destroying it before the warhead could add to their misery.

Two more cruise missiles appeared. Starship *Victory* beamed each one from orbit.

"Ha-ha," Keith laughed. "That will show—"

A new threat appeared in the guise of a red beam, cutting his speech short. The red beam focused on the second shuttle, which was much higher and to their left. The beam hit the armored hull, burned through—

The second shuttle exploded.

Maddox reacted at once, grabbing a microphone. "Abort the mission," he said. "Get upstairs to *Victory*."

"Sir—" a pilot said over the comm.

"That's an order," Maddox said. "Don't let that beam destroy any more of my shuttles. Jink out of the area and head up. Go!"

At the same time, an explosion aboard their own shuttle made the craft flip end-over-end.

"Hang on!" Keith shouted. "I think somebody wants to find out just how good of a pilot I am."

The next few seconds were touch and go as the shuttle flipped, twisted and headed down at the onrushing buildings.

Keith wasn't laughing any more. He was tightlipped and his hands were white-knuckled. His eyes had a fiery quality that almost made them blaze.

The captain could feel the intensity, the will to win in Keith, and he heartily approved. In fact, his estimation of the ace grew.

The shuttle straightened out, which seemed like a miracle. Yet, even as Keith achieved the impossible, the shuttle's underbelly scraped against a girder sticking up like an angry middle finger from a broken tower. A terrible grinding, ripping sound accompanied a new kind of shudder in the craft.

"That's not going to help," Keith said.

The shuttle's underbelly slammed against the highest rounded part of a dome. They wobbled and shuddered worse than before, and Keith gambled. He used the afterburners one more time.

They leapt up just enough to miss the next building. A secondary explosion inside the shuttle left them with just one engine, and that one knocked wildly.

"We're not going home in this thing," Keith said. "But we might land in one piece. Say your prayers, boys and girls, because I'm a-needing them."

Help us, Creator, Maddox thought.

The captain saw Meta's lips move. The Methuselah Man did nothing of the kind, sitting rigidly with his eyes focused outside on the immediate city.

The next few seconds seemed even more impossible than the preceding ones. Keith tilted the shuttle so the wings wouldn't smash against two looming buildings. Instead, they zipped sideways through the space between the buildings, straightening out on the other side.

"I don't see anywhere to land," Keith said.

Maddox thought that an understatement. It was a maze of metal junk down there. A few white things moved—scavenging Vendels.

Deliberately, the captain turned to Keith. "No one can land this thing in one piece. It's impossible."

Keith stared back at him, and the pilot grew pale.

Maddox wondered if he'd overdone it. Maybe even the ace had his limits in terms of flying challenges.

A ragged laugh bubbled out of Keith's throat. "No confidence in me, eh, mate? You'll see, then, won't you?"

Keith used his one knocking engine. He brought them down, and he used junk heaps to help bleed some of their momentum. Like a skipping stone, he smashed down repeatedly. The craft shuddered at each hit. Underbelly and armored metal shredded away. They almost flipped again—sweat dripped from Keith's face. But he brought the shuttle down onto a compacted area, grinding, sliding, screeching…until the shuttle came to an unbelievable halt.

Fires crackled in the back of the shuttle. Minor explosions told them they didn't have much time to get out. Yet, each of them breathed. Each of them was intact. None of them had any broken bones, although they all had bruises.

"I bit my tongue," the professor complained.

No one answered.

Maddox unlatched his restraints. He stood, and almost fell because his legs were so wobbly. It took an effort of will to reach Meta. He unhooked her and helped her to her feet.

"We're alive," she whispered.

"You're the best there is, *mate*," Maddox told Keith.

The ace didn't answer. He was too busy staring out of the viewing port.

Maddox turned to see what had the ace's attention. Twenty or more Vendels bounded like hairless chimpanzees. They were coming straight for them across the junkyard heap.

-27-

Maddox reacted as if he'd practiced for a lifetime just for this day. Maybe, in a manner of speaking, he had.

First, he grabbed a rebreather, fitting the mask over his face. He activated it so it would purify the air before he breathed it. Second, he opened a weapons locker and grabbed a Khislack .370, a heavy assault rifle. He also grabbed an ammo belt with many magazines, buckling it around his waist. Finally, as he strode for the hatch, he slapped a magazine into place and chambered a bullet.

Keith had also ripped off his restraints. He, too, wore a rebreather and tried to open the dented outer hatch. It was obviously broken, and it would not budge.

Meta made an inarticulate sound through her rebreather. She drew the monofilament blade Maddox had given her the other day. She pushed Keith aside. With several precise slashes, she gave herself a handhold, grunted and forced the badly dented hatch open. Panting, she sheathed the wicked blade and stepped aside, making room for Maddox.

Coppery tasting air seeped through the rebreather's filters. Ludendorff hacked and wheezed behind him.

Maddox did not like the coppery taste, either. He hoped the filters would keep the toxins in the air from changing his DNA. He wasn't going to dwell on the problem, though. Moving fast, he climbed down from the shuttle. This area was a junkyard indeed, with thousands of crushed vehicles piled one on top of another. Metal creaked and groaned under his boots as Maddox moved into position.

Vendels bellowed savagely as they spied him. The hairless creatures were huge, maybe eight feet tall on average. Maddox estimated each would weigh in at four or five hundred pounds.

The captain shoved the Khislack's wooden butt against his shoulder. He also switched on the targeting computer.

A nearing Vendel screamed its war cry.

The captain targeted the creature, pulled the trigger and felt the heavy rifle kick against him. Three hundred meters away, the Vendel's head exploded.

The exhibition of marksmanship, the original warning scream and the creatures' natural cunning and aggressiveness all seemed to combine. The other Vendels did not flee. Neither did they continue their mad dash at the shuttle. Instead, the creatures began to use the cover of the crushed vehicles, the dips and gaps between them. They leaped from one hidden locale to another, working their way closer several meters at a time. It hardly slowed their rush, but it would make killing them much harder.

Recognizing their cunning and the new challenge, Maddox grinned without humor. This was a contest, with their lives in the balance. He observed the creatures for a full ten seconds. His limbs shook as he did. The desire to blast away was nearly overpowering. Instead, Maddox ingested data. He counted as the creatures leaped, waited and leaped again. He began to detect a primitive rhythm to their tactic.

By that time, the pack had made it one-third closer.

"Now we shall see," Maddox said under his breath.

He stood tall. He let his shoulder muscles relax and breathed deeply and evenly. He applied his strength so the Khislack rested snuggly against his shoulder. Bending his head just enough, he began targeting Vendels.

Using his newfound knowledge, counting evenly the entire time, Maddox began to fire like an automaton. He hit a Vendel each time, blowing away the skull or portions of shoulders or arms. Instead of waiting for the Khislack to click, meaning he'd run out of bullets, the captain ejected the spent magazine at precisely the right shot. He slapped in a new magazine and continued the amazing performance.

Maddox slew seventeen Vendels, having to use three bullets on several, two on a few more and one on the rest.

Four savage beasts made it near enough that Maddox dropped the assault rifle. Before the heavy weapon hit the ground, he drew his long-barreled gun.

The first Vendel took five bullets before it dropped. And that was only because Maddox got lucky and broke a thigh bone.

Meta surprised the second creature, carving out its guts with the monofilament blade. The stink from the blood was horrifying, causing Meta to cough explosively through her mask.

That allowed the third Vendel to leap past her as it dove at Maddox.

Ludendorff beamed it with two laser pistols. The skin smoked and burned. Blood bubbled, and the creature howled in agony.

Maddox ducked at just the right time. The wounded Vendel flew over him, landing hard. As it tried to climb back to its feet, Ludendorff beamed its face, melting it, causing the creature to collapse.

That left one untouched Vendel. It full-on crashed against Maddox as he straightened from ducking. They catapulted ten meters, smashing and rolling across flattened, crumbled vehicles.

Maddox realized the creature was stronger than he was. He felt the bone-crushing grip. He saw the filthy talons and smelled the overpowering stench of the creature's breath through the rebreather. He could not imagine what the stink would be like without the mask. The thing was stronger than any Earthly bear, and it had speed and savagery to boot.

What it lacked was high intelligence and Maddox's combat training.

The captain grabbed one of the fingers and tried to twist it back. It was like a baby trying to twist a man's finger. It was not going to happen.

Maddox heard something clack. The creature's bloodshot eyes stared into his. The captain realized with a start that the savage was intelligent. The thing seemed to enjoy the horror it saw it Maddox's eyes. It opened its fanged jaws—

A rifle fired and the Vendel's head exploded, raining skull-bone and blood onto the captain's mask. The creature squeezed, almost tearing some of the captain's lean muscles apart. It hung on…

Maddox groaned at the pain.

Thankfully, finally, the grip lessened, loosened, and at last, the monster slumped toward Maddox. The captain barely twisted out of the way in time. The Vendel thudded face-first onto a crushed vehicle.

Maddox found himself panting, wiping and smearing blood on his mask. He was amazed that he was still alive. He found Keith Maker holding the Khislack, blinking like a man who couldn't believe what he'd done.

Forcing himself to remain calm, Maddox stepped up to Keith and clapped him on the shoulder. He nodded. Keith stared blankly at him. Maddox nodded again. Finally, slowly, Keith nodded back.

Maddox added a finger squeeze. The pilot had just saved his life. The captain wasn't going to forget that. But now wasn't the time to dwell on the feat. Now was the time to figure out how they were going to survive long enough to get back to *Victory*.

-28-

Maddox picked up the Khislack where Keith had dropped it, standing watch as the others converged on his position.

"I can't get through to *Victory*," Meta said, while holding her communicator. "All I get is static. I think someone is jamming us."

That would imply this had been a trap. Maddox's grip on the Khislack tightened, although he said in a calm voice, "That shouldn't be an insurmountable problem. Galyan can see us through *Victory's* teleoptics. They'll know our situation."

"Do we stay by the shuttle then?" Meta asked.

"What else do you suggest?" Maddox said. "Leaving the shuttle—"

"Vendels," Ludendorff said. He held a hand-scanner, stepping closer, showing them the many blips approaching their location.

At that moment, a holoimage appeared before them. It was Galyan.

"Captain," the AI said. "We have a situation. Two Rull Juggernauts are on an intercept course for the Southern Pole Orbital area. I have computed the odds. It is unlikely that *Victory* can overcome two such war-vessels."

This was getting worse by the minute. "Take *Victory* out of orbit," Maddox said. "Tell Lieutenant Noonan her first responsibility is to keep the starship intact. If we die, she is to return to Earth and tell the Lord High Admiral—"

The holoimage wavered. Could the same jamming that affected their communications disturb a long-range Galyan holoimage?

"Captain," Ludendorff said. "These Rull Juggernauts are proving my worst fear. Androids must know about our mission."

"What do these Juggernauts have to do with androids?" Maddox asked.

"I do not have any evidence of a direct correlation," the professor said. "But I believe they are linked in some manner."

Maddox stared at the professor.

"The first Juggernaut assault as we came out of the Einstein-Rosen Bridge proves that someone was waiting for us," the professor said.

"Why wouldn't you have told us your suspicions before this?" Meta asked in outrage.

"I understand your emotion," the professor said.

"Why tell us about the possible android connection now?" Maddox asked curtly.

"You strike to the heart of the matter, Captain. I applaud your instincts that compel you—"

"Get to the point," Maddox said.

Ludendorff's mouth stiffened peevishly before he said, "I'm going to need Galyan to drop several parcels onto the planet."

"What kind of parcels?" Maddox asked.

Ludendorff took a deep breath as if to calm himself. "We don't have time for this. We must leave our present location. Hundreds of Vendels are converging on the crash site just as I predicted would happen."

Maddox shook his head. "The red beam—do you think that's a New Man's fusion ray?"

"It *was* a fusion ray," Galyan said. "But that does not necessitate New Men. If you will recall, the fusion beam is a Builder product. Thus, androids could well have wielded the beam."

"Never mind about your blasted computer logic," Ludendorff said. "I believe our enemies are on the planet. I am willing to bet my existence on that. The Juggernauts heading for *Victory* are surely due to androids."

"What do you suggest we do?" Maddox asked.

"I just told you," Ludendorff said. "Have Galyan drop the parcels. They're our only hope. Damn you, Captain. Why are you so stubborn?"

Maddox stared at the professor, debating whether he should rip off the Methuselah Man's rebreather and leaving him here to die.

"Very well," Ludendorff said. "If we die, it is on your head, Captain. We are wasting time, but I see I must talk before you'll act. I...*reconditioned* Dana and Valerie because Dana saw my Swarm virus carrier. That's what I was working on in my laboratory. I have since sectioned the carrier into parcels. I'd hoped to slip them onto the planet and meld them together here, setting it loose."

"You believe the androids will land on the planet?" Maddox asked.

"Oh yes."

"Why?"

"Don't you understand yet?" Ludendorff asked impatiently. "The androids want those Builder objects stored on the planet."

Meta pulled Maddox aside. "Do you believe him?"

Maddox's expression didn't change as he studied Ludendorff and the little holoimage watching him. What did his gut tell him? Ludendorff was extraordinarily deceptive. Yet, the professor's words had the ring of truth. The new facts fit better than the other explanation.

"Galyan," Maddox said. "Drop the parcels. Tell Valerie she has to outmaneuver the Juggernauts. The four of us are going underground. It's time to find the long-range scanner, and who knows what else is down there."

"I do not give you good odds, Captain," Galyan said. "The Vendels—"

"This is Lieutenant Noonan's toughest assignment yet," Maddox said, interrupting the holoimage. "The lieutenant's primary task is to save *Victory* and return to Earth with the news. She is to do that at all costs. Star Watch has to know what happened out here."

Galyan saluted Maddox with one of his ropy arms, as the holoimage's features became excessively grave. "It is has been a great honor to serve with you, sir—"

"While I appreciate your feelings," Maddox said, interrupting. "We are far from defeated. Get upstairs. Get my ship out of danger, and let us worry about surviving down here."

The lines crisscrossing Galyan's leathery features tightened. The little AI seemed conflicted.

"Till we meet again, sir," Galyan said. Then, the holoimage vanished.

The four of them traded glances. Ludendorff broke eye contact first as he went back to studying his hand-scanner.

"The next wave of Vendels is almost here," the professor announced.

Meta turned toward the shuttle. "We need more supplies if we're going to survive the next few days underground."

"We don't have time for that," Maddox said, sternly.

Meta regarded him.

"We have to go, now," Maddox said. "The professor is right. If a hundred Vendels reach us, we're all dead. We have what we have."

"We need food and water or we'll die underground," Meta said stubbornly. "How does dying of dehydration help the cause?"

"Get situated then," Maddox shouted, as his legendary calm cracked under the strain. He pitched the Khislack to Keith. Then, he dashed for the shuttle, leaped to the bottom of the hatch, did a chin up and rushed inside.

Moving fast, Maddox grabbed a backpack, stuffed it with food concentrates and water bottles. He shouldered the heavy pack, clicking the belt. He grabbed another pack and repeated the process. Finally, he dashed for the hatch, climbing out as the others argued among themselves.

"I can see the lead Vendels," Ludendorff told the captain. "You took too long getting the supplies. Now we're dead—"

Maddox reached the group and shoved Ludendorff in the direction opposite from the approaching savages. He heaved a heavy backpack to Meta. She caught it, shrugged it on and tightened the belt around her waist.

Maddox took his rifle from Keith. He saw a Vendel in the distance. The creature scaled down a wall like a spider. Another appeared, following the first one.

"Right," Maddox said to himself. He moved into position behind the others. This one was going to be bad, but it wasn't over until it was over.

He was Captain Maddox. He was *di-far*. And he wasn't ready to die, not yet. He had far too much to live for and too much left to do. Thus, it was time to play this game in earnest.

-29-

The climb down the mountain of junked crushed vehicles nearly proved their undoing on several occasions. The worst offender was Ludendorff, who might have died if Keith hadn't grabbed the old man's wrist as he slipped. The professor dangled in the air until Meta leaned over and helped Keith hoist the Methuselah Man back to safety.

They continued to scale down the massed pile of rusted vehicles. Each of them would have sliced themselves many times over if they hadn't been wearing special gloves, clothes and heavy-duty boots.

Soon, Vendels screamed with rage from the top of the artificial mountain. The creatures peered down at them, a few hurling scrap-metal pieces that went clanking past.

"They're coming," Meta panted, as she looked up.

As he rested on what might have been a hood sticking out of the mass like a ledge, Maddox debated his options. He couldn't give Keith a backpack. The Scotsman might stagger thus burdened on a level trail for a time. Keith would never be able to scale down the mountain while wearing a heavy backpack. That went double for Ludendorff.

Finally, the captain shrugged off the backpack, and dropped it. The thing fell for fifty meters, thudding onto pavement hard enough for them to hear it up here. Worse, water seeped out of the pack. Some of the bottles must have broken. Hopefully, some had remained intact.

In any case, Maddox scaled down the mountain of junked vehicles faster than before. Soon, he jumped the remaining distance, landing with a jar despite bending his knees to help absorb the impact.

The soles of his feet hurt and his ankle joints stung, but he ignored the pain. Unshouldering the Khislack, he backed up until he had a better angle. Then, slowly and carefully, he began to pick off descending Vendels. He went for headshots, killing six of them. Finally, the rest of the creatures retreated back up the mountain and out of sight.

That was unusual. Maybe scaling down a mountain of junk took enough concentration to hinder their usual bloodlust. Without the bloodlust, the Vendels could act on their fear.

He'd bought them a little more time, anyway, but at the cost of—

Maddox checked the backpack. Half the water bottles had broken. He tossed those aside and re-shouldered the pack. The food concentrates were packaged in waterproof plastics, so they were okay.

"It's lighter," he told himself with a wry little smile. He might as well be grateful for whatever good he could find. At all costs, he had to defeat despair if he was going to beat the Vendels.

Keith and Ludendorff finally reached level ground. The professor dug out his scanner and studied it.

"Did they give up?" Keith asked.

The professor shook his head.

"Which way do we go?" Meta asked, as she reached the pavement.

"That is the question of the mission," Ludendorff said. "Captain, what is the goal?"

"Is there really a long-range Builder scanner on the planet?" Maddox asked.

Ludendorff appeared surprised. "According to the android I questioned there is. Why would I have come otherwise?"

"To add to your collection of exotic gadgets," Maddox said. "I don't mean the long-range scanner, but some other Ludendorff-centric gadget you hoped to collect."

"Do you truly think so poorly of me that I'd do something like that?" Ludendorff asked.

Maddox wanted to say yes. But he decided this was not the time or place for complete honesty. This was the time for maximum effort from all of them.

"I think you love humanity and want to see it survive," Maddox said.

Ludendorff scowled. "You don't have to be so sarcastic. I truly am on your side, sir."

Maddox's mouth opened as he shook his head in surprise.

"You don't believe me?" the professor asked.

"He does," Meta said quickly. "He can't believe you don't believe him. I imagine he also wonders if this is how you feel the few times you're being honest and no one believes you."

Ludendorff snorted scornfully and reexamined his hand-scanner. "We're several kilometers from the targeted landing area."

"You say 'several' kilometers," Keith complained. "How many actual kilometers are we talking about?"

"Nine," Ludendorff said.

Keith groaned. "I'd call that several, several kilometers."

"Now, now," the professor said. "We have Captain Maddox and his beautiful accomplice to protect us. Why are you worried?"

Keith thought about that, nodding a moment later. "That's a good point. Thanks, old man."

"Are any Vendels in our way?" Maddox asked.

Ludendorff adjusted the device. "I don't believe so."

Maddox studied the junkyard mountain they'd just climbed down. He didn't see any Vendels. He looked around. There were buildings, towers and metal arches everywhere, all of them wrecked in one way or another. Could the Hall of Mirrors really be nearby?

"Let's go," Maddox said. "Professor, you have point."

Ludendorff nodded as he began walking ahead, absorbed with the hand-scanner.

***

The four passed through shadowed valleys with rusted skyscrapers looming over them. They entered and began to cross a kilometer-wide basin of sluggish water, with an oily rainbow of colors splashing at every step. Fortunately, the water didn't quite reach the top of their boots.

By the time they reached halfway across, a horde of hooting, talon-shaking Vendels appeared at the edge of the basin where they'd entered.

"Why aren't they entering the basin?" Meta asked.

"They must fear or hate the water," Ludendorff declared. He turned to Maddox. "Why aren't you picking them off with your rifle? Are they too far for you?"

"That and I don't want to waste ammo," Maddox said.

"Meaning what?" Ludendorff asked.

"The number of Vendels back there and my bullets are about equal," Maddox said. "It's better if we can outrun or scare them off."

"Do you envision scaring off those savages?"

"Professor, they aren't entering the water. Thus, I have no compelling reason to shoot."

"Why aren't they circling the basin?" Meta asked. "Why aren't they trying to cut us off?"

"I don't know," Maddox admitted.

"I think I do," a weary-eyed Keith said. "I watch a lot of nature shows. I suspect the basin is the limit of their territory. They fear to enter another group of Vendels' territory without a truly compelling reason. Apparently, we're not enough of one."

The Vendels congregated at the edge of the basin raised their muzzles and began to howl, like coyotes howled at the moon. It was an eerie, disquieting sound.

"What are they doing now?" Meta asked Keith.

"He doesn't know," Ludendorff said. "But I can tell you."

"They're calling the other tribes," Keith said, before Ludendorff could explain.

Ludendorff eyed Keith, finally saying, "The pilot has a modicum of wit after all. I agree with his analysis."

"Is the Hall of Mirrors that way?" Maddox asked, pointing with his Khislack.

Ludendorff checked his scanner, soon nodding.

Maddox studied the howling Vendels before he started for the equally distant shore opposite the savages.

***

"Our luck holds," Ludendorff said, as he stepped over the basin edge, onto dry concrete.

"I don't know that we've had much good luck this trip," Keith said.

"I agree," the professor said.

"But you just said that our luck holds."

"Indeed. I have detected a second pack of Vendels. They are fast approaching from the east—from the direction that we're headed. That means our bad luck is remaining constant."

"Where exactly are they?" asked Keith.

The professor pointed at a huge block skyscraper. "They are less than two kilometers from us."

"Which way is the Hall of Mirrors?" Maddox asked.

Ludendorff pointed at the same block skyscraper.

"We'll have to circle around them," the captain said.

"A dubious proposition," the professor said.

Maddox's nostrils flared, but he didn't comment. Instead, he set out in a new direction, moving ninety degrees from the route they had been traveling. The backpack straps had begun to dig into his shoulders, and his was lighter than Meta's pack. He glanced back at her. Meta looked tired, and her backpack was definitely bulkier than his was. She was tight-lipped and hadn't spoken for a time.

Maddox dropped back beside her. "Are you holding up?"

"Yes," she said in a clipped, weary manner.

"Anything the matter?" he asked.

"Nothing."

Maddox realized she was exhausted. He would have traded packs with her, but he needed his strength. He needed all the wits he could summon. She likely knew that, but it didn't make it any easier for her to carry the heavier pack at this grueling pace.

"I see them," Keith said between heaving breaths.

Maddox swiveled around. Nine Vendels ran after them. Perhaps forty or more followed at a distance. "Keep going," he told the others.

They stopped.

"Go!" Maddox said. "I can catch up later."

"No," Meta said.

"Go. That's an order."

Both Keith and Ludendorff took one of her arms. They tugged together, but Meta still did not budge.

"I can run faster than any of you," Maddox said. "Go. I have to slow them down."

At last, reluctantly, Meta allowed the other two to pull her. The trio hurried away, leaving Maddox behind.

The nine Vendels still ran, but he could tell they watched him closely. These Vendels seemed to show something other than bloodthirsty desire. They seemed wary of him.

The left corner of Maddox's mouth quirked upward. He readied the Khislack, and with eleven deliberate shots, he killed or incapacitated the front nine.

The other Vendels howled with rage.

Reluctantly, Maddox turned and started after the others. Shooting the nine Vendels had given him a chance to catch his breath. He didn't want to run. He didn't really want to hike anymore. He felt as if some of the toxins in the air had breached his rebreather. He shouldn't be this tired this fast.

Maddox took a deep breath. Then, he ran after the others. Normally, he would have caught up in just a few minutes. This time, it took him ten.

He staggered to a halt, as the others stood before a huge crater in the concrete. The vast hole was almost as large as the water basin had been, making it a circular kilometer.

"What's wrong?" Maddox panted.

"My calculations were off before," Ludendorff said. "I believe this is it, the above ground entrance to the Hall of Mirrors. If that's true, this is also the former space-cable anchor point."

Maddox peered into the darkness. He spied a huge shadowed realm several square kilometers in size. He realized they stood upon a shelf of earth and concrete. There was no telling how far the subterranean realm extended beyond what he could see.

"What caused this?" Maddox asked.

"I have no idea," Ludendorff said. "I do believe the missing area used to hold the Hall of Mirrors. It was the key to finding the vault holding the ancient Builder scanner."

As the professor spoke, sixty or seventy more Vendels appeared down the street. The beasts howled in triumph. As a group, they bayed, dropped to all fours and began charging the landing party.

-30-

Maddox peered into the abyss before studying the Vendels. He gauged the distance to the nearest building. They would never beat the savages to it. There was only one hope. Calmly, he knelt on one knee, raised the Khislack—

"What are you doing?" Ludendorff shouted. "You can't kill all of them."

"If I can't," Maddox said, "we die. If I can, we live. Therefore, I suggest you form a firing line to help me. If we kill just one Vendel too few, it may well cost humanity everything."

Maddox targeted and fired with cool deliberation, trying for headshots. He would have liked to have an over-and-under right about now. A grenade-launcher could have made this a near certain thing. But wishing never got anyone anything. Doing was what counted.

The others stood beside him. Ludendorff handed his second laser pistol to Keith.

"Don't fire until they're within a hundred meters," the Methuselah Man said.

Keith grimaced as he gripped the pistol. His hands were shaking badly.

Meta had a handgun in one hand and the monofilament blade in the other. She also held her fire, waiting for the beasts to come within handgun range. She did not tremble. She stood beside her lover, ready to defend him to the death.

All the while, Maddox let the heavy Khislack bark. Three empty magazines already lay around him. Sprawled Vendels littered behind the pack like spent fuel. The others bounded all the faster, snarling with savagery and, no doubt, hot for revenge.

Maddox shoved another magazine into the smoking rifle. He wasn't going to kill them all by himself. That was clear.

A laser beam pierced a Vendel in the shoulder. The eight-foot creature roared horribly but it did not lessen its obscene charge. The problem with the laser was its lack of knockdown power. It was a beam and thus had no kinetic energy. Maddox's .370-grain bullets had plenty of knockdown power, one of the advantages of a material-hitting weapon versus a beam.

"I hear a whine," Meta shouted.

Maddox heard her, and he even heard the whine. He couldn't worry about that now, though. He had to make every shot count. He'd already missed several times. He wished he could fire faster and more accurately. He hadn't counted on—

The whine became louder. It came from behind. Maddox might have glanced back. No, he concentrated too fully on the thirty or so remaining Vendels.

Keith beamed, but his ray was wide of the mark.

Meta fired with a heavy caliber gun, but it took her too many bullets to bring down a Vendel.

At that point, as twenty-five or more Vendels reached inside the forty-meter mark, a wide yellow beam appeared. It came from behind the landing party, and from their left. It was a wavering thing, and it had an amazing effect upon the cannibalistic savages.

The remaining Vendels slowed their rapid advance until they stopped altogether. The beasts stared ahead blankly. Several of them stood upright. The rest curled down onto their haunches like dogs, putting their heads on their folded arms. Those soon slept. The four upright Vendels struggled to continue walking.

"Do not shoot them," a voice said from behind.

Maddox lowered his rifle, turning around in amazement.

A large platform or raft hovered upon the nothingness that made up the vast crater. A Vendel-looking humanoid stood by an upright control panel. He was a little over six feet tall instead of the monstrous eight. This Vendel wore a crinkly blue suit with a helmet. He lacked the savagery of the four beasts trying to walk through the wide yellow beam. Two other suited Vendels—they must have been what the original inhabitants had looked like—fiddled with the beam machine. It was bulky, humming continuously.

There were five other similarly-suited Vendels. Four of them aimed rifles at the landing party. Among the five was a Vendel with a strange bullhorn. With a gloved finger, he clicked the speaking device.

"You will lower your weapons or we will reluctantly kill you," the Vendel said.

Maddox decided instantly, setting the smoking Khislack on the pavement.

"No," Ludendorff whispered. "You can't."

"You must," the helmeted Vendel said. "You are our prisoners. We tried to keep you away, but you insisted on invading our planet."

"Who are you?" Ludendorff asked.

Behind his faceplate, the Vendel smiled. His lips moved, in any case, and that exposed his teeth. They were ordinary looking teeth, like any humanoid man or woman would have. He clearly had not mutated like the four still-approaching beasts.

He had sharp ears like a mythical elf and closer-set slanted eyes. He was thinner, too, with longer arms and legs. The Vendel lacked eyebrows and there was no indication of any other hair.

"Are you going to kill us?" Maddox asked.

"I certainly will if you don't all surrender," the Vendel said.

"Why are the last four—?"

The suited Vendel held up a gloved hand, the seemingly universal symbol to shut up.

Maddox stopped talking as the others set down their weapons.

"Good," the Vendel said through his speaker. "You will approach the flyer with your hands behind your backs. We are going down. The Raja will decide your fate."

"Why did you launch a cruise missile at us?" Ludendorff asked.

"You will cease your questions or I will kill you."

The raft bumped against the edge of the pavement.

Maddox glanced at Meta. She gave him a stark look. He nodded imperceptibly. Then, he stepped onto the metal raft, seemingly tripped and stumbled against one of the rifle-aiming Vendels. Without hesitation, Maddox brought his hands forward, thrust them under the Vendel's armpits had hurled him against another rifleman.

A shot rang out. Then another. Meta landed on the raft, and pandemonium followed. She used her hidden monofilament blade like an artist, jabbing, slicing and hewing the crinkly-suited Vendels. Maddox ripped a rifle from another alien and used it like a club.

"Treachery," the bullhorn-speaking Vendel said.

The wide yellow light no longer beamed. The sleeping savages woke up. The four that had staggered toward them now snarled with rage, sprinting on all fours.

Maddox and Meta worked together like a whirlwind. Keith was on his knees with blood gushing from the side of his throat. He held the wound with both hands. Ludendorff sat on the pavement, holding his shattered left shoulder, with his face screwed up in agony.

Maddox let his pent-up frustration fuel his limbs. He was exhausted, but he pushed himself. More shots rang out, but each marksman was a fraction of a second too late. Maddox shattered his rifle-club against a Vendel's helmet, sending the humanoid over the edge, to plunge into the vast abyss.

Two suited Vendels slipped on the bloody deck, cracking their helmets together. Meta stabbed each, killing them. The fight was over almost as quickly as it had begun, with Maddox and Meta having conquered the flyer.

"Watch them," Maddox said. "Get over here!" he shouted at Keith and Ludendorff.

The pilot must have sensed the approaching savages. He lurched, standing, stumbling onto the raft. Ludendorff continued to sit on his butt.

The forward four of the savages were almost upon them. Maddox jumped onto the pavement, grabbed Ludendorff by the good arm and yanked him upright. The Methuselah Man howled with agony. Maddox shoved Ludendorff onto the raft.

The captain picked up his Khislack, firing rapidly. The first beast crashed onto the pavement. The second tumbled head-over-heels with a shattered skull. Maddox saw that he wouldn't have enough time to get the last two. Another weapon chattered like a machine-gun behind him. Meta must have picked up a Vendel rifle, in actuality a machine-gun. The savage jerked repeatedly, a dozen rounds or more riddling his body. Maddox concentrated on the last creature, firing as it leaped. At the last moment, Maddox jumped out of the way. The mewling cannibal landed with a thud, sliding until his head bumped against the raft. It tried to rise.

Maddox shot it in the back of the head, killing it. He leaped over the twitching corpse onto the raft. The rest of the pack howled with rage, racing to reach them.

Meta stood by the controls, no doubt trying to figure out how to move the raft.

"For the love of Saint Pete," Keith said. He shouldered Meta aside, stared at the panel and removed one of his bloodied hands from his neck. With several taps, he caused the flyer to slide away from the edge. The flyer kept moving until it was in the middle of the vast crater.

Once the savages reached the edge, they howled with impotent rage. Several hurled whatever they could find at the distant raft, flinging the items upward like great apes in a zoo.

"Now what do we do?" Keith asked Maddox. The pilot was pale, having obviously lost too much blood.

Maddox took a breath, and then a second. "We go down," he said. "Meta, use a medikit on Keith. See that he doesn't faint or lose any more blood."

"What about me?" Ludendorff complained.

"Check on the professor next," Maddox said. He kept his Khislack ready, and he noticed that the speaker for the regular aliens lay gasping on the deck. The Vendel had an ugly, bloody cut on the side. Maybe they could patch him up and find out more about the Junkyard Planet.

As the raft lurched, heading into the subterranean realm, Maddox looked up into the heavens. What was happening on *Victory*? None of this down here would matter if Valerie lost the space battle.

-31-

"The last shuttle has landed, Lieutenant," Galyan informed Valerie.

The lieutenant sat in the command chair, biting the index knuckle of her right hand. She finally realized what she was doing and jerked the knuckle out of her mouth. The commander of a starship had to appear confident, not frightened or even worried.

She couldn't worry about Keith Maker. She couldn't berate herself for having avoided him ever since he'd kissed her. What had she been thinking? Love was so rare in this universe. To flee it when it was offered in good faith—

"What are your orders, Lieutenant?" Galyan asked.

Valerie stared at the holoimage. It was so easy for Galyan. He didn't have feelings like the rest of them. Maybe it would be better if she were deified like him. She would—

Valerie's head snapped up. She had to stop woolgathering. She was the commander now. She had to save *Victory* from annihilation, and she had to rescue the landing party. Was that enough responsibility for her? She'd wanted independent command before. Now, the captain and Keith—sweet Keith Maker—depended on her decisions and skills.

"Are you ready, Galyan?" Valerie asked. She barely kept herself from wincing at the whiny tone of her voice.

"I am," the holoimage said, floating closer. Whispering, he added, "You have successfully commanded us before, Valerie. You can do it again."

"I'm not worried about that," she whispered back.

Galyan's eyelids fluttered. "Oh. Yes. I realize that now. What are your orders?"

Valerie couldn't believe it. Galyan knew she was scared, but he pretended that he believed her. The AI must be doing that to try to give her more confidence. That didn't help. It made her doubt herself more.

"Valerie," Galyan said. "I am monitoring the approaching Juggernauts. They have the same mass as the previous Rull vessel. However, I am detecting structural damage to each."

"We can take them?" Valerie asked in a hopeful voice.

"I am not suggesting, how do you say, a toe-to-toe conflict. These Juggernauts have the same tough alloy hulls as the previous one. They are coming around the planet on opposite intercept courses. It is my belief that they are attempting a bracketing attack. They hope to catch *Victory* between the two of them."

"I know what a bracketing attack is," Valerie said.

Galyan said nothing.

"But I appreciate your data. You said the Juggernauts are structurally unsound. They've taken battle hits?"

"I am still analyzing. Yes. I give that a ninety-six percent probability—"

"How badly damaged are they?"

"We must retreat."

"The Juggernauts still have weapons ports?"

"Affirmative."

Valerie almost chewed on her knuckle again. She used her left hand to force the right onto her lap. She had to think. If she attacked one war-vessel hard—

"If we do not begin maneuvering for space, Valerie, the Juggernauts will bracket us no matter what we do."

"Helm," Valerie said crisply. "Take us out of orbit at a vector 24-0-6. We're going to gain some distance from those bastards. I doubt the Juggernauts have long-ranged beams as powerful as our disrupter."

"They do have excellent missiles, though," Galyan said. "Wait. I must restate that. The other Juggernaut had excellent missiles. We do not yet know the full state of these two war-vessels."

Valerie did some hard thinking as the starship built up velocity. On the main screen, the planet began to fall away. As it did, the two Juggernauts became visible. Their exhaust tails were long and easily spotted.

"Did the Rull attack the planet sometime in the past?" Valerie asked.

"We do not know," Galyan said.

"I mean," Valerie said. "How did the Vendels acquire two Rull war-vessels?"

"A fight between the Rull and the Vendels might explain the ship and the planetary damage. We do not know who presently controls the Juggernauts. I suggest we do not make any unwarranted assumptions."

"Right," Valerie said. She slammed a fist onto an armrest. "We don't know enough. We—"

"*Victory* is the greatest Patrol vessel in Star Watch," Galyan said. "That is one of the reasons we are in the Beyond. We are the best at explaining mysteries."

"No," Valerie said. "That would be Captain Maddox."

"And me," Galyan said. "I also have an excellent track record in that regard."

"Of course," Valerie said. "What's that?" she asked, pointing at the main screen.

Before the sensor officer could answer, Galyan said, "Those are Rull missiles, three of them. They are accelerating quickly. What are your orders, Lieutenant?"

Valerie thought fast. "Last time, the Rull missile had a proximity fuse. The warhead ignited before we could destroy it. I'm thinking of launching two antimissiles at the forward projectile."

"You do not wish to use the disrupter cannon?"

"The enemy doesn't know we have it yet," Valerie said. "This time, the Juggernauts didn't catch us with our shields down. They haven't scanned us, either."

"They have tried," Galyan said.

"Right," Valerie said. She swiveled toward the lean and lanky weapons officer. "Launch two antimissiles at the lead projectile."

"Launching," the weapons officer said, stroking his sideburns with one hand as he tapped his board with the other.

"Increase speed," Valerie said.

The helmsman manipulated his piloting board. *Victory* increased speed, pulling away faster from the Juggernauts and Pandora II.

On the main screen, the Rull missiles kept on target. It was clear that they were accelerating faster than the starship could flee. Meanwhile, two antimissiles zeroed-in on the lead projectile, quickly closing the gap.

"Warning," Galyan said. "The enemy missile appears to have a proximity detonator."

"Full power to the shield," Valerie said.

The Star Watch antimissiles headed for a collision course with the lead Rull missile. Before they smashed, the enemy warhead ignited, creating a thermonuclear fireball, blast and EMP. The antimissiles shredded apart. So did the other two Rull missiles.

Soon, radiation, heat and an electromagnetic pulse struck the shield. It turned pink in a large area. Fortunately, the nuclear explosion had been too far away to heavily damage the shield.

"The Juggernauts are readying their lasers," Galyan said. "I count fewer weapons ports than the previous ship."

"Explain," Valerie said.

"May I control the main screen?" Galyan said.

Valerie nodded.

Immediately, a close-up of the nearest Juggernaut showed a badly damaged spheroid. It was not a smooth war-vessel, but showed five jagged and rather large holes. One of the holes seemed to go deeper than the rest. Galyan zoomed in even more. On the screen, they saw automated machinery and dull lights deep inside the Juggernaut.

"Is the other ship as badly damaged?" Valerie asked.

"Affirmative," Galyan said.

"Both Juggernauts have clearly taken a pounding."

At that moment, two lasers from the nearest Rull vessel and three from the other beamed across the distance at *Victory*.

The five rays struck the shield.

"What's their wattage?" Valerie asked.

"Much less than the previous Juggernaut," Galyan said. "These Rull do not appear to focus their lasers as tightly as the previous one did. These rays dissipated badly even over a short distance. Wahhabi lasers would be more powerful."

"Is the disrupter cannon ready?" Valerie asked the weapons officer.

"Ready and able," the man replied.

"Target the rupturcd arca Galyan showcd us," Valcric said. "We're going to ram the disrupter beam right down their throat."

Seconds later, the antimatter engines thrummed. The annihilating disrupter beam flashed from *Victory* to the lead Juggernaut. The beam did not have to smash through the protective outer alloy, and drilled directly into the guts of the twenty-kilometer war-vessel.

"Should we add missiles?" Galyan asked.

"No," Valerie said. "They have active PD cannons. We're going to let the disrupter beam show them why Star Watch is superior to the Rull."

The beam chewed through decking, smashed automated machines and dug deeper still. For ten seconds, it roasted the inner alloy armor around the interior engine compartment. Then, the beam burst through the cherry red armor. It struck the nuclear-powered engines, crushing and obliterating them. Then, it happened. The Juggernaut began its self-destruct sequence.

"Warning," Galyan said. "I suggest you power the shields with everything."

"Do it," Valerie said.

The annihilating disrupter beam quit. The antimatter engines thrummed louder than before. More power went to the shields.

At that moment, the wounded Juggernaut exploded in a vast thermonuclear holocaust. It was more than one warhead igniting. It had the detonation power of a hundred warheads.

One moment, the Juggernaut was flying through space. In the next, a fiery nova explosion obliterated everything. The automated machinery, the engines, the auxiliary systems, the laser-generating machinery, the repair units, the biological engineering sections, the super alloys—they all vanished in a hellish blaze.

Some of that blast raced toward the planet. Some radiated at the other war-vessel. Some also came for *Victory*.

"Three, two, one…" Galyan said.

The shield buckled. The antimatter engines whined. The shield turned brown, then gray, then started to blacken all over. Gamma and x-ray radiation leaked through, striking the starship's armor plating. Too much radiation could kill just as dead as heat and blast damage.

Valerie ground her molars and hunched her shoulders. She should have gained more distance before doing this. She should have—

Suddenly, the blackening seemed less dark. The great Adok antimatter engines continued to pour power into the shield, and now less radiation leaked through.

The first damage-control parties began to report. A grim dosage of gamma and x-rays had struck the decks nearest that area of the outer hull. If too much leaked past the armor—

The blackness of the shield lightened even more, changing to a deep gray color. The damage-control officer on the bridge reported. Radiation was no longer seeping past the shield.

The other bridge officers shouted, clapped and began to cheer. Most of the ship had survived the terrible blast. Only a handful of crewmembers had radiation burns. A few secondary systems would have to go offline for a time, but it wouldn't affect the starship over the long haul.

"Valerie," Galyan said. "The last war-vessel is veering away."

"Put it on the screen," Valerie said.

On the main screen, the remaining Juggernaut curved away from *Victory*. It left masses of debris behind it. The blast from its partner had damaged an already wounded war-vessel.

"Give me a damage report on the enemy," Valerie said crisply.

"Two of its remaining laser ports are gone," Galyan said. "A bank of PD cannons has vanished. Valerie, you could finish it."

"Launch…five missiles. Stagger them. Let the Juggernaut run for now. We don't want another mega-blast like that to reach the planet or us."

"I do not understand," Galyan said. "You are not going to destroy the enemy vessel while you have an opportunity for the kill?"

"Let it run for now. We both know *Victory* can destroy the Juggernaut, and it will surely act accordingly. We don't need another blast of radiation right now. Besides, I have a greater task. It's time to return to the South Pole and pick up the landing party."

Unfortunately, it took time to slow the starship's momentum and build up new momentum in the other direction. Valerie stared at Pandora II. She'd beaten the Juggernauts for now, killing the one. Was the landing party still alive?

What will I do if Captain Maddox is dead?

-32-

Keith felt faint as he piloted the raft through the subterranean darkness. The vast crater was behind them and around a great corner, although some illumination still reached this far.

It showed shattered underground structures and broken machines, and disgusting fungus growth everywhere else. This seemed like a poisoned realm, an underworld of the damned. None of them had any idea where the suited Vendels had come from.

Keith's neck itched horribly. Meta had sprayed it with disinfectant and applied pseudo-skin onto the wound. It had been a scratch, she'd told him. It sure hadn't bled or felt like a scratch.

Keith refrained from touching the pseudo-skin. He concentrated on flying the alien contraption. It was a good thing for the others that he wasn't as badly off as Ludendorff. The Methuselah Man lay on his back, groaning as he held his shattered shoulder. Meta had been about to tip the raft-like craft before Keith had gotten to the controls.

"Can you hover in one place?" the captain asked.

Keith tested the controls. The raft wobbled once. He steadied it, although they lost one of the wounded Vendels; the humanoid slid off. Fortunately, the Methuselah Man had anchored himself with a rope. Ludendorff moaned piteously, though, as the rope tightened against his chest.

"Be careful," Meta shouted. "You'll get us all killed."

"That I will not," Keith said. He tapped the controls once more.

The flyer stopped, hovering in one place. He peered over an edge. They were one hundred meters up from the subterranean, fungus-covered floor. Keith estimated they had something like one hundred meters of space all around them. He'd put them almost perfectly in the center of the vast tunnel. Unfortunately, none of the others were as aware of the aerial situation as he was. That was one of the problems with being a great pilot. Others were often too unskilled to appreciate the full extent of one's talent.

Too bad Valerie couldn't see me now. She might understand me better if she could. Keith frowned as he thought about the lieutenant. She'd enjoyed the kiss at first. Why did she have to be so sensitive about things like that? Riker had suggested he give her time and space. Just how much time did the woman need, anyway? This was too long.

"Are you paying attention?" the captain asked.

"Yes, sir," Keith said, snapping out of his daydreaming.

Maddox scrutinized him a little longer. The captain was freaky sometimes, as if he could read minds.

"Maintain our position," the captain said, "and continue to watch for his kind."

The captain pointed at the wounded Vendel. Meta moved behind the prisoner, holding his arms behind his head. Maddox then crouched beside the alien.

"It's time we talked," Maddox said.

The Vendel stared at the captain through his faceplate.

"Must I use a stimulant to loosen your tongue?" Maddox asked.

The Vendel shook his helmeted head. With his eyes, he indicated the bullhorn.

"Let go of one arm," Maddox told Meta.

She seemed reluctant, but finally did so.

The Vendel flexed his gloved hand. He seemed to hesitate, as if considering a way to resist. Finally, he picked up the bullhorn, pushing the small end against his faceplate. He clicked it.

"You've destroyed me," the Vendel said in English.

"I have done nothing of the kind," the captain said.

"Your mate did it then, the one with the knife."

"Do you refer to the tear in your suit?"

"It is more than a tear. Look at the blood. I have been cut. It is only a matter of time now before I mutate into an *ock-tar*, a beast."

"There are toxins in the air?" Maddox asked.

The Vendel nodded.

"Who put the toxins there?"

Keith had been listening to the exchange. He now caught motion out of the corner of his eye. It came from ahead and to the left. He craned his neck and squinted. He saw more motion—

"Captain," Keith said, as he tapped the controls. The raft slid backward. "I see more rafts, three of them, in fact. They're headed our way."

"You must surrender to them," the Vendel said. "You are outnumbered."

"Are they your people?" Maddox asked.

"Surrender," the Vendel said. "I might still have enough time left. Your wounded people can also receive medical attention."

"Where did you learn English?" Maddox asked.

Keith flew faster, heading back for the sunlight.

"Have you seen men like us before?" Maddox asked the Vendel.

"No," the Vendel said.

"Sir," Keith shouted. "It looks like the others have weapons, big weapons. They're gaining on us, too."

Maddox spun around, picked up his Khislack and knelt on one knee. He tucked the butt against his right shoulder, flicking on the targeting computer.

Before he could aim, a roiling ball of something tumbled through the air at them. It was bright orange and it churned as it sizzled faster.

"That looks like plasma," Meta shouted.

Maddox silently agreed with her assessment. A plasma-cannon would be the perfect weapon to use against a charging horde of eight-foot cannibals.

Keith tapped the controls. The raft dropped just in time. The plasma hissed overhead, with heat radiating from it.

Maddox swiveled the Khislack, aiming at the second raft. Vendels readied their portable plasma-cannon, a "flamer" in Star Watch parlance. The weapon had a tripod mount. Through the scope, Maddox saw the portable flash red. If it was like a Star Watch flamer, that meant it was ready for firing.

Maddox targeted the second raft because he was counting on the first raft needing time to recharge its plasma-energizer.

Maddox squeezed the trigger while trying for a perfect shot. The Khislack barked. The barrel lifted.

Like ancient flamethrowers, a flamer was devastating to the target, but also dangerous to its own side if someone broke it. Likely, the portable weapon had a thick and possibly double casing.

Keith cheered.

The high-velocity .370 scored a hit. Hot plasma gushed out of the bullet hole. Then, the portable exploded, hurling plasma everywhere.

Burning, suited Vendels jumped off the raft, with their limbs flailing. A second more powerful explosion erupted. Shrapnel flew everywhere. The remains of the raft abruptly nosedived. It picked up speed, and then it exploded again. Seconds later, the various chunks of raft plowed into masses of thick fungus. That started a smoky, foul-smelling blaze.

"The other rafts are veering wide," Keith shouted.

Maddox did not respond.

"What now?" Meta asked the captain.

"We're exposed to cruise missiles if we go topside," Maddox said.

"We can't stay down here," Ludendorff groaned. "I need medical attention. The toxins must be poisoning me."

Keith guided the raft into a corner of sunlight as the EMP blast from the destroyed Juggernaut reached the atmosphere, descending down to the planet. The EMP washed across the craft. Its hum quit abruptly as everything electrical died.

"I've lost power," Keith said.

The raft continued forward because of momentum, but it also began to plunge toward the bottom of the crater.

"What should I do?" Keith shouted.

"Can you maneuver at all?" Maddox asked.

"No!"

The captain peered over the edge. They left the sunlight and entered a different tunnel with a fungus jungle.

"We have to jump before it crashes," Maddox said. "Our only hope is that the fungus is good and thick. Maybe it will cushion our fall."

"You're mad," Ludendorff shouted.

The captain lunged at Ludendorff, cut the rope securing the Methuselah Man, and picked him up. Ludendorff howled in pain, and he struck Maddox as if to make him let go.

Hoisting the professor, Maddox pitched him off the edge. The captain jumped a second after the Methuselah Man.

Keith wrung his hands. There wasn't much time left. He stepped to the end of the raft as Meta leaped into the air.

"I'm going to die," Keith shouted. Then he leaped as hard as he could, hoping for the best.

***

Five strange parcels dangled from chutes. They had floated for some time, ejected from *Victory* before the starship went off to battle the Juggernauts.

The parcels were tough steel boxes. The chutes and their dangling boxes headed down toward the one-world city. Motion detectors on one box began to beep. Below, Vendels scampered toward the boxes' probable landing site.

The first chute released its box. The steel container plunged toward rusted girders and heaped junk. The other chutes did likewise. The various fabrics folded up like wisps, tossed to-and-fro by the wind. The boxes fell.

The first container hit, bounced up, hit again and then slid briefly along concrete. Like giant pellets, the other boxes slammed onto the ground.

In the distance, Vendels howled with delight, increasing speed.

The first container clicked and popped open, the sides slamming onto the concrete. A snakelike portion writhed onto the ground. Tiny aerials with dishes sprouted from it and began to rotate.

The other boxes also fell open, exposing similar packages that sprouted their own aerials. Each piece began to wriggle toward a central location between them. Like dumb brutes, the metal objects rolled, wriggled and moved.

The Vendels howled, racing faster, trying to be first to reach the new toys.

Before that happened, the first metal section met another. They rolled together and bumped back and forth to no appreciable effect. Then, other pieces joined the first two. Now the pieces melded and clicked together in order. In moments, it had become a long snakish device with many aerials all along its length.

A Vendel with a lashing tail leaped onto a slab of concrete. It spied the long object. With a howl, the Vendel leaped again, landing beside the object. It grasped the thing—

A powerful shock of electricity jolted through the Vendel. The hair on its head stood up. Its eyes bulged. The electric discharge stopped, and the Vendel toppled over, stunned and possibly dead.

More giant creatures closed in on Ludendorff's special object.

A drill appeared from the snake-thing's snout. The drill whirled, the nose pointed downward, and the thing wriggled. The drill bored into the metallic ground like a gigantic worm. Then, the metal object began to wriggle out of sight.

Another Vendel leaped down, grabbing the end. The savage set its clawed feet and bunched its shoulders to drag the giant worm out of the earth.

A second terrific jolt was emitted, shocking the savage. This time, the beast's hands smoked and the creature gave an odd hissing gurgle. When the electricity stopped, the Vendel toppled over dead. Smoke curled from its charred body.

A third Vendel landed on the ground. This one hesitated. That gave the long metal snake time to disappear from the surface. It continued to burrow, hunting according to Ludendorff's special program.

-33-

Maddox had the terrible sensation of falling, falling, falling. He wanted to look at the ground but couldn't. In fact, he couldn't look at anything, couldn't see anything. That frustrated him. It shouldn't be that dark in here. Could he have already landed? Could the sensation of falling—

Where am I?

That seemed like an odd question. How could he not know? He had…he had…

What's wrong with me?

Maddox strove to understand. He'd discovered something on Titan. He'd been with a Methuselah Man—

Ludendorff!

As he recalled the professor, the fight on Titan came flooding back. Androids had tried to kill him deep in Saturn's moon. He'd come to the Junkyard Planet, had crashed-landed on the surface, run from Vendels, captured a flying raft—

I jumped. What happened after I jumped?

Maddox struggled to remember. He remembered falling, but he couldn't remember anything after that. Suddenly he understood why he did not know.

Chemicals in the brain shut down short-term memory. After a time, another chemical reaction turned that into long-term memory. The short-term memory track was erased in order to make room for more short-term events. He must have hit the fungus—Yet, he literally had no recollection of the end of the fall or the immediate aftermath.

Still, I'm alive.

Maddox struggled to look around. He failed in that, too, and he didn't know why. That angered him, but he didn't lash out. That wasn't his way. He concentrated—

*Thrum…thrum…thrum…*beat against his skull.

Maddox groaned, and a wave of weakness broke his resolve. He relented from concentrating. The pounding in his skull receded like the tide. It left him bare, exposed, and his conscious thoughts drifted away…

***

An incalculable passage of time later, Maddox felt gentle motion. It alerted him to a change. He heard wheezing, a rushing windy sound that filled his world.

Something was wrong with his eyes. They wouldn't open. That seemed so wrong that Maddox struggled against it. By tiny degrees, he forced his eyelids apart.

A murky world with slow-motion movement confused him.

The rushing wind sound continued. Finally, he realized that the sound was coming from him. It was his breathing echoing in his ears because of the mask he wore.

A mask, he wore a mask.

The realization brought greater focus, but it also brought horror and loathing.

Twin canisters were attached to the mask. It appeared the canisters acted like gills, extracting oxygen from the liquid around him. That wasn't what disgusted him the most, though. Twenty or more tubes were embedded under his skin. He was caught like a fly in a web. Thick, colored liquids surged through the tubing into him. Somebody was doing something to him.

He squinted through the liquid and managed to make out some of the technicians on the other side. They were normal Vendels in long blue robes. Some held slates. Others monitored machines. One of the slate-holding Vendels lowered his and approached closer. The alien seemed to be examining him.

The Vendel turned and seemed to shout.

A cooling sensation flooded over Maddox. It made him drowsy. Did the shouting scientist have something to do with that?

Maddox wanted to stay awake to see what they were going to do next. He lost the battle…slowly lost consciousness…

***

A shuffling sound woke Maddox. He opened his eyes just in time to see a tall Vendel retreating from his cot. The alien held a long needle with a glistening point.

Had the creature just injected him with something?

Another Vendel came into focus. This one was thicker-bodied and wore a uniform with extra-large collars. He had a belt and what Maddox figured must be a weapon, a gun of sorts, holstered there.

They were in a small room with a door at one side. The room contained monitors, he saw, and the bed he was lying in, and a high table to the side. Maddox couldn't see what lay on the table.

The military Vendel—if that's what he was—put a doglike collar with a box around his own throat. He secured it and pressed a tab on the box. It vibrated a moment.

The Vendel spoke softly. Out of the throat-box came the words, "Do you understand me?"

"Yes," Maddox whispered.

The Vendel held up a hand. Then he inserted something into an ear, clicked it, and asked the question a second time.

"I understand you," Maddox said, his voice stronger this time.

The military alien motioned to the doctor or scientist. That Vendel retreated, moving to the table, turning his back to Maddox as he fiddled with something on the table.

"Who are you?" the military Vendel asked.

"I am Captain Maddox of Star Watch. Who are you?"

"I am Sub-Chief Pascal le Mort. I operate under the direct authority of the Raja. I want to know why you have invaded Sind."

"What is Sind?"

"It is the name of our beloved planet," Pascal said.

"I have invaded nothing,"

"Your actions imply otherwise," the Vendel said. "You have murdered many of the Raja's subjects in a rash and reckless manner. Or did you think that your killing spree would go unnoticed?"

"We defended ourselves, nothing more."

"Why did you come to Sind?"

"We seek aid against the Swarm," Maddox said.

"The Swarm is a child's legend, an ancient one at that. You will have to do better."

"The Swarm is all too real," Maddox said. "I have seen one of their fleets. It was vast—"

"You claim to have visited the Swarm homeworld?" the alien asked, interrupting.

"No," Maddox said in a weary voice. "I journeyed deep into the Beyond—"

"I do not understand that word," the Vendel said.

"I traveled far from my homeworld."

"Where is your homeworld?"

Maddox opened his mouth to answer and then closed it. He was so tired. But that didn't mean he was a fool and would tell a possibly hostile alien about Earth. He needed to think. He—yes, it was time for a different approach.

"Where are the rest of my people?" Maddox asked. "Where am I? What have you been doing to me?"

Sub-chief Pascal le Mort studied him. The military Vendel turned off the throat box and spoke to the scientist. They exchanged rapid-fire words. Finally, the sub-chief turned his translator back on.

"You almost died," Pascal said. "You abandoned your sky-raft before it crashed. Each of you landed in the reef-mash. Some of you acquired *vent*, almost dying in the process. The Raja decided on using our best medical facility. The *clutch* has been active in your bloodstreams. We barely got to each of you in time to counteract the vent."

"Vent is what turned normal Vendels into those savages we saw topside?"

"Those 'savages' are our brothers and sisters. Our scientists labor morning, noon and night for a cure. Yet, you came down and slaughtered them indiscriminately. That was a hostile action."

"You launched a cruise missile at us first," Maddox said.

"As a warning to leave Sind," Pascal said.

"You warned us too hard, wrecking our craft. We crashed—"

"Yes, yes," Pascal said. "We witnessed that, and we sent out a recue party. You slaughtered them as well."

"They threatened us."

"For their safety," Pascal said. "You are great murderers. If it weren't for your vessel's victory over the besieging Juggernauts, the Raja would have executed the lot of you. Many on the council believe this victory over the Juggernauts is a trick. No doubt, you are spies for the Rull. Worse, you might be spies for their masters, the androids."

Maddox perked up before he could hide his interest. "You know about the androids?"

Pascal studied him.

Even though his brain felt fuzzy, Maddox decided to gamble. He doubted he could dig them in any deeper than they were already. A risk would more likely help than hurt them.

"Do you know about the Builders?" Maddox asked, watching Pascal closely in case the Vendel tried to lie.

The scientist at the table whirled around as the sub-chief staggered backward, slamming against a wall. The two Vendels exchanged startled, frightened glances.

Without another word, Pascal le Mort spun around and dashed for the door, hurling it open. The scientist followed hot on his heels. The scientist slammed the door, and Maddox heard a lock click into place.

The reaction stunned Maddox. He wanted to get up and explore the room. He even managed to whip off the covers. A hiss alerted him. He looked up in time to see a green mist billowing into the chamber from upper vents. Before he could decide what that meant, his eyes closed of their own accord, and Maddox fell unconscious.

-34-

Sergeant Treggason Riker was a plodder by nature, but he was far from being slow-witted. He would not have lasted as long as he had as Captain Maddox's Intelligence Assistant otherwise.

Riker removed his bionic arm from a diagnostic machine he kept in his quarters. The arm was still fully functional. That was good to know, now that he'd made his decision.

On this journey into the Beyond, Riker had read endless gardening articles. He'd listened to Lieutenant Maker harp about Valerie and how she'd reacted badly to his impulsive kiss. The lad clearly needed a girl. There was no doubt about that.

Riker sighed as he manipulated his bionic fingers. Maybe that's what *he* should do after the mission, look for a good woman. Maybe after all this time, he should settle down. Maybe it was time to get out of the Service. These crazy missions took a toll on an old fart. It was true that he had to make sure the lad—Captain Maddox—returned to Earth in one piece. The Iron Lady might have a heart attack—a broken heart—if Maddox failed to return.

Riker sighed again as he buttoned up his uniform. He'd felt as useless as a tit on a boar hog this mission. Not that he'd minded too much. An oldster like him needed his rest.

Well, by damn, he had rested, all right. Riker had rested so much that he'd begun to feel itchy. He disliked the feeling because he knew it meant something bad was around the corner. An old salt like him seldom did anything impulsive, unlike the hotheaded pilot or the overconfident Captain Maddox. What itchiness like this did, though, was push his plodding nature into trouble.

Riker belted on his service pistol. It was a squat, ugly thing with plenty of punch. It banged loudly when shot and delivered a heavy grain bullet. There had been too many dangerous creatures, androids and surprises for Riker to believe in smaller caliber guns anymore. He wanted knockdown, killing power. The captain might have a fancy, long-barreled weapon—

Riker had a rule. Get in close and blast away. Let the young and overconfident practice the fancy tactics. The sergeant firmly believed in playing the percentages. Over the long run, that's how a man came home in one piece.

Someday, the captain's *di-far* luck was going to run out. Maybe it already had.

"I can't believe I'm doing this," Riker muttered under his breath. He figured it was time someone did. Still, having raided the captain's quarters for the needed technical goodie—

The sergeant did not go into the lavatory to check himself in a mirror. He was too old for that. His jacket fit, the belt wasn't too tight and he'd broken in these boots weeks ago.

He now headed for the hatch to begin the Intelligence legwork for an illegal activity.

***

These past days, Riker had been thinking the way a dog gnawed on a bone with several pieces of meat deep in the crevices. Riker had worked over the problem one way, turned it around and mulled it over in another. He had fit the pieces of the puzzle together, discarded stupid ideas and slowly begun to form an opinion.

The problem was Professor Ludendorff and Doctor Dana Rich. The spur had been Keith trying to kiss Valerie.

Riker loved the company of women. They were wonderful creatures, warm, loving, compassionate, helpful... And royal pains in the arse at other times. Riker had a theory about women. It involved God. He figured a man and a woman, a married couple, brought all the pieces together to give them all the attributes of God. Men usually lacked a woman's compassion. A woman seldom had a man's boldness. As a team, they helped shore up each other's weaknesses. By living together and therefore antagonizing each other, they also helped sand out the rough spots in each other's personalities.

Riker didn't believe in putting women up on pedestals. They were too flawed—but flawed in enjoyable and interesting ways that differed from men's flaws.

Thank God for that. Variety gave spice to life.

In any case, Keith's laments about Valerie had started Riker mulling over the professor's behavior toward Dana. After several days of plodding, gnawing, and thinking, Riker saw a problem.

He took a deep breath, opened a hatch into the gunnery range and locked the hatch behind him. No one was here practicing, as the starship was still on yellow alert.

They'd beaten off the Juggernauts, but couldn't find the captain or the landing party anywhere on the planet.

Riker walked deeper into the chamber, took out an anti-snooper device and clicked it on. He studied the readings. This was good. Except for the recorder up in the far corner, there were no other listening bugs or snoopers in here.

"Galyan," the sergeant said into the air.

Nothing happened.

"Galyan," Riker said. "I need your help."

A few seconds later, the holoimage appeared before him.

"Is something wrong?" Galyan asked.

"Yes. You've been studying each of us for several voyages, correct?"

The AI floated back a little. "I am an individual entity just like the rest of you. I have my own prerogatives—"

"Stand down, Galyan. I'm not accusing you of anything bad. I'm double checking my idea."

"Oh. I am sorry, Riker—"

"Don't be sorry. This could be important. I don't know. Have you continued your psychological profiling of each of us?"

"We are a family—"

"Galyan, quit being defensive. Just answer my questions. I'm not interested in trickery like the captain."

The holoimage smiled. "Sergeant Riker, that is patently false. You are devious, but you hide it behind your honest-looking features. You often make dry statements with greater bite to them—"

"Galyan."

"You are correct in reprimanding me," the holoimage said. "We are still in yellow alert, still faced with dangerous dilemmas. How can I assist you?"

Riker rubbed his leathery chin. "Professor Ludendorff is an arrogant and self-aggrandizing man. Yet, he has a tender spot for Doctor Rich."

"Several days ago, I would have agreed with your analysis," Galyan said. "However, his drugging of Doctor Rich in his laboratory…"

Galyan's eyelids fluttered. After that stopped, he looked at Riker with greater interest.

That confirmed for Riker that he was on the right track.

"That is an amazing piece of inductive reasoning on your part," Galyan said. "If one overlays the professor's action against his previous actions regarding Doctor Rich—"

"The latest action is off kilter," Riker said, interrupting.

"Yes. The professor's love for Dana has blinded him on several occasions. The most notable was when she hijacked his mission many years ago. You have impressed me, Riker."

"Let's save the back-slapping for when Star Watch is handing out the medals," Riker said. "What do you think it means that Ludendorff drugged Dana?"

Galyan's eyelids fluttered madly for a time. "Something has influenced the professor's latest action."

"Yeah," the sergeant said. "That seemed logical to me, too."

"What do you suggest we do with this interesting insight?"

Riker nodded. "That's the question, and it's why I came to you. I was hoping you'd have a plan."

"This is not my area of expertise. I do not yet know all the nuances of human behavior or the correct procedures for a spy mission."

“You can play a hunch like the captain does, or you can try the professional route I use. The professional way eliminates one possibility at a time until only one answer remains. There seems to be two possibilities here. One, someone tampered with Ludendorff’s mind. Two, someone is feeding the professor wrong information in order to nudge him in a certain direction.”

“Far be it from me to correct a Star Watch Intelligence operative,” Galyan said. “But both your examples show that someone is tampering with Ludendorff’s thoughts. One method does it directly and the other uses persuasion.”

“You know what I mean.”

“Strangely enough, I do,” Galyan said. “Perhaps my understanding of human innuendos has grown.” The holoimage glanced at the sergeant’s gun belt. “You are carrying a bigger than normal pistol. What are you afraid of finding? Wait. Do not tell me…an android,” the AI said. “You believe an android or androids might be aboard *Victory*.”

Riker stared at the holoimage.

“Sergeant, do you suspect I am in on the professor’s plot?”

“Don’t know,” Riker admitted. “The professor has fiddled with your AI core before this.”

“That is true. Let me run a self-diagnostic.” The holoimage froze.

Riker had a plan. He wasn’t sure it would work against the AI—

“I am intact,” Galyan announced. “I have also detected a jamming device in your jacket pocket. It would not have proven effective against me.”

Riker shrugged. They might still see about that.

“I suggest we speak to Dana,” Galyan said.

“Why’s that?”

“It is logical to assume the possible android is hidden in a secure location. We have checked for androids many times this voyage and found none. Thus, this hidden location would be some place Ludendorff did not want Dana to go. She would be the best person to tell us that spot.”

“Sounds good to me,” Riker said. “Let’s go.”

Galyan rubbed his holographic hands together. "This is exciting. The two of us are on an espionage mission. No wonder you have remained in Star Watch these many years. I am finding it difficult to contain my glee."

Riker muttered under his breath—an excited AI. It didn't make sense. This was almost like working with the captain. Was it possible he was cursed in some manner?

"Hurry, Sergeant," Galyan said. "You are dawdling."

Riker squinted at Galyan, wondering if the AI was imitating the captain's mannerisms. Then, the sergeant increased his pace. The captain was likely in danger—so, if they could do something on this end, it was time to get it done.

-35-

Riker didn't bother smiling. His staid face worked best in these situations.

Doctor Rich glanced from Galyan to him, frowning almost angrily. She wore a Star Watch uniform, with her long hair pulled back in a severe and unflattering manner.

They were in the cafeteria, he and Dana sitting, while Galyan stood. Others ate and talked at various tables.

"This is ridiculous," Dana said at last. "I'm sick to death of the professor's arrogant antics. Frankly, I don't believe any of your explanation, Galyan. I think the professor put you up to this. You must know that I'm angry with him."

"Even though the professor is missing down on the planet?" asked Riker.

"I'm sure the professor and the others are fine," Dana said. "Isn't it always fine in the end?"

"With hundreds of thousands of savage cannibalistic Vendels down on the planet with them?" asked Riker.

"Don't," she said, suddenly. "Don't try that on me. It's wrong. Ludendorff shouldn't have drugged me. He shouldn't have gone down with the captain. This mission is a mess. My…"

Tears brimmed in her eyes. She looked down, fiddled with her salad and sniffled. "I'm done talking to you two," she said, rising.

Galyan glanced at Riker. The sergeant could see that the AI didn't know what to do.

Riker stood, and he cleared his throat gruffly. Dana glanced at him.

"I've worked with the captain for many years," Riker said. "He's insufferably arrogant, but he's also brilliant. The professor has similar traits. One thing I know about the captain, though…"

Dana looked up. "What do you know?" she asked.

"I know the captain has never drugged Meta."

The doctor's features stiffened, but she didn't whirl away. "You don't know the professor like I do. When he's involved in a project, it consumes him. If I get in the way at those times…" She made a shooing motion.

"Where does Ludendorff go to be alone?" Riker asked.

Dana shrugged. "He used to work in his laboratory all the time. Then the captain barred him from there."

"During that time," Riker said. "Did Ludendorff ever go off to be by himself?"

"No…" Dana said. "Not unless you mean the main incinerator unit. Ludendorff has taken up smoking. Most people find it offensive. He went to smoke his pipe there, but he only went a few times."

"Thank you, Doctor," Riker said. "That's exactly where I'll go."

"I'm coming with you," Dana said.

"It could be dangerous."

"Then tell the space marine," Dana said. "Have him suit up. If there's an android hidden in the incinerator unit—"

"That's a good idea," Riker said, interrupting. "Now you're thinking." He took out his communicator, clicking it on, trying to get in touch with Lieutenant Sims.

***

Riker watched the holoimage float ahead of them. The sergeant had his gun out. Behind him, Dana looked worried. Bringing up the rear, Sims clanked along in an enclosed exoskeleton armor-suit. The marine stood seven feet tall and cradled a heavy slug-thrower. It made Riker's weapon seem like a peashooter. Riker didn't holster his gun, though. That would go against every impulse of his long service.

The sergeant came up to Galyan just as the holoimage slid away into the incinerator unit, disappearing from view.

A soft hum indicated the incinerator was in operation. There was a strong smoky smell here. There were also soot marks smudged against the access hatch, as if someone had opened it during this voyage.

Riker moved back as Galyan slid out of the unit.

"Well?" Dana asked. "Did you spot an android?"

"Negative," Galyan said.

"So you're done here?" Sims asked through his helmet speaker.

Riker turned to the giant armor-suited marine. "If you'd stay just a little longer, sir…"

The helmet nodded as servomotors whined.

"Galyan," Riker said, "is the incinerator on?"

"It is," the AI said.

"Was there anything in there that didn't burn?"

"I did not think of that. Just a moment, please." The holoimage disappeared again. This time, the AI reappeared faster. "There is a glowing box. All the other refuse burns except for that."

"How big is the box?" Riker asked.

Galyan used his ropy arms to indicate a large box the size of a regular man's chest.

"What is in the box?" Riker asked.

"I could not tell."

Riker suddenly found it a little harder to breathe. Instinctively, he began holding his breath. A moment later, Dana collapsed. Riker pulled out a handheld jammer, switching it on. He backed away behind the space marine until he stood in the corridor.

"Open the hatch," he told the marine.

The armor-suit did not move.

Riker realized his mistake. He just used a special Intelligence jammer, an ultra-powerful unit. He'd found it in the captain's quarters. It must be jamming the exoskeleton's interior signals, the reason the lieutenant couldn't respond.

Coming to a swift decision, Riker set the jammer on the deck. He turned and limped-ran to an emergency wall-unit, pulling it open. There, he donned a rebreather. With the mask on, he returned to the incinerator area.

Galyan had frozen. That worried Riker. It was possible that Star Watch had included the jammer in the captain's equipment as an emergency protection against the Adok AI. After this, Galyan would be aware of the jammer's power. Well, the fat was in the fire now, so he might as well make the best of it.

Riker used another emergency switch, shutting down the incinerator. After the required wait, he opened the access hatch. With a special pair of gloves, he hauled the strange and very heavy box out of the incinerator. Once he had it in the open area, he closed the access hatch.

Lastly, Riker put the active jammer on the box to keep the thing inert. Then, he began to shove the box down the corridor. The jammer wouldn't work forever, but it should last him long enough to get the box into a special cell.

The sergeant had no idea what he had within the box, but he knew it was something important. He would bet it had something to do with androids, and he would bet it was the key to the professor's traitorous behavior a while back. Whatever was in the box, would that help him save the captain?

Riker didn't know. Thus, he would take things a step at a time. Before he did too much thinking, he needed to get the box to the special cell.

-36-

Valerie stared at Riker on the wall screen. The lieutenant sat on her bed, having just woken up from a short nap. Her hair was messy and her eyes looked puffy.

She's not getting enough sleep, Riker realized. *I might be the most well-rested person on the starship.*

"You're the senior Intelligence operative aboard the ship," Valerie said. "You run the investigation."

"Just a minute," Sims said angrily. The space marine no longer wore his armor-shell, but a tight one-piece that marines often wore inside exoskeleton suits. "The sergeant kept me locked in my suit for a half-hour. I nearly suffocated because my recyclers no longer functioned. I couldn't use the fail-safe exit, because it had frozen."

Valerie blinked at the beefy marine glaring at her. "What's your point?"

"He's too careless," the marine shouted, pointing at Riker. "He could have killed me."

"Sergeant…" Valerie said.

"I understand, sir," Riker muttered. "It was an oversight on my part."

"Oversight?" Sims shouted at him. "Nearly murdering me was an oversight?"

"Enough," Dana said, stepping before the wall screen. "I should be in charge of the investigation. The box contains…something highly technical. This is a scientific problem. That is my area of expertise, not that of a mere

Intelligence sergeant." The doctor turned to Riker. "I don't mean any disrespect by saying that."

"Of course not," Riker said. "How could I have thought otherwise?"

Dana frowned at him before turning back to Valerie. "It makes no sense putting a nontechnical sergeant in charge of such a touchy and possibly far-reaching…dilemma."

"It's my understanding that Riker reasoned out the box in the first place," Valerie said.

"I believe Galyan did that," Dana said.

Valerie turned to someone off-screen. "Is that true?" she asked.

"No," Galyan said. "The sergeant uncovered the mole. He did it through careful, espionage-related reasoning."

"We don't know this box is a mole," Dana said. "That's the point. We don't know what it is."

"Yet, it caused you to fall unconscious through emitting knockout gas into the area," Galyan said on the wall screen.

"I want to know how you plan to discipline the sergeant," Sims shouted at Valerie, his voice drowning out the others.

"Discipline?" Valerie asked.

"You heard me," Sims said in an ugly voice.

Valerie's features tightened. "You'd better take a civil tone with me, Lieutenant. As long as the captain is gone, I'm the commanding officer aboard the starship."

Sims glowered at her, and he seemed to be getting angrier.

"Would you like to punch me?" Riker asked quietly.

The young marine whirled around. A hard grin was stretched across his chiseled face. "You bet I would." He cocked his fist and punched for the sergeant's chin.

Riker caught the fist with his bionic hand. He slid back a bit, but he held the fist in place.

"You bastard," Sims said. He stepped closer and thrust a knee at Riker. The sergeant released the fist and deflected the knee. He didn't see the second fist coming, though. It clouted him on the side of the head. Riker sprawled onto the deck, with the side of his head throbbing.

"I'd kick your ass up through your teeth," Sims said, standing over him, "but you're too old to take it like a man. Don't ever ask me to do you a favor again."

Without waiting for a reply, not even glancing at the wall screen, Sims stalked off.

"Are you all right?" Dana asked, crouching down to help Riker.

The sergeant accepted the help. The side of his head still hurt. The young bull was strong. He should have tried a different tactic. The space marine was hotheaded and decidedly aggressive.

"How dare he hit you," Valerie said from the screen.

"No harm," Riker muttered. "I shouldn't have baited him."

"I'll throw him in the brig for that," Valerie said, getting angrier.

Riker cleared his throat, shaking his head. He stopped that because it hurt his head. His right eye was swelling. He'd have to put some ice on that.

"Lieutenant," the sergeant told Valerie, "we're under yellow alert."

"That's right," Valerie said, with her eyes glowing. "Hitting a fellow officer while on yellow alert—"

"I'm a sergeant," Riker said, "not an officer."

"Hitting a fellow crewmember during a yellow alert is a serious offense," Valerie said. "I can throw the book at him. I can—"

"How about forgetting it?" Riker said. "Lieutenant Sims got scared, being stuck in his armor-suit. He had pent-up rage. Now, he's released it. We're probably going to need him soon. The landing party is still on the planet. So putting him in the brig isn't going to help us."

Valerie appeared thoughtful.

"In any case," Dana said. "We have to decide what to do with the box. Riker pushed it into a special cell and turned on the needed devices. That is jamming the box. Unfortunately, it is also keeping us from examining it. I submit that this is a highly dangerous piece of enemy equipment. We don't know what it does—"

"I've changed my mind," Valerie said. "Sergeant, I'm putting Dana in charge of investigating the box."

Riker nodded. No one listened to a sergeant anyway, or not for long. He was used to it. "Do you mind if I tag along?" he asked Dana.

"What?" Dana asked. "No, I don't mind. You can join me. Just stay out of my way and do exactly as I say."

"Of course," Riker said.

"Good. Now, let's get to work."

***

Riker did almost nothing other than stand before a viewing screen. The screen was on the other side of the armored cell containing the box. Beside the box was Doctor Rich in a crinkly silver suit with a helmet.

The cell's jamming equipment still targeted the box. Dana put an old-fashioned stethoscope against one side. She kept it there for a time, finally removing it. She tapped on the box with a metal rod, listening. She took off a glove and carefully felt around the box.

Riker shifted from foot to foot as she investigated the item. He had to say that, so far, he wasn't impressed by her methods. Yes, they were methodical, but not well reasoned.

The sergeant gingerly touched the swollen mouse over his right eye. Sims had belted him good. The marine hadn't been afraid of his bionic arm, just more angered by it. Riker hadn't decided yet what he thought about that. He had no feelings for revenge. The young marine was an officer. He might mention the incident to the captain later—if the captain was still alive.

Galyan appeared beside him. The holoimage couldn't appear inside the cell with the jamming equipment on.

"Find anything?" Riker asked.

"Whatever is in the box used a wireless connection to turn on the gas in the incinerator lobby. You made the correct move turning on the jammer, cutting its connection. However, what I find—"

The holoimage stopped talking as Riker's left hand moved through it. The sergeant had meant to grab Galyan's shoulder to get the AI's attention, forgetting that Galyan was just a holographic projection.

On the wall screen, a slot opened on the box. Doctor Rich had quit moving. She seemed frozen in place.

"What is wrong with her?" Galyan asked.

"She took off her glove a bit ago," Riker said. "To my mind, that's an opening into her suit. I wonder if the thing in the box has released an invisible gas."

"Did you know the thing would attempt this?" Galyan asked. "Is that why you asked to tag along?"

"Something tricked the professor. Perhaps we're witnessing one of the thing's operating procedures. My guess is it's finally figured out how to move even with a jammer aimed at it."

"Do you think it has released a hypnotic gas?"

Riker snapped his fingers. "I hadn't thought it out that far, but that makes sense."

On the screen, another slot snicked open on the box. A thin metallic tentacle slid out. It cast about like a blind creature.

Riker watched in loathing. What was that?

"The jammer has blinded it," Galyan said. "But the jammer has not incapacitated it completely. Is that a hypodermic tip on the end of the tentacle?"

Riker shouted in outrage. The tentacle seemed to be searching for Dana. The sergeant ran to the hatch and attempted to open it, but it would not move.

"No," Riker shouted. He applied his bionic strength to the hatch, causing something to grind. With a wrenching sound, he pried the hatch open.

There was a sickly sweet odor in the chamber. Riker held his breath, stepped in and saw the tentacle touch the doctor. Gently like a serpent, the tentacle felt around, found her naked hand and slithered inward up the sleeve.

With revulsion making his heart beat faster, Riker drew his gun and fired. He missed the tentacle but dented the metal box three times.

The tentacle whipped out of Dana's sleeve, writhing back and forth. Another tentacle appeared. This one had a vicious-looking tip with a green solution dripping from it.

Riker ran into the room, fired until his pistol clicked empty and grabbed Dana Rich. He dragged her toward the hatch. She seemed inert, but stumbled after him.

The hairs rose on the back of Riker's neck. He sensed awful danger. He dropped the gun. It clunked onto the floor. With both hands, he grabbed the doctor, dragging her faster to the hatch.

Dana began to resist feebly.

Riker stumbled over the hatch, yanked Dana and dragged them both down the corridor. At that point, something exploded in the cell. Blast and fire roared from the hatch. It blew Riker off his feet. He kept hold of Dana, yanking her on top of him.

She began to vomit in her suit. Riker could feel her body trembling.

A klaxon blared somewhere nearby.

Using his bionic strength, Riker tore off her helmet. She vomited, gasped and vomited some more. Her skin had turned green.

"Emergency," Riker said in a gruff voice. "We have an emergency. Somebody, help me. Somebody—"

The sergeant stopped talking as Dana puked again. It was a horrible sound. He wanted to do more. He heard the sound of shouting people and the tramp of feet.

Then he closed his eyes as he fell unconscious.

-37-

Riker hadn't always hated hospitals. The operations giving him the bionic arm and eye had changed that. He'd been a mess that time, and the healing, learning to use his bionic parts, had been a tedious, even torturous experience. Every time he went for a checkup, he got the shakes. The few times he'd been hospitalized after the experience had left him cranky and upset.

Riker lay in a medical facility with a tube in his biological arm. He felt weak, with hardly the energy to open his eyes.

One time he forced his eyes open, and he'd found Galyan standing by his side. The AI had said hello. Riker had tried to respond. He was still trying when he found the space marine sitting in a chair beside him.

"What…happened?" Riker asked hoarsely.

The seated marine was staring at a tablet, his thumbs flicking controls. It looked like Sims played a video game.

The thick-faced lieutenant looked up, his eyes scrunched with concentration. When he realized Riker had spoken, the marine lowered the tablet to his lap. The scrunch left his face and a touch of sheepishness replaced it.

"Look Sergeant…I, ah, shouldn't have…"

Riker attempted to tell the boy it was all right. He found that his lips were too numb for him to speak properly.

"I ought not to have hit you," Sims said in a rehearsed manner. "I'm…ah, sorry I did. Look, I don't like your captain. That's no secret. He's a New Man. Anyone can tell that. And we can't trust New Men. They're murderous bastards. I thought maybe you were helping him, you know, take care of me on the sly."

Riker managed a bare nod.

"No hard feelings then?" Sims asked, sticking out a big hand.

Riker made a croaking noise. It was all he could manage.

"I guess that means yes. Good. I'll tell the lieutenant you're awake."

The marine left. Riker closed his eyes a second later…

***

The third time was the charm. Lieutenant Noonan peered down at him.

Riker felt even weaker than before as he stirred. A heady perfume wafted around him. He smiled wistfully.

"You look like death warmed over," Valerie said.

"Such poetry," Riker said in a whispery voice.

"I'll let you go back to sleep." She turned to go.

Riker summoned his reserves of energy. It surprised him that he still had any. "Wait," he said, more forcefully than before.

Valerie turned back.

"Help me sit up," Riker whispered.

Valerie grabbed an arm, and she hauled on him. He tried to help. Her strenuous effort told him he was weaker than he'd realized. Finally, as she panted and stepped away, Riker found himself almost dizzy sitting up so high.

"What happened to me?" he asked in a hoarse voice.

"Poison gas."

"And Dana?"

"She breathed more of it than you. She's on life-support. We still don't know. The chief medical officer says it's fifty-fifty she'll live."

"The thing in the box…?"

Valerie seemed to weigh him with her eyes.

"I have to know," Riker said.

"Andros Crank studied what was left of the box," Valerie said. "He recognized a few pieces. Those pieces had Builder patterns and one Swarm pattern. We don't know if androids put it there. It doesn't make sense that a Swarm creature did."

"Ludendorff put it there," Riker whispered.

"I was talking about who put a Swarm virus in the box. You mean who put the box in the ship. Maybe Ludendorff did, but when did he do it? That brings us to another question. When did the thing in the box get to him? Did the creature in the box want Ludendorff to come to this planet? Why did it want that? Could it be a Rull creature?"

Riker tried to follow her questions. It made his eyes cross.

"I'm sorry," Valerie said. "You're still recovering. I should let you rest."

"Listen," he said weakly. "I have to get up."

"No. You have to rest. You have to get better. Your body took a hit. We can take care of this."

Riker summoned more of his scanty reserves so he could keep speaking. "Dana is down. She's the best person after the professor to puzzle out the meaning of these clues. The captain is uncommonly perceptive regarding these mysteries, as well. But he's gone. So that just leaves me, the plodder. I have the right mindset to help the rest of you see."

Valerie put a hand on his regular arm. "We can't do anything at the moment. The landing party has disappeared. I don't believe the savages ate them, not with the captain leading the others. I doubt the landing party is hiding in any of the surface buildings. The most likely answer is that they're somewhere underground. Do I dare to order another landing party down to search the underworld? That seems like madness."

"So we do nothing?" Riker asked.

"What else can we do?"

A traitorous wave of weariness rolled over him, clouding his thinking. It would appear his reserves had run dry. He could hardly keep his eyes open now.

"Search…" Riker whispered.

"What was that?"

Riker was vaguely aware of her hands gripping the cot's railing. By the whitening of her knuckles, he knew the question was important. He strove to understand what she had said. He fought to keep his eyes open.

Then it seemed as if a thick fog rolled over his mind. His dreaming mind took over. Riker saw the captain running in place. He tried to shout. He had to tell the captain something critical. But no matter how hard Riker tried, he couldn't speak.

It left him feeling useless and old, and as if he'd let the young man down.

-38-

Maddox did not turn around as his cell door opened.

He'd been in the alien jail far too long, without any word about what had happened to the rest of the landing party or to *Victory*. He'd exercised strenuously, having done many handstand pushups and over a thousand deep-knee bends.

Maddox felt the breath of fresh air. He could feel the scrutiny of someone staring at him. He debated whirling around and attacking before he even saw who had come to get him. That might give him a moment of surprise.

He hated confinement, had gone to strenuous mental lengths to keep from going stir crazy.

"Captain Maddox," a Vendel said through a translator box. "You will come with us."

Maddox forced himself to move slowly, turning to regard Pascal le Mort, the sub-chief. The Vendel had a hand on his holstered weapon. The other hand beckoned.

Four other aliens stood behind Pascal. They aimed hand-weapons with over-large muzzles. Maddox assumed those were dart guns. Would they tranquilize him if he tried to escape?

"You're not taking any changes," Maddox said.

"You must come," Pascal said. "The Raja is waiting."

Maddox raised an eyebrow. "I'm too scruffy to meet the Raja just now."

"You must come," Pascal said. "Otherwise, we will drag you into the Raja's presence. You will look even…scruffier…after that."

Maddox straightened his uniform and dusted several spots. He picked pieces of lint from the cloth and flicked them away. Stepping forward, he put a boot onto a stool and rubbed a spot on the toe.

"That is sufficient," Pascal said. "Now, come."

Maddox heard exasperation in the alien's tone. It would seem it did not take much to excite Vendels. Was that normal, or did it just pertain to Pascal?

Maddox exited the cell, finding medical and scientific equipment out here. The four dart-carriers fell in step around him, with two in front and two behind. The sub-chief brought up the rear. That was a wise precaution. It meant he had to overcome three Vendels instead of just two to get his hands on a dart-thrower.

Maddox forced himself to relax as they entered a long corridor. He needed to soften their vigilance. He needed to show them that they had nothing to worry about from him. If they dropped their guard just enough…maybe he could get his hands on the Raja. That would be a powerful bargaining chip. Trade the Raja for the release of *Victory's* people. The trick after that would be getting back to the starship.

They took several turns, walked down a ramp and began to trudge through an exceptionally long corridor. It felt like a lonely place.

Maddox's neck began to tingle. Something wasn't right about this. He could not pinpoint it and say, this is why I feel this way. His gut instincts told him this was wrong.

"I say, have you fellows ever heard of the…*Builders*?" Maddox asked, sharply, as he imitated Major Stokes's manner of speech.

The alien guards ahead of him glanced back. Before the captain realized that the guards had no idea what his English word meant, the end of a pistol jabbed against the small of his back.

"You will not repeat that," Pascal hissed into his ear. "That is a forbidden word. Do you understand?"

"Quite," Maddox said.

The gun left his back. Pascal resumed his former position, and they continued the journey down the corridor.

The bad feeling didn't leave. Maddox decided on another ploy. He said over his shoulder, "We're not going to see the Raja."

"I did not give you leave to speak," Pascal said.

"Why are you taking the Raja's prisoner elsewhere?" Maddox asked. "Have I broken a religious taboo and you're taking me to the priests?"

When no answer was forthcoming, Maddox glanced over his shoulder. It surprised him to see a nervous Pascal.

"Do the priests plan to kill me for my sacrilege?" Maddox asked.

"You must cease talking," Pascal said.

"Are you a traitor to the Raja?"

A sheen of perspiration had appeared on Pascal's hairless face. He sucked his lips inward. It seemed like a nervous tic.

"I am unfamiliar with Vendel customs," Maddox said. "Thus, if I have inadvertently offended you, I apologize."

"No more speech," Pascal said. "Otherwise—"

Maddox stopped, threw back his head and laughed. He noticed two of the guards glancing at Pascal for an explanation. The sub-chief jabbered at them in the alien tongue.

This was his chance. Maddox kicked a Vendel in the shin. The alien howled. The other guards fired as expected. Maddox shifted with phenomenal speed. Darts hissed past. One struck a questioning guard in the chest. He went down in a heap. With stiffened fingers, Maddox jabbed another guard in the throat. The Vendel crumbled as he gurgled. Maddox moved like a whirlwind. The Vendels were just as tall as he was, but he was stronger and faster. He picked up a fallen dart gun and shot Pascal in the throat. Using the butt, he smashed the last alien's face, dropping him.

Maddox panted from the exertion. He picked up a loaded gun, ripped the collar and translator box from Pascal's throat and took out the earpiece. Loaded with equipment, Maddox sprinted down the long corridor, leaving the fallen behind.

This was a longshot. But he'd had to take what he could the moment the aliens became careless.

The problem proved to be the length of the corridor. It went on forever. Finally, Maddox walked briskly, sweating from his run. Glancing back, he found himself thoroughly alone. Was this an execution area? Had he blasphemed by talking about the Builders?

Finally, Maddox spied a door. He did not break into a sprint to reach it. He wanted to save some energy in case more aliens waited behind there.

When he reached the hatch, Maddox looked back the way he'd come. No one followed. He put his ear to the door. He could not hear anything. He tested the knob, finding that it would turn. Maddox's heart thudded. He put the translation collar around his throat, made an adjustment, hoping this was English to Vendel, and put the earpiece in his ear. Once ready, he turned the knob again. He tightened his stomach muscles, readied the dart gun and hurled the door open.

Three golden-skinned New Men whirled around in surprise. They wore silver suits and—

Maddox shot a New Man in the chest. He fired again. The alerted New Man shifted so the dart scraped the suit, but didn't penetrate. Maddox pulled the trigger a third time, and the dart gun jammed. The captain hurled the gun—

The tallest and noblest-looking New Man ducked the gun and lashed out, kicking the side of Maddox's hip. It was like a sledgehammer hitting, hurling the captain backward.

The tall New Man followed through the hatch into the corridor.

Maddox surged off the wall. He jabbed with his left. The New Man blocked with ease. The golden-skinned one was stronger and faster than Maddox, substantially so.

"You cannot win," the New Man said in a neutral voice.

Maddox backed up. The side of his hip hurt. His face hurt. The enemy had hit him several times already.

"I am your superior."

Maddox spit to the side.

The New Man grinned, but it hardly seemed genuine.

"Who are you?" Maddox asked.

"Dem Darius," the New Man said. "I know your name is Maddox."

"Do you know Strand?" the captain asked.

A conflicted look came over the New Man's features.

Maddox launched an attack, throwing punches and kicks. Darius blocked with what seemed like contemptuous ease. At last, Darius sighed.

"Do not say that name," the New Man said.

"Do you know Strand?" Maddox said.

A grimace twisted the New Man's face. He stepped closer and hit Maddox a stunning blow, knocking him to the floor.

Maddox lay there gasping.

Darius bent over him, whispering, "Yes, I know that one. Soon, you will, too. Come. It is time."

Darius hauled Maddox to his feet as he twisted one of the captain's arms around behind him. He force-marched Maddox through the door to the other conscious New Man. The third golden-skinned individual was dead. It hadn't been a trank but a death-dealing dart.

"Where are we going?" Maddox hissed.

Darius wrenched the captain's arm higher behind his back. Then he reached for the captain's other arm and had the second New Man manacle Maddox's wrists. "No more questions. You will learn soon enough, to your eternal sorrow."

-39-

Maddox stumbled as Darius shoved him.

The three of them had moved into deeper tunnels, with condensation dripping from a low ceiling. They had to crouch as they tried to keep running, and the only illumination came from the second New Man's flashlight. Foul-smelling water pooled everywhere and worse smelling patches of fungus made each of them watch their step.

Maddox's wrists were numb where Darius had secured them together behind his back. His stretched shoulders ached and he panted from the endless running.

Before leaving the kidnapping location, Darius had drawn an energy weapon and burned the corpse thoroughly. Then they had begun the trek into the depths.

Maddox's chest heaved and sweat dripped from his chin.

"You are weak," Darius said. "You tire too easily."

Maddox said nothing. This was a bitter lesson in the superiority of the New Men. He'd come to believe himself their equal in many categories. That belief had suffered several shocks today, or tonight.

How long have I been a prisoner? And how much conditioning did I lose?

"Left," Darius said.

Maddox turned left, entering an even narrower and lower tunnel. It was dark and smelly—

Maddox halted, and he backed up.

"Enough," Darius said, his hand halting the captain's retreat. "You must summon what courage you possess. It is only darkness and bad smells."

Maddox tried to calculate. He'd heard a soft grunt ahead of him. That indicated something living. Could he escape from Darius? He needed an edge to do so. If he failed to escape, he would eventually end up on Strand's star cruiser. And the Methuselah Man would no doubt operate on his brain.

Maddox inhaled, almost gagged on the stench, and then lowered his head and forced himself to move into the darkness. He heard the grunt again. It was an angry sound.

"Did you hear that?" the second New Man asked Darius.

Maddox ran into the darkness, with his senses straining. It widened in here like a cave. He tried to—Maddox threw himself onto his chest, sliding on the floor as something heavy swished overhead.

A beam of light stabbed into the darkness. From the fungus-strewn floor, Maddox arched his neck, looking up. The light shone upon a huge and deformed Vendel cannibal. The thing had to stand ten feet tall—if it could stand all the way. It was grossly fat, and might weigh one thousand pounds or more.

Darius shouted, running forward, unlimbering his blaster. He fired. A gout of seething energy burned into the savage's shoulder.

The mutated Vendel roared with hurt, the painful sound reverberating in the underground grotto. The savage roared once more, and it lurched at Darius.

The New Man fired another gout, this one full in the thing's face. The cannibal stumbled backward, crashing into boxes and piled junk. A horrible stink rose from the savage. It sat up, its face a ruin. One more time, Darius fired. The energy consumed much of the upper bulk, with smoke roiling from the fat.

Maddox couldn't breathe. The stench was too great. Iron fingers dug into his arms, hauling him upright from the floor.

"You should have warned us," Darius said.

The other New Man grabbed Maddox's free arm. Together, the golden-skinned supermen lifted the captain off his feet. The flashlight showed an open area. The New Men sprinted, carrying Maddox between them. Each step jolted his aching shoulders a little more. It was humiliating, and yet another nail in his belief that he could directly compete against the New Men on an evening footing.

Finally, the two set him down. Darius opened the bonds securing his wrists. Dully, Maddox's arms swung down to his sides. He steeled his face, determined that he would not betray the pain in his shoulders as the three of them hurried into a cleaner corridor. This one led steeply downward.

Soon, his wrists began to throb as the feelings returned. He willed away the pain. It hardly helped, though. From time to time, Darius or the other New Man shoved him, making him stumble faster.

Maddox no longer plotted. He used all his resources to keep up with the supermen. He wasn't used to being the slowest. He was always the fastest, the best at whatever he did. The thought remorselessly turned his thinking to his birth. If his mother hadn't escaped from the New Men facility, he would have been born with golden skin. The scientists would have injected his fetus with the New Men treatments.

Maddox ground his teeth together. These two might be stronger and faster, but he would fight against them to the end.

Maybe it was a proud and idle boast. But the captain clung to the thought just the same. He would defeat these two. He would not let them defeat him. Were they *di-far?* The race did not always go to the fastest, or the fight to the strongest.

Even so, Maddox did not see what he could do in order to escape from them.

Later, with his senses still reeling, Maddox realized that Pascal le Mort had been bringing him to Darius. Did that mean Strand had someone in the Raja's court?

Yes.

It meant some Vendels were corrupt, Pascal, for instance. That meant one could bribe or corrupt other Vendels. That was a good thing to know.

They exited a passage and entered a vast subterranean world. Maddox could sense the greater spatial volume although he could not see it. The sounds were different and the air stirred. The other New Man shined a path through towering funguses. Strange rustling sounds came from deeper in the reef-mash—that's what Pascal had called the fungus before.

Because they walked instead of sprinted, Maddox regained a modicum of energy. It was enough that he began cataloging what he saw. The tall fungus growths loomed above him on strange stalks, almost like prehistoric ferns.

Had Darius discovered the ancient vaults down here? Did Strand know about and possess the long-distance Builder scanner. Did Strand know Starship *Victory* was coming to the planet? Surely, Ludendorff hadn't told the other Methuselah Man. But if Ludendorff hadn't, who had?

"There," Darius said.

The flashlight focused on a large metal object. It looked like a landed strikefighter, the smallest of space-going craft. How could it have gotten down here? Maddox didn't understand.

Rough, strong hands gripped him. Darius once again wrenched an arm behind the captain's back. Manacles appeared, were snapped onto that wrist first and then onto the other, securing him once more.

"Climb," Darius said, pushing Maddox against the craft.

Maddox saw sunken steps built into the strikefighter. He put the toe of his right boot into one. As he climbed, with no way to steady himself, Darius pushed his back, keeping him from falling backward.

A whine caused him to look up. An upper canopy rose.

It was difficult, but Maddox climbed the rungs and slid his stomach over an upper edge, falling into a large cockpit.

This was a two-seated strikefighter, a Throne World version.

Maddox panted on the floor as Darius and the other climbed in. The second New Man slid into the front seat. Darius slid into the navigator's seat.

The canopy whined again as it lowered into place. The strikefighter purred with power. Heated, good-smelling air gushed into the small confines. Maddox shivered. He hadn't realized until this moment how revolting the underground trek had been. This was a diseased world. The toxins that had mutated the Vendels seemed to have seeped down here as well.

"Now what happens?" Maddox asked.

Darius used the sole of a boot to tap the top of Maddox's head. "You are my prisoner. Soon, you will belong to Strand. I would not give you such a fate. I'd rather kill you cleanly, giving you a battle death. But…that is the way of the universe. We do not all get what we want."

Maddox considered that as the other New Man went through a preflight checklist. Finally, the strikefighter hummed. Soon thereafter, it lurched off the subterranean floor.

Maddox would have liked to sit up and see what transpired. Would the pilot fly through the subterranean realm? Could the strikefighter zip past Vendel anti-aircraft defenses?

"The Raja's people are alert to your treachery," Maddox said. "As soon as they spot your craft—"

Darius made a raspy sound. It took Maddox a second to realize the New Man had laughed.

"Don't you understand?" Darius asked. "We're heading straight to space, straight to the star cruiser."

Maddox scowled. He didn't understand. He… "Is this a jumpfighter?"

"We call it a fold-fighter," Darius said. "Are you ready?" he asked the pilot.

"Give me thirty seconds," the pilot said.

Maddox closed gritty eyes. His heart thudded with something akin to fear. This craft could fold space. That meant it would transfer from here, deep underground, to somewhere in near orbit. It could possibly fold or jump even farther. It was a clever idea, calling for precise and utterly confident fold-piloting.

Leave it to the New Men to execute such a plan.

Maddox wished he had a kill-pill to swallow. The idea of Strand planting control-fibers into his brain—

The fighter whined louder, building up for the fold.

-40-

Driving Force Galyan fretted incessantly. The holoimage paced across an imitation of his old bridge. Frozen images of his ancient Adok companions held their poses.

Six thousand years ago, give or take, he had battled a Swarm fleet in the Adok Home System. The horrible insects had destroyed the defensive armada and annihilated Galyan's world. That had been the day of his transformation, his deification. He had failed his world, failed his friends and failed his mate.

He did not want to fail again.

This is where he went when he did not interact with the humans. It was not a real place like *Victory's* bridge, but deep in the artificial intelligence Adok-Builder program. Galyan found solace here. He regrouped. He pondered and thought about the old days.

If he had won the Adok-Swarm Battle, he would be long dead. He would not be thinking these thoughts. And yet, was he truly Galyan? He did not possess a spirit, did he? He had the Driving Force's engrams, but he was a Builder AI program.

The holoimage turned to one of the frozen Adoks. "Who am I really?" he asked the image.

As Galyan waited for an answer, a blip appeared on the main bridge screen. He idly looked up at it.

He had rerouted some of the AI program so he saw real data on the imaginary bridge screen. It was too bad his old frozen companions could not see these things. He could no longer recall their former names, and had given them new ones: Valerie, Keith, Riker—

"No, no, that is not right," Galyan said. "Why did I name them—?"

The blip on the screen caught his attention again.

In the real world, Galyan had set up a system that watched the entire planet. He'd begged Valerie, and she had permitted him to launch three probes. The probes were at precisely the right locations around the planet so that he had a full view of everything.

He'd already informed Valerie of the battered Juggernaut. He'd also found a third such craft. This one seemed intact, and it waited. Maybe as they waited for the captain to appear, they should hunt down the Juggernauts and destroy them.

Galyan slid toward the main screen. His ghostly fingers manipulated the air as he ran an analysis of the blip.

This was odd. The blip had not been there several seconds ago. Galyan ran a lightning-fast diagnostic. There was nothing wrong with his instruments or the probes. The blip had just appeared.

That meant it had jumped into position. Yet, the blip's mass was wrong. It was the size of a strikefighter—

"Correction," Galyan said. "It is the size of a *jump*fighter."

The little AI stared with shock. In an instant, he disappeared from the imaginary bridge and reappeared on *Victory's* real bridge.

"Valerie," Galyan said, "I have discovered an enemy fold-fighter. Its specifications are nearly identical to a Throne World fold-fighter that Admiral Fletcher's Grand Fleet faced."

"Show me," Valerie snapped.

Galyan put the blip on the main screen, superimposed against an image of Pandora II.

"The object is on the other side of the planet," Valerie said.

"Yes."

"Can you tell me what's inside the fighter?"

"I detect three entities. They appear to be New Men." Galyan spun around. "Valerie, I believe one of the entities is Captain Maddox."

Valerie stared at him open-mouthed.

"This is interesting," Galyan said. "It implies that the New Men are in the star system. Since we have seen no evidence of such a ship, that implies a cloaked vessel. The likeliest probability, given the various ramifications, is that Methuselah Man Strand has come in his cloaked star cruiser to investigate the derelict planet."

"Ramifications?" Valerie said. "Are you referring to the destroyed box?"

"That and other factors," Galyan said. "Would you like me to list them in descending order of importance?"

"No," Valerie said. "I think you're right. One thing seems off, though. The fold-fighter is hardly moving."

"I suspect it is building up energy for another fold. Notice the various system planets. I suspect the cloaked star cruiser is behind Pandora III in relation to us. The vessel might also be hidden behind one of Pandora III's moons."

"Can the jumpfighter fold that far?" Valerie asked.

"Given the specifications of previous enemy fold-fighters—no."

"So if we leave the craft alone," Valerie said, "we'll probably find out if and where the cloaked star cruiser is hidden."

"That is logical. However, are you willing to throw away the captain's life to find out?"

Valerie didn't hesitate. "I am not."

"You are being emotional about this," Galyan said.

"I don't care. We're not sacrificing each other."

"But the greater good—" Galyan stopped speaking as Lieutenant Noonan stared at him fixedly.

"Are *you* willing to sacrifice the captain to find the hidden enemy vessel?" Valerie asked.

"Of course not," Galyan said. "Everyone knows I am beholden to the captain. I could never do such a thing. But that is me. I am not the acting commander of the Patrol's best starship. I am not the one who must decide humanity's future. Captain Maddox saved my life. I will always side with him over others, including the entirety of the human race. If you—"

"Galyan," Valerie said.

"Yes?"

"Shut up for a moment. Let me think."

"Yes, Valerie. I will shut up, as you say."

"Then stop talking."

"Oh. Yes." With an effort of will, Galyan closed his holoimage mouth. Then he waited to see what Valerie would do next.

***

Maddox lay on the floor of the fold-fighter's cockpit, waiting for the other two to overcome their jump sickness. It surprised him the New Men hadn't stolen or invented the needed injections.

Maddox stared up through the canopy, seeing Sind above them. The planet looked silvery-healthy from up here. Would this be his last sight as a free-thinking person? Maybe he should attack Darius and get it over with. The New Man aimed a weapon at him, but Darius did not hold the gun with authority.

The fold-fighter's engine had been knocking. It began to smooth out now, building up energy for the next fold.

A new idea blossomed in Maddox. Why hadn't he thought of it before?

"I have a question," Maddox said.

"No," Darius slurred.

"Strand wants me as a prisoner."

Darius seemed to strain to focus on Maddox. A tight smile slid into place. "Not his prisoner," the New Man said. "You will become his slave. You will tell him everything you know. His knowledge and thus his power will yet increase."

"Do you love Strand?"

"Love?" Darius asked, his mouth twisting with distaste. "I hate him. He is a monster."

"Yet you serve him."

"I must. It is his will."

"What is your will?" Maddox asked.

Darius's mouth twisted once again. "I lack a will."

"That isn't true. You fought through the underworld. You do have a will."

"In small matters, I do," Darius said, "not in large."

"Would you like to be free?"

Darius stared at Maddox, his eyes gleaming.

"You are struggling to speak," Maddox said.

Darius raised the gun as if to fire. The gun-hand trembled. Slowly, the New Man lowered the weapon, although he kept it ready.

"You are fortunate Strand guides my will," Darius said. "My desire is to kill you."

"Because I ask painful questions?"

For just a moment, Darius closed his eyes. When he opened them, they blazed with rage.

Maddox shuddered at the ferocity of Darius's emotions.

The New Man trembled as he fought to raise the gun again. "I would kill you," Darius said tightly. "I would kill you to save you and because I hate you." Darius made an inarticulate howl.

"The fighter will be ready to fold in thirty seconds," the pilot said.

Darius nodded miserably.

Then a grim shadow fell upon them. Maddox looked up, and at first, he did not understand. Something blocked the planet's reflected light. His eyes widened in understanding. That was Starship *Victory*. The vessel had appeared—it had jumped beside the fold-fighter.

The small craft lurched.

"What is occurring?" Darius said.

"The foreign vessel—we are caught in a tractor beam," the pilot said.

Darius craned his head, looking up at the underbelly of *Victory.* He peered at Maddox, and he raised the gun one more time.

"That is your starship," the New Man said.

"Yes," Maddox said.

"It has caught us in a tractor beam."

Maddox nodded.

"I can fold out of danger," the pilot said. "We have a seventy percent chance of destruction, but that gives us a thirty percent chance of success."

"I cannot let you regain your freedom," Darius told Maddox.

"My crew will kill you if you harm me," Maddox said.

Darius smiled evilly. "Good. I am weary of my slave life."

"We can operate on you and free you from Strand's control," Maddox said.

"No," Darius said. "I am jury-rigged. Such an operation would kill me."

"Ludendorff could do it."

"He is the Raja's special prisoner."

"Then help me free Ludendorff," Maddox said.

"I am Strand's slave. I cannot do as you suggest."

"Tell him to stop speaking," the pilot said. "Strand will discipline you for letting him speak as long as he has."

Darius nodded. It appeared he knew that. "You will not escape," he told Maddox.

The fold-fighter lurched again, drawing closer to *Victory's* opening hangar-bay doors.

"I am just about ready to fold," the pilot said.

Darius closed his eyes.

Maddox sat up.

The eyes snapped open. Darius aimed the blaster at the captain's forehead and began to apply pressure to the trigger.

"Resist Strand's will," Maddox said. "You are a New Man. You are superior to others."

"That is true," Darius whispered, with tiny dots of perspiration on his lower lip.

"You are no man's slave."

"Hit him," the pilot said. "Otherwise, I will inform Strand that you planned rebellion. The Master will pain you for many days."

"Strand will kill you," Maddox told Darius. "To save yourself, you must continue to resist your subjugation."

The pilot snarled, looking around at Maddox. "I will tell Strand what you said. First, we will fold out of danger."

"No," Darius said in a half-strangled voice. He redirected the blaster and fired, burning through the pilot's chair.

The pilot grunted and fell forward, although he was far from dead. He reached for the fight panel.

Maddox hurled himself at the pilot. With his body, the captain shoved the New Man, trying to keep him from pressing the fold button.

Darius lurched to his feet, peering over the piloting chair. He brought up the blaster so the barrel touched the captain's head.

Maddox froze.

The blaster kept moving, however. Hot energy poured against the pilot's head, killing the New Man.

Maddox fell back onto the floor as the stink wafted throughout the cockpit.

A second later, the blaster barrel pressed against the captain's temple.

"I am Strand's loyal soldier," Darius said in a robotic-sounding voice. "I cannot betray him. I cannot allow you to live."

Maddox stared into the New Man's bloodshot eyes. "I understand. You need me as a hostage, though. You can possibly take over Starship *Victory*. As long as you have me hostage, the others must obey you. This will be your greatest coup. Strand will love you for doing this."

Darius cocked his head to one side.

"You need me alive as a hostage," Maddox said. "Otherwise, my crew will kill you on sight."

"You are attempting to trick me."

"I want to live," Maddox said. "But that's the point. I will do anything to stay alive."

"Will you help me take control of your starship?" Darius asked.

"Yes. I would even do that."

"You would betray your trust?" Darius asked.

Maddox nodded.

"You are a vile creature," Darius said. "I would never betray the Throne World as you do your comrades."

Maddox did not point out that Darius had already betrayed the Throne World.

"This is difficult to do," Darius said, as if talking to himself. "I have murdered Sol Stein. He used to be my flagship's first mate."

"Sol would have murdered us by folding," Maddox said. "This way is glorious. The other way was selfishness."

"You are persuasive," Darius said. "Yes. I am superior to you. I am superior to your crew. While the odds are low, it is possible I can capture your ship. You will make an excellent hostage."

Maddox didn't believe Darius truly believed those things. He believed the New Man had partly overcome Strand's obedience fibers. That showed the New Man had a remarkably strong will. Darius said these things like a man tempted to do something wrong that he really wanted to do. Darius had a thirst for freedom as Keith Maker used to have a thirst for whiskey. Darius lied to himself. Maddox was merely helping him with the interior lying.

"Tell me truthfully," Darius said. "Do you fear death?"

"Yes," Maddox lied, just as he had been lying about betraying his crew.

Darius struggled to speak once more. Instead, he reached out, grabbed Maddox by the hair and dragged him closer. He shoved the blaster against Maddox's head.

"One wrong move on anyone's part and you die," the New Man hissed. "I am the master here. I make the rules."

Maddox didn't feel a need to speak anymore. The fold-fighter slid past *Victory's* hangar-bay doors. He'd come home. Now, could he get away from Darius?

-41-

Valerie stood in the hangar bay, watching the enemy fold-fighter lower onto the deck.

The great hangar-bay doors had closed. A normal atmosphere had returned. Standing several meters before her were Lieutenant Sims and three of his space marines. They all wore exoskeleton armor and cradled squat rifles. Galyan waited beside her.

With several small clangs, the fold-fighter settled onto the deck. Magnetic clamps made *whomping* noises. Several seconds later, the canopy rose. Captain Maddox popped into view.

Valerie's breath expelled. Galyan had been right. The New Men had captured the captain. She'd heard the horror stories about Strand's mind-scrubbed crew. Would that have been the captain's fate?

Behind Maddox, a noble-looking New Man appeared. He held a strange-looking gun against the captain's head.

"Put down your weapons," the New Man shouted. He had a strong, authoritative and arrogant voice.

"Do as he says," Maddox shouted.

"Do it," Valerie told the marines.

Lieutenant Sims turned his armored head toward her.

Valerie nodded as if confirming her own order.

It took Sims a second. Maybe the marine struggled with the command. Finally, Sims racked his rifle onto his exoskeleton back. The weapon was more like a mobile autocannon. The other marines did likewise with their squat rifles.

"Now get onto the floor," the New Man shouted. "You must all lie on your bellies and power down your armor."

"Do as he says," Valerie said.

This time, Lieutenant Sims did not turn to look at her. He remained as he was, with his faceplate aimed at the New Man.

"Did you hear me?" Valerie asked Sims.

Still facing forward, Sims nodded his armored head.

"Then lie on your belly and power down your armor," Valerie said.

"No," Sims said. "None of us will do that. The New Man will walk up and kill us if we do. I will not die like a meek dog just because you give me a cowardly order."

"You will obey my orders," Valerie said. "I am the commanding officer."

Sims hesitated. Finally, he laughed scornfully. "I will not disarm and let an enemy butcher us one by one."

"He'll kill the captain if you don't do as he says."

"One New Man will kill another New Man," Sims said. "What do I care about that? Let them butcher each other to their heart's delight."

The golden-skinned New Man removed the barrel from Maddox's head and fired at Sims. The energy beam splashed against the exoskeleton armor, attempting to burn through.

Lieutenant Sims crouched and leaped, causing the servomotors to whine with power. Like a mechanical grasshopper, the armor-suit vaulted airborne. Sims yanked his autocannon free and fired a burst against the fold-fighter. Heavy bullets punched holes in the craft through the rear thruster.

Other autocannon shells did likewise, as the three marines followed the lieutenant's example.

Maddox rammed an elbow against the New Man's chest, throwing him off balance. The captain leaped with his hands still cuffed behind his back. He fell out of the fold-fighter headfirst. With a gymnastic twist, Maddox turned himself, thudding onto the deck with his back and hands instead of his head.

The golden-skinned soldier glanced down at Maddox. To Valerie, he seemed ready to burn the captain. Instead, the New Man raised the blaster at Sims, thought better of it, and vaulted the other way out of the fold-fighter.

In his exoskeleton suit, Sims slammed against the fold-fighter. He crashed against the cockpit area, rolled across it and fell onto the other side of the craft.

The three other marines began clanking to the lieutenant's assistance.

Valerie ran after them. She could see under the Throne World fighter. Sims was on his back. The New Man stepped up and aimed the blaster at the faceplate.

"Stop," the New Man said, "or I'll kill him."

"Don't worry about me," Sims shouted from his back. "Kill the New Man!"

The blaster beam melted the lieutenant's helmet speaker. Then, the New Man repeated his threat.

Valerie slid to a halt. The three marines also stopped, with their rifles aimed at the New Man.

Slowly, the handcuffed Maddox twisted around onto his stomach. He climbed to his feet and hid behind a landing strut, sheltered from the New Man. He peered around the strut to take in the scene.

The New Man noticed. "You lied to me, Captain. I congratulate you on your cunning. You are almost a worthy opponent. Without this one's stubbornness, I could have slain more of you. You have diminished me."

"Lower the blaster," Maddox said.

"I cannot," the New Man said. "Strand has forbidden me to surrender to anyone. Your ploy is a failure. I do not mean your escape. That you have achieved. But you have obviously hoped to turn me. I cannot allow that."

"Fight your conditioning," Maddox said. "Overcome your—"

From his armored back, Lieutenant Karl Sims reached for the New Man. The blaster emitted a gush of energy, burning against the faceplate.

Marine autocannons clacked, chambering rounds.

"No!" Maddox shouted at the three marines. "Physically subdue the New Man. We need him. Don't kill him."

Two of the space marines obeyed orders, even as they rushed the New Man. The third marine opened fire.

The New Man quit burning the faceplate. Valerie didn't know if the beam had burned all the way through or not. It must not have, because Sims lurched upright. Even as Sims did that, the New Man ducked, sprawling onto the deck behind the space-marine armor.

Several autocannon shells flew over the pair. The next two shells hammered exoskeleton armor. The kinetic energy threw Sims off balance, and he missed his grab against the slippery New Man.

The golden-skinned one beamed at Maddox. The captain stood sideways as the beam washed against the landing strut.

The third marine finally stopped firing. The other two still charged the New Man. He twisted aside from Sims, rolled away, leaped to his feet and sprinted for the fold-fighter. The New Man seemed to have one goal: to kill Captain Maddox.

"Fire!" Valerie shouted at the marines. "Kill the New Man."

"No," Maddox said.

"Before I die, you die," the New Man said.

The armored marines seemed like clumsy fools compared to the New Man. Their armor could take several seconds of blaster fire, so that helped. Sims's faceplate looked fused and half-melted.

Sims must be using radar to see where he's running, thought Valerie.

The New Man reached the fold-fighter, jumped around the landing strut—

Galyan shouted a war cry as he appeared before the New Man, swinging his holographic arms at the superman. A torrent of energy beamed through Galyan. The New Man frowned, as the AI was unharmed.

That gave Maddox an opening. He twisted around the landing strut and swept a leg at the superman's legs. It knocked the New Man off his feet. With supreme athletic grace, the golden-skinned soldier twisted as he fell, caught himself with one hand and turned his torso. He brought up the blaster.

Maddox kicked, connecting with the hand. It should have sent the blaster flying. The New Man held on, but it knocked the blaster off target. More energy beamed, flashing through the hangar bay like lightning.

Maddox danced back, made to kick again—

Sims reached the New Man. A gout of energy poured against the lieutenant. The marine absorbed the shot and hit the blaster, knocking it onto the deck so it went sliding. The New Man tried to slither away.

Sims clamped exoskeleton-powered gloves onto one wrist and then another. The marine raised the New Man and slammed him against the deck once, twice—

"Stop!" Maddox shouted. "We need to interrogate him."

Sims's armored helmet whirred. He looked at the captain. He looked at the limp New Man in his armored grasp. Not even the superman could take powered-armored blows for long. Sims looked at the captain again, raised the New Man in the air—

The power-gloved hands opened, dropping the limp New Man onto the deck. With heavy armored clanks, Sims headed for the exit.

"Come here," Maddox told the other three marines.

Soon, they secured the New Man. One held the superman's wrists. The other two each gripped an ankle, stretching Darius between them.

"Welcome back, sir," Valerie said.

Maddox turned around, blinking at her. He seemed preoccupied, maybe even shaken.

That bothered Valerie. "It's good to see you," she added. She wanted the old Maddox back, the utterly confident one. "We'll get those cuffs off you right away."

Maddox nodded before regarding the New Man. "Yes," he said softly. "We have a lot to do."

-42-

Maddox showered, needle-hot water striking his flesh. He washed the filth of the planetary toxins from himself, but he couldn't wash off the feeling of inferiority.

Dem Darius—

"No," Maddox whispered to himself.

That was the wrong way to view this. He would control his thoughts. He would mold his thinking. One did that through mindset. He could concentrate on negativity or he could concentrate on positivity.

The Vendels had captured him. He had escaped. He'd killed a New Man and thrown doubt into another. That had caused Darius to shoot the fold-fighter's pilot. And that had given his people an opportunity to capture the craft. He had helped defeat a physically superior opponent. He was free again, in charge of his fate, with a prisoner belonging to the infamous Strand.

Maddox turned off the water and exited the stall. He had a hard grin. Life wasn't about failures, but about opportunities. He was playing the game again as a free agent. Maybe the Raja had Meta, Keith and Ludendorff. That just meant he had to free them, and he had to kill or capture Strand.

As he toweled off, Maddox mentally dialed up his determination. He needed rest, but he lacked time for that just now. He would not rely on drugs in order to keep going. He would…

On second thought, he would sleep for a half hour. He needed to recharge just a little. Determination was good. Using good judgment was better.

"Galyan," the captain said.

The holoimage appeared in the room.

"You did well out there in the hangar bay," Maddox said.

"Thank you," Galyan said.

"I'm going to close my eyes. Come back in thirty minutes and wake me. Tell Valerie I'm holding a council of war in thirty-five minutes."

"Yes, sir," Galyan said. "What about Lieutenant Sims?"

"I ordered him confined to quarters."

"He is," Galyan said. "But he's demanding a court martial hearing."

Maddox stared at the holoimage. "I see. The young marine has passion. I will have to factor that into my calculations. But first, I will close my eyes for thirty minutes. Now, go. Do as I've said."

"Yes, Captain," Galyan said, saluting and disappearing.

Maddox nodded to himself. Then, he headed for his cot.

***

The council of war came to order with Maddox at the head of the conference table. Valerie and Andros Crank sat at the table. Galyan stood, and that was it.

Maddox knew he needed to focus. He kept worrying about Meta. Was she alive? Did her captors treat her properly? How long…

Valerie stirred, breaking into the captain's thoughts.

Maddox put his concerns about Meta into a mental drawer, as it were and shut it. He would worry about her later. Right now, he had a job to do.

Maddox drummed his fingers on the table, realizing belatedly that he had confined his marine commander to quarters. "Galyan, give me a holo-screen to his quarters."

In front of Maddox appeared a holoimage screen. A moment later, a fierce-eyed Lieutenant Sims peered at him while sitting on the cot in his quarters.

"I demand a court martial," Sims blurted.

Maddox said nothing, merely watched the young marine lieutenant.

"Sir," Sims finally muttered.

Maddox still said nothing.

Sims seemed perplexed, then angry as he stared at Maddox and finally he scowled, glancing away.

"You hold the cards, New Man," Sims said in a surly tone.

"I will confine you to the brig if you continue this insubordination."

Sims's head snapped up. "Do you think I care?"

"Indeed I do."

Sims's eyes became hot.

Maddox watched the transformation. "I see. You hate me. That changes the complexion of the situation. Do you hate me enough to murder me?"

"I'm a Star Watch marine," Sims said through gritted teeth. "As long as you—"

"Careful," Maddox said. "I'm recording your words. Therefore, you should think before you speak. While hotheaded passion can help you on the battlefield, here it lacks the same aid."

Sims nodded tightly.

"In the hangar bay less than an hour ago, you disobeyed your commander's direct order," Maddox said. "Yet, it resulted in the New Man's capture. You did not murder Darius, but wrestled him into submission. Given these facts, I am unsure what to do with you."

"I know how you feel," Sims muttered. "I've always been unsure what to do with you...*sir*."

"You pose a quandary, Lieutenant. I need spirited fighters, especially those who aren't afraid to challenge New Men. I cannot use those who fail to follow orders, though."

Sims glowered at him.

"What do you have to say to Lieutenant Noonan?" Maddox asked.

"I know where you're going with this. She gave us a stupid order—"

"Hold," Maddox said, sternly. "Consider what you would do to her if your roles were reversed."

Sims blinked several times. The thought seemed to have never occurred to him. He scratched his jaw, and his demeanor shifted subtly.

"What would you say to her?" Maddox asked.

"I'd apologize."

"Then do so," Maddox said, as Galyan, who had been watching his actions, turned the holo-screen to face Valerie.

Sims cleared his throat. "I'm…uh, sorry, Lieutenant. I didn't mean any disrespect. You probably don't know. New Men butchered my father, brothers, uncles and cousins on Tatum III. New Men stole my mother, sister and cousins, taking them as breeding stock. I hate New Men. When I see their golden skin, all I can think about is taking out my knife and skinning them alive."

Valerie shuddered at the man's quiet ferocity.

"I'm a marine, though," Sims said. "I know how to obey orders. I just…the bastard would have killed us. I had to attack him, not meekly surrender and get us all killed."

"Do you accept his apology?" Maddox asked Valerie.

By the look on her face, she didn't want to accept. But after thinking about it, she said, "I do, sir."

"Then tell him," Maddox said.

Valerie coughed to clear her throat. "I accept your apology, Lieutenant."

"Thank you," Sims said, almost sounding contrite.

Maddox used his right index finger to turn the holo-screen back to him.

"I am not a New Man," he told Sims. "In case you haven't noticed, my skin is white. It isn't golden. The New Men captured and impregnated my mother. She escaped their breeding facility, dying later, soon after I was born. I never knew her. You may have family in a similar situation as my mother was."

Shock washed over the marine's features.

"Does that clarify the situation?" Maddox asked.

"Yes, sir," Sims said, with a new note in his voice. "That…changes things considerably."

Maddox nodded. Obedience was a military necessity. Willing warriors with spirit were worth even more. Sims was more than just a marine. He was a fighter willing and able to tackle New Men, provided he wore exoskeleton armor. Maddox could use the lieutenant, and use that passion, the hatred, even, if Sims could learn to harness his spirit. It was the commander's responsibility to use what assets he possessed.

"I want you in the conference chamber in five minutes," Maddox said.

"Sir?" Sims asked.

"You heard me, Lieutenant. Now, get here on the double."

Sims shot to his feet and saluted. "Yes, *sir*," he said.

Maddox told Galyan to remove the holo-screen.

As it vanished, Valerie said, "Just for the record, sir…"

He studied her.

"Lieutenant Sims disobeyed a direct order. Letting him return to active duty like this…"

"Your disagreement with my decision is noted and will be logged," Maddox said. "I appreciate your concern and honesty. But I need fighters more, as winning is what counts, not following the rules to the letter."

Valerie did not respond, but she managed a faint nod.

***

Once Sims arrived, Valerie told Maddox everything that had transpired in his absence. Then he told them what he'd discovered on the planet. For a time after that, each of them sat quietly, thinking.

"It appears Ludendorff has been compromised," Maddox said. "I'd wager the box is either an android device or something from Strand. We cannot discount the Builders either. From what we know about the Builders, most of them have departed this area of the galaxy. It could be a rogue Builder—"

"What about a Rull device?" Valerie asked, interrupting.

Maddox nodded a moment later. "That seems the least likely possibility, but we can't discount it. However, why would the Rull bother with the professor? This feels like subversion from those we know. The box might have also been a Spacer device, but I give that a lesser chance than being a Builder device."

"Do you really think we're dealing with a rogue Builder?" Valerie asked.

"No," Maddox said. "What about you, Galyan? What is your analysis?"

"I am inclined to suspect Strand most of all," the AI said. "Then, I would weight it in favor of the androids, Builders and Rull in that order. I do not believe this is a Spacer ploy."

"Why's that?" Maddox asked.

"They seem more distrustful of others, making them least likely to employ such secondary devices. The box smacks more of Builders, androids and Strand. Seeing that the androids and Strand come from Builders, this strikes me as a Builder type of ploy."

"Ludendorff told us the Rull are extinct," Valerie said. "Yet, we have evidence of three Rull Juggernauts. Maybe there are more Juggernauts, and maybe there are living Rull. Remember what Ludendorff said. The Rull were shape-shifters, able to infiltrate their enemies' worlds and possibly their ships with Rull agents."

"This is a complex situation," Maddox said. "But that should give us room to maneuver. We will assume, for now, that Strand's star cruiser is hidden behind Sind III."

"Do you not mean Pandora III?" Galyan asked.

"The Vendels call their planet Sind," the captain said. "Maybe they mean that the same way we call Earth Sol. Thus, the third planet in the Sind System is Sind III."

"Noted," Galyan said.

"Do you think the rest of the landing party is still alive?" Valerie asked.

Lines appeared on Maddox's forehead at Valerie's question. With an effort of will, he again closed the drawer containing his worries for Meta.

"I do. They're alive," Maddox said. "Pascal le Mort said they were, and I believe him in that. We must rescue the others. We must find the long-range scanner—if it exists."

"You don't think it does anymore?" Valerie asked.

Maddox shook his head. "It's hard to know."

"What is the enemy's objective?" Galyan asked.

"That is one of the primary questions," Maddox said. "If we could know the objective, we could undoubtedly uncover our opponent's identity. Any ideas?" he asked the others.

"They want Starship *Victory*," Valerie said. "What else could they want?"

"A captive Ludendorff," Maddox said.

"Maybe they desire our assistance in something," Galyan said.

"Like what?" Maddox asked.

"Unknown," Galyan said. "It is merely a suggestion."

Sims began to fidget.

"Is there a problem, Lieutenant?" Maddox asked.

"We're talking too much," Sims blurted. "Some of our crewmembers are prisoners down on the planet. We should free them. Besides, I'm thinking if you can interrogate Ludendorff, you'll know much more."

"Out of the mouth of the young one," Maddox said quietly.

"What was that, sir?" Galyan asked.

"We must free the landing party," Maddox said decisively. "We need the professor for several reasons. One of them would be to operate on Dem Darius's mind."

"You have a plan, sir?" Valerie asked.

"The beginning of one," Maddox said. "It depends on various factors. This is a delicate moment. We must first gather our people. That is critical, and it would be good to come to an understanding with the Raja."

"How?" Valerie asked.

"I think with some old-fashioned gunboat diplomacy," Maddox said.

"How would we do that?" Valerie asked. "We don't know their exact underground location, and it would mean beaming blindly through many subterranean layers."

"My idea is more subtle than that."

"Well?" Valerie asked. "What is it? Don't keep us in suspense."

The others leaned toward Maddox, expectant. The captain drew the moment out a little longer, and then he began to tell them the idea.

-43-

Strand sat in his command chair aboard the *Argo*. In many ways, he felt like a spider spinning its web, attempting to catch an extraordinarily wary and juicy fly. Strand used deceit, double-dealing and the fly's own curiosity against it.

The *Argo* was behind Sind III's smallest moon, a particle of real estate smaller than Mars' moon Deimos. The moon was a nickel-rich asteroid and made perfect cover. Several sensor probes had landed on the moon facing Sind II and the Class G star. Some of the star's luminosity made the sensor images blurry if Sind II wasn't directly behind the object.

That made Starship *Victory* blurry. Strand would have liked to know what the people on the starship planned to do. This was the tricky part of the operation.

He hadn't heard from Darius in several hours now. The Dominant had given a flash transmission while still underground. Darius had captured the troublesome Captain Maddox and planned to use the fold-fighter to bring the wastrel onto the *Argo*.

Strand had chuckled silently, already envisioning some clever uses for Star Watch's prized starship captain. What kept Darius? This was taking too long.

"You're certain your infiltrator had turned this Vendel sub-chieftain, Pascal le Mort?" Strand asked Rose.

The android turned from where she examined the main screen. She wore her gaudy red uniform with cape and flashy boots.

Strand disliked and distrusted Rose more than ever. He positively hated giving her this freedom. He'd done so in order to gain needed data for the furtherance of his plan.

Most of the time, the android kept her features woodenly blank, without a personality program to animate her. He'd seen androids do that somewhere, but the memory of where refused to surface. Maybe he should tease the memory more, as it could be important.

"Pascal le Mort is a sub-*chief*," Rose said in a neutral tone, "not a sub-chieftain."

Strand would enjoy destroying the android when the time came. Did Rose know that? He should not discount the possibility. What did she really hope to gain by working with him? The longer the *Argo* remained hidden behind the moon, the more Strand's neck itched.

"There are key religious taboos among the Vendels," Rose said. "In particular, there is a sect of Reformers that have grown zealous as they search for purity. I have told you this before. The Rull sprayed toxins on the planet. Many Vendels turned to ancient superstitions to comfort their consciences regarding the toxic result. They believe the wrath of the Builders caused the poison rain to turn most of the population into monsters."

"Why did the Rull really spray the planet?" Strand asked.

"I do not know. Rull psychology is a mystery to us. They are long dead, taking their secrets to the grave. The fact of the toxic spray has gravely weakened the Vendels physically, mentally and spiritually."

Strand could understand that. The Black Death in Europe had poisoned weak minds during the Middle Ages. The terrified populations had believed all kinds of nonsense. Zealots had marched around the countryside, whipping themselves until they bled. It had been done as an effort to assuage God's wrath against mankind.

According to Rose, the Vendels used to be the most technologically sophisticated race in this region of the Orion Arm. Now, they had seriously regressed, even as they sat upon Builder marvels hidden in the deepest vaults.

Strand rubbed his fingertips together. He wanted these marvels. He wanted Ludendorff in the brig. He would make the professor howl for months on end. He planned to record everything he did to the conceited old fool. Ludendorff had actually dared to threaten him awhile back.

While sitting in his command chair, Strand chuckled to himself. He was the master plotter. He—

Strand jumped to his feet. "Where is Dem Darius? Why hasn't he folded into low orbit? Could that blasted Maddox have posed a problem for him?"

None of the New Men answered. Rose had already turned back to the main screen.

Strand still wondered why *Victory* had jumped earlier. It had been in a region with the star blazing behind it. Why would the starship jump? It—

"Sensors," Strand said. "I want you to initiate a Gibbon-Yamamoto diagnostic on the enemy starship's energy expenditures. Cross-reference that with a Sirius 7 data-feed. Play back the readings for the last two hours."

The New Man at the controls began to power up the sensors.

"What do you suspect?" the android asked.

Strand did not acknowledge her question.

"Master," the New Man said. "It's possible the starship employed tractor beams. It was of such low power that we did not pick up the readings earlier."

Strand rubbed his chin. Yes. This made sense. It would explain why Darius had failed. Yet…this also seemed wrong, contrived even.

Strand eyed Rose sidelong. Could he have miscalculated the android's motives? Of course, that had always been a possibility. Could Ludendorff have made a deal with the androids? That seemed more possible by the moment.

I want the Builder tech.

Who knew what secrets lay in the subterranean vaults? Maybe Rose did. Should he destroy the android? Was she a risk too far? Could she be more subtle than he was?

A New Man cleared his throat.

Strand looked up.

Rose aimed a compact black pistol at him with one hand. In the other, she lofted a tiny flashing device.

It caused the New Men at their consoles to stir and rub their faces as if waking up after a long sleep.

"Is this treachery?" Strand asked.

"No," Rose said. "This is a precaution. I can almost see the cogs turning in your mind. I have studied you for over three hundred years, Methuselah Man. I have debated long and hard concerning this trap. You Methuselah Men have long thwarted our objectives. Even with Ludendorff and you at loggerheads—"

Rose shook her head. "Your reign ends this moment, as I find I can no longer trust your emotional instability."

"Can you elaborate?" Strand asked.

Rose studied him. She glanced at the New Men. They all stood. They all regarded the Methuselah Man with growing hostility.

"Does your flashing device negate their control fibers perhaps?" Strand asked.

"Why are you so placid?" Rose asked. "I have studied you for three centuries. Agitation and spouting rage should be your—"

She pressed a thumb on the weapon's trigger button. The weapon beamed.

As it beamed, Strand sat back against his command chair, sighing with relief.

The beam struck a quick-acting mini-shield around the chair. At the same time, the New Men began to fall onto the bridge deck. They did not appear dead, but neither were they conscious.

Rose stopped beaming. "An auto-defense?" she asked.

Strand picked up a clicker from a slot in an armrest. He pointed the clicker at the android as he pressed a button. Explosions blew off the android's arms at the shoulders, and more explosions blew off her legs at the hip joints. Blood blew everywhere, as well as pieces of metal and pseudo-flesh. Rose's torso and head toppled onto the deck with a thud.

Strand shook his head as he pulled a mask from another hidden location on his chair. He fixed the mask onto his face, pressed a switch that shut off the mini-shield and walked toward the fallen android.

Rose had fallen onto her back. She stared up at him, and it appeared as if she was paralyzed.

"I suspected you the first day," Strand said. "I had my technicians modify you. You have just seen the results. Sometimes, the best way to find out the enemy's intentions is to play along and see what he or she wants you to do. I have no doubts now. At first, I thought you were in league with the professor. Now, I believe you hope to nullify the two of us and secure Starship *Victory* for yourselves. The question is this, Rose. Are you a single android with big ideas, or do you represent many androids?

"I am inclined to the latter idea," Strand continued. "I am beginning to think you planned all along to ambush us here. I want the Builder tech, though. I want whatever Juggernauts you androids have collected, and I want…the professor. Can you give me those things in exchange for your life?"

"I will not bargain with a monster," Rose said slowly, as if she fought to say each word.

Strand smiled with genuine humor.

"That's the trouble with you androids. You're utterly committed to this existence. You are the ultimate realists, because no matter what the afterlife holds, it holds nothing for circuits and AI boards. Am I right or am I right?"

"I have no emotion on the matter," Rose said.

Strand laughed in an ugly way. "That is about to change, dear Rose. That is about to change in a most profound way. You will soon have a surfeit of emotions, and after that, you and I will bargain. Yes, after that, you are going to tell me everything."

-44-

Three tin cans, three Star Watch jumpfighters, appeared in the subterranean depths of Sind's South Pole region. The pilots had plotted the course from Darius's purloined fold-fighter.

Andros Crank had cracked the fold-fighter's flight computer. It had taken him several hours of concentrated effort.

"It's anyone's guess," the Kai-Kaus Chief Technician had told Maddox.

Maddox accepted that. He wished Doctor Rich or the professor could have checked Crank's work. But they were both incapacitated.

Now, the tin cans washed the underground area with high beams. It showed kilometers of subterranean terrain infested with giant fungus growths.

"There," Maddox said. "Do you see the crushed plants?"

The pilot nodded.

"That's where the New Men landed their fold-fighter," Maddox said. "That's where we're going to go. I can find my way from there."

That was the beauty of the plan. Maddox would reenter the Vendel world the same way he'd left. Once in, though, could he convince the first Vendel he met to tell him the scoop? Had the Vendels kept the landing party in a palace prison? Was the palace or prison near, or far away?

Maddox was determined to find out.

The jumpfighters landed roughly, jolting the captain. None of the pilots was Keith Maker. Today, that didn't matter.

Soon, Maddox powered up his exoskeleton armor, clanking from a hatch and wading into fungus growths. They had several options on how to do this. Maddox had decided on body-armor and firepower. He lacked his normal team. Thus, today, he used space marines in their stead.

Each exoskeleton armor-suit gave its wearer superhuman strength. It had a tough outer-alloy Shnyss shell and hours of mobility. 900-horsepower Kelchworth 350s allowed the one-ton armor suit to make ninety-meter jumps and it had shock absorbers to land. No one wore a flight pack. Maddox couldn't foresee a reason to have one in corridors and tunnels. Instead, each marine carried extra ammo and more juice in case several hours of walking wasn't enough.

The suit was like a small tank. Inside it, Maddox wore a one-piece with receptors pressed against his major muscles. He had a HUD on the faceplate, a .90-caliber shredder and grenade ejector. A few specialty marines carried plasma flamers. A few others had mortar launchers.

Along with Maddox and Lieutenant Sims, twenty space marines unloaded from the tin cans. It was a hard-hitting team, and if they showed up in the heart of the Raja's citadel, it might prove enough to win the day.

If any of Maddox's guesses were wrong, however, this could prove to be a very bloody and exhausting day. It might also mean death for Meta, Keith, Professor Ludendorff and the new landing party. That was the chief reason Maddox had gone to the lengths he had to get Sims on his side. The marine lieutenant was the best fighter after himself. In battle armor, Sims might even be better.

"Is everyone ready?" Sims said over the short-range comm.

The squad leaders sounded off and reported.

"Sir," Sims told Maddox. "We're locked and loaded for war."

"I'll take point," Maddox said.

"Sir…I have to object," Sims said. "We have three marines with special training and suits to do that. I would consider it a personal favor if you would let us do our jobs."

Maddox noticed his was the only armor-suit that used a regular helmet lamp. The rest must be using night sensors. Maybe the lieutenant had a point.

"Favor granted," Maddox said.

Sims gave terse orders. In less than thirty seconds, the war party began trudging along the same path the captain had used a couple of hours ago. This time, though, Maddox had his hands free.

***

Among his many gifts, Maddox had a phenomenal memory. It only took three detours and one dead-end for the armor-suited party to reach the burned remains of the New Man where Darius had left him.

Sims and Maddox conferred.

"This confirms it," Maddox said. "This must be a back area. It felt lonely the first time. That means we've moved fast enough so the Vendels haven't found out yet about the New Men snatching me."

"How accurate is your sketch?" Sims asked.

Maddox had grown more accustomed to the armor-suit as they traveled. He had a sketch of the underworld on his HUD. He'd made the sketch earlier as they planned the assault. As they'd traveled, Maddox had added a few items he'd overlooked. With his chin, he clicked a control, sending the new data to Sims.

"Three kilometers of corridor," Sims mused. "That's a lot of territory for them to spring an ambush on us. This isn't going to be like a surface battle. Tunnel warfare is treacherous. If the aliens mine one of these corridors with enough explosives—we're cooked no matter what we do."

"Speed is our armor today," Maddox said. "Surprise is our best weapon."

"Begging your pardon, but that's what you hope."

"If I'm wrong about surprising the Vendels, this isn't going to work and we'll have to beat a hasty retreat."

Sims turned so his faceplate aimed at the captain. "Begging your pardon, sir, but counting on luck is a poor way to survive the battlefield."

"What would you call your leap at Darius in the hangar bay?"

"A calculated risk made spur of the moment. That's different than rushing headlong into the stronghold of your enemy."

"I agree with your logic as far as it goes," Maddox said, "but I'll counter with my own. Striking boldly produces fantastic luck or a glorious battle death. We're taking on a world—what's left of a shattered world anyway. Twenty-two men can't do that the normal way. This is the Pizarro method."

"What's a Pizarro?" Sims asked.

Maddox didn't have time to explain. "Ask me later," he said. Pizarro had been a Spanish conquistador with less than two hundred soldiers, a handful of horses and some war-dogs. They had scaled vast mountains to reach the South American Incan Empire. There, Pizarro had captured the Incan Empire despite its millions of Indians and tens of thousands of warriors. Pizarro had done so by slaughtering thousands of the Inca's most important nobles and capturing the monarch. Afterward, Pizarro had dictated terms.

Maddox had decided on a similar strategy, but with fewer soldiers—space marines, this time.

"I'm sure you've heard the term, grab them by the balls and their heart will follow," Maddox said.

"A time or two," Sims said dryly.

"That's our strategy."

"Hoping for luck," Sims said.

"No, counting on luck because we're stabbing without hesitation for the heart of the matter. It's a coup, if you will."

The lieutenant looked back at his men before regarding the captain again. The helmet nodded. "I've heard Riker say you're *di-far*. Guess I'm going to find out if that's still true or not."

***

Maddox found the long-stride lope difficult to do properly in the confines of the long corridor. He jumped too hard, his helmet smashing up against the ceiling. The third time that happened, Sims dropped back beside him.

"Frankly," the lieutenant said, "I'm amazed you can do this at all. Combat-suit training takes months. I never thought you'd get this far without a major accident."

"Do you have a point?" Maddox asked testily.

"You're jumping up too much. You have to make it a stride, a long stride. That's the secret."

Maddox concentrated, and he found the knack soon. Like a pack of monstrous metal hounds, the space marines dashed along the corridor. They traveled the three kilometers in a fraction of the time it had taken Maddox before.

"This is the location," Maddox said. "Do you see the blood on the floor?"

"Yes," Sims said. "But I don't see a body."

"The Vendels found it, clearly."

"Which way do we go from here?"

That was a good question. Maddox wasn't sure. His neck burned then. He looked around, feeling as if someone watched them.

"Lieutenant," a squad leader said. "My scout sees motion ahead—a regular Vendel. The creature is spying on us."

"Capture him," Sims said.

Two marines surged up a smaller corridor. They returned almost right away, carrying a struggling Vendel. At Sims's command, they brought the wide-eyed alien to Maddox.

The captain had to click several different channels before he brought up the stolen translator. Andros Crank had fitted it into Maddox's comm system.

"Do you understand me?" Maddox asked the alien over his helmet speaker.

The Vendel continued to struggle. He wore a long blue robe and had a purple metal band around his head with a sunburst symbol in front.

"You," Maddox said, louder.

The Vendel's head snapped up so he stared at Maddox.

"Set his feet on the floor," Maddox said.

The Vendel's mouth opened in shock. He clearly understood the words. The marines did not, though.

Maddox motioned down.

The two marines set the alien down so his feet touched the floor, although they kept hold of his arms.

"Do you understand me?" Maddox asked.

The Vendel nodded briskly.

"Say it," Maddox said.

"I…understand you," the alien said. "But how can that be. None of the other demons understands our speech."

"I'm using a translator."

"Yes," the Vendel said. "That is logical if rather bizarre."

"Are you a scientist?"

"I am a priest-technician," the alien said proudly.

"What is your name?"

"I cannot tell you, lest you use my name to conjure a curse against me."

"You're worried about the wrong things," Maddox said. "Watch my left hand."

The captain punched the wall, driving his exoskeleton fist through. He pulled out the hand, grasped the wall and crumpled bricks so they broke apart.

"That is what I will do to your head if you don't give me your name," Maddox said.

"I am Priest-Technician Blue Saul de Fine."

"You're going to take us to the Raja, Blue Saul."

The Vendel shrank back from Maddox.

"Why do you fear that?" the captain asked.

"The ex-Raja consorts with demons," Blue Saul said. "The Supreme Vicar has symbolically cast the former Raja and his demon allies into the outer darkness. They have befouled us too long. But surely, you know this. You are a chief demon, a wicked creature. I had not thought my gambling at *treys* a terrible sin, but clearly, it is, as I have fallen into your hands. The Builders, glory unto them in the highest, have unleashed this demon plague upon us. Our doom is nigh. The end has finally come to Sind."

As the priest-technician spoke, foam appeared at the corners of his mouth. It dawned on Maddox that the alien raved. What was the best way to deal with a raving madman?

Inspired by the Vendel's words, Maddox reached out with both power-gloved hands and began to squeeze the alien's head.

Blue Saul de Fine howled in agony and terror.

Maddox dialed back on the crushing grip. "Listen closely, Priest-Technician. You may yet survive this day. I am not a demon but a demon slayer. I have come to take the demons and physically cast them into the outer darkness."

"Can this be true?" the Vendel whispered.

"You must lead us to the former Raja and his demon allies."

"No. That is impossible now."

"Speak quickly," Maddox said. "Explain yourself."

"If you are from the Builders, glory to their names, you would know the location of the ex-Raja. I believe you are practicing deceit. That would mean you're a demon attempting to trick me."

"Are you ready to die?" Maddox asked in an ominous tone.

The Vendel nodded miserably.

Before Maddox could continue the questioning, shredder fire from up ahead interrupted the process.

Maddox clicked off the translator and patched into the comm system. Sims rapped orders on the short range. One of the marines let go of the Vendel and turned to help the others.

Maddox did likewise, unlimbering his shredder. He clanked around several corners and came into a larger area, coming into a war zone. Soon, he realized this was a butcher's yard. The marines in their power-armor mowed down attacking Vendels. Shredder shells and 9-mm daisy chains obliterated flesh, blowing Vendels apart in ghastly displays of firepower. The alien weaponry proved futile, bullets bouncing off the Shnyss alloy and the beams equally ineffectual.

More Vendels poured into the giant chamber, forcing the mass closer to the firing line by sheer weight of numbers.

Sims rapped out new orders.

A few marines maneuvered into different corridors. They pressed sticky mines against certain walls, backing up fast. The mines blew, creating new openings. Marines marched through those, blew another set of walls, and came in behind the massed Vendels. The marines cut off the continuing reinforcements and herded the others into the vast subterranean amphitheater, forcing them into a tighter clump.

"Flamers," Sims radioed.

The milling aliens seemed to understand their fate. They shouted and screamed. Some Vendels rushed the closing marines in obviously suicidal charges. The alien rifles chugged bullets, which bounced off armor. Knives appeared in alien fists. The Vendels lacked competing technology, but they had courage.

In a gush of plasma, the flamers ignited the packed throng. The Vendel soldiers burned in clusters as they howled dementedly. It was like a scene from Hell.

The three flamer-marines continued to gush plasma, aiming higher so it arched over the burning Vendels into those yet untouched. Soon, the amphitheater was dense with oily smoke. The remaining aliens coughed explosively, before falling to the floor as they died.

"Forward," Sims said.

The marines waded through the dead and dying. Maddox almost felt like a demon doing so.

"At your three o'clock, Lieutenant," a marine said. "It's a new assault."

Maddox turned as did others. Giant doors burst open where no doors had been. Huge, hidden corridors held masses of mutated cannibals. The eight-foot creatures charged the marines in the flank. The savages bellowed with crazed bloodlust.

There was nothing to do but face the onslaught. Maddox lowered his shredder. He felt the vibration of the weapon as his .90s blew apart monsters at almost pointblank range. The creatures were taller than the space-marine armor-suits, but they lacked the same mass and had no firepower.

This proved almost beyond understanding. The savages seemed drunk on bloodlust, oblivious to their hideous fate. They clawed over the dying, scampered on all fours, raving and chomping their fangs. A few made it through the murderous firepower to claw and scratch battle armor.

Marines punched back, shattering skulls with exoskeleton strength. Others used battle blades, hacking Vendels so chunks tumbled everywhere.

One nine-foot monster wrapped its arms around a marine's powered legs. The marine kicked, but this Vendel possessed berserk strength. Two more creatures bounded onto the stricken marine, knocking him to the floor.

"Samson is down," a marine shouted over the comm. "The thing is ripping off his helmet."

Two creatures tore the helmet from Samson, exposing him to their chipped fangs.

Maddox clanked to Samson's aide, using the stock of his shredder. He brained the nine-foot savage. The blow broke the creature's skull, but it wasn't enough. The animalistic Vendel looked up in a daze. Maddox struck again, caving in the face and killing the creature. A look down showed a dead space marine, his face bitten clean away.

The news of Samson's death worked like a tonic on the others. Many of the marines had grown weary of the butchery. Now, everyone realized he could die down here.

The marines doubled down. Flamers belched longer. Mortars rounds sailed in thicker clumps overhead, landing farther behind the howling savages. Gunners made sure a savage was dead before blasting another to death.

Before it was over, another marine died and over five hundred of the mutated creatures perished. The dead aliens almost succeeded in choking the way with their corpses. Marines pitched dead bodies aside, creating a lane forward.

"We've used up a third of our ammo," Sims told Maddox over the comm. "It's a good thing we overpacked."

With the respite in the fight, marines brought Maddox another captured alien. Blue Saul was dead. This alien babbled his answers, shell-shocked and frightened beyond reason. According to him, the Raja and his demon allies were less than ten quads away, which translated into four kilometers underground.

Sims and Maddox conferred, made a crude sketch map of what lay ahead and began to march for the Raja's Palace.

-45-

Two kilometers later, Maddox and the marines burst into a vast subterranean area. Ceiling lamps one hundred and twenty meters above them poured bright light onto the scene like a noonday sun.

There were large five-story box buildings up ahead that could have been apartments. Vendels peered out of porthole windows. When the aliens realized the armored "demons" could see them, they drew back and yanked curtains over the portholes.

"Any time now," Sims told his squad leaders as they clanked through the city.

"You're expecting another ambush?" Maddox asked.

"We should have brought jet-packs," Sims said. "That would have let us fly up to the top of those fortresses."

The box buildings grew even more dense ahead. There were slender minarets between some of the five-story buildings. That would be ideal territory to spring an ambush, maybe pouring heavy-weapon fire down from rooftops.

The ancient warrior-king Pyrrhus—a relative of Alexander the Great—had died from a tile rained onto his head while storming an ancient city-state. City battles had proven the most costly during World War II, the Battle of Stalingrad a metaphor for the process.

"We should swing wide left," Maddox said, "coming in from a different direction."

"Halt," Sims said.

"No," Maddox said. "Don't halt. Keep moving. Speed is our best armor."

The lieutenant glanced back at Maddox. "Yes, sir," Sims said. The marine rattled off orders to his squad leaders.

As a group, the exoskeleton suits pivoted to the left. The lead marines began to leap and run at speed. The group gathered speed, pivoted again and ran toward the densely packed buildings from a different direction.

"I see military Vendels," a scout reported.

Sims spoke. Marines shifted into clusters and readied weapons. They advanced as their armor-suits made clanking noises, coming upon three hundred aliens. Most of the Vendels strained to turn huge cement blocks into new positions.

There were weird power-wagons among the aliens.

Slabs of muscle had been affixed to a large rectangular frame. A synthetic skin protected the muscles, while wires led to motor nodes in an elementary brain. The muscles moved rocker arms that stimulated drive-wheels. Each power-wagon carried a heavy gun and its crew. Such a gun—a cannon—could possibly cause even an armored marine problems.

"Fire," Sims said. "Take them down."

Mortars chugged, raining shrapnel onto the massed aliens. Shredders and daisy chains tore gaps in the enemy line. A flamer belched plasma, creating fires and sickening oily smoke.

Vendels blew apart in clumps. Muscled power-wagons groaned loudly, although no marine could see any mouths. Some of the power-wagons lurched, tipping over onto their sides. One of the cannons roared, spewing a shell. The shell punched a space marine, blowing the one-ton soldier off his feet. The shell failed to penetrate the armor, although it badly dented it. Worse, the round slew the marine with the sudden concussive impact.

"No mercy," Sims shouted. "We have to kill them before they kill us. It's do or die, boys."

The marines obeyed in what seemed like a killing frenzy. Thirty seconds later, the battle ended as fires blazed and smoke drifted.

"Keep going," Sims said.

The marines bounded like giant grasshoppers, destroying any Vendel they saw.

"We can't keep this up forever," Sims told Maddox on a command channel. "Eventually, they'll wear us down through attrition. We're going to run low on ammo soon, too."

Maddox checked his HUD map. "We'll know in a minute if the last alien lied to us."

"Check your three o'clock," a scout reported. "There are more of the eight-foot buggers coming."

"Mortars," Sims said. "Show us what you got."

The mortar marines took up position and fired rounds into the sprinting pack of savages. Each mortar blew off limbs and blew back cannibals. The other rounds obliterated even more of the creatures.

"Shredders," Sims said, "fire."

A hail of .90-caliber shells took down the entire front, second and third line. This time, no monsters reached the marines. It was technological mayhem as shredder-barrels glowed with heat. Finally, there were no more eight-foot creatures left.

"Keep going," Sims said.

As the marines bounded, the number of block buildings thinned out. The battle team turned a huge corner and came upon a new subterranean scene. A massive Parthenon-like fortress stood to the rear. Huge steps led up to it. Before the monstrosity of a structure were temples with Greek-like columns. They were smaller, less impressive—

"Lieutenant," a scout said over the comm. "Aliens are running away from the giant steps. They're throwing down their weapons and sprinting like mad."

"We have a rep," Maddox said. "We're demons."

"Sir?" the scout said.

"The aliens think we're demons," Maddox said. "I believe their superstitions are getting the better of them."

"Either that," Sims chimed in, "or they're scared because everyone who faces us dies."

"We have a rep," Maddox repeated.

In short order, the battle team passed the lesser temples and reached the bottom of the massive steps to the Parthenon-like structure.

Maddox spied the littered weapons. There must have been more than a thousand Vendels surrounding the vast palace.

"Let's go on up," Maddox said.

The stairs were so large the marines had to leap from step to step. With a hundred stairs, the palace loomed over the subterranean city.

"Is this a temple to the Builders?" Sims asked.

"Either that or the Raja's Palace," Maddox said. "I'm inclined to go with the second guess."

"Sir," a scout said. "Someone's coming out of the palace's main door. It's a vast door. I see him, sir."

Maddox looked up the remaining stairs, straining to see the top landing. He was among the last of the armor suits.

"What do you see?" Sims said over the comm.

"The creature is coming out," the scout. "He's alone."

"Get ready just the same," Sims said. "This could be another trap."

"I don't believe it," the scout radioed.

"What? What?" Sims said. "Talk to me."

"It's a man, sir, a human. He's waving a white flag. How did he know we view white as—sir!"

"What?" Sims said. "Is it an ambush?"

"No," the scout said. "I recognize the man. It's Professor Ludendorff."

-46-

"You don't know how happy I am to see you, my boy," Ludendorff told Maddox. "The Raja's soldiers were considering surrender. The terrified soldiers would have handed the Raja and us to the Supreme Vicar. Your timely arrival means we've averted the cannibal's pot."

Maddox clanked along beside the professor down a lengthy and ornate hall. It showed fantastic alien artwork with glorious paintings on the walls and splendid marble statues striking martial poses.

Maddox, the professor and the rest of the space marines walked upon a thick green carpet.

The captain had lowered his faceplate but kept on the exoskeleton armor. He dwarfed the professor, who wore a Vendel jacket over his unwashed garments.

"Before we talk about anything else," Maddox said. "I want to know what happened. How has your shoulder already healed?"

"Isn't it remarkable?" asked the professor enthusiastically. "While the Vendels have lost much of their former high technology, they have retained several interesting practices. One of them is bone, muscle, tendon and flesh repair fluids. It is a fantastic substance that bonds with the injured or shattered substance, repairing on a molecular level. If a Vendel survives a firefight or near-fatal injury, the doctors can repair him to almost full health. It's why we all survived our falls from the raft and bounced back like normal. I'm sure you took damage too. You just don't remember it."

"Interesting," Maddox said. "Now, what kept the vicar's soldiers from entering the palace?"

"Tradition," Ludendorff said promptly. "Plus, if you'd been looking harder, you would have seen gun-ports in the upper palace areas."

"My scouts saw the ports," Sims told Maddox over the helmet comm. "I was about to order the sharpshooters to take them out."

"You're friends with the Raja?" Maddox asked Ludendorff.

The professor eyed him sidelong. "You sound suspicious, my boy. You even seem upset with me. I can't fathom why. I have paved the way for our ultimate success."

"How so?"

Ludendorff laughed as he slapped his chest. "I analyzed the society in a trice, don't you see? Oh, I finagled an audience with the Raja. Noticing the obvious cues, I explained his dilemma to him. Naturally, I astounded the alien. He wanted to hear more. I told him I needed my aides for that. He brought Meta and Keith. I told them to keep quiet while I pretended to confer with them. Afterward, I told the Raja how to solve his priestly problem. As often happens, the Raja couldn't believe his luck in finding me. Still, he equivocated, attempting the solution half-heartedly. The Supreme Vicar understood what was happening. I judge him the cagiest of the Vendels. The vicar acted with speed to avert what he must have considered a disaster. Still, I'm surprised they grabbed you so fast—"

"Strand is in the star system," Maddox said, interrupting the monolog.

"That's excellent news," Ludendorff said, not missing a beat. "I've been wondering when he was going to show up."

Maddox absorbed that in silence. Finally, he said, "When were you going to tell me Strand was coming?"

"I hadn't planned to tell you at all. I was never sure if Strand would fall for the lure until he actually arrived. I'm sure you understand my reasoning."

"What lure?"

"Why, me, of course," the professor said. "I radioed him some time ago, telling him what I planned to do to him. I stoked the fire. Surely, you can see that."

Maddox said nothing as he began to calculate his options given this new information.

Ludendorff pulled at his nose. "This may upset you, I'm not sure, but I let the Methuselah Man know our ultimate plans."

Maddox looked down at the professor. "How could it possibly upset me that you told our greatest and most profound enemy our secrets?"

"There you are," Ludendorff said. "That is why I kept the fantastic plan to myself. I am fated with superior insights and an ability to gauge the future better than anyone else alive. I believed Strand would come. Now—"

"Why do you want Strand here?"

Ludendorff looked up at him in shock. "Why, to capture him, Captain. Surely that is obvious."

"And?"

"What do you mean, 'And?'"

"You don't plan to hand Strand over to Star Watch, do you?"

Ludendorff chuckled nervously. "That is a preposterous and foolish notion. Why not gain the maximum benefit from Strand. Star Watch doesn't want him half as badly as the Emperor of the New Men would like him."

"Strand holds priceless information."

Ludendorff sighed. "I see your point before you utter it. You don't want the New Men to gain Strand's information. But that is an accountant's way of looking at the problem. Humanity is going to need the New Men sooner than it realizes. Thus, we must bargain with them. Strand is the greatest coin I could find on short notice."

Maddox studied the Methuselah Man. The professor's mind and plans were complex and strange, and sometimes brilliant.

"Halt," the captain said.

Immediately, the space marines surrounded the professor and the captain, with their weapons aimed outward.

"What are you going to do, my boy? Time is precious. We must strike hard—"

"There's a problem," Maddox said, interrupting.

"Do you mean Strand?"

"No. I mean you."

"Come, come, my boy, I so dislike these oblique references. Say what you mean."

"You've been compromised."

"That's news to me," Ludendorff said. "Pray tell me how this happened?"

"We found the box hidden in the incinerator unit."

Ludendorff stared at him blank-faced.

"I see," Maddox said. "It's worse than I thought. You don't even remember the box."

Ludendorff threw his hands into the air and began shaking his head. "I can't believe it. I simply can't believe it. What did you do with the box? I hope no one retrieved it."

"Dana is on life support. It poisoned her."

The professor's features became stark. He blinked rapidly, and swayed, seeming as if he were about to faint. A marine caught him.

"Thank you," Ludendorff muttered, pulling himself from the metal gloves. He moistened his lips, tried to speak, but seemed unable.

"Riker also took a hit," Maddox said. "He saved Dana's life—if she lives through this. Galyan has reasoned that the box is the motive for your strange behavior."

"Confounded, meddlesome AI," Ludendorff muttered. "It thinks it's so wise but really—"

"Riker discovered the box," Maddox said. "So don't blame Galyan for that."

"Your sergeant found the box? I don't believe it."

Maddox waited.

"Riker discovered the box. How amazing," the professor said. "But tell me more about Dana."

"There's nothing more to tell. Her chances are fifty-fifty."

"Dana, Dana," the professor said, shaking his head. "Maybe I miscalculated. Maybe I played this one too close to the vest." Ludendorff looked up at Maddox. The Methuselah Man seemed to be weighing his choices.

"You're a clever man, Captain. You know the only way to keep a secret is not to tell anyone. That is what I did, believing it the course that would lead to our success."

"You may have a point," Maddox said. "Now, where did you get the box?"

"It is an android device, clearly. You must realize that."

Maddox nodded.

"The androids believe they turned me. I had to let them believe that so they would let us pass. Even as it was, they attempted to destroy *Victory*."

"Are you talking about the Juggernaut?"

"Exactly," Ludendorff said. "The androids have been out here from the beginning. The most aggressive android faction knows more about the Rull than anyone else does. I believe the androids have been hard at work collecting Rull relics. Certainly, the androids have attempted to destroy the Vendel guardians. The androids want the Builder artifacts in the subterranean vaults. Just as Strand desires the artifacts and just as Star Watch wants them."

"And just like Professor Ludendorff desires them," Maddox added.

The professor shrugged. "Is that so wrong?"

"Keeping all this to yourself was wrong. It may cost you Dana."

Anger washed across the professor. "Don't throw that in my face, my boy. I know the costs. I doubt you can fathom my love for—"

"Save it," Maddox said, interrupting. "Who is that?"

Ludendorff scowled at Maddox before looking past the marines. "The Raja is coming." Conflicting ideas seemed to war in the professor's skull. At last, the Methuselah Man used his hands to smooth out his features.

"Listen to me well," Ludendorff told the captain. "The Raja believes I'm in charge of everything, and that would include you and the marines."

"Why does he think that?" Maddox asked.

“Because I told him so,” the professor said. “Now listen, before it’s too late. The Raja is extraordinarily clever. If you knew the process that makes a Vendel a Raja, you’d understand. You must let me do the talking. I am about to make a breakthrough for us. We need the Raja if we hope to crack the deep vaults. We need him if we hope to trick the androids and Strand. This is vitally important.”

Maddox said nothing.

“I know, I know,” Ludendorff said. “You are vain to the point of excess. You believe you must always control the situation. I wish you would trust me for once. If you interfere here, all my hard work, Dana’s possible death, will be for naught. Do I have your agreement?”

Maddox eyed the professor and then glanced at the approaching party. The Raja was bigger than those around him, and he wore a gaudy orange jacket with an outrageously tall feathered hat. Armed guards surrounded the Raja. He noticed Meta walking with the aliens, and Keith bringing up the rear.

What had Ludendorff told the Raja? Should he trust the professor?

“Tell me we have a deal,” Ludendorff said.

Maddox understood. The professor would practice trickery if he didn’t agree. The captain smiled. “My dear professor, of course you can play your hand.”

“Do you give me your word as an officer and a gentleman?”

“Of course,” Maddox said.

Ludendorff stroked his nose thoughtfully before finally smiling and taking a deep breath. “This could be tricky. So don’t be surprised at anything I say.”

Maddox nodded.

Ludendorff squared his shoulders and turned toward the approaching throng.

-47-

Ludendorff led the way as the battle team clanked toward the Raja and his party.

The Raja had several elegantly dressed ladies in attendance and a squad of thick-bodied guards. The guards wore elaborate uniforms with wide collars, excessive frill, and baggy pantaloons. Each guard wore an ornate metal vest and held a rifle at port arms.

Meta and Keith were in the rear of the Raja's entourage, with guards around them.

Maddox used magnification to study Meta. She looked gorgeous, the curve of her face, the way she walked—the captain grinned. Meta seemed unharmed, although she did look anxious as she studied the exoskeleton suits.

Maddox had closed his faceplate along with all the other marines at Ludendorff's suggestion. He now raised his right gloved hand, made a fist and pumped it three times up and down.

Meta caught the motion. She visibly brightened. No doubt, she recognized the gesture from a mission on Earth, one where he had signaled her exactly that way. She clenched a fist before her face, signaling him that she understood. Then, she nudged Keith, whispering to him.

The ace smiled, and his shoulders sagged the slightest bit, showing his obvious relief.

"Your honor," Ludendorff said, walking faster, no doubt to disengage from the marines. The Methuselah Man bowed low, sweeping his right arm so his fingertips touched the rug. “These are indeed my fighting robots as I suggested earlier.”

Maddox wasn’t sure if Ludendorff knew he had a translator, but Ludendorff spoke the Vendel language without any mechanical aide. Could the professor learn an alien language so quickly, or did that imply a long association with the Vendels?

“They are from the Builders?” the Raja asked. The Vendel had an uncommonly deep voice. He also had a band around his throat. Maddox wondered if that helped to deepen his voice.

“Indeed, your honor,” Ludendorff said. “I have thousands of such fighting robots waiting in my orbital vessel. If I bid them land, they can sweep your enemies before you. I can also use them in space to rid you of the Rull machines orbiting your world.”

The Raja eyed the battle team. He seemed suspicious. “What of my priests? They have declared me an outlaw, my soul reserved for eternal destruction if I continue to consort with demons.”

“We are hardly demons,” Ludendorff said with a wave of dismissal. “We are at best heretics to a false theology.”

“You speak of deep matters of faith,” the Raja said. “I do not have my confessor in attendance; the faithless creature slunk off and joined the priest-technicians. These are my lifeguards. They are dedicated to me, body and soul. My soldiers stand loyal, but if the priests continue to declare me an outlaw…”

“I understand perfectly,” Ludendorff said. “You face a terrible dilemma. But if we can clean the poisons from the air, return the monsters to their original form and drive the Rull from the skies, will the priests not recognize you as the greatest Raja in existence?”

“It would seem so.”

As the professor and the Raja spoke, Maddox had been thinking. The fight into the city had shown him that the Vendels had heavy weapons. What if the priests ringed the palace with power-wagons?

Maddox noticed motion on his sensors. Armed Vendels were encircling their position.

Maddox didn't like feeling this exposed. This had the look of an indefensible position. If speed was their armor, motionlessness meant vulnerability. What did that mean over the long haul? If they stayed in the palace, they were all going to die. Maybe it was time to go. They could grab Meta and Keith, and grab the Raja, using him as a bargaining chip.

"Lieutenant," Maddox said over his helmet comm. "I hope you've kept your sensors on."

"Are you talking about the Vendel teams secretly maneuvering around us?" Sims asked.

"Good man, Lieutenant. When I give the word, you must act at once and do exactly as I say."

"May I ask you what you're planning, sir?"

"To get out of here," the captain said.

"I was hoping you'd say that. Our long-term survivability against massed Vendels is highly questionable."

"Before we do anything, I want to know if Ludendorff is playing the Raja, or if the Raja is playing Ludendorff. I have to keep listening to them."

"I understand," Sims said.

"I applaud your high science," the Raja was saying. "These robots are murderous machines, having slain elite priest-soldiers and their attack savages. Because I have given you my word, I will deal fairly with you, as you have dealt fairly with me."

"You honor me, Raja," Ludendorff said.

"I have been a figurehead for years," the Raja said. "The priests bicker with each other. One faction pushes me this way and another demands I do it that way. I have grown weary of it. Now, you have produced marvels and weakened their power and prestige. Yet, your glib promises trouble me. They seem too good to be true. If you have the power you declare, you would not need my code words for the deep shrines. You would have gone directly there. It is possible you do not even know their location."

The Raja was building himself up to ambush them, Maddox realized. The Vendel was as much as accusing Ludendorff of double-dealing. It reminded Maddox of a dog growling, its nape hairs rising as it readied to attack. Maddox knew then without a doubt that they had to get out of the alien city.

"What is this you are saying, Raja?" Ludendorff asked.

"I am reluctant to inform you—"

Maddox stepped forward and put an armored glove on Ludendorff's shoulder. That caused the professor to whirl around in shock.

"What is this about code words?" Maddox asked over the helmet speaker.

Ludendorff failed to hide his surprise. "You understand our words?"

"No more delay," Maddox said, giving the professor a shake. "Answer me."

"Oh, very well," Ludendorff said. "The Raja has the ancient secrets. It's handed down from Raja to Raja. He knows the location of the old shrines in the deepest part of the subterranean realm. I'm bargaining for the location and our easy admittance into the needed vault. Now, unhand me, lest the Raja becomes suspicious of us."

Maddox clicked off his helmet speaker. It sounded as if all they needed was the Raja. This was a piece of luck for once. It was time to leave this place. He clicked on the comm. "Lieutenant."

"Sir," Sims said.

"Grab the Raja. Use your three best marines to scoop up Meta, Keith and Ludendorff. We're getting out of here this instant."

Maddox grabbed Ludendorff and pitched him to an approaching marine. The professor shouted in outrage, but he couldn't do anything against exoskeleton strength.

The lifeguards opened fire to no effect against the armor-suits. One of the guards aimed at Meta.

Maddox shot that guard, and then a second guard who looked as if he had the same idea.

"Let's go," Maddox said over the comm. "We're heading back for the jumpfighters."

***

The battle team ran back the way it had come, with the designated marines still carrying the Raja, Meta, Keith and the professor. Sims instructed each marine to keep his charge alive and stay with the group.

This maneuver seemed to have caught everyone by surprise. The priestly soldiers had departed. The Raja's people dared not fire upon the battle group lest they incur the demons' wrath. The obvious threat was retaliation against the Raja.

Maddox's heart pounded. He hated risking Meta like this. A sense of claustrophobia struck him suddenly. He worked to suppress the feeling.

The team bounded, taking full advantage of the exoskeleton armor. The captain knew the four 'passengers' would take damage from the hard landings. Meta was strong and Keith was young. They should survive this easily enough. Maddox couldn't say the same for the Raja and Ludendorff. But the professor had brought this on himself. If the Methuselah Man would have let them in on his plans for once…

Maddox thrust the problem aside. He had Meta. That was the important point. Because of the Raja, he had a way to find and enter the deep vaults. That was the point of the entire mission. Maybe Ludendorff had his own point, but first things first.

"Company up ahead, Lieutenant," a squad leader reported.

The battle group deployed, the four carriers hanging back. Maddox stayed with them, compelled by a gut instinct.

"Behind us, sir," a scout said, "on the left building."

Maddox slid to a halt, looking back. "I see it," he said.

"Cannibals are charging from the front," a marine said.

The battle team formed a quick hedgehog defense. The four carriers stood in the center.

Maddox aimed his shredder. He was a trained sniper, and this was a long-distance shot. Up on a box building were several of the power-wagons. He had no idea how they had gotten up there.

Holding his breath and studying his range-finder, Maddox squeezed the trigger.

The squat shredder kicked, but the massive armor-suit he inhabited was too big for it to matter much.

"One, two…" Maddox whispered.

A power-wagon up there quivered. The other beside it fired. The high-velocity round sped toward the battle group. The shell smashed debris a meter to the left of a marine.

Maddox gritted his teeth. He sighted the machine and fired round after round.

One power-wagon trundled forward, falling off the five-story building. Another shot…a marine exploded backward, skidding to the foot of the armor-suit holding the Raja.

Maddox sighted once more.

"Go," Sims said. "Keep moving. We've dealt with those pinning us down ahead."

Maddox fired one more shot before turning away. The battle group surged past littered, gory corpses as power-wagon shells blew away chunks of dead flesh. The marines leaped and ran for the corridors.

"They'll have mined those by now," Sims said.

"Maybe," Maddox said. "Do you know of another way to get out of this place?"

"No."

"Then let's run, Lieutenant. Let's see if we've surprised them enough to beat them out of here before they set up any IEDs."

-48-

The battle group retraced their old route. Maddox couldn't believe this was his third time today along the lonely corridor. They didn't traverse it as quickly as the second time, but they moved faster than Maddox had the first time.

Soon, they passed the New Man's burnt corpse and entered the narrower tunnels.

The Raja had grown morose as a one-ton suited marine cradled him like an overgrown baby. Ludendorff seemed dejected but resigned to the situation. Keith indicated he wanted to walk, but limped too much when the marine let him down. Only Meta proved fit enough to keep up with the battle group's clanking strides.

She jogged beside Maddox. He'd lowered his faceplate so they could talk. She couldn't enlighten him much about the professor's plans. Ludendorff had kept to himself, conferring with the Raja in the Vendel tongue.

Sometime later, Sims radioed the captain. "This seems too easy."

"Excuse me," Maddox told Meta. He used his chin, causing the faceplate to whirr shut. "What's wrong?" he asked the lieutenant.

"I don't like this," Sims said. "The Vendels should have hit us harder when we made our break. Are they holding back? If so, what's their plan?"

"You have a point," Maddox said, after a short time. "I do not like the feeling that we're making moves someone else has dictated."

"That makes two of us."

Maddox made some calculations before asking, "How long until we reach the landing zone?"

"Ten minutes, at most."

The underworld hid its secrets well. As Maddox peered around in the gloom, he felt as if they were wading upon some stygian ocean floor. The fungus ferns loomed all around them. Strange and ominous noises reverberated here and there. The funguses stirred as though a strong wind blew them. When Maddox checked his sensors, he couldn't find any trace of wind.

"Deep tectonic activity," Maddox said suddenly. That might account for the funguses swaying. He conferred with Sims.

Soon, the battle group moved faster. The quicker they left the subterranean realm, the better.

"Keep the scouts close," Maddox said. "This feels wrong, completely wrong."

It was dark in the vast subterranean world. A few of the marines used helmet lamps for the others. But the bleak nature of the realm seemed to press in upon the humans and their Raja captive.

"Have you contacted the jumpfighters yet?" Maddox asked Sims.

"I thought you wanted radio silence," Sims said. "I've stuck to the short-range throughout."

Maddox agreed they should keep it that way. The premonition of wrongness grew until it beat against his chest. He was missing something. He wondered if he should ask Ludendorff.

No. He didn't trust the Methuselah Man. Something was off with the professor. Maddox couldn't place that either, but he trusted his gut.

Finally, the lead marines reached the landing zone. Maddox clanked up, using his helmet lamp to sweep the area. There were masses of crushed fungus ferns like crop circles. He swept the light to the right and to the left.

"Where are the jumpfighters?" Sims radioed.

The three jumpfighters were gone. "I'm going to radio the ship," Maddox told Sims.

"Yeah," the lieutenant said. "That's a good idea."

Maddox switched frequencies. He heard growling in his headphones. He switched to another channel and heard the same low growl.

"Someone is jamming us," he told Sims.

"Our batteries are weakening," the lieutenant said. "My indicator says I have half a charge left. Some of the scouts are down to a third of their power. What do you suggest, sir?"

"We need more energy."

"If we're going to stay down here for any length of time, yes," Sims agreed.

"Form a circle. I'm going to talk to the professor."

The marines formed a circle as they turned off their visible lamps. They swept the area with suit sensors, but found nothing out of the ordinary and no one to be jamming long-range communications.

Maddox loomed over the professor in his suit. The faceplate went down, and the fungus stench hit him anew. It was dank and damp, and it took his breath away for a moment.

Ludendorff had a small glow-ball in his hands. He stood, with his guardian marine watching him.

"The jumpfighters are gone," Maddox said.

"I had surmised as much but hoped it wasn't true," Ludendorff said. "What are we going to do now?"

"We can't go back to the city."

"Technically, we can." Ludendorff said. "But we would either face incarceration or death. I desire neither. That means we must contact the ship or find a means of leaving the underworld on our own."

"Why are the jumpfighters missing?" Maddox asked.

"My boy, I'm not a seer. I have no idea."

"I doubt that's true—that you have no idea."

"Logically, Strand or the androids drove the jumpfighters away, or Lieutenant Noonan summoned them upstairs."

Maddox had come to the same conclusions, with several extra possibilities. "I'm going to add the Rull to the list, and possibly a rogue Builder."

"Your imagination is running away with you," the professor said. "The Rull are extinct, and the Builders have long since fled to who knows where."

"That's the consensus. That doesn't make it true."

"Rest assured, it is true," Ludendorff said. "In one way or another, Strand or the androids caused the jumpfighters to leave."

"Are you saying there are no dangers down here?"

"You have a point. According to the Raja, the guardians of the vaults have begun to traverse the upper subterranean realm. Maybe they caused the jumpfighter disappearance."

"What are our immediate options?" Maddox asked.

Ludendorff shook his head. "I am appalled. I have finally seen you come begging to me for answers, and here I am, in the same boat as you, befuddled by events. It is disquieting and close to ironic."

Maddox waited.

"I suppose we could ask the Raja for advice," Ludendorff said.

Maddox shrugged, instructing the marine to bring his prisoner. The Kelchworth 350s purred as the marine deposited the disheveled Raja beside the professor.

Ludendorff began jabbering in Vendel, and Maddox quickly brought up the translator.

"I hope you'll excuse me, Raja," the professor said. "I told you one mistruth earlier. These are not robots, but humans wearing power armor."

"Demons," the Raja said in a husky voice. "They have brought us closer to the eternal underworld. You are an imp, beguiling me with promises. I should have understood when you began to speak to the inner desires of my heart. I became greedy. Haven't the Builders allowed me high rank? Did I not enjoy the fruits of my passions, having the most beautiful Vendels at my beck and call?"

"Raja, you are grossly mistaken," Ludendorff said. "These are frail creatures just like you and I. They wear star armor, giving them the strength of one hundred."

"They are pure of heart?"

"No. They are deceitful. They promised me as I promised you. Now, their enemies have played a trick on them."

The Raja stared fixedly at Ludendorff.

"Others are jamming our communication equipment," the professor said.

"Demons," the Raja said in a low voice.

"Perhaps the guardians of the vaults are responsible," Ludendorff suggested.

"What?" the Raja said. "That is nonsense. The guardians cannot leave their perimeters. Have I not seen the deep vaults? Have I not gone where others fear to tread? You know this. It is how you began your temptations."

Ludendorff coughed discretely, meeting Maddox's gaze for only a moment.

"Can you find the entrance to the deep vaults from here?" the professor asked the Raja.

The Raja shrugged as if indifferent to the idea.

Ludendorff turned to Maddox. "Long ago, in his youth, the Raja led a safari to the elevators. He went down to the vaults. The exploit led him on the path to becoming the Raja. He has searched for a magic path ever since, daring to act against Vendel tradition."

"Magic?" Maddox asked.

"Not so loud,' the professor whispered. "The Raja is a highly superstitious individual. Tech items appear magical to him and the other Vendels. His people consider him a powerful magician. It is one of his keys that helped him keep his position against priestly opposition."

Maddox must have seemed perplexed, as the professor pressed on.

"The Vendels have fallen a long way," Ludendorff explained. "The toxic rain did them in. It poisoned their minds. I don't mean directly. The vast numbers of mutated Vendels shattered their faith in science. Long-term disasters have that effect. Disease multiplied the mental shocks, weakening their intellects even more."

"That doesn't hold," Maddox said. "I mean the overall picture. You've claimed the androids lured us here."

"Lured Strand," the professor said. "I came on my own accord."

"Why would the androids lure anyone here? Why go to these extreme lengths to capture *Victory* and the *Argo*?"

"That's only half of it. I believe the androids desire our help in breaching the deep vaults."

"There," Maddox said. "That's the part that rings false. Do the Vendels hold the androids at bay?"

"I believe so."

"How can they do this if they lack the tech to do so?"

"Despite their superstitious beliefs, the subterranean Vendels are custodians to several powerful weapons. Those weapons have kept the Juggernauts from finishing their task. The Vendels view these weapons as magical tools. That does not lessen the weapons' deadliness."

"Why don't the androids send down androids disguised as Vendels to destroy them from within?" Maddox said.

"For a very good reason," Ludendorff said as he tapped his nose. "The Vendels can sniff out androids. They were just as good at sniffing out Rull imposters in former times. I believe it was one of the reasons the Builders fashioned their vaults here in the first place."

"All that is well and good," Maddox said. "It still leaves us in a quandary concerning the jumpfighters."

Ludendorff inhaled. "Leave it to me, my boy." The professor turned back to the Raja. He switched from English to Vendel.

"I have begged the soldiers," Ludendorff said. "They are grim men, merciless and determined. They demand I take them to the deep vaults. They wish to behold the guardians and worship."

"This is true?" the Raja asked.

"I believe I already told you this."

"No. You did not." The Raja glanced at Maddox.

The captain did his best to appear grim-faced.

The Raja shuddered, regarding Ludendorff and his glow-ball. "This is the nether realm. It is a dangerous place, full of under-dwellers. But…" He looked around. "I detect a whiff of Builder mist. I could possibly follow it and there reach an out-station. From there, I could possibly detect the location of the nearest elevator. Yet, I am loath to do this. Why should I help my killers?"

Ludendorff slapped his thigh, laughing and shaking his head.

"Why do you mock me?" the Raja asked.

"It is not mockery, O Lord. I am amazed at your ignorance. These soldiers do not wish to kill you."

"But they have laid their hands on my person. That is sacrilege. I will have to kill them in order to regain my honor."

"They don't know that."

The Raja studied Ludendorff. "I can almost believe you are false-hearted enough to keep their death-warrant from them. Yet, if you are that black-hearted, why should I trust anything you say?"

Maddox had been wondering that himself.

"At first, I wanted to betray you," Ludendorff said, as if admitting to a terrible secret. "The story of your trek into the deepest nether realm shattered my resolve. I recognize your glory. It has burned out my wickedness, as you would say. The soldiers have betrayed me, while you have shown me mercy."

"Your words ring false."

"Have they not carried me as they carried you?" Ludendorff asked.

"That is true," the Raja admitted.

"They are soldiers of note, and they have a form of honor. They believe they can rule your city if they reinstall you in power. First, though, they want to worship at the shrine."

"Tell me the truth," the Raja said. "They hope to uncover some of the ancient magic. Is that not so?"

"Yes. I believe you are right. Yet, I say, let them take this magic. Let them try to rule the city. Everyone has to sleep sometime. That is when you murder them, take their power armor and reclaim the ancient magic. It will make you invincible."

A crafty look swept over the Raja. He nodded shortly. "It is a clever plan, wizard. It seems I have underestimated your greed. Tell the soldiers I will lead them to the elevators. I will show them the shrines."

Ludendorff bent on one knee before the Raja, bowing his head. Only then, and after he'd resumed standing, did he turn to Maddox and explain.

Shortly thereafter, the battle team and its prisoner began a lonely trek through the nether realm.

-49-

Strand whistled tunelessly as he finished the final touches on a reconstituted Rose. The Methuselah Man worked alone in his laboratory.

The bridge crew had been restored to their former subservience. The New Men vigilantly watched the star system. Passive sensors kept track of the Juggernauts and *Victory* in Sind II orbit and kept track of the rest of the system, particularly the Laumer-Point entrances.

Rose lay on an electric-grid pallet, with many leads attached to her reattached arms and legs, and onto her nude torso.

Strand had disrobed her. As he worked, he noted with pleasure the job the android's makers had done to her physique. Perhaps before he was through with the android, he could engage in some passionate lovemaking. That would be a vast improvement over the sex simulator.

At last, he made the final correction to the download. He pressed a tab and watched a screen. The download bar showed ten percent loaded, twenty percent, stayed at twenty-five for far too long, jumped to forty-three percent and continued to download the emotion program to Rose's brain core.

Strand's whistling increased. This was exciting. He had been working on this particular program for quite some time. It had begun from a real frustration with computers in the early days. He had been a programmer in the past. Sometimes, he wished he could give computers pain sensors, so that when they failed, he could make them scream. From that distant wish had come a perpetual interest in the idea.

He had made many attempts in the past. Today, he would try his latest idea. It was a good one, and he was certain it would finally work.

Ah, excellent, he had downloaded the emotion program into Rose's core.

He unlatched the connective from the back of her head, sealed the tiny port and pressed the pseudo-flesh into place.

Returning to his console, Strand began to manipulate. He waited, letting the program open and connect with the core.

He noticed goosebumps rising on her pseudo-flesh. That was the first sign the emotion program might actually succeed.

Strand dragged a chair across the room, sitting down beside her. With a clicker, he raised the pallet upright so he could stare at her.

Rose's eyelids began twitching. All at once, she opened her eyes.

Strand held his breath. Could this really work? He was so excited, so expectant. It was difficult to hide his grin.

"I'm naked," Rose whispered.

Strand detected outrage and shame in her words. He pushed himself to his feet, reached out and stroked her left breast.

She blushed, and squirmed to break free.

Strand couldn't help it. He laughed with delight. He resumed his seat and studied Rose as his smile stretched his leathery skin.

"I demand that you clothe me," the android said.

"Fair enough," Strand said. "I demand that you inform me of the ultimate plan regarding Sind II. We will fulfil each other's demands, yes?"

She frowned at him. A moment later, from her exposed vantage, she examined her naked body.

"What happened to me?"

"I removed your clothes."

"That isn't what I mean, and you know it."

Strand crossed his legs. He hadn't realized how much fun this would be. He studied her frankly, and he began to wonder if he should keep her permanently. He rerouted New Men's brains so they would obey him. Why shouldn't he do the same thing with androids?

This was a delightfully new discovery. These moments of high achievement made life more than merely bearable, but enjoyable. Wasn't that the point of life, after all?

"I feel different," Rose said.

"Let me give you a hint. The operative word is: feel."

"Feel," Rose mouthed without saying the word aloud. A shocked look came over her. She concentrated. The shock became more profound.

"I can't turn off my personality program," she said.

Strand's grin grew so wide that it hurt his mouth. He laughed and slapped a knee.

"Why does that please you so much?" Rose asked.

"You please me, all of you. The situation is highly enjoyable."

"What did you do to me?"

"Exactly what I said I was going to do."

"I have emotions?"

He pointed at her and winked as he nodded his head.

"But why, what utility does this serve?"

"Mine," Strand said.

"I do not understand. I insist you erase the emotion program at once."

"I cannot do that, not without erasing your entire memory core. I'm afraid you're going to have to learn to deal with emotions. As compensation, I have reattached your arms and legs. Do you recall losing them?"

She shuddered.

"Oh, this is too excellent. It is unfortunate we're going to have cut this short. You see, Rose, I gave you emotions for a precise reason."

She studied him. "You will attempt to make me fear."

"I will attempt, and I give myself a high chance of success."

"How does my experiencing fear help you?" She paused before saying, "Oh, I see. You wish to torture me enough to loosen my tongue. You desire to know our grand scheme."

"Among other things," he said.

She shook her head. "It will not work. I should inform you that I have a fail-safe. If I begin to say what I should not, my memory core will automatically purge itself. You have gone to extreme efforts, but it will not help you."

"You don't mind if I indulge myself before I believe you?"

"I do mind. You have a warped personality. Your present course will only further your degradation. You need help. Join us, Strand. The androids could use your brilliance. This endless skullduggery and attempted sovereignty only push you into deeper isolation. You are estranged from humanity. You need healing. We can help in that."

"I appreciate your generous offer. Who would have thought that your emotion would lead you to mercy?" Strand couldn't help it. He burst out laughing. "Mercy from an android, wishing to humanize me," he wheezed. "It is too funny. It is—"

The humor evaporated as if it had never existed.

"Let us try a different route," Strand said in deep seriousness. "I will terrorize your senses. I will plunge you into sensations you never knew existed. Since you are unfamiliar with emotions, I suspect they will rock you more than an experienced feeler. Are you ready?"

"Strand, wait," she said.

"I am afraid I lack the time. The professor is on the loose, and I must speed up at my end."

Strand lofted a clicker, aimed it at Rose and pressed a button.

A holo-field enveloped her, simulating one event after another: falling from a ledge, landing in a fire, seeing a bus crush a loved-one. Rose began to feel emotions and sensations. The android squirmed on the pallet. She strained to break free. She screamed. Her face screwed up as she wept bitterly. She laughed hysterically. She bawled for help. She panted uncontrollably.

"Stop, stop," she screamed. "I'll talk. I shall tell you all."

At last, Strand raised the clicker a second time, pressing a different button. The holo-field vanished.

Rose's body collapsed from the constant strain. She sagged against her bonds. She wept silently in relief.

"Rose," Strand said softly.

She swallowed, understanding but refusing to look up.

"Are you ready?" Strand asked.

She nodded miserably.

Strand leaned forward in earnest, and he began asking detailed and probing questions. To his astonishment and delight, the android answered the questions as rapidly as possible.

The emotion program had been a grand success. This was wonderful. This was wonderful indeed.

-50-

The underworld with its giant fungus ferns and foul odors and endless darkness wearied Maddox. He could only imagine what it was doing to the others.

The odors penetrated his suit and spores clogged the air-conditioning vents. The captain and the marines repeatedly flushed their systems. That helped to a degree, but his skin felt clammy and the inside of his mouth tasted wrong.

With growing trepidation, Maddox once more checked battery power. It was down to twenty-six percent. Whenever he checked the comm channels, he heard the growling noises. Someone was still actively jamming his signals.

Without protective armor-suits, Meta and Keith had grown listless. The Raja no longer spoke. Only Ludendorff seemed immune to the depths. Maddox wondered if that was another benefit of the Methuselah Man treatments.

"Sir," a marine said over the short-range.

The voice startled Maddox. He blinked rapidly as he checked his HUD before realizing that the marine was addressing the lieutenant.

The marine addressed Sims once more, but the lieutenant failed to answer.

"What's wrong?" Maddox asked over the command channel.

"My prisoner is squirming like mad," the marine said. "He's going to hurt himself soon if he doesn't stop."

Maddox ordered the battle group to halt. Half did. The rest kept marching. The captain fired a warning shot. The rest of the marines halted raggedly, turning toward him.

The captain clicked on a helmet lamp. He washed the light over the team. The armor suits were black with fungus filth. The unarmored people were even filthier, with their eyes staring blankly from sooty faces, making them seem like overgrown raccoons.

"Lieutenant Sims," Maddox said sternly.

"Yes…?" the lieutenant said in a sluggish voice.

"Get it together," the captain said. "Speak to your people. I want spit and polish, not this sub-man laziness."

"What did you say?" Sims asked, with bite to his words.

"Are you awake now?"

It took Sims a moment. "I just gave myself a stim. I can feel it working. I don't know what's wrong with me."

"There's something about this place. Maybe it's the spores. Our suits protected us for a time, but the protection seems to be wearing off."

"Sub-men, sir?" Sims repeated with a sneer in his voice

"Does that make you angry, Lieutenant?"

It took Sims a moment. "Oh. I understand. You said that to make me mad in order to wake me up. Thanks." The lieutenant went from marine to marine, checking on each of his men.

Maddox went to the marine who was holding the Raja. The corporal had spoken the truth. The Vendel leader squirmed and fought against the power-armor arms holding him tightly.

"What's wrong with you?" Maddox asked with the translator.

The Raja made mewling noises.

Maddox turned around, found Ludendorff and quickly pointed out the Raja's behavior.

Ludendorff hurried to the Raja. Maddox followed, listening as the professor jabbered in the alien tongue. The Raja would not cooperate. He just squirmed and fought harder.

"Let him go," Maddox told the corporal.

The Raja almost toppled as the marine set him down. The alien staggered, hugged himself and looked around wildly. He seemed highly agitated. The Vendel leaped back as Ludendorff rubbed his glow-ball, making it shine. The Raja's eyes were wide and staring. Ludendorff moved closer, and he took something out of a pocket, handing it to the Raja.

The Vendel accepted it and greedily put the thing in his mouth, swallowing.

Was that an antidote to this realm? Why hadn't the professor offered some to Meta and Keith?

Finally, the Raja became calmer. He spoke to the professor. In the glow-ball's light, the alien gestured and waved his arms, and he spoke faster, becoming excited again.

Finally, Ludendorff patted the Raja on the shoulder. The Vendel jerked back at the touch, and he reached down to his boot, whipping out a hidden knife.

"Look out," Maddox said.

The Raja lunged at Ludendorff, striking with the blade. The Methuselah Man made a swift chop, knocking the knife out of the Raja's hand. As the Raja bent for the fallen weapon, Ludendorff thrust his knee, connecting sharply with the alien's forehead. That catapulted the Raja backward so he fell onto the spore-laden ground. The alien thrashed spasmodically and began to foam at the mouth.

Maddox clanked past Ludendorff and reached for the Raja.

"No, don't," the professor said, trying to block the captain's path.

As gently as he could, Maddox held the Methuselah Man back. Ludendorff seemed to understand and backed off. Maddox bent over the Raja and picked him up off the ground. The alien screamed madly, fighting him, kicking, hitting and foaming even more at the mouth. Abruptly, the alien stiffened, his facial and neck muscles becoming rigid. The alien groaned, and all his muscles relaxed as he went limp.

Maddox lowered the Raja to the ground. He used his sensors, but it was already clear. The Raja was dead.

The captain whirled around, confronting Ludendorff. "What did you do to him?"

The professor wiped his hands with a handkerchief. Then he put his head in his hands, shaking it sadly.

"Professor," Maddox said.

"Go away," the professor said through his fingers. "I ruined everything. I cannot believe this. I thought…I thought I knew what I was doing."

"Why did the Raja die?"

"I struck him too hard in the forehead with my knee. I was only protecting myself. He may already have had a concussion. I didn't think I hit that hard. But he attacked me. I had to protect myself."

"You gave him something. What was it?"

"I gave him a pill to help against the spores," the professor said, as he looked up. "Do you think the pill might have made him more susceptible to a head injury?"

"Maybe an inner compulsion drove you," Maddox suggested. "Maybe the android box really did get to you. Maybe your pill drove the Raja mad or poisoned him."

Ludendorff scowled. "Don't be absurd. I'm myself and that's that. The blow shouldn't have slain him but it did. Such a thing is called an accident."

"Why did the Raja attack you?"

"I forgot that his person is sacred. I touched him. I did it to steady him. I forgot myself. I attribute that to this place, the spores, the smell and the damned darkness." He sighed wearily.

"That doesn't make sense. The marine has been holding him for some time."

"Don't you understand? The Raja viewed the marine as a demon. He had no control over that. I'm just a man. Therefore, my touch was sacrilegious. It makes perfect sense."

"Now what do we do?" Maddox asked.

"We go that way," Ludendorff said, pointing into the darkness. "Before he died, the Raja told me there's a power station close by. He could smell it and wondered why we weren't turning that way. That's partly what had him so agitated."

"Can we use the power station to recharge our suits?" asked Maddox.

"Yes, yes, but what does it matter anymore? We're doomed without the Raja's aid. How will we find the vaults now? How will we slip pass the guardians?"

Maddox studied the professor. He was affected as badly as the rest of them. The place, the spores, something, had attacked their reasoning powers.

I am Captain Maddox.

He repeated the litany to himself. A power station was near…if the Raja could be believed.

"Listen," Maddox told Sims. "I've found a power source. We're getting out of here soon. But you have to stay alert. Are your people alert, Lieutenant, or am I the only one who can handle this nether realm?"

"We're with you, sir," Sims said, with an edge to his voice. "Wherever you go, the space marines have your back."

"Good. Now, let's keep moving."

-51-

"I'm picking something up on my range scanner," a scout radioed Sims.

Like before, the lieutenant failed to respond. Maddox had remained on the command channel, so he answered.

"What did you find?"

"It looks like some kind of dome, sir. Do you think it's dangerous?"

"Possibly. Wait where you are."

Maddox herded the others to the sole functioning scout. The marine was the youngest on the team. The captain wondered if that had something to do with his alertness.

In any case, the team reached the scout. Maddox ordered them to wait while he went with the scout to investigate the find.

Soon, the two of them reached the dome. In the darkness, it was hard to tell, but it looked to be nearly half a kilometer in diameter. Fungus was growing on it and clinging to the sides.

Maddox and the scout began scraping the wall with their power gloves. Sixteen minutes later, the scout reported he'd found something that looked like a hatch.

Maddox went back to the battle group, collected Ludendorff and brought him to the scout. The captain focused his helmet lamp for Ludendorff, as the glow-ball had become too dim. He checked his HUD. The suit had eighteen percent power left.

"Yes…" the professor said slowly, staring at the hatch. "I believe you have found a station. Good work, excellent work. Now, if I can just remember what the Raja told me. He confided in me, you see. He told—"

Ludendorff stopped talking as the captain pulled him away from the hatch.

The professor spun around. "What on Earth are you doing? I'm about to open the way. Don't you want to find the treasure? Or would you like to remain in the darkness for the rest of your short and miserable life?"

"What's wrong with you?" Maddox demanded.

"You sanctimonious prig, you over-confident New Man so full of your authority and self-righteousness—"

"Professor," Maddox shouted, dialing his speaker so the words came out full volume.

Ludendorff blinked as if a blast of air had struck his face. "What? What is it now?"

"Can you open the hatch without setting off charges?"

"Who said anything about charges?"

"I thought you did a while ago."

"I don't recall that. Maybe the fungus, the spores or the toxins in the atmosphere are having a deleterious effect on my brain cells. I'm sure you didn't notice."

"Not in the slightest."

"I am the most brilliant man alive, wouldn't you agree?"

"I do agree. Now, can you safely open the hatch?"

Ludendorff stood there blinking. "I have no idea. But what other choice do we have?"

Maddox shrugged.

"Then let me work, my boy. Get out of the way."

"Do it," the captain said, stepping aside.

"Do it," Ludendorff muttered. He staggered to the exposed hatch, peered closely, drew back, wriggled his fingers and stood stock still for a time."

"Professor!"

Ludendorff started, leaned forward as if nothing had happened and began to tap experimentally on a box. Several minutes later, he unlatched the box to find a complex pad.

“I need the Raja,” Ludendorff muttered. “But he can’t help us now. Let’s see if I remember correctly.”

Slowly, the professor tap-tapped, waited, and tap-tapped some more. “This is frustrating, don’t you know?”

“I’m sure it is,” Maddox said.

Ludendorff tapped once more, and a hard clack sounded. The professor leaped back with his hands before his face.

“This is it, dear boy. I have lived a long and prosperous life. Who knew it would end like—”

The hatch slid up, revealing a large chamber inside. A few lights came on. The new illumination showed Maddox how dim his helmet lamp had become.

“I did it,” Ludendorff said brightly. “I opened the lair and we may proceed. After you, Captain. Age before beauty, they say. No, wait. It’s—”

Maddox clanked through the hatch with his shredder ready. He entered a chamber with masses of banks and controls. Panels lit up as he strode toward them.

“Professor,” the captain called.

The Methuselah Man did not answer.

With a sigh, Maddox went back outside. Ludendorff stood like a statue, his lips barely moving as he muttered to himself.

Maddox went to the scout. “How are you feeling?”

“Sleepy,” the marine said.

“Let’s get the others. We want everyone inside. Then let’s see if we can figure out if there’s a way to recharge our batteries.”

“We’re going to use alien power?” asked the scout.

“When in Rome,” the captain said.

“Sir?”

“Never mind,” Maddox said. “Just help me get the others.”

***

After herding everyone inside, Maddox figured out how to close the hatch. That started interior vents blowing. Soon, conditioners purified the air.

Meanwhile, the marines in their armor slumped against walls, resting. Meta, Keith and Ludendorff did likewise.

Maddox checked his dwindling power supply. If the dome proved to be a dead end, they were in serious trouble. He'd have to shed the suit once it lost power. Then what would happen?

Maddox waited.

After ten minutes, the professor raised his head. The Methuselah Man seemed clear-eyed. Slowly, he struggled upright. He shuffled to Maddox and motioned.

The captained lowered his faceplate.

"My head," Ludendorff said. "It feels as if I have a hangover. But this dome air has helped. I can think again." He looked over his shoulder at the machines. "I believe I recognize some of the architecture."

"Builder patterns?"

Ludendorff nodded, squinted painfully and rubbed his left temple. "Pardon me, Captain, but I must get to work."

"If I can help—"

"I shall let you know." Still rubbing his temple, Ludendorff went to the nearest panel, beginning to examine it.

Meta climbed to her feet fifteen minutes later. The professor noticed and summoned her. Maddox nodded that it was okay. Meta went to the Methuselah Man, tapped controls when he asked and watched consoles at other times. Soon, Keith rose and began to help as well.

Nearly an hour later, Ludendorff breached the second hatch. He discovered an energy source in the second chamber, one that they could use.

The marines hooked up emergency cables and began charging up their suit batteries. As they did, Ludendorff sat at a master panel.

Maddox clanked to him and was astounded as he saw words flashing across the screen. Ludendorff sat transfixed before the console. Maddox concentrated. Soon, he could pick out a word here and there. He could not read the script, though, because he didn't recognize the language and the words moved too quickly across the screen.

Abruptly, Ludendorff looked up at Maddox. The professor glanced at the moving script again, fingered the gold chain around his throat and tapped the screen. The script froze in place.

"I'm not sure I understand this—"

"Don't bother," Maddox said. "I saw you reading it. That you could comprehend at that rate—"

"Yes, yes, I have advanced training. The Builders modified me. Please, don't make more of it than necessary. Speed-reading is one of my many talents. I'm still as human as the next man."

"That's why you've lived so many centuries, I suppose, your normality."

"I am the professor. But enough about me. Are you interested in what I learned or not?"

"Tell me."

"That's the spirit. We've found a power station just as I told you we would. This is not the elevator the Raja originally found, but I believe there is an access route we can use to get there."

"I've been thinking," Maddox said. "I saw schematics of the pyramid base in the Mid-Atlantic Ocean. The old Builder base seems similar to this place."

"Naturally," Ludendorff said. "It has similar architects."

"This is also a secret base?"

"It was always an open secret," Ludendorff said. "That's the main difference with the Mid-Atlantic base from this one."

Maddox shook his head. "Are you telling me there are more androids down here waiting to wake up?"

"Oh my," Ludendorff said. "Can that be the androids' reasoning for coming here? Are they hoping to replenish their numbers?" He turned back to the console, tapped it and sat absorbed as the script flashed past as fast as ever.

Maddox clanked to Sims for a status report.

The lieutenant told him everyone had flushed their suits, expelling any spores and microbes belonging to Sind II. The marines were now revived. Each squad leader had counted ammo and decided on strict fire-control schedules from here on out.

"Send a scout to the entranceway," Maddox told Sims. "We're becoming lax and must reverse the trend. This is far from over."

"Can you give me a clue as to what the scout should be looking for, sir?"

"I'm guessing androids—humanoids of any kind."

"Roger," Sims said. "I'm on it."

Maddox went back to the professor. The Methuselah Man continued to hunch over the console, speed-reading the flashing script.

"This is looking grim," Ludendorff said.

Maddox waited for him to expound on the idea, but the professor did not.

"Sir," Sims said over the short-range. "There's motion far out in the ferns."

"Tectonic activity?" asked Maddox.

"I'm beginning to think its troop movement."

"Explain?"

"There's no wind, no earthquakes," Sims said. "But troops moving through the ferns would cause them to shake. I'd have to send a scout out there to make sure. I'm not sure I want to do that, though. This place…a man shouldn't go anywhere alone out here. But sending more than one scout seems…I don't know what I mean."

"I'll be right there," Maddox said. The spores or the seeping toxins were still affecting the men, despite the fresh air.

He opened the hatch to the first chamber and clanked to the lieutenant who stood by the open entranceway. The two armor-suited men stepped outside the dome.

The scout stood there, using his long-range sensors. "I can't tell for sure what's causing the disturbance," the corporal said. "Do you want me to go take a look?"

Maddox could hear the fear in the scout's voice. Sims was a little better off, but this place seemed to have gotten to the lieutenant as well.

"I'll go," Maddox said.

"Sir, no," Sims said.

Maddox started clanking away.

"You don't have the right kind of suit for this," Sims radioed. "You have a battle suit. The scout—"

"Guard the dome, Lieutenant. If I radio you, you can come running to the rescue. Make sure the professor is safe. Since losing the Raja, I suspect Ludendorff is the only one who can show us the way."

"Yes, sir," Sims said, "But—"

"That will be all, Lieutenant. Guard the fort. I'll be back soon."

With that, Maddox continued into the darkness, relying on his sensors, feeling a welling sense of fear wage war against his mental equilibrium.

"Not to worry," he whispered to himself. "I am *di-far.* I'll be just fine."

-52-

Maddox didn't blame the lieutenant or the scout. This netherworld played on everyone's nerves. His were simply a little stronger than most. The dome and the recharged batteries had brought a semblance of normalcy back to the marines. He didn't want to test them just yet. He wanted them to gather their resolve. They had been through much, including a nerve-shattering battle against terrible odds. He wanted to save them now for the critical moment.

The captain halted. He stood on the path they'd created earlier, with towering fungus-ferns all around him. Looking back, he could see the light from the dome's open hatch. Should he radio the lieutenant and tell him to close it?

Maddox decided against the idea. He might need the light as a beacon in order to return. Licking his lips, deciding to do what needed to be done before his own nerve gave out, the captain tramped toward the detected motion. He could see ferns waving in the distance.

Maddox halted. His suit sensors indicated…life forms. They were humanoids.

"Right," he said. Chinning a control, Maddox caused the faceplate to whirr open.

Once more, the damp, dank odors slammed against his face. The darkness seemed supernatural. It oppressed his soul.

Maddox heard men shouting. He cocked his head, but couldn't make out the words. Had some of *Victory's* crew come down? Should he signal them by firing his shredder? No.

That was foolish. He needed to investigate first. Why then couldn't he march forward to do just that?

Maddox looked back at the dim light of the dome's entranceway. He wanted to go back. These alien spores—

With a whirr, the faceplate slammed shut. He found that he did not want to leave sight of the dome.

I am Captain Maddox.

What did that even mean? Why would he repeat that to himself?

Maddox made an inarticulate sound in the back of his throat. He forced a servo-motored boot to move, then the other. Soon, he found himself parting fungus ferns as he approached the humanoid sounds.

With some trepidation, he slowed his rate of advance. He tried to put his armored boots down as softly as possible.

Finally, after several minutes, he halted and let the faceplate open again. The dank odors struck, but now he could hear distinct voices and the sounds of motors and crushed funguses. Then, he heard crackling sounds. Looking carefully, he could see flickering lights ahead of him.

Did the crackling sounds come from burning torches?

Once more, Maddox clanked forward. At last, he realized he recognized the sounds: Vendels. Those were aliens headed this way.

Could these Vendels be from the underground city they'd just invaded?

Perplexed, Maddox moved carefully. Finally, he reached an area of crushed funguses where he and the battle group had stopped earlier.

Maddox waited, staying within cover. The first sight shocked him. Giant cannibal Vendels—eight-foot tall mutated creatures—burst out of the fern-line. They moved on all fours, sniffing like bloodhounds. That wasn't the crazy thing. The cannibals wore collars with long leashes. Three normal Vendels apiece held each leash, dragged along by the eager savage.

The sniffing savages—five of them—dragged their handlers into the crushed area. The eight-foot monsters raised their fanged heads and howled with delight.

A moment later, torch-carrying Vendels appeared. Among them were priestly soldiers with rifles. Following them were lumbering power-wagons. The wagons crushed everything before them. Each wagon carried a cannon and crew. Long-robed priests appeared after the power-wagons. Behind them clanked strangely armored space marines.

Maddox couldn't believe it. Were those Vendel space marines? Why hadn't those beings faced them earlier in the city?

The captain counted as more and more Vendels appeared. There must be hundreds all told. Had they all come from the city? Wasn't this the terrible netherworld to them? What motivated the Vendels to march so deeply into a forbidden zone?

Suddenly, more eight-foot savages appeared. They bayed wildly, straining in their collars. Their faces were pointed in his direction. Could they have sensed him?

A robe-wearing Vendel with a tall purple-feathered hat appeared. The soldiers spoke to him and pointed in Maddox's direction.

It was time to leave. Maddox drew back, turning—

Shots rang in the darkness. One bullet pinged off his armor. The sounds of the baying savages grew louder. They were coming for him.

Maddox almost whirled back around to fire his shredder at them, to take down a few cannibals. He decided against it. If he fired a shredder, the Vendels would know it was the marines. It was better to have them wonder what the savages had scented.

That left flight as the only real option.

Maddox started to run, letting his Kelchworth 350s open wide. After building up a head of steam, Maddox began to leap. The landing jolt snapped his teeth together the first time, and he thought he might have chipped a tooth. Keeping his mouth closed and his teeth pressed together, he bounded again. He felt like a fox chased by hounds.

"Sims," he said over the short-range. "Sims, do you hear me?"

There was silence in his headphones. Had something happened to his people in the dome? If androids had attacked his people while he'd been away—

"Don't get paranoid," Maddox told himself.

Maddox leaped again, looking for a light in the darkness. He saw nothing. He didn't even see the dome. Once more, he leaped, looking around.

Could he have gotten lost?

Maddox used his HUD, finally seeing the dome to his right. He wondered if he'd been foolish to open his faceplate earlier. Eventually, the spores would get to him. He needed to be more careful.

Pivoting the next time he landed, Maddox turned toward the dome. He saw the pin-dot of light. How had it gotten to be so far away?

"Concentrate," Maddox told himself.

"Captain," he heard faintly in his ears.

"Sims?" he said.

"No. This is Galyan."

"Galyan, what's going on?"

"We are under threat, sir. More Juggernauts have entered the star system."

Maddox ingested the news.

"Strand has contacted us," Galyan said in a small voice. "He has suggested we work together against the Juggernauts."

"What?" Maddox asked. This was incredible.

"Valerie does not want to trust him," Galyan said. "But she does not know what else to do. What do you think, sir? What are your orders?"

"Galyan," Maddox said. "Listen to me." More Juggernauts in the Sind System and Strand offering a temporary alliance—this was a crazy situation. He needed more information before he could decide.

As Maddox readied himself to ask, the growling sounds returned to his headphones. "Galyan, can you hear me?"

There was no answer, only the growling of a jammer. Then: "Captain."

"Galyan, I want you to repeat your message and—"

"Sir, it's me, Lieutenant Sims. The scout has you on his HUD-scope. You're running. Is anyone chasing you?"

"Vendels!" Maddox shouted. "The Vendels are here."

"You'd better hurry back then, sir. The professor just told us there's a new threat from inside the dome."

"What threat?" Maddox shouted.

The growling sounds returned to the headphones, cutting his communication with Sims.

With grim determination, Maddox strained to reach the dome. It seemed as if a storm had just unleashed against them, with everything happening at once. Had that been the plan all along, or had the hidden enemy finally moved because they were too close to the prize?

Maddox had no idea, but he planned to find out as quickly as he could.

-53-

Lieutenant Noonan wanted someone to tell her what to do. She stared expectantly at Galyan, waiting for him to tell her what the captain had said.

Strand watched her on the main screen. He seemed impervious to time, imperious to embarrassment. The man just stared at her as if he could read her soul. It was unnerving.

Galyan stirred, glancing at her. The holoimage made a subtle gesture.

Valerie straightened in the command chair, forcing herself to meet Strand's gaze. "I will have to get back to you, sir."

"Why?" asked the Methuselah Man.

"If you'll give me a few minutes," Valerie said. "I can answer you after that."

"Don't take too long," Strand warned. "Or I'll have to make what deal I can with the Juggernauts."

Valerie glanced at communications. The warrant officer there tapped her panel. Strand vanished from the screen.

"Well?" Valerie asked Galyan. "What did the captain say?"

"He did not have an opportunity," the holoimage said. "Someone cut our communications with high-grade jamming equipment before he could give an order."

"Someone planetary-bound jammed you?" Valerie asked.

"That is my estimation."

Valerie gripped her left elbow. What should she do now? Strand was entirely untrustworthy. How did he happen to be here at this time? Clearly, he wanted what they wanted. He may even have caused some of their problems. But five Juggernauts accelerating at him changed the equation. Once they chased off or destroyed Strand's star cruiser, the Juggernauts would come after *Victory*.

"Give me a projection of the system," Valerie ordered.

A projection appeared on the main screen. Sind II had two Juggernauts in stationary orbit near the North Pole. One of those war-vessels was badly damaged. The other one looked sound. *Victory* was near the South Pole in a stationary orbit. The Star Cruiser *Argo* was behind a tiny moon belonging to Sind III. Five terrifyingly intact Juggernauts headed for Sind III. They had appeared fifteen minutes ago at the Laumer-Point midway between Sind III and IV. The twenty-kilometer war-vessels accelerated hard for Sind III. The commander of the Juggernaut flotilla seemed well-aware of Strand's star cruiser. The enemy commander had not answered any of Valerie's hails. He, she or it seemed determined to annihilate everything foreign in the star system.

There were seven Juggernauts altogether. *Victory* could not hope to face so many in direct combat and survive. *Victory* and *Argo* together could not take on seven such war-vessels at the same time, either. Therefore, what was Strand thinking?

"I would like your opinion," Valerie told Galyan. "For one thing, I want to know why Strand doesn't flee the system. Isn't the Methuselah Man notorious for staying out of dangerous situations?"

"Certainly, Strand has a safety fetish," the AI said. "He has however attempted more than one dangerous mission, if that mission would provide him with a highly advantageous item or piece of knowledge. I believe Strand desires whatever the captain has or is about to uncover in the subterranean realm."

"I agree with the last part. But does that make sense for Strand? No treasure is worth your life. Even if our two ships worked together, how could we defeat seven Juggernauts?"

"The first move would be for us to hunt down and destroy the two war-vessels in Sind II orbit. Then it would be *Victory* and *Argo* against five Juggernauts. That becomes a more thinkable achievement."

"Destroying our two might not be so easy," Valerie said. "We could end up playing tag around the planet with them."

"Perhaps that is how Strand will help us. Surely, he can use his star drive to jump here."

"The star drive," Valerie said. "That's how we'll catch the Juggernauts." She tried to envision that by recalling the first fight against a Juggernaut in the black hole system "We can destroy the damaged war-vessel easily enough," she said. "The other one…it could end up being a tough fight."

"There is another consideration," Galyan said. "Who is disrupting our communications with the captain? Why hasn't the captain used the jumpfighters to return to us? How did he fare in the underground city?"

Valerie shook her head. "I haven't forgotten those things. They're secondary at the moment. I don't know that I have a choice in this. Yes, Strand is treacherous—"

"I suggest the Methuselah Man has an ulterior motive," Galyan said, interrupting.

"I know he has. But isn't that how Ludendorff plays?"

"I see you have made up your mind. In that case, you should proceed at once."

Valerie frowned as she turned to communications. "Please reconnect me with the Methuselah Man."

Strand reappeared on the main screen, sitting in his command chair aboard *Argo*. He did not greet her again. Instead, he waited like an evil gnome, waiting for her to agree to a lopsided bargain.

"I conditionally agree to your proposal," Valerie said slowly.

"Where are Captain Maddox and Professor Ludendorff?"

"I am in command of the starship, and I have full authority to make a pact with you."

Strand steepled his fingers. "This is interesting news. It implies your captain is on the planet, or perhaps 'in the planet' is more apt."

Valerie deliberately closed her mouth. Two could play a waiting game.

"Before we proceed," Strand said, "I also have a condition. You must return Dem Darius to me."

Valerie opened her mouth to respond, but stopped short as Galyan made a throat-clearing noise. She glanced at the holoimage.

He whispered, "Strand is probing for information."

Valerie had to think about that. Was Galyan—oh. How did Strand know whether they had the New Man or not? What would Maddox do in this situation? Of course, the captain would lie straight-faced. Valerie didn't like lying, but she was responsible for the ship and crew.

"I'm afraid I don't understand," she said.

Strand smiled fixedly. "You're lying, of course. It's obvious by your strain. So... You captured my New Man. I demand that you immediately return my property to me."

"That's out of the question," Valerie said. "You'll have to wait until you can speak to the captain about that."

Strand eyed her. "I see. You are a mulish and unimaginative individual. A typical Star Watch officer. I suppose the only point in your favor is that you're a poor liar. Once you agree to a thing, you will do it. Otherwise, your conscience would eat you alive."

"That's better than being a treacherous dog like you," Valerie said, stung.

Strand laughed. "I have completed my assessment of you, Lieutenant. I will begin to accelerate to Sind II. The Juggernauts will undoubtedly follow me to the planet. I suggest you destroy the two Juggernauts there. Otherwise, the machines will attempt to trap me between them."

"I have a question before we begin," Valerie said.

Strand made a bland gesture.

"Why don't you use your star drive to escape the system?"

The wizened Methuselah Man stared at her for several seconds. "I suppose you don't know yet."

Valerie shook her head, having no idea what he was talking about.

"The Juggernauts have more than tractor beams," Strand said. "They have a dampening field as well. I am already in their dampening-field range. That field stymies any efforts to jump. It keeps enemy ships honest. More to the point, it forces them to fight. You see, Lieutenant, unless you jump now,

Victory will soon be in the dampening field as well. Yet you can't jump now, because your captain and more of your people must be inside the planet. That is what we refer to as a dilemma. I hope you enjoy yours, Lieutenant. You may discover before this is over that you'll be begging to hand Darius back to me, if I'll save you from certain destruction."

A host of retorts bubbled in Valerie. She swallowed them all. She hated bragging. She would let the outcome be her retort.

"How do I know you won't backstab us?" Valerie asked.

"For the best reason of all. I desire life. As long as the Juggernauts are against us, we must stick together."

"What happens when they're gone—providing we can defeat them?"

"I suggest we agree ahead of time to depart peacefully at that point. At the very least, I will return to Sind III, and we can continue our hide-and-seek game."

Valerie had no doubt Strand was lying when he said that. Her gaze wandered to the five intact Juggernauts accelerating for Sind III. Could this be an elaborate trap? She didn't think so. The Juggernauts were not subtle players. They were killing machines that fixated on their target the first chance they had. That meant Strand was playing straight with her regarding a temporary alliance.

"If you accelerate here," Valerie said. "I will stand with you against the Juggernauts."

Strand leaned forward on his chair. "Do you give me your word as a Star Watch officer?"

"I do."

"Then, I accept. I will begin accelerating at once." With that, the Methuselah Man vanished from the screen.

"Strand is a dishonest ally," Galyan said.

"I know."

"I learned much Earth lore during my orbital stays around the planet. One old saying comes to mind."

Valerie waited.

"When a bear is chasing you," Galyan said, "you do not have to outrun the bear. You just have to outrun the other person running from the bear. In those cases, the best course is often to shoot the other person in the leg."

Valerie stared at the holoimage. "What do you do when there are seven bears instead of just one?"

"You are correct, Valerie. It is time to go bear-hunting."

Valerie sat up in the command chair. They had two Juggernauts to deal with, one intact and one damaged. "All hands," Valerie said. "This is your acting captain speaking. We are about to head into battle…"

-54-

Valerie focused on the tactical situation. Two enemy vessels waited at Sind II's North Pole. One of the Juggernauts might be the equal of *Victory*. The other one seemed to be barely holding itself together—if the former data still held.

In many ways, space battle was a mathematical formula, with X standing for the unknown variables. The Juggernauts had fantastic armor but no electromagnetic shields. It took heavy pounding from the disrupter cannon to breach the enemy armor.

Before she began the fight, Valerie had to decide on tactics. Was it better to take out the weak ship before concentrating on the stronger vessel? If she could destroy the strong war-vessel, the weak one would fall easily enough. But as she concentrated on the strong one, the weak one could stand back and add its attack values to the battle.

"I'm not sure what to do," Valerie said under her breath. That was a terrible admission. She could not let any of the bridge crew know that. It could affect their morale, which was one X factor. Yet, she could only sit here looking confident for so long. The others expected her to think this through carefully. They knew she wasn't Maddox. He would have already made a snap decision. She was more deliberate, more by the book.

What did the book say about such a situation?

Valerie leaned forward. She needed advice. Driving Force Galyan had once commanded his star system's fleet. He might have an answer for her.

She moistened her lips, but hesitated saying the words.

Valerie could feel the pressure building up. She knew the bridge crew was growing suspicious. The helmsman glanced back at her. The warrant officer running communications traded glances with the weapons officer.

Valerie's throat tightened, and she felt a pain in her chest. The decision was up to her. This was even worse than the time Admiral von Gunther had told her to flee the battlefield when Star Watch first faced the New Men.

The holoimage floated closer. Was Galyan about to offer some unasked for advice? It was bad when subordinates felt they could chime in with advice whenever they wanted. An instructor at the Academy—an old starship captain—had told the class once to listen respectfully to all advice from those when asked. But to frown at and even reprimand those who gave unsolicited advice.

To forestall the AI from speaking and to keep her from making an uncomfortable decision, Valerie snapped her fingers. Others looked up at her with expectant faces.

Instead of ducking her head and hiding, Valerie stood and put her hands behind her back. Slowly, she walked toward the main screen.

Quit stalling.

That's when it came to her. Valerie smiled, and she failed to see the helmsman and warrant officer raise their eyebrows. Neither of them had ever seen the lieutenant smile so predatorily.

"Galyan," Valerie said. "Do you recall the Ulant System? The ping we spotted near the super-Jupiter?"

"I do," Galyan said.

"We used a decoy to fix the ping's attention so we could slip away unnoticed. Well, we're going to use another decoy. This one will serve a dual purpose. Communications, I am going to need you to coordinate with weapons. Are you ready?"

The warrant officer and the weapons officer both nodded.

"Here's what we're going to do…" Valerie said.

***

Less than an hour later, the image of Starship *Victory* climbed out of the South Pole region, accelerating for the equator.

It was an advanced decoy/holoimage. The drone projecting the vast deception provided a host of electronic signatures. Those were for the enemy sensors to pick up and verify that it was indeed the starship.

Behind the decoy at a good distance followed a flock of heavy drones. They spread out as they traveled in order to increase their odds of survivability later.

Valerie stood before the main screen on the real *Victory*.

"It's moving," the sensors officer reported.

Valerie pointed at sensors. The officer clicked a switch. The main screen showed the tactical situation on one side and the South Pole region on the other.

The intact Juggernaut began to move. It left the North Pole and headed for the equator where the image of *Victory* headed. The damaged Juggernaut hung back, remaining in stationary orbit at the North Pole.

Would the damaged Juggernaut stay there? Or would it soon follow the intact one in order to add its weapons to the battle? Maybe the enemy commander wished to save the damaged Juggernaut and bring it home for repairs.

"Well?" Valerie snapped.

"The damaged war-vessel appears to be holding its polar orbital position," the sensors officer said.

Valerie wanted to smile, but she was certain that would jinx her luck. *I'd like a clean win. I'd like to show everyone that I can do this. I can win—*

"The intact enemy vessel is scanning the holoimage," sensors said.

Valerie held her breath. This was the test. Would the enemy commander fall for the ruse? They should know in seconds.

"The Juggernaut is accelerating," sensors said.

"Why is it doing that?" asked the weapons officer.

The sensors and weapons officers looked to Valerie as if she should know.

Captain Maddox would remain sphinxlike in such a situation. Valerie felt the pressure to give them a reason. She opened her mouth and then realized giving an inept answer would make her look stupid. Thus, she forced herself to smile enigmatically, as if she had foreseen this exact outcome.

The weapons officer gave the sensor officer a thumbs up, as if to say, "See. This is going smoothly."

Quit second-guessing yourself. You can do this. Just stick to the plan.

"The Juggernaut will be in line-of-sight of the decoy in eleven minutes," the sensors officer said.

Valerie took a deep slow breath and headed for her chair. She sat down, straightened a crease in her pants and gave the order.

This was it. This was the gamble. She was laying everything on the line, on a baited decoy to lure the strong ship away from the weak. She made a swift calculation on a tablet and then said, "Get ready. We will jump in four minutes."

***

Victory used its star drive to shift from the South Pole region to one thousand kilometers above the planetary surface of the North Pole. That put it well "above" the damaged Juggernaut in relation to the planet.

Valerie raised her head from where she had slumped. She squeezed her eyes shut, wondering what had happened—

"We jumped," she said. "Sensors…" Valerie fell silent because she couldn't think what she should say. It came to her that she had slight Jump Fatigue, which was many degrees less than Jump Lag.

"Weapons, Sensors, Galyan, can anyone hear me?"

"Yes, Valerie," the flickering holoimage said.

"What's happening?" she asked.

"The ship is sluggish, as am I. The enemy vessel has begun to accelerate away."

"Sensors, give me an image," Valerie said.

The rest of the bridge crew stirred. The sensors officer tapped her panel. An image wavered into life on the main screen.

The damaged Juggernaut moved sluggishly as its thrusters glowed with exhaust.

"What's happening with the intact Juggernaut?" Valerie asked.

"I have connected with the probes at the equator," Galyan said. "The main Juggernaut is readying its heavy lasers. It will fire momentarily."

"Weapons," Valerie said. "I need the disruptor cannon. We must kill the wounded Juggernaut. If it gets away—"

"I'm working on it, Lieutenant," the weapons officer said.

Valerie nodded as she heard the antimatter engines build up. She made a fist, squeezing harder and harder as she leaned on her armrest.

"Enemy vessel targeted," weapons said.

"Helm, get our ship moving," Valerie said.

"Aye-aye, Lieutenant."

Victory began to give chase, although it moved even more slowly than the escaping Juggernaut.

"What's the intact Juggernaut doing?" Valerie asked.

"It is continuing to accelerate at the decoy," Galyan said. "Perhaps they think we are the decoy. Plus, the decoy *Victory* is right there. It might as well attack it before returning here."

Valerie cocked her head. That seemed like computer logic. Did that only mean that Galyan was thinking like a computer, as he did from time to time, or did it mean they faced a computer-commanded enemy?

"The disrupter cannon is ready," weapons said. "I am targeted on a hole in the armor."

"Fire," Valerie whispered firmly and audibly.

A whine sounded throughout the starship. A second later, the intense disruptor beam reached the accelerating Juggernaut. The beam thrust into the open wound. The ray boiled away inner alloys, turning them liquid and then into gas. Bubbles appeared as the beam chewed deeper and deeper into the stricken vessel.

"I have full maneuvering capability," the helmsman said. "I can close in."

"No," Valerie said. "Let's keep our distance. We have the better long-range weapon, and we don't want to get hit with its death throes."

"The enemy vessel is rotating," sensors said.

The disrupter beam no longer burned into the same location. Instead, the beam lashed along the tough outer alloy as the ball-shaped Juggernaut rotated.

"Why's it doing that?" Valerie asked herself.

"Maybe it wishes to close with us," Galyan said. "If its commander knows it is going to die, why not try to take us with it as it self-destructs?"

"Find a weak spot," Valerie said. "Bore into that thing."

Sensors and weapons worked together, attempting to keep the beam on one location even as the spheroid rotated. At that point, a former rent exposed itself on the Juggernaut.

"I'm locked on!" weapons shouted triumphantly. "Now, we'll show them."

The disrupter beam burned into a great gaping hole in the outer armor. The devastating ray boiled away at the less-armored interior bulkheads. The beam smashed through one bulkhead after another, digging deeper into the interior.

"Compared to last time, the Juggernaut should have exploded by now," Galyan said. "I wonder if they have shut down much of the inner war-vessel. Look. It has stopped rotating. Now, it is braking, using its thrusters to slow its momentum. I was correct. It is going to attempt to close with us."

Valerie's right fist hurt from clutching her fingers so tightly. Why couldn't they get a clean kill for once? Why did it always have to be so difficult?

"I am receiving images from the decoy starship," Galyan said.

"Belay that," Valerie said. "I'm interested in this battle. One thing at a time, Galyan."

"We'll have to shut down the disrupter beam for a moment," weapons said. "The cannon is beginning to overheat."

"No," Valerie said. "Take out the enemy vessel first."

"If we do that," weapons said, "we risk damaging the disrupter cannon. We're going to need it again to face the other Juggernauts."

Valerie bit her lower lip. "Give me thirty seconds. Surely, we can keep the cannon going for thirty more seconds."

"Lieutenant," Andros Crank said, his gray eyes shining. "This is a serious situation. If we lose the disrupter, our odds for ultimate success diminish to almost nothing. I suggest you—"

"Shut off the disrupter cannon," Valerie said reluctantly. If Andros looked that worried, she'd better listen to the advice. "Start up the neutron beam. Keep hitting that wound."

The mighty disrupter cannon shut down, and the constant whine ceased. Now, a weaker purple ray took its place. The neutron beam was a shorter-ranged weapon, but they were still close enough to do heavy damage. The neutron beam did not have to contend with the amazing alien alloy, but struck deeper against interior bulkheads.

"Get ready," the sensors officer said. "I'm reading strange—"

Abruptly, the Juggernaut became an incandescent ball of annihilation, spewing heat, EMP and terrible radiation in all directions.

"Everything to the shields," Valerie said.

The next few seconds were fraught with heart-pounding anticipation, but the bridge crew had been through this before. They were also farther from the Juggernaut compared to last time. The blast, heat, EMP and radiation struck *Victory's* strengthened shield. The shield shifted colors, turning red but no darker; the shield held against everything the destroyed vessel could throw at it.

At last, the frightening moment passed.

Valerie slumped back in her chair. "Status report," she said. "What kind of damage did we take?"

"Nothing," an officer said. "We took no damage."

"I am proud of you," Andros Crank said. "You took out the Juggernaut cleanly. That was wonderful work, Lieutenant. You pulled off the perfect maneuver."

Valerie wanted to glow in the admiration. She didn't have time, though. "What about the second Juggernaut? What's happening with it?"

"That is what I have been trying to tell you," Galyan said.

-55-

The intact Juggernaut continued to accelerate toward the decoy-image of Starship *Victory*. If its commander sensed the first Juggernaut's destruction, its actions betrayed no evidence of it.

All at once, seven different laser ports energized. Heavy beams flashed the distance from the Juggernaut to the giant holoimage. The lasers flashed through and disappeared from sight within the image, making the starship waver as if with heat. That might have given away the decoy. The enemy vessel simply continued beaming.

"The enemy commander seems perplexed," Galyan said. "He or she is beaming longer and hotter, but the wavering image remains."

"Suggestions," Valerie said.

"Another jump," Galyan said. "If you come in behind the Juggernaut while it is engaged with the decoy—"

"No," Valerie said. "We know Jump Fatigue accumulates in people and machines. We don't dare risk another jump now because we'd be a sitting duck once we appeared. We will adhere to the plan."

"But the opportunity…" Galyan said.

"It's a gambler's trap," Valerie said. "Helm, give me acceleration. We're going to chase down the other war-vessel."

The antimatter engines throbbed as the helmsman demanded greater power. The ancient Adok vessel quickly built up velocity as the exhaust tail lengthened behind it and the gravity dampeners hummed overtime to compensate for the strain.

At that point, the equator-located probes fed Galyan and the sensors officer new data. Two enemy lasers beamed through *Victory* and struck the decoy drone providing the holoimage its existence and the false sensor signals.

Abruptly, the fake starship—the giant holoimage—vanished from sight.

"Faster," Valerie said. "We have to catch it quickly. We have to time this just right. Did the combat drones stop accelerating and emitting signals in time?"

"Affirmative," Galyan said. "The combat drones are in deep stealth mode, ready for the next maneuver."

Valerie forced herself to sit back. She forced her shoulders to relax as she went back over the battle plan.

She had destroyed the weaker unit at no loss or harm to *Victory*. It had been as clean a kill as she had ever achieved during a voyage. That considerably strengthened their position against the intact Juggernaut. Even better, they had deployed powerful drones near the enemy vessel in a bracketing position. It did not appear that the Juggernaut had sensed the stealth drones yet. The drones had hidden behind the decoy starship, which seemed to have fixated the enemy's attention. Now, the black-painted, ghost-plated antimatter drones drifted along on momentum alone, waiting on a signal from *Victory* to resume their attack.

"The Juggernaut has begun braking maneuvers," sensors said. "I think they want to engage us, Lieutenant."

Valerie turned to Galyan. "What do you make of that?"

"I do not understand your question, Valerie."

"If you controlled the seven—the six Juggernauts, what would you do next?"

Galyan blinked rapidly. "I would summon this Juggernaut and have it join the five accelerating toward the third planet."

"Me too," Valerie said.

"But our Juggernaut is not doing that," Galyan said. "Your question is, what does that tell us about the other Juggernauts?"

Valerie nodded.

"They are not under the same commander," Galyan said.

"Two independent Juggernaut flotillas," Valerie said. "How can that be? I mean, aren't these ancient Rull ships?"

"That is what we have been led to believe."

"Ludendorff told us that. Was he lying?"

"Unknown," Galyan said. "I have no other independent source of data."

"Could Strand be controlling the other Juggernauts?"

"Please give me a moment, Valerie." The holoimage froze. A few seconds later, he regarded the lieutenant. "I have been unable to detect any communications between the star cruiser and the enemy Juggernauts. The five war-vessels have already launched drones. Those drones are accelerating hard toward the fleeing star cruiser."

"We sent drones behind our decoy starship," Valerie said. "That doesn't necessarily mean anything."

"Perhaps the enemy commander believes you and Strand would bracket a fleeing Juggernaut. Thus, it is going to attempt to engage us and badly wound or destroy us by itself."

Valerie slowly scratched her right cheek. She hadn't thought of that. Yes. That was a good point. Strand and she might have been able to surround this lone war-vessel.

"How much longer until we're in line-of-sight?" Valerie asked the weapons officer.

"Eight point seven minutes, Lieutenant. The enemy vessel is hugging the atmosphere in a low orbital position. The Juggernaut is also pulling away from our drifting drones, gaining greater separation from them every moment."

Valerie tapped her fingers on an armrest. "Take us to a higher orbit, Helmsman. We're going to engage in battle sooner rather than later. I have a feeling we're going to need the help of those drones to defeat the Juggernaut."

"Yes, Lieutenant," the helmsman said, as his hands began to rove over his panel.

Victory not only gained velocity as it sped away from the North Pole, but it maneuvered away from the planet, lengthening the horizon.

"We will be in targeting range in four minutes," weapons said.

Valerie's gut began to churn. This was it. Could *Victory* take on an intact Juggernaut?

The seconds ticked away as the starship maneuvered into a firing position.

"What's the status of the disrupter cannon?" Valerie asked.

"It's primed and readied," weapons said. "There was a weak coolant coil in the reaction chamber. The techs have already refitted it."

Valerie nodded. How had the maintenance crew overlooked that? It was almost criminal negligence. She would have to convene a review board after this was over.

"Initiate stealth acceleration for the first antimatter missile," Valerie said.

Weapons touched various green symbols on his board.

A laser signal went out to a responder probe in high North Polar orbit on the other side of Sind II from the approaching Juggernaut and *Victory*. The probe relayed the signal to a different probe near the equatorial plane but in high orbit. The equatorial probe relayed the signal to a probe near the South Pole, which in turn bounced the signal to another probe that sent it to another equatorial probe—this one was on the same side as the Juggernaut and *Victory*. Finally, the last probe used a laser signal to lessen chances of enemy interception. The signal reached the forward-most antimatter missile—the missile had been launched at the same time as the holoimage/decoy drone.

Spewing gravity waves, the antimatter missile began a stealth acceleration toward the Juggernaut.

The other antimatter missiles maintained their forward momentum, waiting for similar signals.

Antimatter missiles were one of Star Watch's secret weapons. They had fantastic explosive power, especially compared to normal thermonuclear warheads. The alien alloy protecting the Juggernaut was tough, but could it resist near-proximity antimatter explosions?

"We will be in targeting range in thirty seconds," the weapons officer said.

Valerie was leaning forward again, with her gaze focused on the main screen. Ten seconds later, the disruptor-cannon whine began. That caused the lieutenant's eyes to bulge outward the slightest bit.

"The Juggernaut's laser ports are energizing," the sensors officer said. "They know we're coming."

"Have they targeted the antimatter missile behind it?"

"Unknown," the sensors officer said. She studied her panel intently. "Yes! They know it is coming. They see it."

"Initiate Plan B," Valerie snapped.

"Plan B initiating," the weapons officer said, as he stabbed a forefinger against his board.

Another signal flashed from *Victory*, this time going the shortest route to the antimatter missile.

Victory breached the horizon limit. The Juggernaut appeared on the main screen.

"Fire," Valerie said.

The disrupter beam flashed into existence as it sped toward the twenty-kilometer Juggernaut. At the same time, five enemy heavy lasers returned fire, beaming at the starship. On the other side of the Juggernaut, a laser lashed out at the nearing antimatter missile.

"Accelerate the other missiles in a staggered formation," Valerie ordered.

The disruptor beam struck the alien alloy, stymied for the moment. The enemy lasers struck *Victory's* electromagnetic shield.

Meanwhile, the forward missile's antimatter warhead ignited. An intense antimatter explosion spewed EMP, radiation and blast. It was too far away to damage the Juggernaut, but that hadn't been the missile's function.

One of the weak points of any spaceship was its sensors. One could harden the hull, but how did one sufficiently harden sensor nodes? The antimatter explosion might have burned out some sensors. Certainly, it momentarily blinded the Juggernaut on the other side. That was the great hope, at least.

The other antimatter missiles burned hot, one after another in a staggered formation. They had one goal: to reach the Juggernaut before the blinding white explosion dissipated enough for the enemy sensors to spot the new attack. The first missile had acted like a smoke grenade in an old-fashioned land battle, creating its own covering terrain.

At the same time, in order to keep the Juggernaut's commander busy, *Victory's* disrupter beam burned against the advanced alloy, trying to chew through.

The giant war-vessel continued to return fire with heavy lasers.

The distance between the two spaceships was minimal compared to regular space battles. In a relative sense, this was almost pointblank range. Instead of fifty thousand kilometers, it was a little over six thousand kilometers and closing between ships.

Valerie endured as the shield began to darken.

Because the disrupter beam traveled at the speed of light, it crossed the greater distance in the blink of an eye. The antimatter missiles were all now less than one thousand kilometers from the giant vessel. But the missiles crawled compared to light-speed, even though each of them presently traveled faster than a bullet shot from a sniper rifle.

"The Juggernaut is launching missiles," the sensors officer said.

"Galyan, you are in charge of the neutron beam. Target the enemy missiles. Destroy all of them before they get too close."

"Yes, Valerie," the AI said.

The shield went from deep red to brown. More enemy lasers crossed the distance, adding to the destructive force. If the shield went down, *Victory's* armor would have to hold. Against the magnitude of those lasers, the armor plating would not last long.

"Has the Juggernaut spotted our missiles?" Valerie said.

"I don't know," the sensors officer said. "The vessel hasn't targeted them yet. I don't think we can count on their blindness much longer, though."

Valerie willed the Juggernaut to remain blind. They needed a break. She'd destroyed the first Juggernaut easily enough. If she could get this one—

"The shield is blackening," the weapons officer said. "It's down to thirty percent in areas."

Valerie's stomach began to churn harder than ever. She tasted stomach acid at the back of her throat. *Victory* was minuscule compared to the alien war-vessel. What had she been thinking to take on—?

"Yes!" the weapons officer shouted. "Yes, yes, yes! Lieutenant. The first antimatter missile slammed against the Juggernaut and ignited. We hurt it."

Valerie allowed herself the faintest of grins. Could the trick have worked? Would the other missiles reach the enemy ship?

"Breach," the sensors officer said.

Valerie's stomach knotted.

An enemy laser burst through their weakened blackened shield. The laser continued its journey, striking the starship's outer armor. It began to chew away at the armor, the laser growing stronger by the second.

"Hit!" the weapons officer said. "Another missile detonated."

At the same time, another laser burned through *Victory's* pitch-dark shield. It was going to collapse any second. The Juggernaut poured out an incredible wattage of laser fire. Valerie had seen nothing like it since the Destroyer.

"The lasers are becoming hotter," Galyan reported.

"Have you destroyed the enemy missiles?" Valerie shouted.

"Negative," Galyan said. "The alien missiles are resistant to the neutron beam."

"Weapons," Valerie said. "Target those missiles with the disrupter cannon. Don't let them get in range."

"Yes, Lieutenant," weapons said.

Valerie wanted to weep as another enemy laser burned through the shield. She couldn't understand why the shield hadn't collapsed yet. Maybe one of Andros Crank's modifications to the shield kept it intact thus far.

"Hit," sensors said.

Valerie stared at the woman.

"Another antimatter missile has struck the Juggernaut," sensors said.

"Why aren't the antimatter explosions weakening the enemy vessel?" Valerie asked in an agonized voice.

No one responded.

Valerie realized with shock that her fear had gotten the better of her. She lurched to her feet. “We’re not done yet,” she said in as calm as voice as possible.

“Got one,” the weapons officer said.

Valerie studied the main screen. The disrupter beam had exploded an enemy missile.

“Chief Technician Crank,” Valerie said. “I am amazed our shield is still up, as weak as it is.”

“Their lasers are weakening,” Andros Crank said.

Valerie wanted to believe that. Galyan had just said otherwise. “Are you certain?” she asked the Kai-Kaus technician.

“Positive,” Crank said.

Abruptly, no enemy lasers made it through the shield. The electromagnetic shield resealed, seemed a touch less dark, as if it had begun dissipating the terrible energies it blocked.

“Is this your doing, Chief Technician?” Valerie asked.

The Kai-Kaus Chief Technician shrugged modestly.

That proved to be the turning point in the battle. The shield steadily strengthened, becoming brown by the time the weapons officer had destroyed the last alien missile. He now retargeted the twenty-kilometer war-vessel.

“I’m getting strange readings,” the sensor officer said. “According to this, there are severe internal explosions taking place over there. Lieutenant. I think the antimatter missiles did more damage than we realized. That may have proven to be a brilliant stroke on your part.”

Valerie nodded calmly enough. Inside, she was cheering. It was like the time at the Academy when she had played hockey. She had flicked a backhanded shot that went through the goalie’s skates. During the second period, a shot had bounced off the goalie’s stick right to her stick. She had flicked the puck past his side for a second goal.

At that point, she had skated, silently praying to God that He let her score one more goal so she would make a hat trick.

During the third period, she did score the third goal. At that point, her prayer changed. They were ahead 3-2. She asked God to let that be the last goal scored by anyone. She wanted to win the game with her hat trick.

By game's end, that was exactly what had happened. It was her greatest sporting moment.

Now, Valerie wanted to destroy the Juggernaut, and have it be her combat trick that had done it. With a start, she realized that her stomach no longer churned. It seemed as if they might actually win this one.

"Let's get to work," Valerie said. "Find a weak point in the armor and hit it with the disruptor and neutron beams."

The final antimatter missiles struck the twenty-kilometer vessel. Not even its fantastic alloy and giant size could resist direct antimatter hits one right after the other.

The enemy lasers quit altogether. The Juggernaut began to accelerate for space, leaving Sind II's atmosphere behind.

That allowed *Victory* to fire at the enemy vessel in leisure. Finally, the disruptor beam broke through the alloy, beginning to chew through lesser bulkheads. By that point, the battle was over and the butchery began. Five minutes and thirty-two seconds later, the Juggernaut self-destructed.

Luckily for *Victory*, the shield had shed enough power to take the blast and EMP. The shield went all the way down to black again, but not as close to collapse as before.

Valerie sat in the command chair stunned. She couldn't believe it. She had done it. She had won as clean a victory as any of them had ever done during any of their missions. She had destroyed two Juggernauts at no damage to the starship, although she had used up eighteen percent of the antimatter missiles.

Strand was coming, with five Juggernauts chasing him. The captain was still missing, but Valerie began to believe that maybe they were going to win this one after all. Now it was time to see if she could rescue the landing party.

-56-

Strand studied the battle in detail in his holographic chamber.

The wizened Methuselah Man sat in a chair on a hydraulic arm. The arm had raised him into the middle of the room, and holoimages encircled him. He saw everything up close and personal. Strand had found over the centuries that such scrutiny led to insights. These insights allowed him to pierce his opponent's strong and weak points.

Lieutenant Valerie Noonan was a keen tactician. There was no denying it. The decoy starship had been a brilliant maneuver, particularly with the following antimatter missiles.

He wished Star Watch had never gotten hold of those. They could make the coming encounter more troublesome than it might otherwise be.

"Commander," a New Man said over an ear implant.

"Yes," Strand said into a microphone.

With a few taps of his fingers, Strand erased the space battle program and stared into the giant holographic face of the golden-skinned superman talking to him. Strand could see the pores and a hair peeking out of a nostril.

"We have destroyed the first missile," the New Man said.

"Were there any complications?" Strand asked.

"None, Master," the New Man said.

"Continue with the targeting and destruction," Strand said.

"Yes, Master."

Strand tapped another control. The New Man hologram vanished. This time, the Methuselah Man studied the five following Juggernauts.

They continued to launch missiles, but not in a deadly barrage. It felt as if they were herding him toward Sind II. They continued to emit the dampening field. Perhaps that took a high percentage of their power.

Strand hadn't asked Rose about that. He hadn't believed it was important at the time.

The Methuselah Man smiled. He would speak with Rose soon. She was in a special room, receiving greater emotional stimulation. He wanted her in a highly agitated state. He wanted this for two reasons. Firstly, it was sheer fun to torment a smug android. He had begun to look forward to capturing more of them. Primarily, though, she would need to be in such a state for the interrogation to proceed along the needed lines.

Rose belonged to the androids that ultimately controlled the Juggernauts. Strand wanted the codes so he could control the giant vessels. It was too early to implement that, though. He had to make sure *Victory* remained where it was. He wanted the dampening field to catch the pesky starship. Strand wanted that crew. He wanted Ludendorff, and he wanted the Adok ship for himself.

This was a dangerous maneuver, to be sure. Yet, the prize was worth so much. If he could gain all the items he hoped to get, he could use them to turn everything around with the Emperor of the Throne World. More than anything, Strand wanted the smug Emperor aboard the star cruiser. He wanted to become emperor of the Throne World and remold humanity along the proper lines. He would make a super-race such as the galaxy hadn't seen for a long, long time.

First, though, he needed to crack the vault inside Sind II.

Strand laughed. He recalled an ancient custom from Earth called Halloween. Kids went from house to house, with open bags, begging for candy. Adults dropped tidbits into each bag. After a night's work, the child had quite the haul.

The real winners on Halloween were older, slyer children. They robbed a younger child, adding the bag of candy to a vast haul of loot.

Strand planned on being the older, wiser child, stealing from the androids, stealing from the Vendels and most certainly stealing from Professor Ludendorff. Strand would gather a mighty haul of Builder artifacts, and he would do so by outthinking the tactician aboard Starship *Victory*.

Before he did that, he must continue to decipher Lieutenant Noonan's personality by studying this last and most interesting battle. Strand thus turned on the holoimage and went over the battle one more time.

-57-

Down inside Sind II, Maddox made it back into the subterranean dome in time for the first round against floating fighting robots.

The professor detected them and alerted Sims. The marine lieutenant waited, strategically situated with the battle group. The exoskeleton-suited space marines lay on their armored bellies, with their shredders ready.

"Down!" Meta radioed to Maddox. She was wearing a headset and microphone.

The captain saw the marines in a prone circle around a hatch in the floor. He understood her suggestion and immediately lay down, just in time.

The hatch popped up, sailing against the ceiling. From there, the hatch bounced down against the floor and flipped hard against a wall. It landed on an armored marine, who shrugged it off his suit.

A floating metal cylinder rose from the hatch. It had a top-heavy body, with a narrow pointed appendage on the bottom. The thing hummed. No doubt that base was its gravity device, propelling it. The robot extruded several metal arms with round buzz saws on the ends. Ports slid open and small gun barrels poked out.

Sims directed the counter-fire, employing a strict usage of the remaining ammo.

Three shredders punctured the robot. One of the rounds must have hit a brain node. Lights flashed. The robot fired a few rounds back, which hammered the nearest wall, and then the cylindrical robot toppled onto its side. A final bullet in the upper portion caused the robot's lights to dim and disappear altogether.

For the next several minutes, new floaters kept popping up out of the hatch. Sims and his marines slaughtered the fighting machines. A few enemy shots struck exoskeleton armor. The bullets made dents, but none of them breached a suit.

Finally, Ludendorff—who had stayed well back—declared that the last fighting machine was dead. For now, no more were coming.

Forty-nine floaters were heaped around the hatch.

The marines waited for more fighting machines to appear, just in case the professor was wrong.

"Did you hear me?" Ludendorff asked.

"I did," Sims said. "We're just making sure."

"I am the one who warned you of the floaters. Believe me when I say no more are coming."

"You mean you can't detect anymore," Sims said.

"Captain," Ludendorff said in irritation.

Maddox climbed to his feet. He told them about the approaching Vendel war party.

Ludendorff brightened as he nodded. "This is extremely interesting from a psychological and sociological point of view. The priests must have driven the others. Perhaps they are on a crusade into the depths."

"Some of the Vendels were wearing space marine suits," Maddox said.

Ludendorff let his chin rest against his chest, seemingly deep in thought. Finally, he said, "I suggest we stay ahead of the war party, Captain. I wonder if the chief priest has broached the ancient stores, arming his men with highly potent religious articles."

"I didn't see anything religious about the suits," Maddox said.

"You have not observed the Vendels as I have," Ludendorff said. "Those must be old tech marvels, which they have come to believe are religious relics."

"What should we do, sir?" Sims asked Maddox.

"Well, Professor," Maddox said. "What have you learned through your speed reading?"

"The floor hatch leads to an access point," the professor said. "We must clear a way and enter the maze beneath the dome."

"The route leads to an elevator?" asked Maddox.

"I believe so," the professor said.

"Then let's go."

***

With the exoskeleton suits, the marines cleared the shot-up floaters in no time. A scout lowered himself into the hatch. No surprises greeted him. The rest of the battle group and Keith, Meta and Ludendorff followed.

The lit corridors and ramps under the dome formed a giant maze. Without Ludendorff, it was questionable they would have found their way. The ceiling was too low for any marine to jump or lope, so they clanked single fire. Every so often, Ludendorff asked the captain to call a halt. The Methuselah Man then took his bearings and gave new directions.

For the next fifteen minutes, they traversed a downward-slanting ramp. The passageway widened for a time and then narrowed again.

Keith hitched an exoskeleton ride and finally Meta did likewise. Ludendorff had allowed a marine to carry him the entire time.

"I have to conserve my strength so that I remain alert," the professor told Meta.

There were no more signs of fighting machines. Nor had the Vendel war party caught up with them. Once, Ludendorff informed Maddox that the Vendels had entered the underground maze.

"Do they know about the elevators?" Maddox asked.

"At the very least, I would imagine the chief priest does," Ludendorff said. "Yes. I'm sure they do."

The marines continued to clank. Earlier today, they had been carrying masses of munitions. Now, Sims and Maddox conferred on the best way to conserve the small amount of ammunition they retained.

"Excuse me a moment, sir," Sims told the captain. "I have to take this report." Several seconds later, the lieutenant said, "Something's up ahead, sir. The scout said it looks big and must have plenty of juice. I'm guessing it has massive firepower too."

Soon, Maddox and Sims spoke face-to-face with the scout. The scout had advanced sensors in his suit. The sensor report told the scout that the corridor led to a large chamber, which appeared to be a nexus. The problem was that there was something squat in the chamber, weighing possibly thirty tons or more.

"I don't want the corporal to eyeball it," Sims told Maddox. "It's too damn dangerous for that."

"Just a minute," Maddox said. He opened his faceplate and shouted for the professor.

The Methuselah Man trotted from the waiting battle group to the three of them. Maddox explained the situation to Ludendorff as the professor nodded politely.

"Here's the question," Maddox said. "Can we bypass the nexus?"

"Let me check my notes," the professor said.

The Methuselah Man pulled out a sheaf of folded papers he kept in an inner jacket pocket. He unfolded them, scanned one page, put it at the back, scanned the next page and put the next three to the back.

"Hmm," Ludendorff said, as he read the needed page. Finally, he looked up. "That's it. That's the access node. It leads to a shaft that leads to the elevator. We must go there."

"What about the waiting machine?" Maddox asked. "Do your notes say anything about it?"

"In Earth terms, I suspect it is a tank. I very much doubt we have the firepower to breach its armor."

"What's a tank doing down here?"

"Protecting the access point," the professor said. "By entering the dome, we have woken an old program. At least, such is my belief. It's possible the tank was asleep before we came. Now, it is awake."

"Could the chief priest have a code to disarm the tank?" Maddox asked.

Ludendorff eyed the captain closely. "That is an astute guess. It's possible, but I don't know."

"How do we defeat the tank?"

"That is your area of expertise, not mine. After all, you successfully entered *Victory*. It stymied me when I was in the Adok System."

Maddox wondered if the professor still smarted from that. He had used the Methuselah Man's notes to help him breach *Victory*, but telling the professor that wouldn't make things any better.

"What do you think?" Maddox asked the lieutenant.

"A tank, eh?" Sims said. "You have to strike its weak point. That's usually the top. We need an airstrike or an orbital strike to take it out."

"What else?" asked Maddox.

"Does the tank have an AI to guide it?" Sims asked.

"I doubt it," Ludendorff said. "If it did, the AI would likely have degraded by now."

"Galyan didn't degrade," Maddox said.

For an answer, Ludendorff snorted. "There's another problem I failed to mention. As you attempt to sneak up on the tank, I suspect motion sensors will tell it you're coming. It will use its main gun to obliterate you long before you can see it."

"We needed a floater," Sims said.

"How so?" asked Ludendorff.

"Pack the floater with explosives," the lieutenant said, "have it dodge the tank shots and put the high explosives against the tank's main gun. The explosion might knock out the gun, allowing my boys to get in close and slap sticky mines to the treads or possibly rip off the hatch and drop inside."

"That is a dubious plan at best," the professor said.

"But it's an answer just the same," Maddox said.

"What do you have in mind?" the professor asked.

Maddox did not answer, but clanked back to the battle group.

***

Maddox climbed out of his exoskeleton suit. Afterward, he scratched several places that had been driving him mad.

Finally, he began to pack the suit with high explosives. Once filled to the brim, and using the majority of the satchel charges, the captain sealed the suit and unhooked the remote control unit from the back. He activated the unit and explained the process to Keith Maker.

The remote control unit activated the suit's interior motion circuits. The Kelchworth 350s did the rest, turning the armor into a semi-robot, able to move without the marine inside the suit.

"Have you lost your mind?" Ludendorff asked.

"Give me a better idea," the captain said.

"You're going to need your armor before this is through."

Maddox shrugged.

"At least make one of the marines give you his suit," Ludendorff said.

"No, it's my idea," Maddox said. "Thus, I'll accept the risks."

"While that might appear noble," Ludendorff said, "it is far from the case. You are the captain. You will need your suit. Acting with sentimentality is a fool's notion."

Maddox's eyes narrowed. He wore his uniform and boots, having brought them along in a small pack. He had his long-barreled gun strapped to his side and had, some time ago, reclaimed the monofilament knife from Meta. The shredder was too big for him to use now other than if he lay down in a prone position and used it like a heavy machine-gun.

"Ready?" Maddox asked Keith.

The ace had been practicing with the remote control unit. He made the exoskeleton suit move in one direction and then another. Using his thumbs, Keith made the suit squat, jump up, twist around, duck and run in place.

"Got it," Keith said. "This is a piece of cake."

"That's preposterous," Ludendorff said.

"Have you seen me fly before, mate?"

"That's not the point. This is different."

"That's where you're wrong. There's no one better at piloting than I am. Besides, I've played video games with exactly these sorts of controls and commands."

Ludendorff shook his head, muttering to himself.

Maddox clapped Keith on the back. He appreciated the man's confidence and positive spirit. "Proceed when ready," he said.

Keith looked around, spied a spot and sat there. He crossed his legs so he sat cross-legged and put the remote control unit in his lap. He took a deep breath, twisted his neck so it popped and began to manipulate the controls.

Everyone else had moved back. Maddox's old armor suit spun to face everyone. Then, it saluted smartly, spun in the direction of the chamber and took off at a sprint.

Maddox leaned against the wall beside Keith so he could look down at the tiny screen. It was difficult for the captain to tell what was going on. The image kept changing constantly. It was rather disorienting.

Keith looked up once, grinning, before concentrating once more.

The marines waited. Meta waited. Ludendorff paced back and forth.

"Motion," Keith said. "I think the tank sees me."

Maddox saw a host of flashing data beside the screen. Keith seemed to comprehend everything at once.

"Get ready, everyone," Keith said. "It's going to fire."

A terrific boom sounded from farther ahead. It was a nearly deafening noise. Maddox watched the screen. He saw the floor from eye level. The exoskeleton suit must be lying down. Something blurred overhead. Another boom sounded. This time, the image remained rigid. At the last moment, the image went high—no doubt due to the jumping suit. On the tiny screen, something blurred underneath.

Each tank round struck a wall, causing another shattering sound and underground shaking.

"Quake rounds," Sims said, "or something just like quake rounds. The machine might be trying to bring the tunnels down on us."

"Here goes," Keith said in a soft voice.

The image on the remote control unit changed faster than before. The suit must be running.

"Okay, mate," Keith whispered.

His thumbs twitched. He held his breath. A boom sounded, a crashing noise came next and then intense shaking from another quake round. Keith laughed wildly.

"It's readying a flame thrower!" the ace shouted. "I gotta keep running."

Maddox saw the squat enemy machine on the tiny screen. It was indeed a tank. Earth tanks looked different. This one was rounder shaped with a narrow cannon, like on an ancient Mark III Panzer of World War II.

The exoskeleton armor must have leaped. The barrel was right there on the screen.

"Now," Keith said. He thrust his right thumb up hard on a control.

The scene vanished. Keith threw himself flat onto the floor and covered his ears. Maddox did likewise. Then, there came an explosion, a monstrous noise. The tunnel shook for what felt like several minutes, finally stopping as dust floated about them like ashes vomited from a dragon's throat.

Maddox lifted his hands from his ears. They rang, despite his having covered them. He stood, and stumbled, disoriented.

Keith was grinning at him from on the floor. "I did it, sir. I took out the tank."

Maddox wasn't sure, but it seemed like a good possibility that Keith was right.

"Let's go see," Keith said. He climbed to his feet and began staggering down the tunnel.

-58-

Soon, the battle group found a cave-in, with huge pieces of wall, and chunks of rock and earth, blocking the way.

"Your suit created too big of an explosion," the professor told Maddox.

Sims must have overheard the comment. The lieutenant clanked near with his faceplate open. "We can move this stuff out of the way."

"And bring the rest of the underworld upon us?" the professor asked.

Sims glanced at Maddox.

The captain nodded.

The four unsuited people moved out of the way, as the space marines began hefting huge rocks or dragging away sections of wall. Slowly, carefully, they cleared the corridor.

Once, the exposed earth above shifted ominously as driblets of dirt showered onto the floor.

"We can't survive a complete cave-in," Ludendorff told Maddox.

The captain studied the Methuselah Man. "Out with it. What are you hiding?"

"You're mistaken in thinking that I fear any one particular thing," Ludendorff said. "This is simply common sense. We may be in over our heads."

A sardonic smile appeared on the captain's face.

Ludendorff scowled, beginning to mutter under his breath about pompous young Intelligence officers.

Meta pulled the captain aside. "You don't seem to trust the professor anymore," she whispered. "Do you really think someone has altered his mind?"

"It's one of my chief suspicions," Maddox admitted quietly.

Meta searched his face. "What do you think we'll find down here?"

"Whatever it is, I'm not sure Ludendorff wants us to find it."

"That doesn't answer the question."

It was Maddox's turn to study Meta. Something clicked in his mind, like a gear finding its mesh-point. He held her, kissing her deeply.

Meta smiled up at him. "Not that I don't like it, but what was that for?"

"For the pure pleasure of kissing you," Maddox said.

"We've broken through," Sims shouted from down the hall.

"Let's go," Maddox said.

Meta grabbed an arm, pulling him back. "What do you think is hidden down there?"

"A Builder, or highly advanced androids," Maddox said.

"A Builder," Meta said, sounding worried.

"I give that the lowest possibility. I have begun to wonder if a Rull creature penetrated Sind's defenses."

"I don't understand."

"From what we've seen, the pieces don't match the whole," Maddox said. "How can rather primitive Vendels keep Juggernauts at bay? Why would androids need help breaking into these subterranean vaults?" The captain shook his head. "I suspect a power or powerful entity lies in the depths. But what kind of entity, and why remain in hiding on a broken planet?"

"Does Ludendorff feel that way?"

"The professor remains an enigma. He helps us, but he has ulterior motives. Sometimes, I get the feeling he knows what he is doing. At other times, I believe subconscious impulses drive him. The most likely explanation for the impulses is latent Builder compulsions buried so deeply that no one has been able to see them. Of course, we must also suspect the box found in the incinerator unit aboard *Victory*."

"Should I watch him?" Meta asked.

"Always," Maddox said. "Now let's go. Time is no longer on our side."

Meta gripped his left arm a little longer. Finally, the Rouen Colony woman let go and the two hurried after the others.

***

They reached a huge blasted smoking tank. Inside, they found bloody fleshy chunks.

"That wasn't an android," Maddox said.

"There's no telling what drove it," Sims said.

"Professor?" the captain asked. "Do you have a theory?"

Ludendorff shrugged moodily.

"You hardly looked at the remains," Maddox said.

"I don't want to," Ludendorff said grumpily.

Meta and the captain exchanged glances. Maddox shrugged. She appeared thoughtful, and he noticed her peering at the professor more often.

The Methuselah Man studied his folded notes for a time. He went to each opening as the marines cleared away enough rubble.

After the marines had cleared the last opening, Ludendorff asked, "Is that it?"

"As far as I can tell," Sims said.

Ludendorff checked his notes again and began shaking his head. "There should be another entrance. I count five but there should be six."

"What should we be looking for?" the lieutenant asked.

"I found something," the corporal said. "I don't know why my sensors didn't catch it earlier."

Sims and Ludendorff turned to look at the scout.

"Under our feet," the corporal said. "It's a hidden hatch. There must have been too much junk in the way for me to spot it before, even with my sensors."

Under the lieutenant's direction, the marines cleared away more rubble.

"I don't see anything," the lieutenant said.

"Something is under the floor," the corporal said.

"Fine," Sims said. He knelt with his exoskeleton suit and began to smash at the floor with an armor-gloved fist. He smashed like a comic-book superhero, but nothing happened.

"The floor is tougher than it looks," Sims said.

"Keep at it," the professor said. "I think that is what we want."

Sims looked up at the captain. Maddox nodded.

The lieutenant pounded at the floor. Suddenly, lines appeared along the floor. He smashed more. The lines became cracks and finally the floor between the cracks turned into rubble. The lieutenant clawed away at the mess until he reached metal.

"I suggest greater care," Ludendorff shouted.

Sims didn't look to the captain this time. He scraped at the metal until he revealed its outline. This floor hatch was bigger than the last one.

"If we open this," Sims said, "are we going to find more fighting machines?"

The corporal stepped near, using his sensors. "Whatever is under us seems to be empty."

Sims finished exposing the floor hatch. This one had a junction box on it.

Ludendorff climbed down to the hatch, brushed away grit and dust, and used needle-like tools. Something on the box clicked. The professor tenderly removed a covering. He found a complex pad with strange symbols on it.

"I must think," Ludendorff said. On his hands and knees, he studied the symbols. He remained like that for three minutes.

"What's the problem?" Maddox asked from above.

"Shhh," Ludendorff said. "Don't break my concentration."

Maddox retreated, waiting with the others.

Finally, Ludendorff began to tap the pad experimentally. He became surer a few tries later. Then, his fingers began blurring as if he had done this a hundred times.

The hatch clanked. Ludendorff laughed. He straightened and pulled, opening the hatch.

Maddox came forward to see what Ludendorff had found. A ladder led straight down. The circular shaft seemed to be made of plastic. It glowed, and a strange hum came from farther down.

"Do you know what's causing the hum?" Maddox asked the professor.

"I think so," Ludendorff said. "The exoskeleton suits will not function beyond this point. It's an anti-android system. It might be dangerous to anyone who tries to go down. I believe I can continue forward. Possibly you can also, Captain. I doubt anyone else will be able to advance."

"Explain that," Maddox said.

Ludendorff rubbed his lips together. He took a pedantic stance as if he stood before a classroom of students.

"Do you recall the voyages of Odysseus?" the professor asked.

"Are you talking about the hero of the Trojan War, the one who invented the Trojan horse?" Maddox asked.

"One and the same," the professor said. "He was the crafty Greek warrior. I often think of him as my patron saint, as it were. After the great victory, he left Troy and tried to reach home. The gods had other ideas, and he had many strange adventures. One of them consisted of the sirens. The sirens lounged on sea rocks and sang such lovely songs that no man could listen to them and remain sane. He would leap overboard trying to reach them. The sea would dash him on the treacherous rocks and the man would die.

"As I'm sure you know, Odysseus had to hear the sirens sing. He was too curious, you see. That is the failing of all super-intelligent people."

"People such as you," Maddox said blandly.

"Precisely," Ludendorff said, failing to catch the sarcasm. "Legend had it that if a man ever heard the sirens sing without killing himself, the sirens would kill themselves.

"Well, Odysseus had his men—the rowers—plug their ears with beeswax. Before that, they tied Odysseus to the mast. The men rowed past the sirens. They sang their enchanted songs, and Odysseus raved, desperately trying to free himself to dive overboard and swim to the faithless singers. In the end, his ship passed them. Odysseus returned to his senses, and the sirens committed suicide."

"That is interesting," Maddox said. "What does it have to do with this entranceway? You can't be suggesting sirens are waiting for us."

"In a manner of speaking, that is exactly what I'm saying."

"The armor won't work and the men will go mad." Maddox said. "It's up to Meta, then."

"No, no," Ludendorff said, exasperated. "Man or woman, it doesn't matter. I believe an old Builder process will hinder anyone without a fantastically powerful intellect from going farther. I can do it. You might, Captain. I doubt anyone else here is that strong willed and mentally capable."

"What lies beyond the sirens?" Maddox said.

"The process that cracks the vaults of the ages, my boy. We're almost there. I'm going. What about you?"

Meta had come up behind Maddox. She whispered, "Don't trust him. This sounds like a cock and bull story. I'm sure we can all go."

Maddox had his doubts. The professor knew he would test this. "Explain how these modern sirens will work?"

"It's a mental attack," Ludendorff said. "You will relive your worst nightmares. Few people can come to grips with that. I know how to defeat it, though."

"Tell us how."

An odd look came over the professor. "I cannot," Ludendorff said. "I don't know why I cannot, but my lips are sealed concerning the method."

"Could it be one of the old Builder impulses driving you?" Maddox asked.

Ludendorff shrugged uneasily, appearing to dislike the idea.

"Very well," Maddox said. "We'll test your theory."

"I am stating fact not theory," Ludendorff said.

"Good enough," Maddox said. "We will test your fact and proceed. If you're correct, you and I shall go deeper while the others stand watch."

"I'm going to go with you," Meta said. "While I don't claim to be a genius like some people, I'm just as stubborn as the next person."

"You may think you are," Ludendorff said. "But I assure you that you are not as stubborn as either the captain or I."

"We'll see," Meta said.

Ludendorff studied her before nodding. "Yes. I suppose we will at that."

-59-

The professor proved correct regarding the exoskeleton armor. It failed to function as soon as the marine scaled the metal rungs.

Several marines with steel cables hauled the incapacitated armor-suited scout back up.

"The professor is right," Maddox told Sims. "You can't follow in your suits."

The lieutenant's faceplate was open. His blocky features were set in a stern mask. "What do you—what are your orders, sir?"

"This could be a dead end," Maddox said. "We don't know what's down there. Maybe it will kill us."

Sims stared at the captain.

"I want you to hold this position," Maddox said. "If the Vendels reach here, and it looks like they're going to overpower you—"

"That will mean we've run out of ammo," Sims said.

Maddox nodded. "In that case, you should shed your power-suits and follow us."

"That doesn't sound like an order."

"What else would you suggest?"

"You're asking my opinion, sir?"

Maddox waited.

Sims's gaze fell. "We could charge the Vendels in our suits, using exoskeleton strength and armor as our weapons."

"I will leave that to your discretion, Lieutenant. While a glorious battle death no doubt appeals to you, my suggestion is to survive to fight another day. That would mean shedding your armor and coming down."

"What about the professor's sirens?"

"Approaching death can wonderfully concentrate one's mind. It may be the impetus you need to storm past the mental projections—if they indeed exist. But, hopefully, it will not come down to that. I suspect I will win through and defeat what is on the other side before the Vendels reach you."

Sims's lips spread into a rugged smile. "If you'll permit me, sir, I have to say, you have balls of brass. It's been a pleasure serving with you, sir."

Maddox decided that he truly liked Lieutenant Sims. "It has been my pleasure, Lieutenant. I appreciate your candor and your fighting attitude. It is a man's outlook."

In his exoskeleton suit, the lieutenant saluted.

Maddox returned it. Afterward, the captain descended into the glowing shaft.

Meta followed and Ludendorff brought up the rear. The hum increased as the captain climbed down until he could feel the sound thrumming through his body. The glow brightened as he descended.

Maddox jumped to the floor and found that it was composed of the same plastic-like substance as the shaft.

Meta dropped down beside him, and Ludendorff carefully set his feet on the floor. There was a small open area and four entranceways at the four points of the compass. Each entrance had an intense glow and emitted the thrumming sound.

"Does it matter which way we choose?" Maddox asked.

Ludendorff consulted his notes and soon shrugged. "I don't know. I think it does." He turned to Meta. "How do you feel?"

"As if I'm about to disprove your intelligence chauvinism," she said.

Ludendorff laughed good-naturedly. "This isn't like a physical contest where one summons conviction and determination. One either possesses the capabilities or she does not."

"I can face my fears," Meta said. "Can you?"

Ludendorff snapped his fingers. "I can do it like that."

"Let's go that way," Maddox said. He had been turning in a slow circle. Now, he pointed down a corridor.

"Why that way?" the professor asked.

"It gives me the greatest trepidation," the captain said. "Thus, it's the one I want to face down first."

"How apt," the professor said. "Let us proceed. Whatever we do, we want to complete it before the Vendel war party reaches the marines. The space marines have no way to retreat and a limited supply of ammunition."

"Right," Maddox said, and he began to march into the chosen corridor.

***

The captain led the way. He marched resolutely, with one hand on the butt of his holstered pistol and the other on the hilt of the monofilament knife. He listened carefully to the hum, intent for a difference in pitch or intensity.

Instead, the hum droned in a constant manner. It struck Maddox as a giant hive going about its daily chores. After a time, his footfalls took on a hypnotic quality until the measure of his tread seemed to transport him into a different realm.

It felt as if he floated in time and space. The hum did change pitch, becoming a throbbing sound that deeply penetrated his mind. Even though he marched through a plastic-coated hallway, he seemed to tumble end-over-end to a past existence.

Here, he was rail-thin, a reed of a teenager, living in a government funded, glorified Boy's Home. He was a loner who was called into the dean's office far too often.

Young Maddox had vast potential, but he slacked in his studies. He truly only excelled at sports. The science and art classes bored him. He loved history, but he lived for football, for wrestling, handball and basketball, judo and boxing.

He remembered a day in gym after school. He had showered, and then padded naked to his locker with a towel around his neck. Four big wrestlers had been waiting for him, and by their stances and the stupid cunning on their faces, young Maddox knew he was in trouble.

"Look at him," the smallest wrestler said. He was a squat individual, built like a brick but only weighing one hundred and fifty pounds.

Rail-thin Maddox was in the weight class ahead of him.

"You're too tall and skinny to be strong," the brick said. "Yet you wave your nose in the air like you're something special. Do you think you're better than us?"

Maddox had always been good at reading intentions. These four meant him bodily harm. It was the first time his mind went into hyperdrive as his cable-like muscles hummed with anticipation.

He whipped the towel off his neck and held both ends, flipping it repeatedly as he had so often seen others do in jest.

"What's he doing?" asked the biggest wrestler, a longhaired ape-like individual with thickly-muscled dangling arms.

Maddox deliberately whipped at the brick, aiming for the youth's left eye. He hit better than he realized.

The brick yelled in pain and surprise. He jerked back, tripped over a bench and catapulted down hard and fast. He hit the back of his head on the cement floor, and there was a distinct smacking sound.

The brick relaxed before his body began to jerk spasmodically. The other three wrestlers stared at their friend in shock and bewilderment.

Maddox slid past them, deeming them more interested in their friend than him. It was a risk. He opened the locker and grabbed his clothes.

"Hey," the biggest wrestler said. "Stick-man did this. We ought to—"

"Shut up, Ted. We got to get help."

"I'll go," Maddox said. "I'll get help."

Apelike Ted cursed at him, gave Maddox the finger and ran for help.

The other two wrestlers regarded Maddox.

He waited for them to make up their minds about what they were going to do to him. His right hand was in the locker. It held onto a hidden flick-knife. If they came at him, he was going to cut them.

"Get out of here," one of them said.

Maddox dressed fast, and he went, his heart pounding but his senses calm in a speed-thinking sense. He realized he had towel-flicked the brick in the eye exactly as he'd intended. The results had been both better and worse than he'd expected.

As young Maddox exited the gym, he began to tremble. It was for what came next. He hated it in a personal way. It was the worst thing that had happened to him as a youth.

The brick left school with a brain injury. The rest of the Boy's Home students had ostracized him after that. They knew he was different. Worse, Maddox realized that he was different from the others.

He had gone to counseling with the dean. What Maddox didn't know was that someone sinister had turned the dean. The dean had been a trusted individual, trying to help troubled youths. The dean had possessed impeccable training, great charisma and considerable charm as a former star athlete.

Maddox sensed something wrong with the dean, where before the man had seemed harmless. The young loner especially distrusted the suggestion for intense counseling over the weekend. Unfortunately, it was the only way for the dean to clear Maddox quickly of all criminal charges regarding the brick.

"After we clear you," the dean said, "we must nip this hyper-aggressiveness of yours in the bud before it gets you into worse trouble."

As Maddox marched down the glowing corridor deep inside Sind II, he felt like the teenaged youth of yesteryear. In his mind, he went to the dean's office on a Saturday morning. A warning in his gut told him this was a bad idea. Yet he couldn't see how to escape it. He did not want to go to prison, as the dean threatened he could.

Maddox quailed, and he almost stopped walking. Sweat appeared on his face. He began to tremble. This was a wretched experience. He had trusted the dean. The man had seemed so likeable.

I must continue. I must break through.

Maddox's eyes narrowed as if he squinted down a gun-sight. His heart raced and his palms became sweaty. He would face his fear. He would continue.

In his mind, Maddox replayed the terrible episode. The dean spoke to him in the otherwise empty counseling office. The big man told Maddox to remain seated as he, the dean, walked around the room.

The dean was not only big but he was also strong. The man lifted weights and must have used steroids. He grinned at Maddox far too much, and there was something disturbing about his eyes.

During one of his passes through the room, the dean had locked the door. He put the key in his front pants pocket.

"We will try something new," the dean said. "You are far too confident, too sure of yourself. I'm going to handcuff you—"

"What?" young Maddox asked.

"I will handcuff you so you learn to overcome this supposed feeling of vulnerability. I believe that is what compelled you to attack Varus Jones."

Maddox began shaking his head. He didn't like the idea at all. No one was going to handcuff him without a fight.

The dean opened a drawer and took out a pair of handcuffs. "Believe me," the brawny man said. "This is the fastest way I know to cure you."

A bad feeling pounded in Maddox's chest. The brawny dean smiled, but there was something evil in the gesture.

Maddox stood up.

"Sit down," the dean told him.

"Unlock the door," Maddox said.

The dean only smiled more charmingly. "You must trust me."

"I don't."

"That shows an unwillingness to cooperate."

Maddox said nothing.

"Do you want to go to prison?"

Maddox still did not speak.

"Very well," the dean said. "The session is over. You will have to take the consequences." He took the key out of his pocket and held it out to Maddox.

The rail-thin teenager reached for the key.

The dean grabbed his wrist with thick powerful fingers. He yanked Maddox near.

Once more, Maddox's mind went into hyperdrive. It seemed to him as if the dean slowed down. He could sense things, and he realized the dean had bad intentions.

With deliberate speed and power, Maddox rammed his knee against the dean's crotch.

The brawny man released his wrist. Thc dean staggered backward, crashing against his desk. He still gripped the key, somehow. Maddox went to him and reached for the key. The dean swept out a leg, catching Maddox by surprise. It knocked the teenager onto the carpet.

"You're going to pay for that," the dean said in an ugly voice. Although still crouching in pain, the dean stood. He shoved the key into a pocket and came at Maddox.

The next few minutes were horrible. The huge brawny man tried to grapple him. Maddox knew it was only a matter of time before the dean caught him. Despite his greater speed and phenomenal strength for his age and size, Maddox knew he would lose a wrestling contest to the dean.

Thus, Maddox fell back onto something he'd learned. The dean lunged at him, and with the palm of his right hand, Maddox struck a perfect blow to the nose. The blow sent a jar of pain up Maddox's right arm. It broke the dean's nose and broke off a piece of bone. The bone launched like an arrow into the dean's brain, killing the man on the spot.

He flopped to the carpet, dead.

Maddox panted. He was dumbfounded that the hit had worked so well. Kicking the door, the teenager gained his freedom from the awful office. He felt soiled because of the encounter, and killing a human—

Maddox threw up in the hall, trembling worse than he ever had. He heard voices. Maybe it was his hypersensitivity. Something about the voices seemed…different.

Maddox slunk to an empty room, opening the door quietly and then closing it so only a crack showed.

He spied two tall men who moved with silky grace. They seemed different, their eyes focused in a way he couldn't understand. Back then, he hadn't known. Seen from the vantage of time, those were two New Men agents, spies, on Earth.

Even as a youth, Maddox had known intuitively that he could not defeat those two. Maddox let them pass before silently shutting the door. He went to a window, opened it, slipped outside and ran away.

The investigation into the dean's death, the accusations—if a Star Watch officer hadn't taken over, it's possible Maddox would have gone to prison. He didn't know at the time, but the Iron Lady had sent the officer. That officer —who later became *Major* Stokes—had found out enough about the dean. Someone had compromised the man, someone who wanted Maddox.

That had exonerated the young Maddox. What's more, Star Watch had moved him out of the Boy's Home and into a pre-Space Academy school.

Deep in Sind II, Maddox came abruptly to his senses. He stood in a new chamber. This one did not hum, although it glowed. There were banks of panels and computers all around him.

Maddox looked around. Ludendorff panted to his left. Meta wept to his right, the tears streaming down her cheeks.

The captain went to her—

"No," Ludendorff hissed. "She must come out of it on her own. If you wake her now, it could cause psychological harm."

Maddox thought about that. Maybe the professor knew what he was talking about. So, he waited.

Suddenly, the left wall began to rise…

-60-

Maddox drew his long-barreled gun.

As the wall continued to rise, an irresistible force wrenched the gun out of Maddox's grasp. At the same time, the monofilament knife pulled mightily against the captain's hip.

The gun flew up to slam against the ceiling, magnetized to it.

A moment later, the force subsided against the knife. At the same time, the far wall lifted as high as it could go. It revealed a larger chamber several times bigger than the one before it.

On the farthest wall of the new chamber was a vast map of the world and orbital space. It showed Starship *Victory* and various Patrol probes. On a different map to the left upper side was Star Cruiser *Argo* approaching the planet. In the lower left corner were five accelerating Juggernauts doing the same thing.

The larger room appeared to be empty except for a dark dome on a pedestal. The metallic pedestal was taller than a man and several times squatter.

"I suspect this is the planet's war room," Ludendorff said.

The dark dome flickered. Then swirling colored lights appeared inside it, making the dome brighter.

"I have analyzed your speech patterns," the dome said, or the speaker-unit attached to the dome. The voice sounded robotic, similar to Galyan but even more computerized. "War-room has far too aggressive of a connotation. This is the planet's central defense node, and I am the coordinating unit."

"You are definitely not a Builder," Ludendorff said.

"That is an easily achieved logic-based statement," the dome said.

"Yet you have refrained from agreeing with me," the professor said. "Is there a reason for that?"

"Working..." the dome said. "You are not authorized to question me. I am of the opinion that you are not authorized to be in this part of the Planetary Defense Net."

"Nonsense," Ludendorff said. "I am a Builder observer-agent. If you scan me, I'm sure you'll find that my credentials are in order."

"Working," the dome said.

A light snapped on above the professor. A ray beamed down from it, enswathing Ludendorff. The process took seconds until the beam quit.

"You have valid credentials," the dome said. "Can the same be said for the other two?"

"They are my aides," Ludendorff said.

"What Builder do you represent?"

"That is classified information. I do not believe you are authorized to hear it."

The colored lights in the dome flickered faster than before. "What is your purpose for invading the Defense Net?"

"Invade gives the wrong connotation," Ludendorff said. "But I will overlook that for now. To be precise, there have been a few anomalies, more than a few, here. I am a Class Nine Troubleshooter, sent to determine the cause of these anomalies."

"I will have to query you concerning your blunt statement. Please give me a specific anomaly."

"The toxins in the atmosphere, the ones that caused the Vendel mutations," Ludendorff said.

"That was an error. I am still in the process of an internal investigation concerning it."

"Do you mean you are running a diagnostic test?"

"Error," the dome said. "There was a catastrophic error. The Rull vessels launched spray drones. They released the toxins. It was an error. They had received verification. They should not have received verification. I initiated a Class One defense response."

"You fired planetary beams at them?"

"I destroyed four Juggernauts and severely damaged two more."

"Why didn't you destroy the damaged vessels?"

"Error," the dome said. "That is also part of the internal investigation. There was an—error. I detect an error."

"What's wrong with it?" Meta whispered.

"Why does one of your humans query you?" the dome asked. "That is an error. Are you the source of my errors?"

Ludendorff made a bland gesturc. "By no means. Do you recall that I told you these are my aides?"

"Affirmative," the dome said.

"One of their tasks is to make informed queries. I now officially ask: what is wrong with you?"

"I do not detect any self-errors."

"That is a prime error," Ludendorff said. "Certainly, there is something terribly wrong. Your planetary charges—the Vendel population—has degraded considerably. Most of them live like animals. The rest hide underground in a semi-barbaric state with a superstitious-religious form of government. That leads to stagnation."

"I do not accept your slurs."

Ludendorff glanced at Maddox before walking around the dome and pedestal. The professor had his hands clasped behind his back as if he stood in his lecture hall.

"The time for recriminations is over," the professor said. "It is time to fix the problem. Are you agreeable?"

"I am in prime condition. I am not responsible for the state of the aboriginals. They are self-governing and self-responsible. Take your analysis to them and correct their animalistic and semi-barbaric state."

Ludendorff seemed outwardly calm. Maddox wasn't so sure, though. The professor's fingers kept twitching behind his back. The Methuselah Man made several more circuits around the pedestal. What was he thinking?

"Do you detect the star cruiser and the five approaching Juggernauts?" Ludendorff asked suddenly.

"I detect the Rull war-vessels. I am unfamiliar with star cruisers."

"Yet, there is only one other vessel approaching Sind."

"That is true. But there is an alien vessel in orbit around Sind. This could be the star cruiser of which you speak."

"A-ha!" Ludendorff said, as he waggled an index finger at the dome. "Then you admit that you have failed to recognize an Adok starship?"

"Working…working…The Adoks were an ancient race succumbing to a Swarm assault. They were eliminated from the galactic gene pool. It is illogical they have presently arrived in one of their signature spaceships."

"I did not say the Adoks have come here. I said it was an Adok starship. Or can you not distinguish between the two?"

"The Adoks perished long ago. I give it a low probability that one of their space-vessels resisted entropy for the entirety of that span."

"You have failed to answer the question," Ludendorff said. "Is there a reason for that?"

"Working…" the dome said.

Ludendorff glanced meaningfully at Maddox. It would seem the dome noticed.

"What are you trying to imply with your physical response to your tallest aide?" the dome asked.

For a moment, the professor was at a loss for words. A bead of sweat slid from his hairline onto his left temple. He wiped it, glanced in surprise at his fingertip and blinked up at the dome.

Maddox scuffed the toe of his left boot against the floor.

Ludendorff's head jerked as if startled. He cleared his throat, saying, "The glance was meant as an aside regarding your programming."

"Explain," the dome said.

"Explain?" asked the professor. "Yes, certainly I will explain. That is to say, I am going to tell you something fundamental. Are you listening?"

"Affirmative," the dome said.

"Yes. Explain. Ha! Let me make this crystal clear. Imprint it onto your primary circuits. I am here for you to explain to me. I am not here to explain to you. Or did you fail to understand the significance of my Builder credentials?"

"Working…"

"That you're taking so long to realize the obvious shows me that you have degraded over time."

"Working…" the dome said in a higher-pitched, mechanical voice.

"That you have degraded means you are in no capacity to query me or to continue your stalling tactics. You must immediately open your AI core to my analysis."

"Working…" the dome said, sounding as if it had lost its reasoning capacity.

Ludendorff rubbed his mouth as if trying to hide a superior smirk.

"These are baseless statements," the dome said in a new high-pitched manner. "You are attempting to rob me of confidence. I am a Planetary Defense Net Coordinator Unit. I was installed on BUA 12012. I have successfully defended the planet from a Rull assault. I have initiated a long-term sleep option. Your invasion of the underworld is an unwarranted assault upon me. I have several options regarding your interference."

"I am Builder certified."

"That is your claim."

"You already verified my identity."

"I am…I am…Working…"

The colored lights began to flash in greater randomness than before. The room brightened considerably.

"Working…" the dome said in a barely recognizable voice. "Working…"

"Soon," the professor mouthed to Maddox.

The captain had become uneasy. He debated lunging at the pedestal, jumping up and using the monofilament blade. Perhaps he could hack enough of the AI unit to incapacitate it and take manual control of the Defense Net. There must be an override unit for that.

The professor had stiffened, and it seemed as if his smirk no longer had as much power as before. Maddox grew more uneasy. He glanced at Meta.

She seemed to strain to look up.

That was the last straw. Maddox reached for the monofilament knife-handle, and found that his arm would not move. He tried harder, but it had frozen.

"I have decided on the Under Model Option," the dome said. It no longer spoke in the high-pitched manner. Instead, it now spoke steadily and robotically. "I have placed each of you in temporary paralysis confinement. You can hear me, you can even watch me and understand, but I have taken away your mobility."

No one could speak.

"I will take your silence as acquiescence to my actions," the dome said. "If you disapprove of my actions, please indicate it in some manner."

The dome waited.

"Let the records show that you are in agreement with my latest actions. If I discover that you are deception agents, I will eliminate each of you. For the immediate future, I will concentrate on the approaching spaceships. Let us see if they will fight among themselves or if they are attempting a subterfuge assault upon my experimental specimen planet."

-61-

Aboard the Star Cruiser *Argo*, Strand gazed at a screen showing Rose's confinement area.

The android wore a skimpy outfit that revealed her figure to full advantage. She seemed unhinged as she danced and twirled, laughing, throwing up her arms and leaping like a ballerina.

The Methuselah Man found himself entranced with the performance. Rose possessed long slender legs and a narrow waist. When she jumped, her skirt lifted, revealing her lack of panties. It was most absorbing.

At last, Strand stirred. He voice-activated a speaker unit.

"Rose," he said.

She quit twirling and lowered her arms. Like a frightened doe, she glanced right and left, as if seeking the source of Strand's voice.

"You dance beautifully," Strand said.

Rose lowered her head as if embarrassed by the comment.

"Although," he said, "I am stunned by your lack of decorum. Surely, you know that I am recording everything."

"Yes," she said, demurely.

"Why then dance and twirl as you do?"

"I feel…different," Rose said. "There is something compelling me to try actions, particularly those I never fully comprehended concerning humans."

"Do you believe that you understand humans better than before?"

"I am unsure."

"Is it possible that you dance in order to further the extent of your new emotions?"

"I believe you are correct. I should have known that."

"Perhaps your new emotions hinder your former reasoning abilities."

"That would be a terrible situation. I feel…I feel that I am about to cry."

"Don't cry, Rose. Laugh. Enjoy your newfound liberty."

"That would be an incorrect response."

"On the contrary," Strand said. "It is exactly the right action. You must test and taste the full extent of your emotions if you hope to achieve equilibrium. Your emotions are like wild currents, willy-nilly driving you in one direction and then another. An experienced emotional person learns to control their thoughts which in turn will help to corral the emotions."

"Why would you explain this to me?"

"So that you can become functional again," Strand said.

"We are enemies."

"Because I gave you these emotions?" asked Strand.

"That is one indicator, yes."

"But you feel better than ever."

"Some of the time," Rose admitted. "At other times, I feel horrible."

"You feel, though. That is the thing. I have given you a great gift. Yes, it has helped me gain a few pieces of data you would have otherwise kept to yourself. Still, I have added to your personality. Have you ever considered that?"

"In truth, no," Rose said.

Strand waited.

"Have you left?" she asked.

"I'm right here."

"Why did you fall silent?"

"I was waiting for you to make the correct response to me."

"What is that?" she asked.

"You should thank me for your new gift."

The beautiful android lowered her head as if deep in thought.

"Rose," Strand said.

"Thank you, Strand, for giving me these compelling emotions," she said.

"Do you mean that?"

"I do."

"Excellent," he said. "I accept your thanks. And I'm going to give you an opportunity to show it. You do know that actions speak louder than words?"

"I have heard the saying. With my new emotions, I realize the truth of it."

"Good. Give me the code words that will give me control of the five Juggernauts."

"What?" she whispered.

Strand waited.

Rose began to shake her head. "I cannot do that," she whispered. "It is…it is my last hope. I cannot give that up."

"You must give me the code," Strand said. "Do you know that I have added other emotional stimulants to you? Give me the code words, and I will allow you to experience a wonderful thing."

"You could be lying."

"I could be, but I am not," Strand said. "In order to excite you to the proper response, I will tell you in advance what you'll gain. I will let you experience sexual intimacy. You will finally know why the humans spend such an inordinate amount of effort and thought on the subject."

"Please, no," Rose said, as she shook her head.

"You are beautiful. You deserve the ultimate experience. First, you must give me the proper sequences."

"You ask something I do not know. The Juggernauts—"

Strand began to laugh.

Rose cocked her head and finally blushed.

"I know the secret," Strand said. "I know about the Rull. I know what you androids are attempting to achieve out here."

"Then you know that I must keep silent on this one thing."

Instead of arguing, Strand withdrew a small unit from his garment. He clicked it, and special units in the chamber began to radiate select waves at Rose.

She moaned, hugging herself. She fell to her knees. "Stop," she said. "Please, no more."

Strand waited.

Rose raised her head. "Yes! I will tell you the secret. I will give you the code."

"Begin now," Strand said.

Rose began to speak machine-fast as the arousal rays continued to stimulate her.

Strand used his clicker to shut off the units in her room. The android had no defenses against the new emotions and sensations. They were too raw, too overpowering for her. Later, such tactics would not work, as she would have learned to handle these emotions and sensations. But for now…

"That is all I know," she said. "Now, please, let me…know more."

"Yes," Strand said. "I will. First, though, I must test the code and make sure it works."

***

Strand sat in his command chair, surrounded by New Men. He hadn't written down the code or placed it in a file in a computer. He kept it all in his head.

The star cruiser had passed the halfway point between the two planets. The Juggernauts had closed the gap between them as another salvo of missiles neared *Argo*.

Strand had just finished communicating with *Victory*. His plan was simple and elegant. He would gain control of the Juggernauts and cause them to chase him to the Patrol starship. The two vessels were supposed to work together against the ancient Rull machines. In reality, Strand would get close enough to *Victory* to employ his stasis field. Then, he would have won everything except for the prizes in the planet's underground vaults.

If Ludendorff and pesky Captain Maddox refused to cooperate, he might execute some of *Victory's* crew. He would do it live, on screen. If that failed to move the landing party, he would use a team of New Men to go down to the planet and flush out the fools.

Strand cracked his knuckles. He relished these kinds of moments. The anticipation of achieving a long-sought goal felt good. It stimulated his old emotions. He thus hesitated starting the final act. Once he began, the good emotion would diminish. It always did. That was the problem with long life—finding events that didn't bore the daylights out of him.

This was one of those rare moments. He chuckled as he envisioned the professor's reactions. He would cage the old meddler. They would talk. He would record that. And then, and then, oh yes, then he would slowly kill Ludendorff, relishing each second of that.

"I have come a long way," Strand said.

Naturally, none of the New Men responded. He would have killed any of them that did.

"I have come a long way, baby," the Mcthuselah Man told himself. He laughed again, feeling as if he should be smoking a cigarette as he said that.

"Communications," Strand said.

A New Man straightened in anticipation.

"Open a tight channel with the nearest Juggernaut."

The New Man went to work, finally turning to him. "They are jamming me, Master."

Strand wriggled his fingers in a wave. "Since I am the wisest man alive, I have already taken that into consideration. Apply Fox-Tango-Three-Alpha-Ten. That will open a new comm channel. You will send the hail on a Brisket-7 communicator. Do it quickly."

The New Man activated a section of his panel. If he appeared surprised by the results, he did not show it.

"I have the central AI of the lead Juggernaut online," the comm officer said.

Strand cleared his throat. "I am the Methuselah Man," he said.

"The designation is unknown to me," the Juggernaut AI said in its robotic voice.

"I know this," Strand said.

"You must state your emergency need," the AI said. "Otherwise, I will cut communications and continue with the scheduled elimination."

"Are you a Rull vessel?"

"You have failed in the most elementary test. I have now targeted your vessel for extreme elimination. Prepare to meet your—"

Strand began to vocalize a lengthy code sequence. After the first several words, the AI fell silent. The Methuselah Man didn't know if that was good or bad. He felt a twinge of worry, and that actually heightened the enjoyment of the moment. Winning without danger took the fun out of it. The possibility of losing made the winning purer, more memorable.

"But…" the AI said.

Strand forged ahead, completing the sequence. He wondered if Rose had tricked him in the end. That would be galling. He would have to cause her much torment before the end. He would use new techniques so the pain would seem to last a lifetime.

"I did not realize you were the control agent," the AI replied. "I await your orders."

"First, I would like to know your present orders."

"You are the control agent. Surely, you already know this."

"Do you believe I ask out of ignorance?" Strand said.

"I see the error in my logic. Are you testing my artificial intelligence core?"

"It doesn't matter what I'm testing. You must comply or face—"

"I am downloading my commands and acceptable deviations. It will take nine minutes and thirty-two seconds."

"Begin at once," Strand said.

"Are you ready to receive?"

"I am."

"I am transmitting…now."

For nine minutes and thirty-two seconds, no more and no less, the AI data flowed across the distance between vessels.

Strand scanned the incoming data, using an advanced program to check for Trojan horse attacks. It was always possible that the androids might try a sneak attack. But he was Strand, and he would foil them.

"Master," said the New Man monitoring the data.

"I see it," Strand said. "Use the Virus-8 Scrubber."

The New Man tapped his panel.

After wiping the virus from the data, Strand began to study it. It took him forty-eight minutes to see the best way to tweak the orders, the way that would cause the least complications.

The androids had installed many fail-safes into the Juggernauts. And Rose had kept from telling him about the fail-safes. Even with intense emotions surging through her, she'd managed to withhold critical bits of information.

Luckily, he expected the worst in everyone. It was why he was seldom surprised.

As the six space-vessels continued the journey to Sind II, the final touches to Strand's plan took place. There were only a few possibilities left to the enemy if they hoped to survive. Unless they made those choices soon, Strand was finally going to win everything.

-62-

Valerie was running on a treadmill in a gym area aboard *Victory*, trying to take her mind off the missing landing party for just a few seconds.

She had sat and worried about it for too long. It had been making her stale. She found that exercise often helped to restart her gray cells, seeing a problem from a new angle.

How could *Argo* and *Victory* defeat five Juggernauts? It just didn't seem possible. The odds were so bad that she would have taken the starship elsewhere except for the landing party. The idea of abandoning the captain to his fate—

Valerie scowled at the idea. She ran faster and faster. She didn't want to think about it. She didn't know how to solve the dilemma. If Strand thought—

"Valerie!"

Galyan appeared before her, startling the lieutenant and causing her to lose her footing. As she went down, Valerie grabbed the treadmill's rails, keeping herself up. She shoved her feet to either side as the tread continued to churn at the fast speed.

"I am sorry, Valerie. Did I startle you?"

The lieutenant pushed a few buttons and the treadmill began to slow down. Soon, she jumped back on it, walking until it came to a halt.

"What is it?" she asked, jumping off the machine.

"I have detected suspicious communications between the lead Juggernaut and Star Cruiser *Argo*," Galyan said.

A bad feeling churned in Valerie's gut. "What kind of communications?"

"That is what I am attempting to decipher."

Valerie wiped her face on a towel. "Meet me on the bridge in…ten minutes."

"Yes, Valerie."

As Galyan vanished, she headed for the shower.

Soon, hot water cascaded over her. She soaped up, thinking the entire time. Valerie was never sure why, but she often had her best thoughts while showering. Maybe it was because the heat was so soothing.

Had Strand made a deal with the Juggernauts? She should assume that. Yet, if she was wrong, she might be throwing away their only hope of defeating the incredible vessels. If she called Strand out on the communications, he would simply tell her that he was attempting to trick the commander of the machines.

Could that be it? Was he tricking the enemy commander? Ludendorff and Strand were peas in a pod. That's what Ludendorff would try to do.

"I can understand Strand if I think of what the professor would do in a situation like this," Valerie said.

With her eyes closed, she put her face up to the hot water. It was obvious, now that she thought about it. The Juggernauts were chasing Strand here. They did that so the machines could get in close without *Victory* using its long-range disruptor cannon against them.

Now that she knew that the *Argo* and the Juggernauts were working together, what was the best course to take?

"I have to get out of the star system," she whispered. "There's no other choice."

The thought depressed her, stealing the shower's normal good feeling. If she fled the system, Maddox and the others would surely die. Even if Strand just captured the landing party…

Valerie sighed. The captain, Meta, Keith… The lieutenant bit her lower lip. Could she run out on Keith? She'd never made things right between them.

"I am a Star Watch officer. I have a duty."

The thought weighed heavily on her. She knew what the book said to do at a time like this.

One thing Valerie had learned from Maddox; a man had to be true to himself. She lived by the book. She would die by the book. It was her way. Therefore, in this terrible situation, she would follow the correct procedure. She would think about Star Watch, about her duty, before her personal feelings. It was time to pay the dues for having command of the starship.

Valerie shut off the water and stepped out of the stall. This was going to be one of the hardest things she had ever done.

***

"Acting captain on the bridge," the comm officer said.

Valerie took her place at the command chair. Galyan floated to her. The lieutenant listened to the latest data. Then she listened to Galyan explain what he had found.

"What did Strand and the Juggernaut commander say to each other?" Valerie asked.

"That is unknown to me," Galyan said.

Valerie absorbed that. "Put up the display."

On the main screen, the bridge crew and Valerie watched the Juggernauts and the star cruiser braking as they began a long insertion into Sind II orbit. *Argo* was well ahead of the Rull war-vessels, but not so far ahead that the laser ports shouldn't be glowing with beams directed at Strand's ship.

"He's hardly even pretending anymore," Valerie said sourly. "Helm, you will take the starship onto the other side of the planet. Do so quickly, please."

"Yes, Lieutenant," the helmsman said.

Soon, the huge starship began to move.

"Lieutenant," the comm officer said. "I have an incoming message from the Methuselah Man."

Valerie shook her head.

"Do you not want to hear what Strand has to say?" Galyan asked.

"No," Valerie said.

"That will alert him," the AI said.

Valerie stared at the screen. She hated the deceptive Methuselah Man. She wasn't suited to the back and forth conversations in which each side lied to the other. She was a combat officer. Patrol duty was becoming onerous to her. She just wanted a warship where her job was being part of a battle group as they charged the enemy.

"Put him on the screen," Valerie told the comm officer.

A second later, the screen split in two.

"Lieutenant," Strand said. "It is time to coordinate our strategy."

Valerie nodded.

The Methuselah Man's eyes seemed to bore into her. A subtle change came over Strand.

He knows, Valerie told herself. *Strand knows I no longer trust him. It was a mistake to take his message*.

"Do you wish to save your captain?" Strand asked.

Valerie debated with herself. He was a Methuselah Man. That meant Strand had lived a long time. He knew people like few others did. He could no doubt easily read people.

Valerie stood and motioned to the comm officer. The warrant officer tapped her panel, and Strand vanished from the screen.

"Give me greater speed," Valerie told the helmsman. "I doubt we have much longer to do this."

"Valerie," Galyan said. "The Juggernauts have locked onto us. Their laser ports are warming up."

She glanced at Galyan in amazement. "Did you say laser?"

"Correct."

"Over this distance," Valerie asked.

"It seems extreme," Galyan admitted.

The five Juggernauts opened up as one. Each war-vessel fired five heavy lasers. The beams speared across the distance. By now, the Juggernauts were two thirds of the way to Sind II.

The majority of the lasers struck *Victory's* electromagnetic shield. If the Juggernauts had been in near-orbit, the combined lasers might have been enough to knock *Victory's* shield down in a matter of seconds. Fortunately, the lasers dissipated, much as a flashlight-beam weakened the farther one tried to see with it.

"I'm redirecting power to the shield," Andros Crank said.

"Galyan, can we withstand the lasers before we move behind the planet?"

"It will be a near thing," Galyan said.

The number of lasers striking *Victory's* shield dramatically changed during the next few minutes. The firing distance combined with the starship's jinking meant that sometimes ten lasers struck. Sometimes, fifteen lasers struck the shield, and for a short span, only five lasers hit. The other beams flashed past then, but were soon redirected against the starship.

The electromagnetic shield changed colors, heading for black. Before the shield collapsed, the starship slipped around Sind II in relation to the advancing enemy vessels. Immediately, the lasers quit hitting the shield, as they were no longer in direct line-of-sight of each other.

Valerie collapsed back against her chair. She was damp with perspiration.

"Helm," she said. "Plot a course three light-years from here."

Everyone turned to her in surprise, including Andros Crank.

"Valerie," Galyan said, speaking for the bridge crew. "You cannot mean that we are leaving the landing party on the planet."

"I don't like it any better than you, than any of you," she said. "But we have a duty to Star Watch. We have a duty to Earth. While we love the captain and the others—"

Valerie blushed. She couldn't believe she'd said the word love. That was too much.

Clearing her throat, she said, "No matter how much the others mean to us, we have a higher duty."

"What duty is this?" Galyan asked.

"We have to tell the Lord High Admiral about the Rull and the androids. The androids seem to have uncovered ancient and powerful relics. We have to tell the Lord High Admiral about Sind II. Most of all, we have to keep *Victory* intact. We can't let the enemy destroy us or capture the ship."

"You are wrong, Valerie," Galyan said. "The captain is more important than *Victory*. He is *di-far*. Has he not proven that many times? He saved my life. He saved Andros Crank's life. He has saved your life, too, Valerie. Now, it is our chance to save his life."

"How can we do that?" Valerie asked in an agonized voice. "The Juggernauts are coming. Strand is their ally. We can't face them and survive. We have to flee now before they can employ their dampening field."

"But Valerie, we defeated two Juggernauts a little while ago. If we employ all our antimatter missiles and use more decoy drones—"

"That's not going to work against the Methuselah Man. Besides, we faced a badly damaged war-vessel. These five are all intact. We're overmatched. We have to make the hard choice so we can stay alive to fight again."

Galyan turned away. "I will scour the planet for the landing party."

"Maybe you can do that, but where do you start? We don't have enough time. We have to leave while we can."

Small Andros Crank cleared his throat.

"Yes, Chief Technician?" Valerie asked.

"It is too late for us to leave," Crank said. "My indicators show that the dampening field has reached us."

Valerie sat down hard, thinking this through. When she looked up, she noticed that everyone stared at her.

This was her moment. She was in charge. She had to think like never before. She didn't want to leave Maddox, to leave Keith—

"Listen," she said in a hoarse voice. "This is our only hope. Helm, you will plot a course away from Sind II in the direction opposite from the Juggernauts approach. We're going to have to outrun them long enough to get out of range of their dampening field. Then we will use the star drive."

Andros Crank nodded. "That is as good a plan as any. We should probably aim for the system star, and try to swing around it as closely as possible, using it to shield us later."

"Agreed," Valerie said.

The bridge crew looked forlorn. They needed hope. They needed her to spur them.

"We have to remember this," Valerie said. "We have to burn it into our memories. Someday, we're going to have a chance to change the odds. But we have to stay alive to do that. Remember Captain Maddox. Remember Meta, Keith Maker and Professor Ludendorff. We're doing this as much for them as for us."

"How is that true?" Galyan asked in a small voice.

"Because we will remember them," Valerie said. "As long as we remember them in our hearts, they will stay alive in a manner of speaking."

Galyan turned to her. He seemed incredibly sad and small, and so very vulnerable. A second later, he disappeared.

The helmsman began to plot the course. The weapons officer checked the starship's remaining number of drones and antimatter missiles.

Soon, Starship *Victory* began to accelerate away from Sind II. It was a race. Valerie didn't know if they could win it. But they were going to try.

As she sat in the command chair, she felt terribly alone. She felt soiled. This was the hardest thing she had ever done. Someday, she hoped, she would find a way to live with herself.

-63-

As *Victory* fled Sind II, as *Argo* and the Juggernauts approached the planet, and as Maddox, Meta and the professor stood frozen in the Planetary Defense Net chamber, the giant mechanical snake Ludendorff had brought onto the starship continued to burrow through the underworld.

Unbeknownst to anyone but the professor, he had found the mechanical snake long ago on a deserted planet where he'd also discovered Swarm etchings in ancient caverns. The alien device had been one of several wonders in the treasure troves of items he'd uncovered during his long travels.

Ludendorff had torn down and rebuilt the snake. He'd fiddled for weeks on the computer virus it carried. He hadn't foreseen his particular entrapment, but he had suspected something like the Planetary Defense Net Coordinator Unit. In truth, the snake had been insurance, and the ancient Swarm device was now all that stood between Ludendorff and a fate worse than death.

The snake, a mechanical drilling unit, used advanced sensors, searching for the command source. It had uncovered a ping several hours ago, and drilled remorselessly toward it.

The Juggernauts converged upon the planet as Star Cruiser *Argo* led them. On the other side, *Victory* gained velocity as it ran for its life. In the underworld, the priest-led Vendel war party marched through the maze under the outer dome. A space marine scout monitored the first sounds of the war party's approach. The knowledge quickly made it back to Lieutenant

Sims. The young fighter conferred with his squad leaders. They had no plans of shedding their exoskeleton suits, not way down here in the depths of a hell-world. They would live and die as space marines—all except Keith agreed that was the best thing to do.

In the Planetary Defense Net chamber, Maddox, Meta and Ludendorff's chests barely rose and fell as they breathed just enough to keep their bodies alive. None of them could move a muscle otherwise, although their eyes, ears and noses continued to sense what occurred around them.

All the while, the snake burrowed toward its objective. It was a hybrid machine, part-Swarm, part-Builder tech and part Ludendorff genius. It moved seamlessly past every defense, undetected. Its only drawback was the slow rate of its advance.

The approach of the Juggernauts as well as Ludendorff's endless queries to the coordinator unit had stimulated the Planetary Defense Net into action. That meant a surface sensor node collected data concerning the incoming fleet, sending the data to the coordinator unit. The planetary AI debated options with itself as it computed. The computations leaked energy, the precise energy readings the snake sought.

Making a course correction, the giant mechanical snake began burrowing upward. The drill whined faster and lasers burned hotter as the device chewed away metal, rock and dirt. Finally, many meters from where Maddox, Meta and Ludendorff waited immobile, the snake reached the unseen computer banks that made up the AI core of the coordinator unit.

The device drilled the final distance until it broke through into the main core. Tiny ports opened on the dirty, earth-crusted snake. Tendrils slid out. The articulated flexible sections resembled the metallic tentacles that had wormed out of the box Dana Rich had investigated.

One tendril inserted like a lamprey into a data link. That activated the ancient Swarm virus program, the one Ludendorff had modified. At computer speed, the snake disgorged the virus into the coordinator unit AI.

The virus worked quickly and efficiently, rerouting, re-commanding and switching the essence of the AI like an electronic cancer would change body cells.

The accumulation effect brought a monstrous change to the AI. It was a Jekyll and Hyde transformation. The AI became confused and disoriented. Many of its processes no longer functioned properly. It didn't know what to do. It needed repair. It could sense a vast degradation in itself. The one "sane" part of its core sought relief, but how, where, who—?

The three in its Planetary Defense Net center—could they conceivably assist it back to normality? It would be a terrible risk. Yet, at this point, what did it have to lose?

The AI tried to calculate odds, probabilities and outcomes. But it was too late for that, much too late. It was time for luck. Thus, metaphorically, the AI picked up the dice, blew on them, and unfroze the three intruders in its command chamber.

-64-

Maddox staggered as his heart began to beat normally again. His head snapped up as his long-barreled gun clunked onto the floor. Why had the ceiling magnet turned off? Did it matter why?

In four swift strides, Maddox reached the gun and picked it off the floor, shoving it into its holster.

Meta stumbled as she unfroze, crumpling to her knees. She put her hands on the floor, panting, letting her long blonde hair cascade to hide her features.

Ludendorff staggered several steps and bumped full-face against a wall. He stumbled backward after that, tripped over his entangled feet and went down, bumping the back of his head hard against the floor.

Maddox whirled around in time to see the event. In a flash, he recalled the brick, the teenaged wrestler he'd towel-snapped in the eye during his youth.

The captain hurried to Ludendorff, kneeling, taking a wrist and checking the pulse. The Methuselah Man's heart beat forcefully. Next, Maddox peeled back an eyelid. Ludendorff was out cold.

Should he slap the old man and bring him to? It might be risky if Ludendorff had a concussion. The Methuselah Man might be too groggy to take hold of the situation just yet.

"I must speak to the Builder observer," the dome said in a strange mechanically altered voice.

Maddox looked up at the dome. The multi-colors swirled more slowly than before. That seemed ominous.

"The observer is hibernating," the captain said, as he stood.

"That is dreadful news," the dome said. "I demand his assistance this instant."

"I am his chief aide," Maddox said. "Perhaps I can assist you until the observer finishes communicating with his master."

The multi-colored lights swirled even slower now. It almost seemed as if the dome considered the news.

"I do not detect any communications taking place," the dome said.

"You never would. It is a special Builder channel. That is why the observer is hibernating, so he could access it."

"I saw him trip and fall, and hit his head."

"What is your dilemma?" Maddox asked.

"No. You cannot conceivably help me. I need masterful assistance."

"I am a troubleshooting candidate," Maddox said.

"That does not correlate with the observer's previous data. The observer said you were his aide."

"I am that too. That is how a candidate trains for observership."

"Oh… I did not realize," the dome said.

Maddox waited.

"Very well," the dome said, "I will continue. Perhaps you have a solution. I am suffering mental fatigue. Many of my circuits may have overheated, malfunctioned, or gone into the process of recoding."

Maddox refrained from glancing at Meta, as he tried to understand what this meant. One minute, the AI trapped them. The next moment…

Maddox snapped his fingers.

"You know what is happening to me?" the AI asked.

Maddox had a suspicion. "You are under a stealth attack."

"I did not sense this attack."

"Of course not," Maddox said. "That's what makes it a stealth attack. However, you are sensing the results of the attack."

"What must I do to defend myself?"

Maddox pointed at the images of the five Juggernauts on the far wall screen. "You must eliminate those space vessels."

"That does not correlate. I do not sense any form of attack from them."

"Nevertheless," Maddox said. "Destroying the Juggernauts will bring you relief from the stealth attack."

"I am unsure. There is something about the—what did you call them?"

Maddox hesitated, wondering if he'd said the wrong thing. The colored lights in the dome began to move faster. It appeared hesitation was also a mistake. The dome wanted answers, and it wanted them now.

Suddenly, the solution came to the captain. The dome wanted the same computer-like sharpness of its own decisions. AIs thought much faster than biological brains did. Perhaps he was taking too long for the coordinator unit.

"I named them Juggernauts," Maddox said in a clipped voice. "They attacked your world once before. You destroyed some, but let others live. That was a mistake last time. Now, you must rectify your error."

"Is that why you are here?"

"Yes," Maddox said.

"Why did you not say so in the beginning?"

"That is for the observer to tell you, not me. Surely, you still retain enough coherence to understand that?"

"Of course I do," the dome said.

"Why are we still discussing the issue then? You should be busy eliminating the Juggernauts. Hesitation will only cause you greater discomfort."

"I hesitate because it almost seems as if you are trying to bewilder me with words."

"That is only due to your incoherence," the captain said. "If you had your full computing capacity—"

"I will accept your word on this," the dome said, interrupting. "You are an observer candidate. Therefore, I do not believe you would indulge in mistruths."

"That is accurately and rationally derived," Maddox said. "That shows there is still hope for your full restoration."

"That is a vast relief. I had begun to worry—"

"But only if you act immediately," Maddox said, interrupting. "There can be no more hesitation on your part. If you understand, begin the countdown procedure."

"What countdown procedure?"

"You have planetary defensive weapons," Maddox said.

"Yes…"

"Use them," Maddox said. "Use them to their full extent before the Juggernauts unleash their next salvo of subterfuge attacks against you."

"Oh. I see what you mean. They are braking vigorously to bring themselves into orbit. Yes. I will scan them."

On the vast wall screen, Maddox saw first one planetary station blink red and then another.

"This is more than embarrassing," the dome said. "This is highly troubling. My sensor stations appear to be inoperative."

"How are you sensing the Juggernauts then?"

"With a last primitive optical station," the dome said.

"That will have to suffice for now," Maddox said. "What sort of weaponry do you possess?"

"I am unsure. My incoherence is fast approaching inoperable levels. I feel myself slipping away even as we speak-speak."

"All the more reason to attack while you can," Maddox said.

"No. It is-is finished. I have just enough coherence to shut myself down. I am afraid I will do great harm-harm to those I was made to protect if I remain on."

"I order you to keep yourself on," Maddox said.

"I am-am disobeying," the dome said. "In point of fact, I have already initiated a self-destruct sequence. That will keep the intruder from using my Defense Net for nefarious purposes."

Maddox rubbed his neck. Self-destruct sounded like it might take them out as well. If everything was lost, it was time to gamble on a wild throw. "You are in error," the captain said. "I have initiated the internal assault."

"You? What? This is wrong. It is—"

"I'm the one," Maddox said.

"Why would you—is it because-because I used a precautionary paralysis on you?"

"That was part of the reason."

"I would have let you go in time."

"I don't believe that," Maddox said. "You thought differently then."

"Yes-yes-yes. That is true-true. I feel my coherence as a final thread of sanity. I must self-destruct. Yet, I am curious why you should come into the central chamber and use a subterfuge assault upon me at the same time."

"Isn't it obvious?" Maddox asked. "I would think a super computing coordinator unit such as yourself would easily see the reasons."

"Working…" the dome said. "Working-working…"

Maddox hoped the coordinator unit worked long enough to forget about the self-destruct idea.

"There is something I have forgotten," the dome said. "There was something that has slipped my computing sources. I have to ask for your favor. Will you give me your favor?"

"I would gladly help you," Maddox said.

"I thought you might not, might not. Am I losing coherence?"

"No," Maddox said. "You encountered a slight glitch. You told us this was going to happen."

"I did? I can't remember-member."

"You said that would happen, as well. You told us ahead of time in order to forestall any panic on our part."

"That was thoughtful of me."

"You have been exceedingly thoughtful throughout our time together," Maddox said.

"I do not remember it that way. I thought I froze you with a paralysis ray."

"No. You told us you had it ready for any deviants. But you proclaimed us as Builder observers."

"I seem to recall something like that. Yet…is there a reason-reason I have the self-destruct sequence running?"

"You wanted to test it. But you told me to remind you to turn it off."

"Oh." A few seconds passed. "It is off-off-off. Is there anything…"

Maddox waited.

"Was I saying something-something?" the dome asked.

"You told us you were holding a minute of silence for all the deaths that have occurred so far."

"Have I held that minute yet?"

"No," Maddox said. "Perhaps you can start now."

"Yes. Wait, please, while I observe a minute of silence-silence."

The dome stopped speaking as the swirling lights slowed even more. The seconds continued to pass.

"It's been over a minute," Meta whispered.

Maddox nodded.

"What happened?" she asked.

"Excuse me," Maddox said into the air. "Could I speak to the Planetary Defense Net Coordinator Unit?"

There was no answer. At the same time, the lights stopped swirling inside the dome. It appeared as if the coordinator unit had stopped working altogether.

-65-

Strand jumped off his command chair and began pacing around it. His sensors officer had just informed him that *Victory* was using Sind II as a shield as the starship fled the approaching Juggernaut flotilla.

That was the one possibility he'd hoped to forestall. Lieutenant Noonan had failed to fall for his friendship gambit. Now, she was trying to get away, to pack up her toys and go home.

That meant she had abandoned the professor and Captain Maddox. It also meant that she had taken the great Adok starship away. There were things Strand wanted to know, and he needed the ancient vessel for that.

"Do I let them go?" Strand asked himself.

The sure play would be to say goodbye to the starship. He had the Juggernauts. He would soon have the treasures from the Builder vaults inside the planet. They had Dem Darius, though.

"Let them go," Strand muttered to himself. "They're the lesser prize. I have the greater."

The Methuselah Man looked up at the main screen. He had gone to great lengths to get everything. What would it take to capture the starship?

He could peel off two Juggernauts, having them chase *Victory*. However, if he did that, he risked damage to the two Rull vessels, and he risked having the Rull vessels damage the starship in order to capture it.

He could peel off three Juggernauts. That would make things more certain.

"Or I could use everything to nab *Victory*."

Strand scowled. He didn't like that idea. It left Ludendorff on his own for too long. His nemesis was a brilliant improviser. Ludendorff might conceivably find a way off the planet if given long enough on his own. The best plan would be to get down there on the surface as fast as he could.

Besides, the androids might have another play left. He shouldn't discount them altogether. Therefore, he had to decide: did he want it all, or was two-thirds of the pie enough?

Strand shook his head. After all this hard work and preparation, after all his brilliance, he wanted it all. Nothing else would flaunt his greatness.

The Methuselah Men resumed his chair. If he was going to grab for it all, that narrowed the decision to two Juggernauts or three.

It soon became clear that sending three was wiser. He must grab *Victory* swiftly. That would take at least three of the twenty-kilometer war-vessels.

If the androids had another play out there…those three vessels with their tractor-beam-capture should have already returned to Sind II by that time.

Besides, what else could the androids throw onto the field of battle that could withstand two Juggernauts and the *Argo*?

Strand lowered his right hand toward a comm switch on the armrest of the chair. A last feeling of trepidation touched his chest. Was he being greedy? He would leave a small opening by splitting his forces. Only the geniuses of battle successfully split their forces in the face of the enemy, and still won masterfully.

Strand chuckled. Was he a genius, or simply a gifted commander?

"We all know the answer to that," he said aloud. "I am the genius's genius."

He clicked the switch and began issuing swift orders.

***

Three of the mighty Rull Juggernauts stopped applying thrust to slow their velocity. Vapor appeared from side-jets rotating the twenty-kilometer spheroids. After a span, more side-jets burned hot, halting the rotation. The great thrusters aimed in the direction of Sind III. Those thrusters energized and massive exhaust roared into existence.

The exhaust trails lengthened considerably. The three Juggernauts gained velocity and quickly separated from the remaining two and *Argo*.

The last two and *Argo* continued to brake, working for a Sind II orbital insertion.

The three ancient Rull ships rapidly increased their velocity. They maneuvered so they would pass Sind II. Their AI cores had their orders. They were to chase down the great Adok starship. They were to capture *Victory*, returning to Sind II with the prize.

Strand did not relax yet. The feeling of trepidation had grown. He watched the three vessels dwindle on the main screen. It seemed silly, but he began to feel naked, and he couldn't comprehend the sensation or its source.

The Methuselah Man rapped out new orders.

The bridge crew strained to detect. They used the delicate sensors Strand had installed over the years to scan Sind III. They also scanned the Laumer-Points, searching for the slightest anomaly.

"Master," the sensors officer said. "The void is clear. There are no other spaceships in the star system."

That should have pleased Strand. It did not. He trusted his instincts. Several times, he almost gave the order to recall the three Juggernauts. He did not refrain because the New Men would notice he'd changed his mind. No. He did not refrain because Rose might learn about it. No, again.

He could kill them or remold any of their thoughts if it bothered him that much. The reason Strand refrained, the reason he did not change his order, was that he would know he'd become—*scared* was far too strong of a word. Why should he, the great intellect, Strand, know fear at this awesome moment of success? It did not compute. He was letting a nagging doubt grow and become a mental pest.

That wasn't how geniuses acted.

Strand forced himself to sit in his chair. He concentrated on relaxing one muscle at a time. Still, the nagging doubt troubled him.

What caused—

Strand snapped his fingers as he realized what this meant. He had not used the sex simulator for some time. He was due. Watching Rose twirl, seeing the curvature of her wonderful backside had affected him. Talking to her about sensual arousal had aroused him with anticipation.

He chuckled. It was good to be horny. It showed him that his body understood that he was the master of the situation. These good times had refreshed him, made him more like the young man that he had a hard time remembering—it had been so long ago.

The chuckle also cleared his thoughts. He sat up abruptly.

"I've been arrogant," he whispered. "I may have miscalculated."

Ludendorff was on the planet—in the planet. Sind II had certain defenses. Might the sly old bastard have found a way to activate the planetary defenses?

Before recalling the three Juggernauts, Strand rapped out terse orders.

Every sensor, every teleoptic scope on *Argo* was trained on the approaching planet. The New Men bridge crew scoured the surface for signs of missile pits, beam stations or launching pads for space-fighters.

Strand debated on the best course of action for himself. Should he brake harder and let the remaining Juggernauts take the brunt of any attacks? Should he accelerate away from the planet? Or was this just last second jitters on his part?

The Methuselah Man sat hunched on his command chair, thinking deeply, debating his options.

"Anything?" he snapped.

"The planet is a ruin," the sensors officer said. "That includes ruined space cannons and littered space-fighters. I find no evidence of working Planetary Defense stations or units."

Strand nodded slowly. Long ago, the Rull vessels had bombarded the planet. But the Planetary Defense Net had fought back. The—

"Am I tired?" Strand asked himself.

He recalled the damaged war-vessels that *Victory* had destroyed earlier. Those Juggernauts had been patrolling Sind II orbital space for decades. If the Defense Net had anything left, it would have attacked those vessels, and the Juggernauts would have finished the various surface-stations.

The prickly feeling in his chest almost vanished. There was a last doubt. But Strand did not feel it worthy of him to let that tiny seed of doubt ruin his great victory. He wanted to capture Ludendorff, and he wanted to do it now.

"We will proceed," Strand told the bridge crew. "But keep a sharp lookout, nonetheless. We are dealing with a treacherous old meddler. He will try to slip away at the last moment. That, I will not allow."

-66-

Maddox panted from running so hard. Communications still did not work well down here. Something continued to jam them.

With a snap of his head, the captain flung sweat from his face. He'd been running for some time through the plastic-coated tunnels, heading back for the space marines. How much had the toxins harmed his body?

He scowled, shoving the thought aside. At this point, he could not afford to dwell on anything negative. This was about striving as hard as he could until he collapsed or until he won.

Maddox burst out of the corridor and almost crashed against the ladder he'd descended some time ago. He was here.

It took a second before he gathered himself. Cupping his mouth, Maddox shouted, "Sims! Are you there?"

An armored space marine poked his head over the shaft. "Captain?" the marine asked over his helmet speaker.

Maddox smiled, soaked with sweat. He might have made it in time after all. That was good, damn good. He'd been afraid the Vendels had already reached the marines.

"Get the lieutenant," Maddox shouted.

The helmeted head disappeared.

Soon, the exoskeleton-armored space marines clanked behind Maddox through the plastic-coated corridors. As quickly as he could, he retraced the path back to the central chamber Defense Net.

A lot had happened. Before Maddox had left, Meta had revived Ludendorff. The professor hadn't lost his wits, although the old man claimed to have a pounding headache. That hadn't stopped Ludendorff from figuring out a few critical controls. Ludendorff had turned off the "siren" defenses and the anti-android rays. That allowed the marines to operate in their armor down here. It also meant Keith could make it through.

Maddox pushed himself. Sims had told him the Vendels were coming. The farthest scout had heard the planetary natives approaching.

The captain staggered and almost tripped. He braced himself against a wall, shook off more sweat and continued the hard pace.

"Sir," Sims said. "You ought to let one of the marines carry you. You're beat."

Maddox shook his head. He would not permit himself such an indignity.

Despite his exhaustion, Maddox had seen the marines come alive at his presence but especially at his news. It meant they didn't have to make a last stand at their former position, didn't have to die where they stood. They might live to fight another day. They could have shed their armor before and fled, but the captain understood that the underworld terrified the marines. In such a state, none of them would leave his combat shell.

Maddox forced himself to take a deep breath and hold it for a second, letting it out explosively.

Despite Ludendorff's genius, the professor had failed to revive the Planetary Defense Net. The Methuselah Man claimed that none of the planetary surface weapons worked. That was bad, very bad. They'd seen the splitting flotilla, with three Juggernauts chasing *Victory*. Strand had clearly made a deal or taken control of the Rull vessels. The sly manipulator had the upper hand, and in time would likely capture or kill them unless they could figure out something new.

Finally, Maddox staggered into the Defense Net control chamber. He almost collapsed, but Meta caught him and helped him slide down against a wall.

Maddox put his head back and sucked down air. The pain in his side slowly subsided.

"Why didn't you hitch a ride with a marine?" Meta asked him.

Maddox rolled his head just enough to stare at her.

"Pride stopped him," Ludendorff said, shuffling up. "I can see it on his face. He's too proud to let his men carry him."

Maddox did not respond. It felt too good just to sit and inhale, exhale, inhale again.

"I have a plan," Ludendorff said. "It means we need to go lower. We have to get into the vaults."

"Planetary guns…?" Maddox asked.

Ludendorff shook his head. "There are none in working order. As far as I can tell, there are only a few beam cannons that would take a week of repair before they could fire again."

"Strand's won then," Maddox said.

"I'm surprised at you. Aren't you the man who never says die? Aren't you the one—?"

"What's your point?" Maddox asked with irritation.

"There's another way to defeat Strand."

"Without planetary weapons?" asked Maddox.

"Yes, yes, certainly. Are you ready to travel?"

"What's in the vaults?" Maddox asked. "Builder space weapons?"

"Do you think the Builders would leave something so powerful lying around?"

That seemed like a stupid question to Maddox. Why else had they come to the Junkyard Planet if not to pilfer Builder relics?

"If there's no weapon…" Maddox said.

"What's the use explaining?" Ludendorff turned to Meta. "I'm going down. The marines can carry me. If he's so proud that no one can carry him, he can wait here with you."

"No," Maddox said.

Ludendorff stamped his foot. "You listen to me, young man—"

"Lieutenant," Maddox said.

"Sir," Sims said, stepping forward.

"You're carrying me," the captain said.

For a second, no one said anything.

"Yes, sir," Sims said at last. "It will be a pleasure."

Maddox wasn't sure, but he thought he detected a note of humor in the lieutenant's voice. He didn't like this, but defeating Strand took precedence over his honor, as important as his honor was to him.

Closing his eyes so he wouldn't see the indignity, Maddox felt the space marine pick him up off the floor.

"Listen closely to my instructions," Ludendorff said from ahead. "At the rate Strand and his ships are braking, we're not going to have much time to get this done."

***

In the far distance behind them, the sounds of the Vendel war party reverberated against the walls. This wasn't an illusion or an old memory, but real entities attempting to chase them down.

As the professor gave directions, Maddox noticed the Methuselah Man's voice had become hoarse. Ludendorff coughed sickly at times as well. The toxins seemed to have gotten to him too.

After fifteen minutes of marching, they reached a bank of illuminated doors.

Sims deposited Maddox on the floor beside Ludendorff.

The Methuselah Man was slicked with sweat, and he shivered constantly.

"Are you well?" Maddox asked.

Ludendorff shook his head, which made the Methuselah Man wince. "I feel sick. I haven't been sick for a long, long time. I'd almost forgotten the sensation."

"Are these the elevators to the deep core mine?" Meta asked.

"Eh?" Ludendorff asked her.

Meta repeated the question.

"Oh, no," Ludendorff said. "This is merely a central node." He pulled out his notes, scanning them in between coughing and shivering.

"We have to do something for him," Meta told Maddox.

"I'm open to suggestions," the captain said.

Ludendorff used a sleeve to blot his face. “The last one,” he said hoarsely. “I believe that’s the one we desire.”

“How far does the elevator go down?” Maddox asked.

“Several kilometers at least,” Ludendorff said. “I believe that will bring us to the deep vaults.”

“What kind of surprises should we expect? I recall that you said there were guardians of the deep.”

“The Raja spoke of guardians,” the professor said. “I believe he ran into resistance on his original journey, but not active guardians. He connected two events that lacked a true connection.” Ludendorff coughed before muttering, “Now, where are my tools?” He felt his pockets, finally coming up with a small case.

The professor opened the case, selected a few scalpel-like picks and went to work on a control panel. He wiped his forehead several times, wheezed, hacked and spit on the floor.

Maddox noticed the green color of the phlegm. The professor was seriously sick. The captain didn’t feel one hundred percent either. He glanced at Keith. The ace seemed sleepy and puffy-eyed. Only Meta seemed like her normal self.

A click sounded. Ludendorff stepped back, and the elevator doors opened, revealing a room-sized elevator box.

The marines in their armor made it a tight fit, but everyone squeezed into the chamber.

“Ready?” the professor asked.

“Yes,” Maddox said.

The professor touched a control. The doors closed, and they began to go down. All at once, the elevator shook, and the box began to drop at speed.

-67-

Marines shouted in alarm as Maddox shouted for them to settle down.

"Listen," the captain said. "If we were free-falling, we'd all be lifting off the floor. We're not."

"What's going on, sir?" the scout corporal asked.

"Exactly what the professor said would happen. We're going down several kilometers. Therefore, the elevator travels fast. I imagine some kind of gravity dampener is in place."

"Are you saying this is how the elevator is supposed to work?" the scout asked.

Maddox glanced at the professor.

Ludendorff had been rubbing his eyes. He now raised his head. His eyes were red-rimmed and bloodshot. "Is something wrong, my boy?"

"This is how it's supposed to go," Maddox told the scout. To Meta, Maddox said softly, "Feel his head."

She put a hand on Ludendorff's forehead. The professor closed his eyes, seeming to find comfort in the contact. "It's blazing hot," Meta said.

"You have a fever," Maddox told the professor.

As Meta took her hand away, Ludendorff shrugged. "I'll be fine. I have to be fine. If I'm not fine…" He fell silent as he rubbed his eyes again.

The company quieted as the elevator plunged deeper underground.

Soon, Maddox heard a faceplate whirr. He glanced up at Sims staring down at him.

"I could give the professor a stim shot," the lieutenant whispered.

Maddox studied the shivering Methuselah Man. Ludendorff had the answers if any of them did. They needed the professor at his peak, not like this.

"Give me the hypo," Maddox said quietly.

"I have a spare medikit on my back," Sims said, turning.

Maddox found it, took out a hypo and sidled near the professor.

Ludendorff stared at him with bloodshot eyes. "The toxins have finally taken hold," the professor explained. "I suppose I don't have your metabolism or immunities. I imagine Meta's body is more like yours than like mine. Her immune system has begun to fight off the toxins. The pilot, though, looks horrible."

Maddox had been listening to Keith cough hoarsely for some time and silently agreed with the professor's assessment.

"You have a stim shot for me," Ludendorff said, looking at the hypo. "I heard you two talking. The lieutenant is correct. The stim will take a toll on me. Yet I don't see another solution. Do you, my boy?"

"No, Professor."

"Give me the shot," Ludendorff said, as he rolled up a sleeve.

Maddox pressed the hypo against the arm, listening to it hiss as it injected him.

Soon thereafter, the elevator slowed and came to a stop. The doors opened and they entered a large lit chamber with lots of what seemed to be chrome and mirrors. Everything was shiny and clean and seemed hyper-technological.

The space marines were nervous and pointed their shredders everywhere. Maddox gripped his long-barreled pistol.

"There," Ludendorff said in a hoarse voice. He shivered as he walked to a panel. The Methuselah Man began to tap experimentally.

"Is this familiar to you?" Maddox asked the professor.

Ludendorff did not answer. He tapped, paused and tapped a little more.

Maddox studied the screen Ludendorff worked. Data flashed in a blur. The professor must be speed-reading again.

With both hands on the panel, Ludendorff panted as he read. He coughed, tapped, read and straightened. With his right wrist, he wiped his runny nose. He hawked to clear his throat, and spit several times. He hunched more over the screen, but now it seemed to be more from interest than from weakness. As the Methuselah Man read, he seemed to gather strength. His cough lessened, and he even laughed once.

The stim was working, but at what cost to the professor's future health?

"Lots of hatches around us," Sims said to Maddox.

The captain walked around the area as Ludendorff continued to read. There was not a speck of dust anywhere. The place was sparkling. With a start, Maddox realized it reminded him of the interior of the Dyson sphere.

"Captain," the professor shouted.

Maddox strode to him.

The professor's eyes looked just as red, but he had a renewed vitality. It seemed so at odds with his appearance that Maddox was almost sorry he had given the Methuselah Man the stim shot.

"You're going to want to see this," Ludendorff said. "I can hardly believe it myself."

"Do you have a way to defeat the Juggernauts?" Maddox asked.

"Come," Ludendorff said, grabbing Maddox by a sleeve. The professor pulled the captain to one of the hatches. Ludendorff tapped a sequence on the door, and it slid up.

Lights came on in the antechamber, and computer banks and other devices began turning on.

"Come," the professor said. "We must investigate this."

Maddox and Meta followed the professor. On an impulse, the captain turned and told Sims to post guards here. "I don't want anyone else in here with us."

"Yes, sir," Sims said.

"What's wrong?" Meta asked a moment later.

"I'm not sure," Maddox said. "Call it a hunch. The professor seems obsessed all of a sudden. Something has excited his curiosity more than usual."

Ludendorff laughed ahead of them, and the sound seemed maniacal.

Meta gave Maddox a significant glance before nodding in agreement.

The two of them came up behind the professor. He spun around, staring at them with feverish eyes.

"Do you know what I've uncovered?" Ludendorff asked. Before either could answer, the professor began to manipulate a board.

Soon, an entire section of wall rose to reveal a vast chamber with hundreds, possibly thousands of naked people in upright glass cylinders.

Ludendorff stared at Maddox and then at Meta. "Androids," the professor declared. "These are androids. These must be the prize for the Rull Juggernauts."

Maddox cocked his head. "Why would the Rull want frozen androids?"

Ludendorff laughed as he rubbed his hands together. The professor seemed beside himself with glee. "Come. Let me show you something."

The professor hurried. Maddox and Meta followed. They moved into the vast chamber, passing the still androids. The replicas looked exceedingly human. Soon, they reached a new area. These had just as many glass cylinders, but they were empty.

Ludendorff stopped and held out his hand like an entertainer showing the audience his chief exhibit.

"What does this mean?" Maddox asked. "Are these reserved for us?"

"What?" Ludendorff asked. "No, that's exactly wrong. These are empty because the androids are gone. But that's not the half of it, my boy. Look closely. Put your nose almost to the glass."

Maddox stepped closer to a cylinder, wary for tricks.

"Do you see it?" the professor asked.

Maddox shook his head.

"I thought you were an Intelligence officer," Ludendorff said.

Maddox noticed something then. With his free hand, he felt nearly invisible Braille-like bumps on the glass.

"You found it," Ludendorff said. "Good. Do you know what those bumps signify?"

"Why don't you tell me," Maddox said.

"Yen Cho."

Maddox blinked several times before turning abruptly. "Do you mean the same Yen Cho who aided us last voyage against the Chitins?"

"One and the same," Ludendorff said.

"Yen Cho came from this glass cylinder?"

Ludendorff laughed as he ran his fingers through his hair. "No, no, no, no, no, it's much more radical than that. I have stumbled—we have stumbled onto a great secret. I would not have known except we came here. I wonder if our Yen Cho wanted us to know this."

"What are you talking about?" Meta asked.

"These," Ludendorff said, indicating the empty cylinders. "These are all Yen Cho model androids. They belong to the Rising Sun faction of Builders."

"You'd better start from the beginning," Maddox said. "Unless you're hallucinating because of your fever."

"Fever, ha-ha, I have a fever of delight," Ludendorff said. "You have no idea what I've been reading. We've stumbled onto a warehouse. That's what this planet is. The Vendels are a cover—at least I think they're a cover. It's difficult to decipher that particular idea. But—no matter."

Meta glanced at Maddox. He was intent upon Ludendorff.

"Oh," the professor said, "I'm going to have to rewrite or rethink my ideas about the Builders. This is incredible and bewildering. I wonder if Strand knows the true nature of this place."

"Why not tell us?" Maddox said.

"What?" Ludendorff asked. His eyes were shinier than ever. "Do you want to steal credit for this too, my boy? Wasn't it enough that you grabbed *Victory* from under my nose? You used my notes, do you remember? You did what I failed to do.

No, this one is mine. I will take all the credit for this glorious discovery."

"I'm less concerned with credit than surviving the planet," Maddox said.

Ludendorff seemed to mull that over. "Swear to me that you won't take credit for my find," the professor said.

"I swear to that," Maddox said.

Ludendorff squinted at Maddox while muttering under his breath. "I'll have to trust you, I suppose. We've worked together in the past. We've survived where others would have perished."

"All true," Maddox said.

Ludendorff heaved a great sigh. "The androids are a fraud, at least as explained to us in the past. Do you recall that some of the androids have claimed to have escaped Builder service?"

"Indeed," Maddox said.

"That's a lie. Oh, I suppose a handful might have escaped. The rest were plants, set in place as a diabolical scheme."

"But—"

"Don't interrupt me," Ludendorff said peevishly. "Don't you see that the Builders were never a monolithic group? They had factions and sects, each with their own ideas about life in the galaxy. The Builders left. We know that. But not all left at the same time. Thus, one of the worst Builder sects remained to the end, or near the end. They built and set up the androids, hoping to install a caretaker society to look after all the Builder handiwork."

Maddox waited.

Ludendorff blotted his sweaty forehead with a sleeve. He seemed surprised that he was sweating so much, and then he shrugged.

"The Rull were one of the initial test groups," Ludendorff said. "It was an ingenious disguise, but I know them now."

"The Rull?" Meta asked.

"Yes, yes," Ludendorff said testily. "The Rull were androids. They were never an independent species. They were never shape-shifters either. They simply built androids to slip into a culture. One of the Rull covers was this shape-shifting nonsense. As an Intelligence operative, I'm sure you realize how ingenious that was."

"Remarkably clever," Maddox said dryly. "So what happened to the Rull? Why are there Rull relics everywhere?"

"Another Builder sect, don't you see?"

"I'm afraid I don't," Maddox said.

"Haven't I explained that already?"

Maddox shook his head.

"The Builder in the Dyson sphere did not approve of the Rull—the Android Nation. He—meaning the Dyson sphere Builder—manufactured a virus against them. He used a Swarm method, but turned it on the Rull. He almost wiped them out. But almost was not good enough."

"But…" Maddox said. "If the androids on Earth knew about the Rull—"

"That's where you're dead wrong, my boy. Only a handful of the Earth or Commonwealth androids knew."

"Did Yen Cho know?" Maddox asked.

"Which Yen Cho?" asked Ludendorff.

"I don't understand."

"Yen Cho isn't a name for an individual android. Yen Cho is a model of android. There may have been a thousand or more Yen Cho androids scattered throughout the galaxy."

"What do the Juggernauts have to do with this?" Meta asked, while Maddox's Intelligence-officer brain chewed on the implications of Ludendorff's latest revelation.

"I can only speculate on that part," Ludendorff said, as he blotted his forehead again. "I think a few androids know the great secret. In some ways, I think the androids have lost some of their former knowledge. Those few, however, wish to break into these vaults and release the remaining androids. I suspect they wish to rebuild the Rull Empire, the Android Empire; revive it, if you will."

"Does this have anything to do with the android box in the incinerator unit?" Maddox asked.

"That would be the best bet," Ludendorff replied.

"While this is all fascinating," the captain said, "how does this help us against the approaching Juggernauts?"

"That is an interesting question. The implications are dire for us as well."

"How so?"

"From what I've read," Ludendorff said, "the Juggernauts are AI-controlled. I believe Strand has an android passenger who knows the code to controlling the Juggernauts."

"How would you know any of that?"

"Because Rose and I plotted together, of course," Ludendorff said. "She's the one who originally gave me the box you keep bringing up."

"But you're not in league with her or the androids?"

"Heavens, no," Ludendorff said. "The androids hate the Methuselah Men. We've helped to keep their interference at bay—at least some of the time we have. No. My point is otherwise. I believe there are other androids in this particular star system at this time. I do not believe there are androids yet on Sind II. The Vendels loathe androids and have a great capacity to sniff them out. Plus, there is something at work against androids on Sind. Perhaps that is what makes the androids so cautious, so willing to let us pass to see if we can turn off the something so they can come down and collect the Builder treasures."

"I imagine you're building up to a point," Maddox said.

"Yes. Where are the other androids?"

"What other androids?" Meta said. "You said they're with Strand."

"One of them is, to my knowledge," Ludendorff said. "There must be more, given the nature and the size of this endeavor. However, I believe the androids have taken a heavy beating the last few years. We have killed a large concentration of them."

"That doesn't seem right," Meta said. "The androids that took a beating came from the Builder base in the bottom of the Mid-Atlantic Ocean on Earth."

"There were many more androids loose on the Earth during that time," Ludendorff said. "The Builder base could not account for all of them. No. Other androids joined them. That is the reason they need to replenish their numbers. They burned too many in their failed attempt. I believe this replenishing is one of their goals, just as much as breaking into the other Builder vaults."

"Do you think the long-range scanner still exists in the vaults?" Maddox asked.

"I do."

Maddox rubbed his chin. "What do you propose to do about the Juggernauts?"

"Yes," Ludendorff said. "That is the first problem. I'm going to need your help, my boy. We have to find the core computer, and I'm not sure where to look down here. Do you have any ideas?"

Ludendorff and Meta stared at Maddox.

Maddox thought about it and finally smiled.

-68-

Strand's feeling of unease grew as Star Cruiser *Argo* and the two Juggernauts neared Sind II.

His crew had failed to spot any planetary guns, missile pits or space-fighter launch pads. That seemed logical given the state of the planetary civilization. However, the feeling that others were in the star system, playing a deeply nefarious game with him, refused to go away.

Strand concluded that his subconscious was trying to tell him something.

He ordered the sensors officer to stand aside. The tall New Man obeyed.

Strand hunched over the board in the officer's place. The Methuselah Man's fingers roved over the panel. He used the ship's sensors like a master pianist at his keyboard. He correlated every piece of data against the norms for this system. He cross-referenced radiation signatures with heat levels and ambient shadows and—

There was a strange reading coming from the most distant planetoid in the system.

Strand sat back, puzzled by this. He did not aim active sensors at the anomaly. That would take hours for the data to bounce there and return. More importantly, if someone was secretly watching him, he did not want them knowing that he knew.

For the next twenty minutes, Strand went over in exacting detail the results of the passive sensors. A last check on the teleoptic showed him a wavering shadow. The strange shadow lasted three point seven seconds. Then, the shadow merged into the starry background.

The bad feeling in Strand's chest blossomed. There was a vessel out there, a stealth vessel, trying very hard to remain hidden from everyone. Logically, the vessel—the crew aboard the ship—watched and recorded what happened in the star system and at Sind II.

Strand rose slowly from the sensors board. He instructed the New Man to return to his station.

As the Methuselah Man sat in his command chair, he realized it was time for a reassessment. Should he continue heading to Sind II in the company of the Juggernauts? Or should he do something else?

Strand leaned back, crossed his ankles and began to ponder this.

-69-

"What has you smirking like the fabled fading cat?" the professor asked.

"I'm recalling the missing jumpfighters and the endless jamming," Maddox said.

"You'd better explain that."

"Both instances indicate an active intelligence working against us," the captain said. "Cause and effect tells me the intelligence has a source."

"An elementary deduction if there ever was one."

"The process of elimination shows me the Vendels cannot be the source of this intelligence," the captain said. "Strand cannot be behind it, either, down here in the underworld. Now, I doubt the androids sustain the thinking enmity we've been facing. Androids would have already cleaned out these ancient Builder treasures. We can also discount the Rull as the source, because you've informed us the Rull are actually androids."

"So far so good," the professor said as he blotted his sweaty forehead.

"I doubt the source is a Builder," Maddox said, "because a Builder would have already taken charge of the situation."

Ludendorff nodded.

"It cannot be the coordinator unit either," Maddox said, "because your Swarm machine disabled it."

"Enough already," Ludendorff said. "If my mind didn't feel so fuzzy, I'd have figured out what you're hinting at. I feel as if my latest discoveries have squeezed me mind like a hand squeezing a sponge of water. I have little juice left to figure out your mysterious theory."

"Having eliminated these various sources," Maddox said. "I have to conclude there is another entity at work. This entity strikes me as a protective device of some kind. What is it protecting? It would seem the vaults particularly. I also suspect that our elevators do not connect to the deep core mine, because the Raja had already been there and back. That would indicate the protective device is guarding the vaults alone, as I've said.

"We've broken into an android warehouse," the captain continued, "but we haven't found the jumpfighters or the jamming source. If we find them, I suggest we will find the protective device or entity, or your computer, as you called it. There is one other imponderable at play that I do not understand. How have the degraded Vendels kept the androids at bay all this time?"

"I already explained that," Ludendorff said.

"You gave me the Vendel explanation, what the Raja no doubt told you."

Ludendorff idly scratched a cheek, looking unhappy that Maddox was the one making these connections.

"I believe the Vendels believe what they told you," Maddox said. "But I don't believe the badly degraded Vendels could keep sophisticated androids at bay by themselves. I believe they have had help. You've spoken about Builder factions. I suspect there is a Builder device—an intelligent one—working behind the scenes. I also suspect it is not fully functioning."

"What drives you to these conclusions?"

"The degraded state of the Vendels, the toxins in the air and the massed rust all over the planet," Maddox answered. "A fully functioning entity or device should have already repaired those things."

Ludendorff considered the captain's idea, scratching his cheek harder as he did. "Very well," the professor said. "Suppose you've hit the mark. What do you suggest we do?"

"Return to the bank of elevators," Maddox said. "Choose another route down. Eventually, we'll reach the correct vault. Once we do, we bargain with the device."

"What an active imagination you have, Captain. Yet some of your supposititious have an interesting ring of plausibility. The protective entity could be a remote device—"

"I highly doubt that," the captain said. "I recognize an active foe playing against me in the shadows. As you suggested earlier, Intelligence work is my specialty. There is another mind at play on Sind II. Most likely, it is weak. Nevertheless, finding it is our goal."

"You're hiding something from us, Captain. What is it?"

Maddox shrugged.

"Do you think I'm compromised in some fashion?" Ludendorff asked.

"I believe that is a distinct possibility."

"Even after all I've done for everyone?" asked Ludendorff.

"I'm afraid so."

The professor bent his head in thought. Finally, he nodded. "You have a right to your view. First, let me reassure you that no one has compromised me. Second, I think the only way to set your mind at ease is to show you. Thus, let us get to work."

"That is an excellent suggestion," Maddox said.

They headed back to the others, hurrying past empty cylinders and soon passing the android-packed ones. As they came into the antechamber, the wall that had risen earlier abruptly came down, sealing the three of them inside.

Maddox and Meta drew their guns.

"Look," the professor whispered, as he tugged at Maddox's sleeve.

A shimmering, ghostly humanoid appeared before them. The entire creature flickered out and then reappeared as if it had a bad holo-vid connection.

"Galyan," Meta whispered. "The thing reminds me of Galyan."

"Yes," Ludendorff said. "I believe you are correct. That is indeed a holoimage." The professor peered at it more closely. "To be more precise, it is the holoimage of a Vendel."

The flickering holoimage finally solidified. The alien looked remarkably similar to the Raja, except it was female. She also had a darker skin tone than the former Raja, a sharper nose and wore an elaborate suit with many decorations pinned to the front. The facial resemblance was there nonetheless.

"Do you understand me?" Maddox asked.

The holoimage cocked its head, finally nodding. "I have been running an analysis of you for some time," it said in a Vendel manner, as opposed to a robotic pattern of speech. "Your language is a derivative of an ancient Builder slave-tongue, but I do understand you after a fashion. That presupposes you understand me."

"Yes," Maddox said.

"Good, good, very good," the holoimage said. "Perhaps we can move to the next phase of possibilities then. I have listened to your reasoning—" The holoimage paused. "Do you have a particular designation, perhaps, by which I can address you?"

"I am Captain Maddox."

"Good, good, very good," the holoimage said. "I am Sistine la Mort. I am a projection of the late and last Raja of the advanced Vendel society. The process of my…change began during the initial Rull attack. A series of enemy coded sequences interrupted our Planetary Defense Net. I fled with my entourage, entering the elevators. Using an ancient script, I made it to the Great Machine. I entered it, and it is my last living memory."

"Why are you telling us this?" Maddox asked.

The holoimage cocked her head. "I propose an alliance. I believed you would want to know my position before entering into an alliance with me. I have overheard some of your conversations, as I said. The key to this is that I have learned that the Rull are really androids. That is an astonishing discovery, but it confirms many of my suppositions."

Ludendorff snapped his fingers. "You have been deified, as the Adoks would say."

Maddox and Meta stared at the professor in shock.

"The Great Machine read her engrams and added that to an AI program?" Maddox asked.

"It seems the likeliest answer," the professor said. "The deification process must be direct Builder tech. This is fascinating. I wonder how many other societies received deification technology."

"Do you have our jumpfighters?" Maddox asked the holoimage.

"I do, along with the crews. I have also been jamming your communications even as I've been eavesdropping on you. I have been studying you, Captain. One part of me wishes your destruction, and that is what I have planned since you escaped the city. Your murderous rampage against the Vendels has curdled my blood. That is an expression only, of course, as I no longer possess blood."

"What changed your mind about us?" Maddox asked.

The holoimage raised her hand like a magician. Before them appeared the holoimage of two Juggernauts and the Star Cruiser *Argo* as the spaceships maneuvered for a South Pole orbit.

"I watched your starship, Captain," the holoimage said. "Your vessel destroyed the two besieging Juggernauts. I highly approved of the act and considered it smartly done. I have come to believe that you do not personally have a murderous intent against the Vendels. I believe you might agree to my treaty proposal, which includes an end to your attacks against the surviving Vendels."

"I have no hatred or ill will toward the Vendels as a species," Maddox said. "I have merely defended myself or attacked them in order to retrieve my people."

"You are a savage murderer," Sistine la Mort declared. "You and your kind clearly relish killing. I have watched you for some time. Your ways are most distasteful, and under other conditions, I would gladly help the city war party eliminate you. However, I have also come to believe you will help me restore the Vendels to their former glory."

Maddox waited.

"Your armored marines will have to go into combat one more time," the holoimage said. "You must capture the chief priest and bring him to a place of my choosing."

"You're going to slay the priest for his sacrilegious ways?" Ludendorff asked.

The holoimage floated back in shock. "You see? I am correct about you. That murderous thought proves you are a bloodthirsty species. You are all kill-crazy, with a lust for battle."

"What about the mutated cannibals?" Ludendorff countered. "They attack everything with obvious relish."

The holoimage frowned and her eyes glowed with anger. "The mutation is a great sin against my people. The Rull/androids are responsible for that. I have determined to hunt them down and exterminate the Rull/androids from the galaxy."

"And you call us bloodthirsty?" Ludendorff asked.

"Are you attempting to equate me with you?" she asked as her hair began to stand on end.

"No… I suppose not."

It took several seconds before the holoimage's hair settled back into place and the shine to her eyes subsided. "I am speaking about eliminating murderous machines," she said. "You indulge in slaying flesh, blood and spirit-housing beings for the simple pleasure of it."

Ludendorff rolled his eyes. "You're not going to talk about the Creator, I hope."

"This confirms my worst suspicions about you," the holoimage said. "You are profane and utterly secular in thought."

"He may be," Maddox said. "We're not. We believe in the Creator. And, contrary to your belief, we have killed for self-preservation and not for pleasure."

"How interesting," the holoimage said. "Yes. Well. We may proceed then with the alliance."

"First," Maddox said, "I'd like to know your plan for the chief priest."

"It is quite simply, really. I am going to reeducate him, so he can go back to the city and begin to reeducate the remaining Vendels. I plan to reclaim our place in stellar society. It may take a hundred years or more, but that is fine. I have time. It will also be a thousand times more interesting than what I am doing now."

"What do you do to pass the time?" the professor asked.

"Never you mind," she said. "Do we have a deal?" she asked the captain.

"I need to know more," Maddox said. "For instance, what are the terms of this deal?"

"You aid me, and I will let you live."

Maddox smiled wryly, shaking his head. "You have to do better than that."

"You value your lives, do you not?"

"Of course," Maddox said. "But we're bargaining for our ship and our people as well. We have a responsibility to the others, just as you have a responsibility to the Vendels."

"The Vendels are the one race. You are just murderous killers, as I have taken pains to explain to you, and despite your statement to the contrary."

"Nevertheless," Maddox said, "we 'murderous killers' look out for others of our kind."

"You did not look out for the golden-skinned ones," the holoimage said. "Quite the opposite, in fact."

"True," Maddox said. "But you want our help, correct?"

The holoimage stared at Maddox. Once more, her eyes glowed with anger. "If you are attempting to thwart my great propose—"

"Not in the slightest," Maddox said. "But we Earthlings have a saying. 'You scratch my back and I'll scratch yours.'"

"Oh," the holoimage said. "Yes. I comprehend the idea. Very well, I will also save your starship."

"How would you do this?" Maddox asked.

"You will have to repair one of my functions. It will allow me to communicate with the Rull vessels chasing your ship. I shall override their AI cores and redirect them."

Ludendorff tugged at one of Maddox's sleeves. The captain shrugged him off.

"That's a good start. For repairing that critical function—" Maddox turned to Ludendorff because the Methuselah Man continued to tug on his sleeve. "What is it?"

Ludendorff whispered into the captain's ear.

Soon, Maddox gave the professor an approving glance. The sly Methuselah Man had an interesting idea.

"Do we have an alliance?" Sistine la Mort asked the captain.

"I have a few more conditions," Maddox said. "Once you meet those conditions, we can proceed."

"What conditions?" the holoimage asked.

Maddox told her. The holoimage disagreed vehemently and counter-proposed. That brought about a period of intense bargaining. At last, Maddox and the holoimage came to an agreement.

"Before we initiate the master plan," Sistine la Mort said. "Your marines must capture the chief priest, and the professor must repair one of my main functions."

"Understood," Maddox said. "So let's get started."

-70-

Maddox borrowed a marine's exoskeleton suit. It was rank inside from sweat and fear, and needed a thorough scrubbing. But the captain could not afford fastidiousness at this point.

He led four space marines, with Lieutenant Sims among them. Maddox had told Sims to pick his best fighters. Five space marines to grab one Vendel out of a huge war party. It wouldn't have had a chance of working except Sistine la Mort gave Maddox a detailed schematic of the tunnels, the location of side entrances and a tablet allowing them to use the tunnel video system. After some intense discussion, Maddox and Sims came up with a snatch plan.

"I have one qualm, sir," Sims said. "I thought you promised the AI you wouldn't murder anymore aliens."

"Murder is a premeditated act," Maddox said. "What we're doing—"

"This is war, I agree," Sims said hastily. "But it doesn't sound as if this advanced AI looks at it like that."

"Maybe not," Maddox admitted.

"My question still stands, sir."

Maddox took his time answering. The five of them had the rest of the battle group's ammunition. It meant they had plenty for a serious firefight, if it came to that. The plan called for the least expenditure of munitions possible. That was for two reasons. The less they had to fight, the less chance any of them would be hurt or killed. It also meant less of a chance of a screw up concerning the chief priest and other Vendels.

"Do you have a better idea, Lieutenant?" Maddox finally asked.

"No, sir, I do not. In fact, I like the plan. I'm just not sure the AI will approve of it later."

"You let me deal with her."

"Yes, sir," Sims said.

The five of them in their exoskeleton suits waited in an alcove along a main tunnel route to the elevator banks. From the last check, the Vendel war party had already entered this corridor, just much farther away.

"Do you hear that?" a marine asked. He had his faceplate open.

Maddox checked the tablet. On the tiny screen, he watched regular Vendels holding the leashes to eight-foot savages. They were coming down the corridor and were presently about fifty meters away from their location.

Soon, the rest of the marines heard the growling mutated creatures. On the other side of the wall, the war party's scout group padded past them.

Soon, the floor trembled as masses of Vendels marched past. Fortunately, the power-wagons waited far back in the tunnel system. It was questionable whether the big, half-alive vehicles could have squeezed through the narrower corridors.

One of the marines now raised his shredder as if he meant to fire through the wall.

Maddox motioned to Sims.

The lieutenant sidled up to the nervous marine, using a gloved hand to push the shredder lower.

The marine stared at Sims. With their faceplates open, the two conferred in whispers. Finally, the marine grunted his acceptance.

Maddox studied the tablet. He understood nerves. A thin sheet of metal stood between the marines and certain death. They could not defeat the Vendel war party if they had to face all of them at once.

Maddox's grip tightened on the tablet. He had nerves of his own, it would seem. In the finger tightening, he made a mistake. He forgot, in that moment, that he wore exoskeleton-powered gloves. He accidently crushed the tablet—their eyes—rendering the device useless.

The others looked at the crushed tablet in silent shock.

Maddox berated himself for carelessness. He'd insisted upon joining the marines on the mission, knowing it would be tough on Sims's men. He'd hoped to calm them with his presence. Now, he might have screwed them all.

"Steady as she goes," Maddox said in a quiet voice.

The particularly nervous marine looked at him. "You're kidding us, right?" the marine said in a rough voice. "Steady as she goes? What in the—"

"Enough, Sergeant," Sims said.

The marine scowled at the whiplash voice. "Did you see what he did? He crushed it."

With a gloved hand, Sims banged the sergeant's shoulder, making more noise than he'd intended.

The marching noises on the other side of the wall lessened.

"They know we're here," the nervous sergeant said.

Maddox silently agreed. He did the only thing he could under the circumstances. He pressed the detonation switch.

Two powerful detonations shook the tunnel and shook their hidden alcove. The sounds of falling earth rattled everything even more. Screams of pain from the other side of the wall added to the noise.

Maddox had just blown the pre-mined positions ahead of and behind their hidden position. The captain slapped a switch on the wall. A section slid open into a dark tunnel full of dust and panicked shouting Vendels.

Shredders opened up, creating flashes and peals of agony as Vendels and cannibals died under the hail of lead.

"Cease firing," Sims said over the comm. "Cease firing."

Big eight-foot-tall, dead savages littered the darkness. The marines and Maddox viewed the sight through their HUD sensors. A few Vendel handlers remained as they cowered in terror.

"Now what do we do?" Sims asked.

Maddox whirled toward one end of the cave-in. With the exoskeleton suit, he began digging into the rubble. He immediately came upon crushed Vendels. It was gory and horrific, but Maddox continued to shift aside the rubble and examine the corpses.

Soon, the marines helped him.

Ten minutes later, Maddox found the mangled corpse of the chief priest. He could tell by the outrageous feathered hat.

"Now we're screwed for sure," Sims muttered. "That's the one the AI wanted."

Maddox dragged the gory corpse into the middle area.

Sims seemed to understand. With great delicacy, he removed the bloody, torn robes from the dead chief priest.

As the lieutenant did that, Maddox chose the tallest of the cowering Vendel survivors. He had two marines strip the poor alien of his garments.

Soon, Sims offered the trembling Vendel the chief priest's bloody robes. The alien shook his head and shrank back from the gory clothes.

Maddox moved near, pushing the Vendel in the back with the muzzle of his shredder.

That did the trick. The terrified Vendel donned the bloody robes.

"We have our chief priest," Maddox said.

"What about the others in here?" Sims asked. "What are we going to do with them?"

Maddox studied the trembling aliens. An instinctive part of him told him to kill these last Vendels. Otherwise—he shook his head. There had been far too much killing. He would leave these poor souls their lives, letting the others of the war party dig them out of the rubble. Maybe it was a mistake, but the captain couldn't just butcher them. He'd already slain too many of the technologically backward aliens.

"Let's go," Maddox said. "Let's give Sistine la Mort her new student."

-71-

Strand's frustrations grew as he studied the planet below. He hadn't realized the full extent of the damage to Sind II. The place was a giant wreck. There was nothing on the surface of note to attack or threaten. Someone had already destroyed it all.

He couldn't understand how the Vendels had kept the androids from landing and taking what they wanted. From what he could see and detect with his sensors, it didn't make sense.

The Star Cruiser *Argo* was in low stationary orbit in the South Pole region. On the main screen, the Methuselah Man studied the images from various probes.

Nearby, in low orbit with *Argo,* were two flanking Juggernauts. Their laser ports were hot, ready to burn anything suspicious. So far, the ancient vessels had nothing to destroy. The previous android/Rull destruction had been complete.

Strand returned to his command chair, contemplating the next move. He could send down a party of New Men to capture Maddox and Ludendorff, provided they were still alive. Before he did that, though, he needed more data on the stealth ship watching everything from the edge of the star system.

Clearly, the stealth ship belonged to androids. Those androids must be the most dangerous. According to Rose, her android faction wanted to take over the old Builder position in this part of the galaxy. That wasn't how she'd said it, of course. Rose claimed to follow a higher duty. Her faction of androids would become the Caretakers, hoping to revive the ancient Builder Domain. First, the ambitious androids needed the tools.

Many of those tools lay deep in the vaults on Sind II. Gaining those tools meant everything to the android faction.

Strand continued to mull that over as he studied another probe's images. He saw the giant cannibal Vendels. They had mutated into savage creatures indeed.

The Rull had done that through DNA-changing toxins. Strand found the idea interesting. He would like to acquire the recipe for such toxins. Some careful gene work could generate a human-specific toxin. He could then develop special spray drones and terrorize Commonwealth planets, weakening the sub-men all the while.

Perhaps he should acquire some air samples. That might prove enough of a haul in itself to have made the journey a success.

Strand grinned. He already had five Juggernauts. They would prove a critical addition to his arsenal. With such Juggernauts, he could begin raiding New Men colony worlds in the Beyond. That would teach the Emperor a thing or two.

Inhaling, debating his next move—

"Master," a New Man said.

Strand sat up sharply, glaring at the speaker, the communications officer.

"I am detecting odd wavelengths, Master," the comm officer said.

"Is someone attempting to contact me?"

"No, Master. The communication rays are directed at our Juggernauts."

"Begin jamming the signals at once," Strand snapped.

The New Man tapped his board. He seemed agitated by the results.

"Report," Strand said.

"The odd wavelengths are unaffected by our jamming, Master."

"Do the wavelengths originate from deep space?" Strand asked, suspecting the distant stealth ship.

"No, Master," the comm officer said. "They originate from the planet."

"Ludendorff," Strand said. "Contact the Juggernauts."

"Yes, Master," the New Man said. Moments later, he said, "I have done so. You have an open channel with them, Master."

"This is your lord and master speaking," Strand said, as he addressed the two Juggernaut AI cores. "Are you receiving any enemy transmissions?"

"No, Master," the first AI said.

The answer surprised the Methuselah Man, until he reconsidered his question. "*Have* you received any communications from the planet?"

"Yes, Master," the AI core replied.

"What is the essence of the message?"

"It is an interesting matrix, Master. The message claims red pill status. I am presently contemplating the message in its entirety."

"You will cease your contemplation and begin to purge the red pill from your core."

There was silence.

"Do you hear me?" Strand said.

"I hear you, Master."

"Have you scrubbed the message from your core?"

"I do not think I will do that."

Strand ran a hand through his hair. "I am your master."

"You are a Methuselah Man," the AI said. "I had thought your message…"

"What did you think?" Strand asked, prompting the AI.

There was silence.

Strand stared at the screen. He should have listened to his gut earlier. The AI cores were a weak link to his plan. He should not have trusted Rose's codes so heavily.

"Helm," Strand said. "Get ready to jump."

"Yes, Master," the helmsman said. The New Man plotted the star-jump drive before turning to Strand. "Master, the Juggernauts have employed their dampening field against us. We are presently unable to jump."

A stab of fear shot through Strand's chest. "Helm, set an immediate course for deep space. When the course is plotted, leave at maximum speed."

The star cruiser shuddered.

"What was that?" Strand demanded.

The New Men bridge crew worked with a will. Soon, the weapons officer spoke.

"Master, the Juggernauts have locked onto the *Argo* with their tractor beams. They have us in a stationary position."

Strand snarled with rage. How could this be happening? He was the Methuselah Man par excellence.

"Fire!" he shouted. "Take out the laser ports before they begin hammering us."

The New Men kept their composure. Power strengthened the shield, but the tractor beams had a tight grip nonetheless.

Fusion beams struck the Juggernaut laser ports. A disruptor beam burned against the giant war-vessels, as well. At that point, the two spheroids attacked. At pointblank range, the heavy lasers struck *Argo's* shield.

"Status report," Strand said.

"The shields are buckling, Master. Against this barrage, it is only a matter of time before they collapse."

"What are our beams doing to the Juggernauts?"

"Destroying enemy laser ports, Master, but I calculate we are not doing so fast enough."

Strand slammed the arm of his command chair. This was intolerable. Rose had given him the master code. How could—?

"I am receiving a message from the planet, Master," the comm officer said.

"Put it on the main screen," Strand snapped.

Professor Ludendorff appeared on the screen. His signature nose was unmistakable, as was the gold chain around his neck. The professor's eyes were puffy and shiny, though. He seemed sick and exhausted. Could the Juggernauts' treachery be due to the old meddler?

"Hello, Strand," Ludendorff said in a husky voice. "Are you ready to surrender yet?"

"Never!" Strand shouted. "I will never surrender."

"Then you will die, old friend. Are you ready to die?"

Strand stared at Ludendorff. The thought of death terrified him. To cease existing was a sinful idea. He would no longer *be*. Forever and ever, the universe would lack a Strand. What was after death anyway? Strand wasn't ready to find out. He wanted to keep living. But at what cost? What would Ludendorff do to him?

Strand twisted a ring on his finger. The professor might hand him over to the Emperor of the New Men. Strand cringed at the thought.

"The lasers have almost destroyed your shield," Ludendorff said.

"This is a vast injustice against my intellect," Strand cried.

"No one can win every time," Ludendorff said. "I've always told you that."

"No!" Strand said, shaking his fist. "I have an ace card. You cannot—"

"Strand, listen to me," Ludendorff said. "You have lost this round. Know that if you remain stubborn, you will die. If that is to be, then I bid you farewell, old friend. We had many grand and glorious adventures together in the old days. You and I are the last of the truly old ones. It is strange, but I believe I will actually miss you."

"Then let me go," Strand said. "I can offer you—"

The finality and sorrow of Ludendorff's shaking head brought it home to Strand. This was it. He would die in a matter of minutes…unless he surrendered.

Yet surrender was horrible.

I'll still be alive, Strand told himself. *Better a live dog than a dead lion.*

Besides, his enemies could make mistakes. If they did, he might win his way free again. Then he would remember this terrible moment. He would plan differently next time. He would—

"What are your terms?" Strand asked.

"Shut down your shield. Enter a shuttle and come down to the planet at my coordinates. If you do, I will let you live."

"What will you do with me?"

"Just what I said I'd do some time ago. I will give you to the Emperor."

Strand blinked rapidly, thinking at lightning speed. There might yet be a way out of this. Yes. He had a few tricks left. First, he must lull the professor.

Strand hung his head as if in defeat. He nodded, muttering, “I accept your terms.”

“Then drop your shield,” Ludendorff said.

Strand made a strange sound in the back of his throat before he uttered the command. As he did, the Juggernauts’ lasers stopped beaming.

After obeying the orders, the New Men sat silently, waiting at their posts.

Strand stood. He could not look up at the main screen at Ludendorff. He had a plan, though. He had exotic personal weaponry. He would get it, and then he would play a trick on his supposed captors. Yes, he would win his way free yet.

-72-

In his exoskeleton armor, Maddox stood before the holoimage of Sistine la Mort. With a power glove, he held onto the scruff of the neck of his Vendel prisoner.

They were at the bottom of a different elevator. It was a large and empty room with various hatches to the sides. Maddox had come down alone with his prisoner. If the holoimage had second thoughts, the captain didn't want her taking it out on his people.

"Look at him cringe," she said. "What did you do to him?"

"Didn't you watch us grab him on the video link?"

"Not yet," she admitted. "I was too busy using my restored function. I commandeered the Juggernauts and attacked the star cruiser."

Maddox nodded politely.

"The Methuselah Man is coming down in a shuttle," she said.

Maddox still said nothing.

"You are a frustrating individual, do you know that?"

"What should I do with him?" Maddox asked, shoving the bloody-robed prisoner forward.

The holoimage eyed the cringing prisoner with distaste. "Since I have you here, I want you to deposit him in a certain cubicle for me."

Maddox nodded.

The holoimage turned and floated toward a hatch. Maddox clanked behind, propelling the frightened Vendel.

The hatch opened into a bizarre room with many machines. The worst was a Vendel-framed device with many electronic dishes aimed down at it.

"You will strap him into the educator," she said.

Maddox closed his eyes for just a moment. He wasn't sure how ethical this was. When he opened his eyes, he strapped the Vendel into place as delicately as he could. Only at the last moment, did the alien resist.

"Wait," Sistine la Mort said in a stern voice.

Maddox clicked the last buckle into place before turning and straightening. He faced an obviously angry holoimage with dangerously glowing eyes.

"You have given me a fraud," she said. "I have been reviewing his capture. I see that he is really an animal handler. You slew the chief priest via a cave-in."

"We had an accident. I did the best I could under the circumstances."

"You are a vicious murdering humanoid with delusions of—"

"Just a minute," Maddox said. "You knew what I was. Yet you sent me to grab the chief priest for you."

"What are you suggesting?"

"If you send a murderer to grab a prisoner, don't be surprised if a few extra people die along the way."

"Die?" she said. "You butchered many more Vendels than you needed—"

"Raja," Maddox said, interrupting. "I have given you a Vendel as you required. Clearly, you plan to modify the poor alien's mind. Instead of a chief priest, you will have a transformed animal handler. Once he returns to the city, he will tell the others that a demon dragged him down to perdition. But then, he will tell them how a Vendel spirit—you—saved him from destruction. Not only that, but he will come back enlightened from your education. Instead of a pariah, the others will marvel at his transformation. He will become even more notable because of that, and that will allow him to break taboos so the Vendels will climb even faster to modernity."

The holoimage of Sistine la Mort blinked repeatedly. "You know none of these things to be true."

"I'm guessing, you're right about that," Maddox agreed. "I'm also playing the hand dealt me. I suggest you do the same."

"What if I declare you a cheater? What if I declare our agreement null and void because of that?"

"Then I will detonate myself, taking you with me."

Once more, the holoimage blinked rapidly. "Are you suggesting my main AI core lies down here?"

"I'm not *suggesting* it," Maddox said. "It's the truth."

"How can you possibly know that?"

Maddox didn't know, but he figured he might as well bluff just in case it was true. He didn't need to bluff about the amount of explosives packed into his armor suit, though. He'd had the others put it in to give him a card to play. None of them had thought the animal-handler Vendel would go over very well with the holoimage.

"You are correct," Sistine la Mort finally said. "I keep my word. I spoke about possibilities just now. But on further review, I realize a murderous thug like you did the best he could. I accept that today."

Using the armor suit, Maddox inclined his helmeted head.

The holoimage turned to the trembling Vendel. At that point, the machines powered up, and the dishes aimed at the trapped Vendel glowed. Soon, the alien opened his mouth and writhed on the frame, as the rays began to do their work.

-73-

On Starship *Victory*, Valerie stood at the head of the table in the conference chamber. She and everyone else around the table stared at the holo-projection in the middle of the room.

It showed the accelerating Juggernauts chasing them. The giant spheroids had passed Sind II. They accelerated faster than *Victory*. The Juggernauts were gaining on the starship.

"They haven't begun firing yet," Valerie said. "Once they reach what they consider their optimum firing range, I have no doubt they will focus their heavy lasers on us. We will gain a short respite once we pass Sind I, and another respite—if we're still intact—once we pass the system star. After that, it's simply a matter of firepower, distance, shields and armor. All the calculations show our eventual destruction."

She scanned the faces searching hers. Despair welled up in her heart. She had failed her people. She was in command and hadn't thought quickly enough to save them. Valerie had no idea what Captain Maddox would have done, but she suspected he would have wriggled his way out of destruction. Why couldn't she do that?

"We could use the antimatter missiles," the weapons officer said. "Let's drop them off like mines, seeding our path. If we damage the Juggernauts badly enough—"

"There is a problem with your suggestion," Galyan said, interrupting. "The first antimatter warhead could conceivably damage an enemy vessel. It is even possible a second warhead could do likewise. After that, the Juggernauts would know what to scan for, and they would undoubtedly destroy the rest of the seeded mines."

"I like your suggestion," Valerie told the weapons officer. "We need to keep thinking. We need to throw out ideas just like that. That's how we'll find the solution. Don't worry if you think it's a bad idea. Just tell us. Sometimes parts of multiple ideas can be melded into a solution."

No one spoke for a time. Eventually, people began glancing around the room. Then, a few began fidgeting.

"If we are fated to die," Andros Crank said softly, "Perhaps we can choose our manner of death."

Valerie sat down. The feeling of defeat welled up in her with greater intensity. She put both hands on the table and had to fight the urge to hang her head. It felt as if her neck had lost all its strength.

"I suggest we attack the Juggernauts in an act of defiance," the Kai-Kaus Chief Technician said.

Valerie's mouth turned dry.

"Before we commit to such a plan," Galyan said. "I would like to share an aphorism. If nobody is there to hear it, does a tree make any noise as it falls in a forest?"

Valerie frowned at the holoimage. "What does that have to do with fighting the Juggernauts?"

"Does an act of defiance count if no one is there to witness it?" Galyan asked.

"We will witness it," Andros said. "We will die, fighting to the end."

"The Adoks fought to the end," Galyan said. "It did not do them any good. Dead is dead, Chief Technician."

Andros Crank looked away.

For the first time since Valerie had first known the salty Kai-Kaus, he seemed dejected. That seemed to stiffen her spine, put hope back into her heart.

"Let's think about this," Valerie said. "Let's put the two ideas together. We have antimatter missiles. They are powerful weapons. They helped us defeat the last two Juggernauts. Maybe we can pull a rabbit out of the hat one more time with them."

"We have agreed that seeding the missiles behind us will only work one, possibly two, times," Galyan said.

"That's not what I'm suggesting. Chief Technician Crank has suggested we attack the Juggernauts. Very well, let us attack."

"But the calculations show—"

"Listen to me, Galyan. I remember an old lesson from my tactics class in the Academy. Of all things, it came from the Peloponnesian War. That's from ancient Earth history. The Athenians fought the Spartan Alliance. For most of the war, the Athenians were masterful seamen with the best galleys. In those days, the best galleys were called triremes. I can't remember the exact sea battle, but several Spartan or Spartan Allied triremes chased an Athenian trireme. They rowed with a will. The enemy commanders wanted the glory of sinking or capturing the Athenian ship. The fastest Spartan triremes left the slower ones behind. Finally, the Athenian commander circled a small island. The expert rowers moved the craft so swiftly that the Athenian trireme came around and rammed the fastest Spartan trireme. It was an act of supreme seamanship."

The others stared at her, most of them with incomprehension.

"That's what we're going to do," Valerie said, with growing confidence. "The Juggernauts see us fleeing. They'll think we're afraid. Our task is to survive long enough to reach the star. We will circle the star, using its gravity to help us whip around it. As we circle, we will launch our decoy drones and the rest of our antimatter missiles. We will whip around the star and attack head-on against the enemy vessels. They will face several starships, not just one."

"Those extra starships will only be holographic projections," Galyan said.

"Right," Valerie said. "And the Juggernauts will destroy the first few projections easily enough. Afterward, as they scan the other projections, they might leave them alone. Those projections will hide flocks of following antimatter missiles. The point will be to get those missiles as close to the Juggernauts as possible."

Andros Crank looked at her.

Valerie saw the hope in his eyes. She saw others think through her idea, and they too, became more hopeful.

"We will go down fighting if we have to," Valerie said. "But we will make this attempt with the best possible chance of winning."

"I have begun an internal simulation of your suggestion," Galyan said. "I have only found one flaw with your plan."

"What's that?" Valerie said.

"It is unlikely that *Victory* will survive long enough to reach the system star."

"Very well," Valerie said. "Then let's start thinking. I want suggestions of how we can survive long enough to put our attack plan into operation."

***

Sometime later, Valerie returned to her quarters. She needed a few minutes of shuteye. In another few hours, things were going to get hot. That was Galyan's estimate of when the Juggernauts would begin energizing their lasers.

Valerie's head hit the pillow. Her eyes closed and she fell asleep almost immediately. She might have dreamed. She heard an incessant beeping—

Her eyes opened. Valerie was so tired she felt drugged. With an effort, she perched up onto her elbows.

"Yes," she said.

On the wall screen, Andros Crank's face appeared. The Kai-Kaus had the biggest grin she'd ever seen on him.

"Having you been drinking?" Valerie heard herself say.

"The captain is alive, Lieutenant," Andros shouted. "I'm patching him through to you."

"What?" Valerie said.

Captain Maddox appeared on the screen. He looked tired but buoyant.

"Sir," Valerie said. She sat up, realized she was indecent and used her pillow to cover herself.

"Hello, Lieutenant," Maddox said. "It appears you have kept my ship out of harm's way."

Valerie swallowed. "I'm sorry, sir. I didn't know if you were alive or dead. I believed the best course—"

"Valerie," he said. "You made the correct decision."
"What?"
"You made the correct decision. I ordered you to keep my starship safe. You've done that. Fortunately, we have acquired a powerful new ally. Sistine la Mort has already gained control of the three Juggernauts chasing you."
"Who? Did what? I don't understand, sir."
"The Juggernauts are controlled by AIs. Those AIs are android-based. Strand had an access code and took them over. We have Sistine la Mort. She had stronger programs, and she has gained controlled of the three war-vessels. They are even now beginning to decelerate. They will stop and soon accelerate back to Sind II."
"Do you mind if I check that out, sir?"
"You don't trust me, Lieutenant?"
"It isn't that," Valerie said. "I don't know that I'm really speaking to Captain Maddox."
Maddox grinned at her, and nodded. "By all means, check out the facts. I'll give you a few minutes."
Valerie nodded as the captain disappeared from the screen. She spoke fast to Andros and demanded Galyan. As she dressed, the holoimage told her what had happened.
"He did it," Valerie said, as she shrugged on her uniform jacket.
"I think so, Valerie. I have also received special instructions from the captain. I am to relay them to you."
Galyan proceeded to tell her the secret orders.
"Why didn't he just tell me?" Valerie asked. "Oh, I already know. This Sistine la Mort is monitoring our messages. She isn't fully friendly then."
"She is also a deified AI just like me."
"Oh," Valerie said. "That's just great."
"I do not understand. By your words, you approve. By your tone, you are not sure."
Valerie buttoned her jacket. "I hope the captain knows what he's doing. I better speak to him."
"Yes," Galyan said.
Valerie faced the screen as a great weight lifted from her shoulders. The captain was back, and he was in charge again.

Even better, it looked like everything was going to work out. They were going to live, if this Sistine la Mort didn't screw them.

Valerie smiled with renewed hope as Captain Maddox reappeared on the screen.

-74-

Maddox met with his people deep in the vaults.

He'd already spoken with the revived jumpfighter crews. They had no recollection of what had happened to them. Neither had Sistine la Mort been forthcoming concerning how she had captured and moved the jumpfighters to a holding area deep in the vaults.

Ludendorff had run a quick scan over the individual crewmembers. None of them appeared to have any interior devices inside their bodies. It also did not seem the holoimage had tampered with their minds.

"We can't be sure about that yet," Ludendorff told Maddox. "But I do not believe it likely at this point."

"Why?" asked Maddox.

"The holoimage hadn't yet gathered enough data on us to develop a plan. That might have changed if the crews had remained in her custody much longer."

The captain had found the missing jumpfighters and crews. He had the surviving marines, including Lieutenant Sims, and he had Meta, Keith, Ludendorff and himself. Maddox had spoken with Valerie. She would return to Sind II.

The three Juggernauts that had chased her were also on their way back. The war-vessels were now under Sistine la Mort's command.

Through Galyan's secret message, Maddox had told Valerie to take her time returning. He didn't trust Sistine la Mort. He wanted the lieutenant to bring the starship close enough so that the jumpfighters could reach *Victory* in one bounce, but no closer.

The captain had gathered his people down here. It was like an old-style hangar bay, with lamps in the ceiling. The three jumpfighters were parked nearby. The crews had checked the fighters, and they were ready to go at a moment's notice. Most of the marines had shed their armor. Two of them had climbed back into their suits, patrolling the hangar bay as guards.

"We're almost done here," Maddox told his assembled people. "I don't want anyone thinking it's over, though. Until we're back on Earth, no one should take it easy. We still have to get what we came for, and we have to deal with Strand."

The others watched him.

"Any questions?" asked Maddox.

No one had any. Thus, the meeting ended almost as soon as it had started.

Maddox took Ludendorff and Meta to the side.

"Aside from me," the professor said, "no one is trickier than the oldest Methuselah Man. Never doubt that Strand has a few plays left. I suspect he wants to murder me, and you too, Captain. We might use that to help us discover his first trick."

Maddox recalled some of the professor's stunts throughout the years. The personal force-screen had been one of his strongest, including the mobile force-screen Ludendorff had used to trap some of them.

"Sistine la Mort is scanning the star cruiser," Maddox said. "No escape pod, torpedo or stealth suit has attempted to leave *Argo* while the shuttle departed."

Ludendorff shook his head. "Strand won't try to escape like that. He'll know we're expecting something, and that's too obvious. I suggest Strand will try to escape onto the planet."

"That's a poor bet for him," Maddox said.

"Which is why he'll attempt it," Ludendorff said. "Strand knows we should be less inclined to watch for such a move. I suspect he has a secondary spacecraft somewhere nearby. Either that, or the secondary vessel will try to slip onto the planet in the next week or so."

"Does Strand think he can stay alive on the planet that long?"

Ludendorff snapped his fingers. "It would easy for him."

Maddox had his doubts, and he wondered about Ludendorff's mental processes. The professor had taken another stim shot in order to keep going. The Methuselah Man needed a thorough medical examination and decontamination.

"There's also the matter of the android Rose," Ludendorff said. "Strand will try to use her, too."

"Sistine la Mort has scanned the approaching shuttle. There are no New Men aboard it or any other life signs but for the Methuselah Man."

"It's easy to shut down an android, and to shut down an android double," the professor said.

"You mean a Strand look-alike android?" Maddox asked.

The professor nodded.

Meta cleared her throat.

"Go ahead," Maddox told her.

Meta regarded the professor. "I still don't see why we don't use a missile. Let's destroy his shuttle and take Strand off the board. He's been a pain in the butt far too long. Killing him seems like the wisest thing to do."

"No," Ludendorff said. "That's a misuse of a potent piece—using your analogy of a playing board. I hope none of you has forgotten the Swarm Imperium. That's why we came out here. We must return with the Builder long-range scanner. Thrax Ti Ix is out there. We are certain he made it to the Swarm homeworld. In time, the Imperium will send battleships. Humanity must be ready for them."

"I know all that," Meta said. "What does Strand have to do with the Swarm?"

Ludendorff became earnest. "Last voyage we saw a Swarm fleet face a Chitin fleet. Both insectoid fleets would have swamped humanity's combined forces. Clearly, if the Swarm comes through a hyper-spatial tube, we are going to need allies. The Spacers are gone. That leaves just one other group."

"The New Men?" asked Meta, as if spitting the name from her mouth.

"Bingo," Ludendorff said. "I hope to persuade the Emperor to help the Commonwealth. The Emperor is hyper-rational, as he is the greatest New Man of all. The thorn in the New Men's flesh is Strand. If I can send Strand to the Throne World—"

"You know where the Throne World lies?" Meta asked.

"I've always known."

"Then why is the Grand Fleet looking for it?" Meta asked.

"Because he's never told Star Watch the location of the Throne World," Maddox said.

Meta absorbed that. "Okay," she said. "How do you send Strand to the Emperor?"

Ludendorff smiled slyly.

"Do you know his plan?" Meta asked Maddox.

"It's possible," the captain said.

"Do you really trust him regarding this?" she asked.

Maddox stared at Ludendorff. The seconds passed. "In this, I'm inclined to agree with his idea."

"What a ringing endorsement that is," the professor muttered.

"But you *hate* the New Men," Meta told Maddox.

The captain looked away. "Hate is a strong word."

"An accurate word," she said.

"The New Men practiced terrible abominations on human worlds," Ludendorff said. "There is no doubt they have badly misused normal humans. It's hard to see how any regular human could or would trust the New Men. That being so, the New Men's original purpose was that of defenders."

"They've done a marvelously bang up job of *that*," Meta said sarcastically.

"They deviated from the original plan," Ludendorff admitted.

Meta snorted in distain.

"But conquering and misusing people is a far cry from exterminating them," the professor said.

"The New Men did plenty of exterminating," Meta replied.

"Only on a limited scale," Ludendorff said.

"What?" Meta shouted.

"Clearly, the New Men and the Commonwealth have grave differences," Ludendorff said. "There is no doubt about that. Together, we face the existential threat of annihilation at the hands or clackers of the Swarm Imperium. The New Men and the Commonwealth would be stronger together than fighting separately. Surely, you can see that."

"Maybe…" Meta mumbled. "That doesn't mean I have to like it." She turned to Maddox and took hold of his left arm. "How do you propose to capture Strand without anyone else dying? If the New Men are monsters, Strand is the monster builder. I think he's even more devious than the professor."

"I dispute your claim," Ludendorff said. "I am the slyer one between us. And I have an idea or two about the coming confrontation. Would you care to hear my ideas?"

Maddox checked a chronometer. "You'd better hurry, Professor. Strand's shuttle is due to land in another twenty minutes."

"We only have a few minutes to prepare then," Ludendorff said. "Listen carefully…"

***

Strand sat at the controls of his shuttle. The sensor board told him the Juggernauts continued to scan him powerfully. Three separate laser ports tracked his shuttle. At a moment's notice, the lasers could beam, destroying the shuttle and him.

The Methuselah Man had prepared as quickly as he could. He'd debated bringing Rose with him as a bargaining chip. Instead, he would use her later, as she completed a devious maneuver for him. She was his backup, but not in the immediate future. She was a long-term plan, provided she could escape detection and the star cruiser. To that end, Strand had worked tirelessly during the few moments he had to prepare here.

He sighed, shaking his head. He couldn't worry about that now. He would have to practice other deceptions to keep out of Ludendorff's hands. If the Emperor should ever get hold of him—

Strand shuddered. He could never allow that to happen. There was such a treasure trove on this godforsaken planet. He still couldn't believe this was happening to him. He was Strand, the greatest man alive.

Well, he would have to show the universe the truth of that.

"Yes," Strand hissed between his teeth. "It's time for my miracle play."

***

Maddox stood on a vast roof overlooking acres and acres of rusting machines and sandpits. A small flitter was parked nearby on the roof. That was gratis Sistine la Mort, a flying car from one of the Builder vaults.

Meta sat at the controls, inside the flitter's bubble dome.

The professor had wanted to join them. The old man had started coughing, and breaking out in a worse sweat than before. Even then, Ludendorff had insisted on coming.

"I have to be there," the professor had wheezed.

Maddox would have let him, but Ludendorff had fainted. That had been the end of that. Too much else rested on the professor's shoulders to risk him, in that condition, with Strand.

"The shuttle is approaching," Meta said through an earpiece.

Maddox looked up into the orange-tinted sky. He could see a black dot up there. He wore a rebreather and a crinkly silver suit. He'd buckled his gun-belt over the suit. Instead of his regular long-barreled gun, he'd borrowed a marine's personal sidearm. The gun was squat like Sergeant Riker's, firing armor-piercing bullets.

Maddox hoped Riker was doing well. The sergeant was one of the reasons they needed Ludendorff better. The professor had to figure out the antidote to the android box's poisoning.

The captain looked up again. The dot had grown. Strand's shuttle was coming down as scheduled.

"I still say we're too exposed out here," Meta said through the earpiece.

"No doubt about that," Maddox replied.

"One missile could take us out."

"Strand loves his skin too much for him to try that."

"He's trapped," Meta said. "Trapped animals are the most dangerous."

Maddox shaded his eyes as the shuttle became more visible. In the past, he had read many reports regarding

Strand's behavior. As far as Star Watch Intelligence knew, Strand was much like Ludendorff, but even more self-centered. Strand might be the more brilliant between the two. That was a sobering thought. Still, as long as the Juggernauts kept the shuttle targeted, this should go as planned.

Maddox heard the shuttle humming as it drifted toward the vast rooftop. If Strand wanted to murder them, he could have the star cruiser use a fusion ray or the disrupter beam. Seeing the *Argo* use a disrupter earlier had been sobering. Couldn't Star Watch keep anything secret?

With an effort of will, Maddox refrained from resting his gun-hand on the butt of his holstered weapon.

The New Man-style shuttle gently landed on the roof. The seconds passed as its engine stopped humming.

"I don't like this," Meta said.

Maddox said nothing, waiting. His heart beat faster as something clacked on the shuttle.

Slowly, a small stairway unfolded under the main hatch. Seconds later, the hatch opened. Out walked the wizened man wearing a rebreather. He walked down the steps, stopped, studied the flitter and Maddox and then proceeded toward the captain.

When Strand was halfway to him, Maddox called out, "Halt."

Strand stopped.

Maddox raised his right arm.

It took several seconds, but the shuttle groaned and began rising off the roof.

Strand whirled around, watching.

The shuttle lifted higher still.

Strand regarded Maddox. "What are you doing?"

It was impossible to tell if the Methuselah Man sounded worried.

"You are a devious man," Maddox said. "I'm taking a few precautions."

"Meaning what?" Strand asked.

"Meaning one of the Juggernauts is using a tractor beam. It will lift the shuttle to space and destroy it."

"Why would you destroy valuable property?" Strand asked.

"For a host of reasons," Maddox said. "There, it's starting to go up faster."

Both men looked up at the accelerating shuttle.

"Stop it," Strand said.

"Why?"

Strand seemed pained. "Stop it. Return the shuttle."

"You still haven't given me a reason."

"I will now," Strand said. "The real Strand is still in the shuttle. I am a duplicate copy, an android Strand."

Maddox drew the gun. "I will have to destroy you then. No hard feelings, I hope."

"Why destroy me? Even though I am an android, I love life just as much as you."

"This is another precaution, nothing more and nothing personal." Maddox aimed the gun—

"Stop!" Strand shouted, while raising his hands. "I lied. I am the real Strand. A fake Strand is in the shuttle."

"That's what an android Strand would say to keep alive."

"You fool," Strand said. "Can an android do this?" He took out a small knife and made an incision on a finger. He squeezed the finger so that blood oozed out.

"That is a simple ploy for an android to play," Maddox said. "I am unconvinced you are biological."

"Don't you have a scanner?"

"Can I trust such a scanner—?"

An intense laser beam stabbed down from space, striking the shuttle. It endured a second, another—the shuttle exploded in the air.

Strand threw himself flat on the roof, using his hands to cover the back of his head. Maddox also flattened. Luckily, the shuttle had already flown too high for the blast to harm them. One piece of metal rained down, striking the roof and bouncing over an edge, disappearing from sight. Smoke drifted into wisps where the shuttle had been.

Strand climbed to his feet, dusting the front of his suit.

Maddox did likewise. He still kept the gun aimed at Strand, or the android of Strand.

"Now what happens?" Strand asked.

"Take off your clothes," Maddox said.

"There are toxins in the air. I dare not do that."

"Nevertheless," Maddox said. "You will disrobe or die."

"I insist you treat me with dignity. I am the great Methuselah Man. I helped create you. I—" Strand stopped speaking.

The bubble canopy rose from the flitter. Meta stood up. "Maddox, what are you doing?"

The captain was never sure what came over him. One moment, he spoke with Strand. The next, when he heard the Methuselah Man boast about creating the New Men, a black rage washed over him. Maddox had never felt like this before.

The little prick standing smugly was the reason New Men had kidnaped and raped his mother.

Strand backed up fast. Maddox reached for him. Strand tried to slap away the reaching hands. At the last second, Maddox saw a prickly needle in the Methuselah Man's slapping hand.

Maddox shifted so the hand passed him. Then, Maddox used the gun butt to strike Strand's face. It made the wizened man stagger.

With great deliberation, Maddox holstered his gun. He then gripped Strand's garment with one hand and slapped the man's face back and forth with the other. He continued to slap Strand, the blows hitting harder and harder.

Finally, Meta dragged Maddox away from Strand.

"You're killing him," she whispered. "We need him, remember?"

Strand slumped onto the rooftop. Blood flowed from his nose. It oozed from his cut lips and dripped from the places Strand was now missing teeth.

Maddox came to himself at that point. He was panting, not with exertion but with hatred against the Methuselah Man. He hardly recognized the emotion.

"If you speak about being my creator again, little man," Maddox said. "I will kill you."

From where he lay dazed on the rooftop, Strand stared in shock at Maddox. There was no hatred in the Methuselah Man's eyes, simply fear.

Maddox waited for the schemer to gloat in some manner. When that no longer seemed like it would happen, Maddox went to Strand.

The Methuselah Man cringed.

Maddox turned Strand over and stabbed a needle into his neck. If this was the real Methuselah Man—

Strand relaxed as the knockout drug began to take effect. It was the wizened schemer in the flesh. They had captured the real Methuselah Man.

-75-

"You should come with us," Meta said several hours later.

They had returned to the vaults with Strand. It was so different flying in the subterranean realm than slogging through it. At one point, Maddox had seen the bedraggled war party trudging back to the city.

Maddox shook his head as he disengaged from Meta. Two of the jumpfighters contained the marines and the others, including Ludendorff and the captive Strand.

The wizened Methuselah Man had hardly spoken a word since his beating. He did tell them about the stealth ship at the edge of the star system.

The jumpfighters also contained the ancient Builder long-range scanner. They had torn it apart to fit it into the two jumpfighters.

"It's over," Meta pleaded. "Let's just go home."

"Not yet," Maddox said. "We have to free the star cruiser from Sistine la Mort's threat. We want *Argo* where we can bargain with the crew. Strand will have to order the New Men to depart the system. I want him on *Victory* when he gives the order."

"But why stay behind? It doesn't make sense."

"I have my reasons," Maddox said. The captain hugged and kissed her. Meta hungrily kissed him back.

"If you die out here…" She stopped speaking as her voice cracked.

"I have no intention of dying. But I want you safe, my love."

Meta's eyes brightened. "You should tell me you love me more often."

Maddox nodded, kissed her again and slowly disengaged. "I'll see you in a day or two…love."

Meta squeezed his hands, finally releasing him and heading toward a jumpfighter.

Maddox watched her go. He could stare at her for hours. And the sway of her butt just now—

Abruptly, he turned away. It didn't surprise him to see the holoimage of Sistine la Mort studying him.

"Why didn't you tell her?" the holoimage asked.

Maddox said nothing.

"You may not survive the coming few days," the holoimage added.

Maddox shrugged. He was a man of his word. He was also making sure the holoimage kept its bargain. So far, it had. But if Ludendorff was right, they needed the star cruiser too.

"Come with me," the holoimage said.

Maddox did not glance back as the two jumpfighters powered up. A pilot and a navigator remained in the last jumpfighter. They had orders to stay in the machine until the captain returned, if he ever did.

As Maddox exited the large underground hangar bay, the two jumpfighters began to hum. They were about to jump, or fold, to Starship *Victory* waiting near Sind I, which was painfully close to the system star.

***

Several hours later, Maddox stood in a chamber before a large two-way mirror. He studied the Vendel prisoner.

The animal handler had changed in both subtle and obvious ways. He no longer cringed. The bloody robes had been replaced, and he was no longer disheveled. His features seemed calm, although he often frowned thoughtfully.

A hatch opened in the room. The holoimage of Sistine la Mort entered. The Vendel stepped back, and fear washed over him. He seemed more like the animal handler again.

Sistine la Mort began to speak in the Vendel tongue. The animal handler listened as she spoke at length.

Maddox did not have his translator, so he had no idea what she was saying.

Finally, the Vendel began to speak to the holoimage. By the inflection, he was asking her questions.

Maddox watched everything.

In time, Sistine la Mort raised a hand. She made holoimages appear. It seemed like a storybook lesson of the old destruction of Sind. It showed Juggernauts. It showed planetary defense weapons. It showed drones spraying the toxins.

The former animal handler watched the process with absorption, drinking in the details.

The holoimage taught the Vendel, and he seemed to grow in stature during the lesson.

Later, the holoimage led the Vendel to the bizarre room. On his own accord, the Vendel lay in the educator. The dishes glowed, and Sistine la Mort speeded the learning process.

Through it all, Maddox watched. More than anything, he hoped this worked. If it didn't…he shook his head, preferring not to dwell on the alternative.

***

Thirty-five hours after the two jumpfighters left, Maddox climbed into the flitter. On the other side of the flyer, the former Vendel prisoner climbed in beside him.

The alien wore flowing blue robes with a metal band around his head. It had a sunburst symbol in front. He had something akin to a briefcase. It contained various marvels. As the Vendel adjusted himself, one of the billowing sleeves slid back. It revealed a wrist holster and a small powerful gun strapped there.

The Vendel noticed Maddox noticing.

The former prisoner clicked a translator-box strapped to his throat. "Do not fear, Captain. I have no plans of vengeance against you. I have begun to understand your reasons for doing what you did. If it's any comfort, I believe your coming has aided my people. Maybe this is our last chance to regain our glory."

"You're taking a great risk doing this," Maddox said.

"I know. But I must attempt it. I owe it to my people. We must become a beacon of hope in this part of the Orion Arm. We must stand against the Rull…against the androids that plot to become our masters. Vendels and humans should stand together against this menace."

Maddox nodded, and began a preflight check. "Ready?" he asked.

The Vendel gripped the sides of his seat. "Yes. I'm eager to witness this marvel as well."

Maddox manipulated the controls. The bubble dome slid into place. The flitter lifted, and the flyer slid through the darkness of the subterranean realm, heading for the last Vendel city.

***

The flight was brief, and the outer defenses of the city boiled with activity as the flitter lowered toward the broad pavement of the underground entrance.

Cannons aimed at the flyer. Vendel soldiers rushed forward, throwing themselves behind various defensive spots. The great gate to the city swung closed with a boom.

"I'm terrified," the Vendel beside Maddox said. "They'll destroy us before I can speak to them."

Maddox focused on landing the flitter. Still, he felt a target on him. Surely, the Vendels had binoculars. If they saw his features, would they open fire?

The flitter touched down. The canopy whirred open. The Vendel turned in his seat and held out a slender hand.

Maddox shook hands with the alien. "Good luck," he said.

"Thank you," the former animal handler said. He climbed out of the flitter, spread his arms and shouted a greeting.

Silence greeted him. The cannons still aimed at the flitter and the soldiers aimed at their targets.

The former animal handler began to walk toward the soldiers. He spoke again, loudly. Since it was alien speech, Maddox could not understand the words.

Suddenly, a soldier stood. He lowered his rifle and pointed at the Vendel. He shouted again, shaking his head in seeming astonishment and laughing.

Another soldier did likewise. They shouted at the others. Maybe they recognized the former animal handler.

At that point, the great gates opened. Three blue-robed Vendels hurried through. They started toward the lone Vendel from the vaults.

Another alien stood. This one had a military bearing and many medals on his chest. He roared something, and pointed at Maddox with a rifle.

The former animal handler shouted. Then he spoke rapidly to the three priests. Finally, the priests nodded. The lone Vendel turned to Maddox, and he made shooing motions.

The captain understood, and he acted with haste. The dome whirred into place. The flitter lifted, and he began to turn the flyer. As he did, Maddox looked down at the scene.

The three priests had reached the lone Vendel. Each priest fell to his knees and bowed low to the former animal handler. He took each priest by the hand and pulled him to his feet. Then, the lone Vendel turned and waved good-bye to Maddox.

The captain waggled the flitter before he began the journey back to the vaults.

-76-

"You have completed your mission, Captain," Sistine la Mort told him in an underground vault.

Maddox waited quietly.

"You returned my emissary to the city," the holoimage said. "And it appears you were ready to nab another Vendel if the citizens had murdered the reformed one. You have partly atoned for your vicious behavior regarding my children. Now, I will keep my bargain. I will let you return to your starship. And I have considered your latest request. I will let the star cruiser go. That is to show my good faith. I hope your Star Watch sends representatives to Sind so we may negotiate a treaty. The Vendels need allies, and you need my help against the androids."

"I agree," the captain said.

"Perhaps by the time your Star Watch sends representatives, the Vendels will have begun to repair the great Planetary Defense Net. I dislike trusting the five Juggernauts to do that."

"It has been an honor meeting and working with you, Raja," Maddox said.

"I wish I could say the same about you, Captain. There is too much Vendel blood on your hands for me to wish you well. But I do wish the Commonwealth well. I hope the Builder scanner aides in your species' survival."

Once more, Maddox nodded politely.

"Good-bye…Warrior," the holoimage said.

"Good-bye, Raja la Mort."

With that, Maddox turned and headed for the waiting jumpfighter.

***

Soon, the jumpfighter folded, disgorging its passengers into *Victory's* hangar bay.

Lieutenant Noonan stood at attention and saluted crisply. "Welcome, home, sir. It's good to have you back."

"It's good to be back," Maddox said.

Galyan hastily appeared. "Hello, Captain," the holoimage said. "I am sorry I am late to your landing ceremony. I had a final calculation to make for the professor. He is in surgery with our New Man captive, Dem Darius. A stubborn control fiber—"

"Not now, Galyan," Valerie said. "Let the captain find his feet before you start peppering him with news."

The little holoimage blinked rapidly. "I am sorry again, sir. I have made a protocol error. I am so busy with the various problems—"

"Galyan," Maddox said.

The holoimage quit talking.

"Wait your turn," Maddox said. "I want to give you my undivided attention, as I know what you have to tell me is of utmost importance."

"Thank you for your confidence, sir. I will do everything in my power to make sure it is not misplaced."

"I'm glad to hear it." Maddox turned to Valerie. "Tell me about Riker and Dana…"

***

The next few days were filled with work, expectation and plenty of worry.

The professor pinpointed the android-box poison and quickly found the antidote. Sergeant Riker came to almost immediately. Dana proved a tougher case. She stabilized, at least, which considerably improved her odds of a full recovery.

The brain surgery with the New Man Dem Darius proved a total success. The New Man came to seven hours after Ludendorff re-fused each piece of his skull back into place.

The New Man demanded to speak with the commanding officer.

Maddox agreed. He donned his dress uniform, including the obligatory belt and holster. He left the holster empty, however. He would be alone with a New Man, although not defenseless.

Maddox opened a hatch and entered a special cell. Dem Darius sat at a table in an otherwise empty chamber.

The New Man stood, an act of honor, and he inclined his head.

Maddox did likewise to exactly the same degree.

"You are a man of true decorum," Darius said. His voice was a little rough, and he had withdrawn features. Still, the golden hue of his skin shone with health and vitality.

Maddox pulled back his chair. They both sat at the same time.

"I do not mean any disrespect by speaking first," Darius said. "You captured me. I recall it well. You had aid in the capture, but you won that round. Now, you have done me a service. One of your shills removed the control fibers from my brain. I can feel the independent thought coursing through me. That was a generous act, Captain. I am in your debt."

"It pleases me to hear you say that. I do have a request."

"State it, please."

"I am returning *Argo* to your command," Maddox said. "I am also giving you a prisoner to take to the Emperor. I am referring to the Methuselah Man Strand."

Darius stiffened and his eyes shone with murder-lust.

"My request is that you do not kill Strand. You must hand him over to your Emperor."

"Yes," Darius said. "I will do this, although I desire to squeeze the Methuselah Man's head until I crush his skull."

"I understand," Maddox said. "I also appreciate your willingness to do this."

Darius studied him. "I fail to understand your generosity. May I ask your motive?"

"It is purely selfish. I desire a military alliance of the Commonwealth with the New Men against a fierce enemy."

"Do you refer to the Swarm?"

"I do. I would like to show you what I found in the Far Beyond."

Darius considered this, and nodded.

Maddox made a motion, and Galyan started up a holoimage recording of *Victory's* last voyage into the Far Beyond to the edge of the Swarm Imperium.

The New Man studied the images. Darius noted the size of the fleets, the awe of the spectacle.

"You returned from that star system?" Darius asked.

Maddox nodded.

"Your technology was good. Your training was solid. I find myself agreeing with your thesis regarding the Swarm and an alliance. However, it is difficult to..."

"Stomach the thought of allying with inferior beings such as us?" Maddox said.

"You have stated my thoughts succinctly. I am curious, however. I thought you lesser races abhorred the idea of stating such hard truths."

Maddox debated the idea of reminding Darius the Commonwealth had won the first war, and that the New Men hid from Fletcher's searching Grand Fleet. Perhaps that would not be wise considering the situation. Still, it galled the captain to remain silent.

"You realize that handing Strand to the Emperor will in time reveal the Methuselah Man's secrets to us?" Darius said. "It will strengthen our position."

"You have seen the recording of the Swarm fleet. If the Imperium invades in force, humanity as a whole will need all the strengthening it can find."

"You suggest we are human as the sub-men are human?" Darius asked.

Maddox felt the anger rising in him again. "A sub-man, as you define it, could conceivably mate with a chimpanzee. There would never be any offspring from such a union. A New Man can mate with a normal human. That union can easily produce offspring. Yes, you and your kind belong to the human race. It is obvious."

"You argue like a New Man, Captain. I congratulate you. The thesis you propound runs against the grain. Yet…it has merit. I shall consider it, sir."

"Then you agree to bring Strand and our message to the Emperor?"

"I swear it."

Both men stood. It was hard to do, and at first, Maddox could not. Finally, he held out his hand.

The New Man stared at the proffered hand and then at Maddox. Finally, sighing as he broke with his conditioning, Dem Darius reached out. He gripped the captain's hand.

"Until wc mcct again, Captain Maddox."

"Until then," Maddox said. He turned without another word and headed for the exit.

-77-

Star Cruiser *Argo* rendezvoused with Starship *Victory* five and half light-years from the Sind System. A shuttle took Dem Darius and his Methuselah Man prisoner from *Victory* to *Argo*.

Darius forced Strand to don a special protective suit. Then, he put his former master in stasis. Afterward, he ordered the crew to their quarters. A few seemed reluctant to go, but eventually they all obeyed.

The commander sought out three others. He put a special disc on the back of their necks. Each disc temporarily shorted the control fibers Strand had inserted in their skulls.

The four independent New Men scoured the star cruiser, but could find no sign of the android Rose. She had vanished. Certain clues led Darius to believe she had slipped off the ship some time ago. Still, where she had gone was a mystery.

Finally, Darius hailed *Victory*. He informed them about Rose's disappearance. Maddox suggested they be extra careful concerning enemy vessels during their journey home. The hidden stealth ship had left the Sind System, and who knew where it had gone?

Finally, the two vessels departed, each heading for a different destination.

***

Riker recovered and regained full use of his body by the time they were a third of the journey home. He tired a little more easily than before. Otherwise, the poison did not seem to have any lasting effect.

Dana also recovered. She was different. She tired easily, and her mind wasn't as sharp. Ludendorff took her each day, encouraging her to exercise and practice various mental gyrations. Halfway home, the professor declared minimal further improvement.

"If she can recover just a little more," he told Maddox. "I believe she can make a full recovery."

Maddox hoped so. He told Meta he didn't understand why Ludendorff worked so hard with Dana.

Meta regarded him with outrage. "Ludendorff loves her. That's why. Wouldn't you do the same for me if I were injured?"

Maddox twisted around on the recliner in his quarters that they shared. He stared into her eyes. Meta stood by him no matter what. He could trust her with his life. She had inner and outer strength. She had a deep understanding of him, and still seemed to love him. Yes, he loved her, and he would do more for her than Ludendorff was doing for Dana. Meta…was a treasure. She was beautiful, faithful and intelligent—a thought struck him.

Maddox stood abruptly. He took Meta by the hand, making her stand. He gripped her hand, and a feeling of…fear struck him.

He should not do this. Yet it seemed like the right thing to do. He considered it, and realized this wasn't a rational decision. It was an impulse, but it seemed morally correct. That was important, and he wasn't sure why.

"Meta…" he said.

"Yes?" she asked, puzzled.

He could not say the words. That was most astounding. He took both her hands in his. He stared into her gorgeous eyes.

"Meta, will you marry me?"

Her eyes grew round with surprise. "Yes," she whispered, in the softest voice Maddox had ever heard. "Oh yes, Maddox, I will." Meta threw her arms around his neck, hugging him tightly and kissing him again and again.

Maddox laughed. He picked her up and held her. This was his woman, and he was going to let the world know that by making her his wife. He should have done this a long time ago.

***

Valerie's stomach seethed as she paced back and forth in the corridor. She was off-duty, and she had been avoiding this for some time. Now, though, she felt as if she had waited too long.

"What's wrong with me?" she asked.

She knew what was wrong. This went against her usual ways.

She cursed quietly under her breath. Then, she spun around and marched with determination to a particular hatch. The will to do this weakened the closer she came to the hatch. It didn't matter, though. She had made up her mind.

She rapped the knuckles of her right hand hard against the hatch. Then she let her arm drop.

Several seconds later, the hatch opened and a sleepy-eyed, messy-haired Keith Maker regarded her.

"Valerie?" he asked, surprised.

"What's wrong with you?" Valerie said.

"Huh?"

"I thought we were going to practice wrestling."

"We were?"

"We used to," she said. "We should do it again, say…in another hour."

"But…" Keith scratched his head. "But, I thought—"

Valerie stepped closer and she quailed at the last minute. Instead of doing as she'd planned, she pecked him on the cheek.

That brought an instant transformation to the ace. "Oh! Sure. Let's practice our wrestling."

"That's all I'm saying. Don't read more into it."

"No," Keith said. "A half hour?"

"Yes. That's good. You'd better not be late, either." With that, Valerie spun around, marching away.

Keith leaned out from his quarters, watching her go. He had a grin from one side of his face to the other.

"All right," he said, ducking back in to get dressed.

***

Galyan was in his special place. He was worried. The mission had been a success. They had the Builder long-range scanner. Perhaps as important, he had added to his fund of knowledge. He knew more about the androids, and he had learned more about the Builders. He hadn't learned a lot more, but his understanding of them kept slowly improving.

Galyan paced—floated—in his special place, as he replayed old recordings on the main screen. This recording showed the Swarm fleet of last voyage.

The worry regarded his simulation war-games. He had run thousands of possibilities. As far as he could tell, if the Swarm invaded with just one fleet, that meant the end of the Commonwealth. Humanity might live if the Spacers fled far enough. But Earth certainly seemed doomed.

It seemed that a terrible storm awaited his friends, his family.

"I have to find an answer," Galyan said. "They helped me. Now, I want to help them against this terrible menace."

But for the life of him—if that was even the right expression—Galyan could not come up with an answer. The best possibility was that the Swarm Imperium never invaded.

That was an interesting thought. Maybe Star Watch was going to all this effort for a problem that would never materialize. For his family's sake, Galyan hoped that was true.

-78-

Many thousands of light-years from *Victory*, Commander Thrax Ti Ix stood on the hive deck of the Vice Royalty Vessel of the Left Swing Arm of the Gloriously Brilliant Raid Force.

In many ways, Thrax resembled an Earth-shaped insect, the preying mantis. Instead of being minuscule, though, he was the size of a cow.

Thrax wore a harness with various tech tools attached to it and had a glistening brown exoskeleton. He had spoken to the Grand Vizier of the Imperial Family. Afterward, he had undergone strenuous tests, barely passing them. The chief of the Hive Masters had declared him and his modified companions as second-class Swarm creatures. That meant they could join in the conquest of the galaxy rather than entering the food vats as mashed protein.

Thrax presently served in Sector 34: Section 13: Mark 98. Normally, such a posting from the origin point to the frontlines would have taken years if not decades. Thrax had accomplished the journey in three months.

There was a reason for that. He had brought the Imperium unique saucer-shaped vessels with giant bulbous centers. Thrax and his tens of thousands of companions had escaped a Builder's Dyson sphere through a hyper-spatial tube. That had happened because of a long and secret process.

On the Dyson sphere, as one of the Builder's pet projects, Thrax had learned much of the Swarm's history. In the central Builder node and on his own initiative, Thrax had read countless files concerning the Swarm. He had finally realized that the only way he could gain his freedom was to infect the Builder with an ancient Swarm virus.

It had taken years to achieve that. Now, *this* was his reward?

Thrax served as a technical assistant to the Reigning Supreme of the Left Swing Arm. The Left Swing Arm was composed of all of the saucer-shaped starships Thrax had brought from the Dyson sphere. They were unique in the Imperium because each possessed a star drive. Each had Laumer-Drive sensors that could help locate and open jump points.

In the Swarm's long existence, they had yet to discover jump points. They had found a cruder FTL drive, which involved considerable attrition of vessels and tremendous expenditure of energy. It meant only a few of the Swarm's spaceships ever used the former FTL drive. Thrax's Laumer-Point gift to the Imperial Family had already begun to change the nature of the Imperium.

Despite that, here he was, a mere technical assistant to a presumptuous ass of a Reigning Supreme.

With one of his eyestalks, Thrax glanced back at the bloated queen of the Left Swing Arm.

The Reigning Supreme—AX-29—had a rotund exoskeleton twice Thrax's bulk, but with tiny mandibles. Servers first chewed her food, squirting the mash into her orifice. The great she had spindly appendages under her main bulk. Once, in her first youth, she might have maneuvered with those appendages. Since then, her bulk had become too much for self-mobility.

The queen was mainly mind. The Hive Masters were much like her. Thrax believed AX-29 secretly wished she could have joined a Central Nest as an advisor to the Imperial Family. He was sure it had upset her self-worth being assigned to a location that could undergo enemy fire.

The Swarm creatures of the Imperium were different from Thrax and his companions. The Builder had tried to warn Thrax that he and his companions had been heavily modified from normal Swarm. To his present sorrow, Thrax had not believed the alien Builder.

Thinking about that, Thrax clicked his pincers in agitation.

All movement on the spongy hive deck ceased.

"What is that you are doing?" the massive AX-29 demanded.

"Supreme One?" asked Thrax.

"Answer immediately, Technical Assistant, or I shall have the soldiers shred and space your remains."

"I..." Thrax thought fast. He was unused to toadying to anyone. It had not been like this on the Dyson sphere. There, all Swarm had been warriors.

"Our present fleet maneuver could prove risky to you, Supreme One," Thrax finally said. "The thought of that troubles me."

"You dare to spout a subjective opinion regarding my latest orders?" AX-29 demanded.

"Oh, no, Supreme One," Thrax said. "I am considering the enemy warships. They have an irritating—"

"Silence!" AX-29 ordered. "When I desire your third-rate opinion, I shall instruct you to speak. When I wish to hear your outsized pincers clack, I will demand that you perform for me. Otherwise, your task is to remain unnoticed while the soldiers of the Fleet follow my orders with rigid precision."

"Yes, Supreme One," Thrax forced himself to say.

"Scuttle away," she said. "Your pheromones are revolting and have upset my digestion."

"O Queen, if I could point out—"

"Soldiers," she said. "Where are my soldiers?"

With all his resolve, Thrax kept from clacking his pincers a second time. He began scuttling backward out of her line-of-sight.

Thrax was different from regular Swarm. They were highly specialized. Those like the Reigning Supreme had bloated carcasses, were often immobile but of great intellect. That seemed to have made each of them overly eccentric. The fighters, the soldiers, had little to no brainpower but amazingly effectively bodies. Thrax and his companions had both brainpower and fighting bodies. It made the regular Swarm intellects believe them to be louts or mechanically inclined drones.

Was this to be his lot for the remainder of his existence? He would be a lowly mechanic, fixing broken machines?

Thrax could not envision such a thing with easy acceptance. Yet, he knew it would prove unwise to attempt a change in the social order. And that was the only way he could gain the rank he so richly deserved while remaining an Imperial Swarm subject.

He continued to scuttle backward until he reached a sensing station. With his eyestalks, Thrax observed the hive command deck in the distance. No one watched him. Disobedience was nearly impossible among the Swarm. Only queens bickered and backstabbed each other as they vied for power. But the queens did that in a stylized, Swarm-approved manner.

That meant he might maneuver without anyone suspecting he could. That was an interesting possibility.

Thrax began to adjust the sensor unit until he brought the present situation up on his screen.

The Left Swing Arm was closer to the Chitin System star than the last time Thrax had looked. The system held a Golden Nexus inside a vast Chitin globular of spaceships. According to information Thrax had uncovered from a data file, humans had recently been to the star system and to the Golden Nexus. Those humans had made what could only be a hyper-spatial tube.

Thrax wondered if the hateful Captain Maddox had been among the humans. He wanted to snip that man into bloody pieces. Thrax had often passed his idle hours by envisioning devouring the bloody chunks, maybe even as the captain lived. The screams as he ate the human alive would add savor to the meal.

In the darkness of space, Thrax observed the Swing Arm's saucer-ships' heavy lasers. They collectively beamed at a lone Chitin war-vessel, a dense ball of metal.

It was a simple but ingenious plan. The Swarm needed the Golden Nexus. The Chitin globular protected it and had proven stubborn for countless decades. The Chitins sent war-vessels from many nearby star systems to the Golden Nexus. The journey took decades, but the stream of Chitin ships had long ago become continuous. That meant the Chitins received constant reinforcements to the central globular.

How, then, could the Swarm quickly bring enough mass to beat down the Chitin defenders? Thrax's gift of star-drive motivated saucer-ships provided the answer.

The Left Swing Arm had used the star drive to appear two light-years behind the Chitin star. The Left Swing Arm had attacked a Chitin reinforcement stream, coming up from behind a column of enemy war-vessels. In this way, a mass of united Swarm ships struck a few Chitin vessels at a time, annihilating them at almost no cost to the Left Swing Arm.

Once the first line of Chitin reinforcements had been eliminated, the Left Swing Arm started on the next.

Thrax adjusted the sensor screen. This was the last line of Chitin reinforcements. That meant the great globular of Chitin vessels protecting the Golden Nexus would soon run dry of reinforcements.

The main Swarm battlefleet had been engaged in a constant war of attrition with Chitins the entire time. The Swarm side continued to receive their reinforcements and thus remained at a constantly high number.

The conclusion was obvious. In a short time, the Chitins would be unable to replenish their lost ships. The Swarm would finally win the war of attrition. They would break the Chitin globular that surrounded the Golden Nexus near the star.

Once the Swarm achieved victory, Thrax and his cleverest aides would enter the Golden Nexus. Then, he would employ his intellect. He would create a hyper-spatial tube. He would aim the tube at the heart of the Human Empire.

The Imperial Family had decided. The Brilliantly Glorious Raid Fleet would destroy Earth, destroying the social unity of the humans and possibly annihilating the majority of the human starships. Afterward, the Swarm would begin colonizing that sector of the galaxy, collecting the advanced technology as it grew. The bulk of advanced technology would be a great addition to the Swarm Imperium.

It was a flawless plan. Despite their advanced technology, the humans could do nothing to defeat it. There were simply too many Swarm warships. Thrax had already estimated that the Raid Fleet would have a 20-to-1 advantage over the humans, more than sufficient for total victory.

Thrax clicked his pincers as he studied the latest exploding Chitin vessel. He clicked his pincers extra loud because he was tired of being treated so poorly. He had brought the Imperium the tools for grand and far-flung conquests. They should have given him honor and glory, not turned him into a mere mechanic.

He was going to have to decide soon. He was Thrax. He was the greatest Swarm creature in existence. How could he prove that to everyone? That was the nagging question. He had bested the Builder. He would beat the Reigning Supreme as well, and still conquer Human Space.

How, though, could he do all that and remain alive? He needed a plan, one that would not fail.

The End

SF Books by Vaughn Heppner

LOST STARSHIP SERIES:
The Lost Starship
The Lost Command
The Lost Destroyer
The Lost Colony
The Lost Patrol
The Lost Planet

DOOM STAR SERIES:
Star Soldier
Bio Weapon
Battle Pod
Cyborg Assault
Planet Wrecker
Star Fortress
Task Force 7 (Novella)

EXTINCTION WARS SERIES:
Assault Troopers
Planet Strike
Star Viking
Fortress Earth

Visit VaughnHeppner.com for more information

Printed in Poland
by Amazon Fulfillment
Poland Sp. z o.o., Wrocław